TWO OF A KIND

"I hate those pilgrims," Bearclaw Johnson muttered. "Hate the smell of them. Hate the sounds of their axes. I don't blame the injuns for fightin' to keep 'em out of their lands. I love this country, Falconer, and I don't want to see it destroyed. That's what they do. Destroy the land and everything on it."

Falconer laughed softly. "We showed them the way, Bearclaw. You and me and our kind. That's the irony of it all. They're coming because we filled in the empty spaces on the maps and loudly sang the praises of this land. They're coming and there's no stopping them."

"We could stop 'em," Bearclaw said. "Yes, we could. Them plow pushers are weak-kneed cowards. No match for the likes of us."

Falconer leaned forward. "Hear me, Bearclaw. Leave them alone because if it's war you hanker after, you won't win it."

That was that, then. Falconer had chosen which side he was on. And if it meant going up against another mountain man for the sake of folks who were taking over the wilderness that both of them used to call their own, so be it. . . .

Jason Manning

PROMISED LAND

A SIGNET BOOK

SIGNET
Published by the Penguin Group
Penguin Books USA Inc., 375 Hudson Street,
New York, New York 10014, U.S.A.
Penguin Books Ltd, 27 Wrights Lane,
London W8 5TZ, England
Penguin Books Australia Ltd, Ringwood,
Victoria, Australia
Penguin Books Canada Ltd, 10 Alcorn Avenue,
Toronto, Ontario, Canada M4V 3B2
Penguin Books (N.Z.) Ltd, 182–190 Wairau Road,
Auckland 10, New Zealand

Penguin Books Ltd, Registered Offices:
Harmondsworth, Middlesex, England

First published by Signet, an imprint of Dutton Signet,
a division of Penguin Books USA Inc.

First Printing, July, 1996
10 9 8 7 6 5 4 3 2 1

Chapter One

Lillian Tasker awoke and looked at the walls of her room and felt like a stranger in her own house.

Sitting up, she brushed stray tendrils of mahogany brown hair out of her hazel eyes and breathed a melancholy sigh. Her back ached and she thought, ruefully, *I am getting old.* Where had all the years gone? She must have misplaced at least a dozen. The four-poster bed was packed up in the wagon along with almost everything else she owned, and she had spent a restless, dream-haunted night on the floor with some blankets and the star pattern quilt her mother had made for her as a wedding present seven years ago. *I was sixteen then, and so naive. That means I am only twenty-three years of age. So why do I ache so from just one night on a puncheon floor?*

It wasn't as though she had led a pampered life. Far from pampered, in fact. Her father, dead now after wasting away for two winters following her mother's sudden and fatal illness—when they had buried Annie Birch they had buried her husband Jacob's will to live, as well—her father had been a hardscrabble farmer, first in Pennsylvania, later just down the road to Springfield from here, in Illinois. He had wanted sons more than anything in this world, and, as is so often the case when a person wants a thing so bad, he didn't get his wish. Instead, Annie had given him three daughters—four if you counted poor little Mary who had died in her crib one dark February night when the ice covered the windowpanes like thick cataracts in the eyes of an old person, and the wind had howled like starving wolves around the cabin's eaves.

As a result, Lillian and her two sisters had done their share of farmwork from the time they were big enough to brandish a hoe, resulting in a degree of ambivalence toward farming in Lillian from a rather callow age. So, what had she done? Gone and got herself married to a farmer, of course.

Will Tasker had made many promises to her. One being that he wouldn't be a farmer for long. But every business venture he had gone into all starry-eyed with reckless optimism yet blind to the consequences of failure had died a miserable death. Lillian had never held that against him. She hadn't married him on account of foolish promises. She wasn't quite that naive. No, she had married Will for a different set of wrong reasons. Because he was tall and good-looking with broad shoulders and strong hands and a winsome smile and when he touched her something wondrous and warm and wet happened to her body. So she had agreed to marry him, for purely selfish reasons, to have that touch all to herself whenever she wanted it.

Pretty soon, though, his touch had ceased to work that magic on her. But not before she had borne him a son. Fate had a wonderful knack for the ironic. Her father had desperately desired a strapping son or two, and ended up with three daughters, while Will had said, "I want a precious little girl, darlin', one who looks just like you." And he had gotten a boy. Little Johnny, still asleep in the loft. Six years old now, but in many ways much older. When the Ohio River had taken his father's life, Johnny had done a lot of growing up in a very short time.

Will's death had not hit Lillian all that hard, really. She had grieved, but more for her son and what he had lost than for herself. It had occurred to her, sometime before the keelboat Will had been traveling on had been smashed into kindling by a sawyer, that she had no longer loved her husband, and the inevitable next step had been speculation as to whether she ever really had loved him. She had resigned herself to living out her life with him, nonetheless. Because he was a decent man, and good to her, and worked hard to provide for his family, even though his big, silly dreams had sentenced them to a hand-to-mouth existence, just one small disaster away from destitution.

Will had built this cabin, and it had weathered seven bitter Illinois winters quite handsomely. Lillian let her eyes roam across the well-fitted floor and walls of the cabin's only bedroom, every inch of it hewn by Will's capable hand. But she simply could not bring herself to feel guilty about leaving this place that Will Tasker had sacrificed so much blood and sweat and toil to make for her. Today she was beginning a new chapter in her life. It was time to stop looking behind her at the past.

Throwing the quilt aside, she stood and glanced out the room's solitary window. It was still dark, with just a suggestion of the dawn pearling the eastern skyline. She lit the candle by the light of which she had read her Bible the evening before, and folded up the quilt and the blankets. Then she shed her frayed-at-the-edges nightshirt. As she reached for her plain brown gingham dress she caught a glimpse of her own reflection in the window's darkened glass—and froze, standing there as before a mirror to gaze critically at her body.

Childbearing had not ruined her—her belly was flat, her breasts, though smallish, were still firm. The farm had not waited for her to recover from having Johnny, and the hard labor she had endured from "can see" to "can't see" six days a week—with the Sabbath being a day of rest as the Good Book commanded—had whipped her back into shape. Her skin was still soft and alabaster white where her dress had sheltered it from the elements. But her hands—she looked at them, back and front, with disgust—her hands were dark and ridged with calluses, the fingernails cracked and beginning to yellow. And her face . . . She moved closer to the window, peering as one would at a passing stranger who looks vaguely familiar. Yes, there were lines there, around her eyes and chiseled like parentheses around her mouth. Lines that had not been there a few years ago.

Melancholy came creeping back into her soul, and she realized how unhappy she had been, especially since Will's death, but even before, so that at times she had wondered if she had ever really been happy, or even knew what true happiness was. Still, she liked to think of herself as one who did not wallow in self-pity, and reminded herself that she was on this day embarking upon a journey that might by some miracle deliver her unto happiness.

Will's brother had written her from the Oregon Territory after her husband's death. Of course, Warren Tasker had been the perfect gentleman, making no mention of his true motives. But Lillian had known from the start that his concern for her went beyond the fraternal. He had been jealous of Will for capturing her hand—she had seen it on his face at the wedding. He had left Illinois shortly thereafter to seek his fortune out West, and recently he had been urging her to come to Oregon, and painted a pretty picture of her prospects if she did so. Warren could be very persuasive, and she had never been shocked or put off by his well-disguised entreaties. The Taskers were a family of Tennessee ridge runners, and in that society a widow being taken in by a dead man's brother was not an unheard-of arrangement. Warren wanted her for his bed, and she knew it, but that hadn't deterred her.

In the course of her correspondence with Warren she had never given him any reason to think she was accepting the offer he wanted to come right out and make but never had done. She refused to let herself cogitate overlong on the situation—she would handle that if and when it arose. It all seemed rather nebulous and far away—two thousand miles away, if what she had heard was accurate, and many unforeseen things could happen between here and there.

But suddenly, standing there nude in the empty bedroom, looking at her reflection in the window glass, by the dancing light of a guttering candle, Lillian Tasker felt very alone. It had been so long since a man's touch had ignited the passion pent up inside her. She hugged herself, and her arms brushed up against her penny brown nipples and made them hard, and she gasped, remembering—it hadn't been so long that she couldn't remember what it was like. Quickly she turned away from the window, shame hot on her cheeks, and donned the gingham dress. Time to get cracking. Oregon was calling her.

Stepping out of the bedroom, Lillian paused to listen for the sound of Johnny's breathing in the loft above, but heard no sound. Assuming nonetheless that her son was still fast asleep, she tiptoed across the room to the big stone fireplace. Sitting on her heels, she stirred up last night's embers, added some kindling from the box near at hand, and soon had a spirited blaze going which slowly dispelled the night chill lingering in the cabin.

She wondered how many times she had built a fire in this hearth. It had always comforted her. Second thoughts ambushed her. What on earth did she think she was doing? She had given up the security of this land and this house—for what? The untold perils of the frontier? A man's glowing description of some faraway promised land she might not even live to see? She was placing her six-year-old son's life at risk because she was tired of her situation and longed for—what? Adventure? Romance? Escape? In truth, all three. She scolded herself for being so childishly selfish. A mother should always do what is best for her child, and think of herself last.

Worst of all, they were going it alone, just her and Johnny. She had heard about "Oregon Societies" forming up in certain towns, whose members pledged to make the westward trek together and look out for one another through thick or thin. But she belonged to no such collective, knew of none personally, and was venturing forth into the great unknown all on her own, in hopes of finding an emigrant train in Missouri which would take her in.

She rose, suddenly listless, without any energy, and tried to bestir herself with the reminder that it was too late to change her mind. The place was sold; Mr. Hanrahan had given her a fair price, which was quite unlike Mr. Hanrahan, but then he admired her figure and had hoped to curry her favor with his generosity. She had needed the money to buy the overland wagon, as their run-of-the-mill spring wagon was unsuited to frontier travel and would not have survived the journey.

The wagon she had bought was built of seasoned hardwood capable of taking extreme temperatures, river crossings, and mountain travel. The "prairie schooner," as it was called, had a flatbed ten feet wide, with two-foot sides and a double thickness of canvas as rainproof as sailcloth could be. Its slats were caulked with tar, and spare tongue, axles, spokes, and wheel rims were stowed underneath the bed in a possum sling along with a coupling pole, a pair of hounds, and an extra kingbolt. Grease buckets, two water barrels, and heavy rope came with the wagon, too. Throwing in the six oxen for the team, the whole outfit had cost her four hundred dollars, leaving her only two hundred out of the farm's sale. A dollar an acre, that was what that repulsive Mr. Hanrahan, whose eyes undressed her every time they met, had given for the place.

Half of the two hundred had gone to pay off their bill at the store in town and lay in provisions for the trip. The man who had sold her the prairie schooner, Ezra Jones, had told her what she would need. Jones had planned to make the trek himself, but his wife had left him, taking up with a smooth-talking whiskey drummer, a blow which had knocked every bit of Oregon Fever out of Ezra Jones.

Following his advice, Lillian had laid in two hundred pounds of flour, a hundred and fifty pounds of bacon, twenty of sugar, ten of salt, and ten more of coffee, in addition to dried fruit, saleratus, rice, tea, chipped beef, dried beans, vinegar, mustard, and tallow. The medicine chest contained blue mass, quinine, cathartic elixir, and a flask of whiskey. She had also purchased powder and shot for the rifle. All was packed into the wagon, along with her bed, rocking chair, several trunks, and a few odds and ends. Tessie, the milk cow, and Blue, the gelding, were tied up to the prairie schooner's tailgate.

She went to the door to look out and make sure all

was in order. Blue had a habit of slipping a tether and wandering off at the most inopportune times. But the horse whickered softly at her from the end of his rope. Lillian smiled. Ol' Blue was always ready for anything. But Tessie looked rather unenthusiastic. The oxen were already in their traces—she and Johnny had struggled with the hitch well into the night. Poor Johnny. He had to be exhausted. But they would need to get better with the team. Couldn't afford to spend half the day trying to get the beasts into their leathers.

Then she saw her son, over beneath the elms where they had erected a headstone for Will. Will's body had never been recovered from the river, but Lillian had ordered the stone anyway. Johnny was kneeling beside it now, and Lillian's heart went out to him. She wondered how long he had been out there. He was fully dressed, but March nights in Illinois could be quite cool.

"Johnny. Johnny, come here."

He ran to her, brushed the unruly hair out of his face, and Lillian could tell he had been crying, but he was trying to put on a brave front, and she made no mention of his tears.

"You should be wearing your coat, Johnny," she said, a gentle scold.

"I'm sorry, Ma. I just . . . just wanted to say goodbye to Pa."

"I know, darling."

"Do you think he's sad because we're leaving, Ma?"

She put an arm around him. "No, I think he understands." What else could she say?

"Ma, do you think it's true, what they say about the pigs in Oregon?"

"What do they say?"

"That they waddle around under great big acorn trees, so fat they can hardly move, and they're already cooked, with knives and forks sticking out of them so's you can just cut off a piece whenever you're hungry?"

She laughed. "Now where did you hear that?"

Johnny shrugged. "I dunno. They say there's lots of true wonders in Oregon. Do you think that's so, Ma?"

"I think we had just better go and find out. How about it?"

"I'm ready."

Now she was the one who, quite unexpectedly, had to battle the tears. "You go warm yourself by the fire while I load up the last of our things."

Carrying the blankets and quilt out to the overland wagon, Lillian heard the sound of an ironshod horse on the road down in the trees, and a moment later she saw a solitary rider emerge from the shadows of the wood. Recognizing the swayback gray as belonging to Mr. Hanrahan, she swore under her breath. She went back inside to fetch rifle and Bible, putting them in the schooner's box as Hanrahan arrived in the yard.

"So you're going through with it, are you, Mrs. Tasker?"

"Hello, Mr. Hanrahan. Yes, of course I'm going." She said it as though she had never had a moment's doubt.

Hanrahan negotiated his bulk out of the saddle and to the ground. He wore a dark blue frock coat and yellow nankeen trousers, and his gold vest was pulled tautly over a prodigious belly. Long side whiskers framed a moon-shaped face and partially covered pockmarked cheeks. He had the eyes of a ferret, and an unhealthy pallor to his skin. The sun was just peeking over the eastern skyline, and it cast his shadow over her.

"I had rather hoped you would change your mind," he confessed with a lugubrious smile.

"No. There is nothing to keep me here, Mr. Hanrahan."

"Well," he mewed, and Lillian saw a glimmer of desperation in the eyes that roamed in bold trespass along her willowy frame, "I wanted to speak to you about that very thing. You know, I am a man of no small means, Mrs. Tasker. And I have long admired you. You are a fine figure of a woman. I could take care of you. And the boy, too, naturally."

Lillian's temper flared. The nerve of this man! But she tried to maintain her composure.

"What would Mrs. Hanrahan think?" she asked.

Hanrahan flinched. He was a businessman who had made his money in canal building twenty-five years ago. Now he dabbled in a variety of going concerns. His wife was a stern, matronly woman with, in Lillian's opinion, a singularly unpleasant disposition. She didn't know it, but Hanrahan had married her twenty years ago because she came from a family of wealth and position, and he had never loved her, in fact could not bear to even touch her these days. Mrs. Hanrahan was active in the temperance and abolitionist societies. She seldom had a nice thing to say about anyone. In a way, Lillian couldn't blame Hanrahan for seeking feminine affection outside the home, as his wife seemed not only unaffectionate but not very feminine.

"Naturally, she would not have to know," replied Hanrahan. "I could make, uhm, certain arrangements. You and the boy would live quite comfortably, I assure you. In Springfield, let's say."

"You want me for your mistress, then."

Hanrahan made the mistake of thinking that Lillian was actually considering his proposal. Stepping closer, an oily smile on his lips, he touched her arm. His touch was clammy, repugnant to her. But she defiantly stood her ground.

"Your husband has been dead for—what is it, now?—two years. You must be very lonely. I could take care of you, Lillian. You would want for nothing."

"Except self-respect. I may be desperate for a man's attention, Mr. Hanrahan, but not *that* desperate."

Hanrahan took offense, as she had intended that he would. He took a step back, an ugly expression on his face, looking like a man who had been slapped, hard.

"What?" he rasped. "Oh, so you think you're too good for me, is that it? I should have just had my way with you and been done with it. Yes, that's precisely what I should have done." And he looked like he was of half a mind to do it now.

Fists clenching, Lillian fired a glance at the cabin. Johnny was standing there in the doorway, struck by the morning sun and standing still as a golden statue. That her son had overheard the exchange made her furious at Hanrahan. She whirled, climbed up to the prairie schooner's box, and brought down the rifle.

"How dare you speak to me in that way," she snapped at Hanrahan. "If you do not leave this very instant I shall put a bullet right between your eyes."

"You forget, this is my property now. You can't throw me off . . ."

Lillian raised the rifle to her shoulder.

"I am a pretty good shot, Mr. Hanrahan," she warned icily.

"You wouldn't dare." But Hanrahan's voice quavered a bit—he was not speaking from conviction.

"I would dare anything," she replied.

Hanrahan muttered unpleasantries as he hauled his red-faced bulk into the gray's saddle.

"The frontier will eat you alive, Lillian Tasker," he said with relish, a parting shot. "I hope your bones bleach in the desert sun. No, better yet, I hope some savage buck gets his dirty hands on you. The thought of what he will do to you gives me pleasure."

"It would," she said, reproachfully. "Now git."

Hanrahan turned his horse and kicked it into motion, his back stiffened with the starch of indignation—and fear. Would she shoot him in the back? He wouldn't put it past her. Clearly she was quite mad. Only a madwoman would venture West alone, with only a snotty-nosed kid for company. He hadn't really thought she would go through with it. But obviously she had lost her senses, the bitch.

Chapter Two

For the thousands who went west in the year 1843, the journey began in earnest in the towns springing up like weeds along the lower Missouri River. Chief among them were St. Joseph and Council Bluffs. Of course, most emigrants had to travel for weeks to reach one of these so-called "jumping-off places," for they came in large measure from Illinois, Iowa, Indiana, Kentucky, Tennessee—and some from as far away as Pennsylvania and New York and Virginia.

Most of them were young, with the confidence and energy of youth to sustain them. They believed hard work today would result in a better life tomorrow. They were lured by the promise of free land, for, in order to populate the vast new territory west of the Mississippi River, Congress had passed the first Preemption Bill in 1842. This allowed the settler to "squat" on a piece of land and, as long as the trees were cleared and a house built and a field plowed—in other words, if the land was "homesteaded"—he would be allowed to purchase it, subsequent to a government survey, at the minimum auction price.

It was an offer very attractive to the people who had endured the long Depression which had swept the country in 1837. Numerous banks had failed. By 1839, wages had fallen an average of fifty percent across the board. Horace Greeley had used the New York *Trib-*

une as a soapbox from which to exhort the people to go West. Wheat sold for a paltry ten cents a barrel and you couldn't get a penny for corn. By 1843, the nation was bearing witness to a major westward exodus.

The promised land were the distant territories, called Oregon and California. Mexico still, technically, possessed the latter, but it was a land of milk and honey, or so they claimed, an earthly paradise where the sun never stopped shining. The Pacific Northwest was rich beyond all imagining. England laid claim to part of Oregon, and a thousand English settlers were farming the Puget Sound area, while the Hudson's Bay Company had made its mark as far south as the Willamette Valley. But Mexicans and Englishmen didn't worry the American pioneer. The United States was destined to encompass the whole continent, after all. This they firmly believed. And as for the Indians, well, the Indians did not till the land nor did they build upon it. They were nomads, so they had no legitimate claim upon the land.

In 1843 there already existed a clearly blazed trail to the western paradise. Up the Missouri until the Big Muddy joined the Platte—the wide and alkaline-heavy Platte, "moving sand" as some had described it, so shallow and muddy fish could not prosper in it, and people could not bathe in it or drink its water. The trail on the northern bank was called the California Road, and only later would be known as The Mormon Trail.

The emigrant leaving a Missouri jumping-off place in mid-April, after the winter mud had dried up a bit, was lucky to reach his destination in October. First stop was Fort Kearney, in the Nebraska Territory. Next came Fort Laramie, in Wyoming, six hundred miles from the starting point. By then it would be summer.

Beyond Fort Laramie lay Sioux country, and then the mountains, beyond landmarks like Independence Rock, where mountain men had carved their names in the stone. The trail rose to the eight-thousand-foot divide at South Pass. Beyond South Pass lay Fort Bridger, then Fort Hall. By now the emigrant would have come one thousand miles. He would be only halfway home.

At Fort Hall those bound for Oregon would turn north, following the turbulent Snake River, then west to the Columbia and the fabled Willamette Valley. But from Fort Hall on the journey became more difficult. Summer would be on the wane, and a brief autumn would warn of imminent hail and rain and snow. One mountain range after another would obstruct the pioneer's path. At the Blue Mountains wagons would have to be hoisted with ropes and pulleys to the rimrock. Two hundred miles later a new and even more fearsome obstacle—the Dalles, the canyon of the Columbia River, where the cliffs were too steep to negotiate, and the emigrant had to take to the river on flimsy ferries tossed about by raging, roaring rapids.

In 1843 the emigrant reaching a Missouri jumping-off place knew what lay ahead. Hundreds had gone before, and those who had survived the ordeal sent word back, spreading the Oregon Fever, and they all seemed to vouch for the promised land. It was there. It really existed. It really was worth all the hardship.

It took Lillian Tasker and her son Johnny three weeks just to reach a jumping-off place on the Missouri River. For the first few days they made poor time, no more than ten miles a day. This was in part due to the fact that Lillian had to acquaint herself with maneuvering the prairie schooner and a team of plodding oxen—quite a different proposition from driving a spring wagon pulled by a brace of mules.

She was aware that a great debate currently raged concerning the relative merits of mules versus oxen for the westward trek. Lillian had decided that while a mule might travel faster and could endure the summer heat with more aplomb than an ox, the mule required good, firm roads and abundant grass or grain to make a go of it. But there was no guarantee of good roads or adequate graze where they were going. Besides, the eight oxen she had purchased cost three times less money than a team of only six mules would have.

She had heard that in Africa oxen were used as saddle animals; a stick was driven through the cartilage of the beast's nose, and to either end of the stick was attached a leather thong, bridle fashion. The ox's nose was extremely tender, and this rather cruel device made the animal more manageable than would have otherwise been the case. Lillian hoped she would never have to find out. She could not abide cruelty to animals. Then, too, it was said that the Plains Indians were less likely to steal oxen than mules. Oxen were less likely to stampede. And in an emergency they could be slaughtered for food, and there was hardly anything less palatable than a tough, stringy mule steak.

Of course, Lillian entertained high hopes of avoiding the red savages of the frontier. She had heard all manner of stories about them, all of them terrifying. But Ezra Jones had tried to reassure her on that score. "Chances are you won't see hide nor hair of 'em," he had told her. "There ain't that many of 'em to start with, and the Great Plains is a mighty big space. In the summertime they're chasin' after the buffalo herds, or making a game of stealing another tribe's ponies and women. If you do happen upon an Indian, whatever you do, don't show him you're afraid. An Indian truly admires courage, and he might test you. But show fear and he'll go for you the way a wolf goes after sheep."

Lillian had to assume Jones knew what he was talking about—the man had fought in the Black Hawk War ten years back. She wasn't sure how much courage she could muster if confronted by a Sioux warrior. And the awful things Mr. Hanrahan had said! She shuddered when she recalled them.

Their progress was also hampered by uncooperative weather. A storm swept down from the northwest, with a cold and slashing rain, winter's final encore performance, or at least she hoped as much. They crossed the Mississippi by ferry upriver from the sprawling frontier metropolis of St. Louis. Lillian was leery of cities, having never set foot in one. Her mother had warned her long ago that cities were cesspools of iniquity, where male predators victimized poor little country girls. She turned the overland wagon north, taking a well-established river road north to the confluence of the Mississippi and the Missouri.

In April the Big Muddy was a wild and raging beast. Lillian heard the river long before she actually laid eyes on it. At its mouth the Missouri injected a flood of chocolate-colored water into the placid green of the Mississippi. The Missouri surged against its banks, carrying away great trees, which mixed with the carcasses of buffalo, logs, and underbrush in a reeking flotsam pulled up against dangerous snags—the bleached bones of dead trees implanted in the bottom mud and protruding above the surface.

There seemed to be hundreds, if not thousands, of these snags, and Lillian wondered how the fur trappers had ever managed to get their keelboats up this river. The snags hadn't been the worst of it. At least you could see them. There were "rafts"—logjams clogged with sand, forming natural dams around which the river plunged in narrow chutes. There were "sawyers," too, like the one that had taken Will Tasker's life on the Ohio—logs caught by their roots and limbs just beneath the surface, bobbing violently up and down unseen in the murky water, waiting to rip the guts out of an unfortunate boat. Sandbars and quicksand were commonplace, as well.

Lillian kept the prairie schooner well away from the treacherous banks. The Missouri frightened her. In a way she thought of the river as her introduction to the Wild West. Was this any indication of what the rest of the frontier was like? The Big Muddy had a disposition even more unpleasant than Mr. Hanrahan's—or even Mrs. Hanrahan's. It was saying to her *I'll kill you if I can, just give me half a chance.*

Finally they arrived at St. Joseph. Lillian counted on finding a caravan here which would take her in. There were plenty of other emigrants about. The town fairly overflowed with them. Dozens of camps ringed the outskirts, and Lillian gave up counting at a hundred and twenty prairie schooners. Her spirits soared to see these people. People just like her and Johnny. Farmers in homespun and mule-ear boots and wide-brimmed hats, women in gingham or wool dresses, and so many boys and girls. Johnny watched the children, his curiosity tempered with reserve. There had been so few children in the vicinity of the farm for him to play with, and Lillian realized how lonely her son's childhood had been thus far.

"I'm sure you'll make some nice friends during the journey," she told him. "Wouldn't you like that?"

"I won't have time," he replied solemnly. "I have to look out for you now, Ma, with Pa gone."

Lillian suppressed a bittersweet smile, and answered

with an earnest nod. "Well, that's true, but maybe you'll find a little spare time for play. I won't be much trouble."

St. Joe prospered catering to the needs of the pioneers. Numerous businesses occupied raw clapboard buildings, some the worse for wear after a few years of withstanding the raw elements of the open prairie. Lillian stopped the oxen team in front of a likely-looking place. Donnell's Mercantile. She had to strain at the leathers to get the job done, but after three weeks she had developed a new set of muscles in her shoulders, arms, and fingers. She had never been a weakling to begin with, having spent all twenty-three years of her life sowing and reaping the good earth.

Setting the hand brake and wrapping the reins around the pole, she was about to descend from the wagon's box when Johnny caught her by the forearm.

"Ma! Look!"

She glanced at him, saw the awed expression riveted to his face, and followed the direction of his gaping stare.

Two men were strolling side by side along the board sidewalk fronting the buildings on this side of the wide, rutted street. One was an Indian, wearing leggings and bone breastplate, beaded moccasins, and a blue breechclout, a red three-point blanket draped over one broad shoulder. His hair was cut in a roach, like the mane of a horse, and stiffened with red clay. His copper skin was painted with stripes of vermilion. His companion looked no less wild, a white man in grayish yellow buckskins, black with grime above the knees and under the arms and in the crotch. He wore an eagle's feather in his flop-brimmed hat. Lillian could scarcely see his face for the tangled beard that covered it.

The white man was talking in an animated fashion to his Indian companion, speaking in a guttural tongue that sounded much of the time like he was trying to clear his throat of a stubborn obstruction. They were coming toward the wagon, and they were downwind, too, because Lillian could smell them a good ten paces away. They reeked of bear grease and rotgut whiskey. They fairly reeked, too, of the unfettered and adventurous spirit of the frontier, and Lillian found herself gaping right along with her impressionable son. These men were of an entirely different breed from the sod-busting kind she had known all her life. Not better, necessarily. Just different. They passed right by the wagon, and only the Indian spared her an inscrutable glance. Her pulse quickened a little, but she wasn't afraid.

"Was that a *wild* Injun, Ma?" asked Johnny breathlessly.

"Not too wild, Johnny." Her son had no acquaintance with Indians. Illinois had been cleared of the wild ones some years before his birth. There were a few to be seen on the streets of towns like Springfield, drunkards all, reduced to wearing the tattered cast-off clothing of white men, and doing menial tasks for a mere pittance just to buy a little food and a lot of cheap whiskey.

It came to Lillian then that perhaps the Indians had every right to resist the onslaught of the white man. In her circle the red man was considered just another varmint, to be done away with, with no more thought given to it than one would give to killing a wolf or a rattlesnake. But they were just people, after all, with quite different ways of playing the game of life, and it hardly seemed fair to expect them to play that game by the white man's rules. If they didn't, though, they were exterminated, or at least driven off of their land.

Lillian shook her head and climbed down from the wagon box, turning to help Johnny down.

"I can get down on my own, Ma."

Lillian mumbled amused apologies and went to the door of the mercantile, pausing there and pretending to look inside while actually watching Johnny's reflection in the window glass as he scrambled down the offside wheel. The wheel was a bit taller than the boy, but Johnny was strong and agile and very well coordinated and Lillian told herself not to worry about him falling down and hurting himself. She told herself, too, that she mustn't smother him. These days a boy had to grow up in a hurry, and on the frontier that was even more the case. By age ten, or twelve, Johnny would have to be able to do just about everything a grown man could do. It was just that he was all she had, now, and if anything happened to him, well, she doubted she could survive the blow.

Johnny was the main reason she missed Will. She could mend tack and shoe a horse and plow a field with the best of them, and she could teach Johnny how to do all those things, and more—how to shoot, how to make cartridges, how to set a rabbit snare, how to mend a fence or patch a roof. But she could not teach him how to be a man. Only a father could do that.

He joined her at the door and they went inside. The place was claustrophobic, so filled was it with goods of every description. Airtights, blankets, coats, rope, fabric, guns, hats, knives, boots, gunpowder in little wooden casks, crackers in big wooden barrels, axes and farm implements, bonnets and dresses, quinine water and elixirs, steel traps and fishing hooks, marbles and licorice sticks in big glass containers on the counter top.

"May I help you?"

She asked the clerk if he had some citric acid, an

anti-scorbutic she had forgotten to stock in the medicine chest. Johnny was gazing with such rapture at the licorice that she couldn't resist buying him a stick. It was, she mused, probably the last licorice until Oregon.

"I'm bound for the Oregon Territory," she informed the clerk, a bored, pasty faced young man with watery, owlish eyes magnified by thick-lensed spectacles.

"Isn't everybody?"

"I was wondering if you could help me."

"No," said the young man, sarcastically, "I've got to stay here and help my uncle run this place."

Lillian smirked. "I'm sorry. I haven't made myself clear. I would like to join up with a wagon train. Who should I speak to about that?"

"Nine out of every ten people you meet out there in the street. They're all headed West. But not me. I don't have the fever. I got better sense."

"You're not being very helpful."

"Lady, I'm busy."

"You're a brat," said Lillian, snatching her purchases off the counter. Turning, she saw a towheaded man standing there smiling at her. "What are you grinning at?" she asked crossly.

"Beg pardon. Name's Wilkerson. Tom Wilkerson. I couldn't help overhearing. You say you're bound for Oregon?"

Lillian's eyes narrowed suspiciously. Was this another Hanrahan? Another scoundrel bent on taking advantage of a young woman on her own?

"I am," she said.

"My family and I are going that way, too."

"Family?" Lillian's face brightened.

"Yes, ma'am. Wife and two of the prettiest daughters a father ever had. Is this strapping young lad yours, by any chance?"

"Yes. Johnny, say hello to Mr. Wilkerson."

"Hullo."

"Fine-looking young man. Yes, ma'am, there are twelve wagons in our company. We've all come from Indiana, except for Judd Pollock and his family. They come from the Sandusky country. We're looking for a guide here in St. Joe. Think maybe we've found one. Man named Spellman. We're going to meet with him this afternoon. Why don't you come along?"

"You mean, join your group?"

"Sure. Why not?"

Lillian beamed. "Why not?" She put out her hand. "My name is Lillian Tasker, from Illinois."

Chapter Three

Tom Wilkerson's party was camped just west of town. He introduced Lillian and Johnny to his own family first. His wife Molly was a plump woman with a round, pleasant face. When she smiled, which was often, dimples appeared in her cheeks. The two daughters, Edna and Phoebe, were mirror images of their mother—same fine complexion, same dainty feet and hands, same round, dimpled face, hair the color of cornsilk.

Molly treated Lillian like a sister she hadn't seen in years. Lillian had wondered if she might not turn out to be a little jealous, her husband going off into town and coming back with a young widow woman he wanted to enlist in the company. But Molly Wilkerson appeared quite secure in her marriage. It was obvious she and Tom loved one another very much, and Lillian envied them the security of a rock-solid relationship against which the storms and vicissitudes of life broke helplessly like waves upon a rocky shore.

Edna and Phoebe, aged eight and six respectively, were extremely well-mannered. They tried to coax Johnny into playing with them, but he resolutely snubbed their advances. Chattering gaily, they ran off together, Phoebe mischievously yanking on her older sister's pigtail. Lillian apologized to Molly. "Johnny lost his childhood when his father died. Besides, he hasn't been exposed to very many children, and doesn't know how to act."

"Maybe that will all change now."

"I hope so."

"It must have been very difficult for you, without a husband, to provide for yourself and your son. I don't honestly know what I would do if anything happened to Tom."

"We've managed."

"I admire your courage, I truly do. In your shoes I could not have come even this far."

Some of the others in the company wandered over, curious about the newcomers. There was Jonathan Holsberry and his daughter Grace. Holsberry was the one man in the group who did not look like a farmer, and, in fact, he turned out to be a physician. He was tall and spare and looked like an ascetic. In addition to household belongings and some medical equipment and supplies, he carried a trunkful of books in his overland wagon. Homer, Plato, Shakespeare, Dryden—did Lillian like to read? She confessed that in the past she had had precious little leisure time in which to indulge, but yes, she did love books. Of the Birch sisters she was the only one who had actually enjoyed attending school, in the winter months when their help was not quite so desperately needed around the farm. She and her sisters had ridden an old sway-back mule named Jericho—named such because when he brayed it was as loud as the Israelite trumpets which had toppled the stout walls of that Canaanite stronghold. Eight miles to and from the little school-house, and Lillian had almost always had her nose stuck in a book coming and going. Holsberry was delighted to find someone else who appreciated literature, and he invited Lillian to borrow a book anytime she wanted. Tom Wilkerson laughed in a good-natured way.

"Poor Jonathan, stuck with a bunch of unlettered plowpushers." Holsberry took the joshing with good humor.

Holsberry's daughter had been appropriately named. She was a beautiful woman-child of fifteen years. Her problem was that she knew she was beautiful. Within a few minutes of making her acquaintance Lillian knew Grace for what she was, a hot-blooded, impetuous, vain, and selfish vixen convinced she was God's gift to men, even though at her age she didn't know a fraction of what she thought she knew about the male of the species.

The good doctor, of course, doted on her. *She must remind him of his wife, who died in childbirth,* thought Lillian, and she couldn't help but wonder if Holsberry's wife had been cut from the same cloth as the daughter. If so, she must have made the doctor's life a living hell, for he was a plain, stodgy, mild-mannered man. Odd, how sometimes opposites were attracted to one another. Holsberry pampered Grace, while she had him wrapped around her little finger. In his eyes she could do no wrong. He would always refuse to see her faults. All this Lillian could tell in a glance.

She could tell, too, that Grace was a shameless flirt. She gave Tom Wilkerson a sidelong smoldering glance and let her shawl slip just a bit off one bare shoulder—she was wearing a Spanish-style blouse that revealed quite a lot of her shoulders, and her breasts, as well. Let the shawl slip, but not for long—the afternoon sun might, God forbid, blemish her soft, alabaster skin. Lillian wondered how well she would stand up to the hardships of the long trek which lay ahead. Probably not well. She was unaccustomed to hardship. Her father had made certain of that. But there were things on the frontier that Doc Holsberry would be incapable of protecting Grace from.

Wilkerson treated Grace with cool courtesy, and without so much as a glimmer of desire in his eyes. He was a man who knew what he had in Molly and his two daughters, and he wasn't going to be lured into temptation. Molly seemed to know this about him, and she did not raise a fuss over Grace sashaying about and cutting her eyes at Tom. Grace was lucky, decided Lillian, who would not have taken so kindly to Grace if Will had been the object of her bared shoulder, come-hither glance routine. While he was alive, Will had never given Lillian cause to be jealous, but that, she suspected, was due in large measure to a lack of opportunity rather than an abundance of character on his part; there had been a weakness at Will's core, an inability to be satisfied with the blessings God had provided, a desire for more and better that had manifested itself in all those get-rich-quick schemes, but could have just as easily cropped up in another way, with sirens like Grace Holsberry. Lillian was glad Will wasn't here, for it spared her having to put Holsberry's daughter in her place.

Lillian suspected it was Grace rather than her own presence in the camp that attracted the Norwood men to the Wilkerson wagon. Ted Norwood and his two sons, Clete and Jake, had come West with a pair of wagons. The Norwoods weren't farmers, but they were the same breed of man. Ted Norwood was full of talk about his big plans for the Oregon Territory. He intended to build a lumber mill and open up a blacksmith shop. His iron-thewed sons were built like their father, with broad shoulders and barrel chests, ages twenty and eighteen respectively, tall and good-looking and as full of a young man's powerful desires as their father was full of dreams. They might have paid Lillian more attention if Grace hadn't been present with her shawlwork and sultry eyes and saucy hips, but Lillian's feelings weren't hurt. She was, instead, rather amused to see how the Norwood brothers jostled each other as they hovered around Grace like dogs in heat. They were young boys trapped in the bodies of big strong men, and Lillian looked forward to watching the rivalry between them develop as they vied for Grace's affections. So long as it didn't go too far, of course. Girls like Grace could cause even brothers to have a falling out.

There were two families present who were much like the Wilkersons—the Pollocks and the Blakemores. Young people with little children who had the look of good solid farming folk. Judd Pollock was in search of greener pastures and elbow room. Taciturn, humorless, he couldn't abide living where you could see your neighbor's chimney smoke when you stepped out the door of your cabin. Daniel Blakemore had come to Indiana from Pennsylvania, and upon finding the best bottomland already claimed, had decided to chase the setting sun a little further.

Then there was Lomax who, with his partner Abney intended to forsake farming when they reached the promised land. Their two wagons were loaded up with all manner of goods, in which they had invested every dollar to their names. Lomax was in his thirties, and Abney about ten years younger, and both men were bachelors. They had been acquainted with one another for quite some time, but Lillian had always believed that it was a mistake for friends to go into business together. Wilkerson confided in her that the two men were constantly at odds, in order to explain the curt manner in which they greeted her. "They're worse than a pair of old spinster sisters," said Wilkerson. "Always snapping at each other. I reckon the partnership will be dissolved long before we see Oregon."

The Durant family also owned two wagons, and Lillian knew why when Wilkerson introduced her to them. There were seven members of the family—Norris Durant and his wife Sadie, her father and mother, their thirteen-year-old son Billy, and six-year-old Brace, as well as a baby daughter named Sally. Norris Durant was a dour man. His brows were knit together in a perpetual frown. His wife Sadie struck Lillian as being a very unhappy woman, who cowered like a kicked dog every time Norris spoke to her. He barked orders like an army sergeant, and everyone in the family snapped to it when they heard his gruff voice. The older boy seemed to have a rebellious streak in him, while the younger, Brace, was quite shy. Since Brace was the only boy in the company who was Johnny's age, Lillian had hopes they would become playmates and friends. Assuming she could convince Johnny that it wasn't necessary for him to take over his father's role as man of the house.

Finally there was Lee Donaghue, a widower, who had come West with his ten-year-old daughter Lisle to—as he frankly admitted to Lillian—escape the memory of his recently departed wife, who had died eighteen months earlier, struck down in the prime of life by cholera. The tragedy had left an indelible mark on Donaghue. The horror of it still lurked in his melancholy eyes. He looked like a man who had not yet recovered from a terribly debilitating illness. Lillian's heart went out to him.

"I can well imagine what you are going through," she told him. "I lost my husband not all that long ago."

Donaghue's expression brightened a little, and he stuck out a hand. Lillian took it, and Donaghue held on to her like a man drowning in a fast-running river grabs hold of a rope thrown to him by a rescuer on the bank.

"Some days," he said, "I can hardly find the will to get up out of bed. Life would be altogether pointless, except for my daughter, Lisle."

"In time it will become easier to confront the day," said Lillian, speaking from experience as she gently but firmly pulled her hand free.

"That Lee Donaghue," said Molly Wilkerson later, "is a good-looking man, isn't he? A shame what he's had to go through."

Lillian agreed, recognizing Molly's remark as the opening salvo in a campaign to play matchmaker. *I will have to be careful around Lee Donaghue,* she mused. *He is in a fragile state, and if I am careless with his feelings he will shatter like thin glass.*

Late that afternoon the man called Spellman arrived in camp. Tom Wilkerson called everyone to gather around.

"This is the fellow Daniel and I told you about. He has agreed to be our guide."

Spellman stepped forward, taking charge of the situation. Lillian admired the colorful quillwork on his long, fringed buckskin jacket. In addition to the jacket, he wore durable stroud trousers tucked into high black boots. A straw planter's hat, adorned with two eagle feathers, shaded flinty eyes in a square face, most of which was covered with a beard the color of rust. His was a stocky build, but there wasn't much fat on his bones, and at six foot six he loomed over everybody.

He took a moment to scan the faces of the pioneers. *He is taking our measure,* thought Lillian. *Looking for the grit and the mettle he knows we will need for the task ahead of us. Perhaps, too, he is gauging us individually as to our chances for survival, picking out in his mind the ones who won't make it to Oregon.*

"My name is Amos Spellman. Let me tell you a

little something about myself. I was born in Alabama thirty years ago. My folks moved to Texas and I had the great good fortune to fight the Mexicans in '36, alongside General Sam Houston at San Jacinto. I am right proud to inform you that I was the man who captured the General Santa Anna himself." He noted with satisfaction that the emigrants were duly impressed by this revelation.

"Later, I rode with the Texas Rangers and fought the Comanches. Ladies and gentlemen, I am here to tell you that no more fierce fighters exist than the Comanches—except the Rangers. We were but a handful, but we whipped those warlords of the Plains. Whipped 'em good. After the Texas frontier quieted down I got restless. The spirit of adventure infects my blood and I suppose it always will, until someone cuts my veins and lets it run out of me.

"So I rode West alone. Tangled with the Comancheros, and the Apaches. Lived in the mountains for a spell. The fur trade was a losing proposition by that time, so I spent my days exploring the high country. I know those mountains, and the plains you must cross to reach them, like the back of my hand. One day I had occasion to rescue a small party of emigrants, much like this one. They had lost their way and found themselves trapped by an early snow. With my help they survived the winter. I came to admire their pluck and determination. Knew then what my mission in life was to be, and since that time I have escorted hundreds of folks just like you through the wilderness to the promised land."

He should change his name to Moses, thought Lillian wryly. She was a bit put off by Spellman's bombast. No false modesty in this man, that was certain. He talked like one of those traveling salesmen her father was always running off the old home place. Spellman was a salesman, and he was selling himself. "Always be wary of the man who beats his own drum too loudly," her father had told his daughters. "It's been my experience he ain't half the man he claims to be."

Spellman was still rolling along with his deep rumbling voice and slow-as-molasses Southern drawl.

"Mr. Wilkerson here has informed me that you are all bound for Oregon. That's fine. Oregon is a splendid country, and you will no doubt prosper there. But first you must get there. And to do that you must pledge now to do as I tell you at every turn. There may not be time for me to repeat myself, and I am unaccustomed to doing so anyway. You must put your trust in me."

"How come I ain't never heard of you" asked the dour Lomax.

Lillian smiled. At least there was one other in the company who wasn't swallowing Spellman's tale whole-hog.

"Probably because you haven't asked the right people. The people who *know*."

"We all agreed we need a guide," said Wilkerson, scowling at Lomax. "And they don't grow on trees, I can tell you. Daniel and I spent a whole day and part of another in St. Joe before we lucked upon Mr. Spellman."

"If you would like references," said Spellman with, Lillian thought, a hint of sarcasm, "ask Jim Bridger, or Sam Houston, or the first Arapaho dog soldier you meet."

"We'll rely on you, Mr. Spellman," said Daniel Blakemore.

Spellman nodded, approving of this blind faith from a man who scarcely knew anything about him. "Call me Amos. Experience has taught me that a few hard-

and-fast rules must be applied to an enterprise such as this one.

"Even in a party this small we must have seven captains. Each captain will be on duty one night a week. It will be his job to protect the camp and the stock during the night. Mr. Wilkerson and Mr. Blakemore, whom I have met, will, of course, serve in this capacity." Spellman proceeded to select five more men—Lee Donaghue, Ted Norwood, Judd Pollock, Norris Durant and Abney. Lillian gave Spellman credit for passing over the Norwood brothers. They were young and therefore prone to being irresponsible; perhaps Spellman had made note of the fact that they were paying more attention to Grace Holsberry than to his own words. Lomax's scowl deepened as Spellman passed over him as well. No doubt his earlier remark had rendered him *persona non grata* where Spellman was concerned, and Lillian had a hunch that in the future Spellman would call upon Lomax to do absolutely nothing, as a kind of punishment for his daring to question Spellman's bona fides.

"When we stop to make our night camp," continued Spellman, "we must always circle the wagons. The lead wagon will turn to the right, the next wagon to the left, with the others that follow alternating to the right and the left. There must be no gap in the circle thus made. The tongue of one wagon must reach the gate of the one in front of it. The animals will be kept within the circle during the night. After dark, no one will be allowed to venture from the wagons without my permission. Is that clear?

"Finally, any and all disagreements which may arise between members of this company which are not of a family nature will be settled by me. This organization will not function as a democracy. My word will be the law. You must sustain me in all of my decisions."

"Now wait just a doggone minute," rasped Lomax, who had decided he had nothing to lose by speaking up. "We pay you two hunnerd dollars to take us to Oregon, ain't that so?"

"That is correct," said Spellman.

"Then, way I see it, that means you work for us. What you're saying is, if you tell us to do something that's just plain stupid, like throw ourselves over the edge of a cliff or something, we got to do it. I'm telling everybody straight out, that doesn't sit too well with me."

"If a majority of you decide to remove me," said Spellman equitably, "I will go, with no hard feelings. But believe me when I tell you that my mission from this day forward will be to deliver all of you safely to the Oregon Territory, and I will pursue that mission with all my heart and soul. Your fate is in capable hands. You have my word of honor, and that word means everything to me. Without honor, a man is not a man."

Starting with Tom Wilkerson, every man in the company stepped forward to give his hand to Spellman. In so doing they wordlessly pledged to follow his lead in the months to come. Even Lomax, rather begrudgingly, participated in this ritual. Spellman took his leave then, advising one and all to be ready to break camp at first light on the morrow.

As the others dispersed to their respective wagons, Lillian approached Tom Wilkerson. "I want to discuss my paying a fair share of Mr. Spellman's wages," she said.

"The two hundred has already been collected, so . . ."

"I will not go unless I have paid my fair share," said Lillian, adamant.

Wilkerson smiled. "I reckon that would come to twenty dollars, then."

With a nod, Lillian turned to her wagon. "I will have Johnny bring it to you shortly."

Donaghue appeared at Wilkerson's side, watching Lillian walk away. "That appears to be one fine lady," he said. His voice had a wistful quality.

Wilkerson chuckled and clapped Donaghue on the shoulder. "Lee, you're looking a lot better today than I've seen you look in weeks."

Chapter Four

That evening, spirits soared in the camp. Tomorrow, at long last, they would embark on the great adventure. They would be well and truly on their way to the promised land. Someone had gone into St. Joseph and bought a basketful of eggs. Everyone was delighted to partake of this luxury, as eggs would undoubtedly be in short supply for the duration of the trek. The Pollocks and the Durants were transporting some chickens in stick cages, but of course the birds had been jostled over hundreds of miles of rough roads already, and had long since ceased laying eggs.

The country all around St. Joseph had been virtually denuded of trees and brush as, in years past, pioneers and townspeople had harvested all available firewood. Not to be deterred from having a big bonfire—and cooked eggs washed down with hot coffee—cow, buffalo, and oxen chips were gathered. The resulting blaze was not as spectacular as would have been produced by a wood fire, but no one complained. Daniel Blakemore broke out a fiddle and began to play. He was soon joined by Abney, who demonstrated a genuine talent for cajoling sweet sounds from a mouth organ.

They played "Money Mush" and "Zip Coon" and several other tunes. Tom Wilkerson got the ball rolling by taking his wife Molly in a light-footed spin around the fire. The Norwood brothers descended like vultures on Grace Holsberry. She danced with Clete first, then Jake, then Clete again, and so on. That seemed eminently fair to everyone except the Brothers Norwood, neither of whom looked kindly on having to sit out every other dance.

Edna Wilkerson asked Johnny if he would care to dance with her. Lillian thought that was a very sweet gesture on her part, but Johnny was mortified by the prospect, and flatly refused, without even a "thanks anyway." Edna's feelings were a little bruised—Lillian could see it in her bright blue eyes—and once Edna had walked away she scolded Johnny for his rudeness. Quietly, so that no one else would notice.

"She was only trying to make you feel welcome," she told him. "You could have at least said thank you."

"I don't have time for dancing," said Johnny stubbornly. "I'm watching out for wild Indians. Somebody's got to."

"I don't believe there are any wild Indians within a hundred miles of St. Joseph, Johnny."

"You never know. What would Pa think if I let you get scalped and murdered by red savages?"

Lillian had to smile. "I feel quite safe with you around, Johnny. Nonetheless, I want you to go and apologize to Edna."

"Do I have to?"

"You most certainly do."

"Yessum." Head hanging, Johnny shuffled a few steps and turned back. "But I still don't have to dance with her, do I?"

"No, though it wouldn't hurt you to."

When Johnny reached the Wilkerson family he discovered to his chagrin that Edna was dancing round the fire with Billy Durant. Lillian watched her son watching Billy with a funny look on his face—and she smiled again. It was never too early to learn a lesson about missed opportunities.

Sitting there on the blanket beneath a sky ablaze with uncountable stars, Lillian watched the others dance and play and felt quite content. These people on the whole had made her feel right at home, and she considered herself fortunate indeed to have met Tom Wilkerson in that St. Joe mercantile. This was a small company, and two thousand miles of hardship and peril lay ahead, but she had never been more confident that she would make it to the Oregon Territory. She had sold the farm and moved out because she had felt she had to escape—her own past had been suffocating the life out of her—and the odds of reaching her destination had not—and could not have—deterred her. But now she knew she would see the promised land, that it was God's will that she see it; it had been no happy accident that Tom Wilkerson had been in Donnell's store at that precise moment. Furthermore, she knew deep in her bones that life in Oregon would be rich and rewarding. She had made the right decision, after all. Of that she was certain, and she could scarcely wait until morning came, and the beginning of the journey.

Then she spotted Lee Donaghue standing over by his wagon on the other side of the fire, and the lurid dance of the flames cast flickering shadows over his haunted face, and he was watching her with a kind of desperate, wistful intensity, and she was suddenly afraid that at any moment he might muster up enough courage to come across and ask her to dance. Not that she would mind dancing—it had been so long, and she liked to dance—but she didn't want to with Lee Donaghue, and by so doing perhaps feed the obsession of a man consumed by loneliness. He needed someone to help him come to terms with his loss, to deal with the pain; Lillian knew what that was like, just as she knew it would be a terrible mistake to try to help him. Those wounds had to heal by themselves. It was an ordeal a person had to endure alone in order to become whole again.

To prevent an unpleasant situation from arising, she stood up and stepped out of the light of the fire, having to go beyond the wagons to escape Donaghue's gaze, and the great silent, dark, mysterious prairie stretched out before her in all its majesty, and the wind sweeping across the sea of grass brought the pungent aroma of the rich, cooling earth to her nostrils.

A shadow separated itself from the wagon to her left, and the breath lodged in her throat, and then she recognized Abney. He wore a sheepish expression, and held a half-empty bottle of whiskey down at his side, as though he hoped she might not notice it in the darkness, but she caught a whiff of his liquored breath as he mumbled apologies for having startled her.

"Hope you won't make mention of the fact that I was, uhm, indulging, Miss Tasker."

"Nothing wrong with strong spirits, in moderation."

"It's just that Lomax, he's a teetotaler. His old man was a drunkard. Used to beat up on Lomax, and his mother, too. Now me, I don't ever get falling-down drunk, you understand. Really, I don't. Just that, every now and again, I need a little nip to settle the nerves." He smiled, holding up the bottle like a child who has been caught with something he shouldn't have. "Liquid bravemaker."

"What are you afraid of, Mr. Abney?"

He glanced out at the night-shrouded expanse of prairie. "I don't mind telling you, I'm afraid of *that*. Of what's out there, waiting for us."

"What *is* out there?"

"That's the big question, isn't it? It's the not knowing that wears down the nerves."

"We'll be fine, Mr. Abney. You'll see."

"I admire your courage, miss. But I've got a bad feeling in my gut. I can't shake it, try as I might. I think we're all going to come to grief."

"Then why, may I ask, are you coming along? You really shouldn't, you know, if you feel that way."

Abney gave her a funny look. "Because I've got nothing back there. No good reason to stay."

Lillian nodded. She knew the feeling. "I won't tell Mr. Lomax," she promised as she turned away and went back to the fire to round up Johnny. It was time to turn in. Tomorrow would be a long day.

As she lay in her blankets beneath the prairie schooner, her son sound asleep beside her, the rifle lying on the other side of her, sleep eluded her. She kept thinking about Abney, trying to drown his fears with strong spirits, and part of the Lord's Prayer kept repeating itself, over and over, in her head—*Yea, though I walk through the valley of the shadow of death, I will fear no evil . . .*

Amos Spellman arrived with the sun the following morning. Despite the previous night's festivities, everyone in the company was up early. The wagons were packed, the teams hitched, breakfast had been cooked. Everyone—except, mused Lillian, for Mr. Abney—was eager to be on their way.

Spellman was mounted on a handsome sorrel with three white stockings and a blazed face. Beside him trundled a wagon—a hidehunter's high-sided wagon with a canvas tarpaulin strapped across the top, smaller than a prairie schooner, but a rugged and reliable conveyance nonetheless. The man in the box who handled the four mules in the hitch wore a long gray duster. Lank black hair brushed his shoulders. His complexion was dark; his features had a fierce cast. Lillian didn't like the looks of him at all. Apparently no one else did either. Tom Wilkerson spoke for the others when he demanded an explanation from Spellman. Who was this man, and what was he doing here?

"His name is Breed," replied Spellman. "I know him by no other. He is half Mexican, half Apache. We met some years ago on the Llano Estacado. He saved my life. I was hard-pressed by a band of pesky Comancheros, in the Canyon of the Palo Duro. The scourge of the West Texas plains, folks, those Comancheros. They are robbers and cutthroats without peer in the long and sorry history of mankind. We are exceedingly fortunate that our route will take us well north of their customary range."

"That still doesn't explain why he's here," said Wilkerson.

"He's here because he rides with me. He will prove his worth to this expedition many times before we reach our destination. He speaks no English, but he is acquainted with a dozen Indian dialects. I know some Comanche, and that is how we communicate. He is far and away the best tracker I have ever had the privilege to know, and he is a crack shot with both pistol and rifle. When you purchased my services you bought Breed's as well, and you will come to be very glad that you did."

Wilkerson glanced at Daniel Blakemore, who shrugged.

"But why didn't you tell us about him before?" asked Wilkerson.

"Would it have made any difference? Listen. If you want your money back you will have it, and no hard feelings."

"We'll have hell to pay finding another guide this late in the year, Tom," said Blakemore, worried that his friend might scotch the whole deal with Spellman just because he didn't like the half-breed's looks.

Wilkerson nodded. "Keep the money, Mr. Spellman. Just get us to Oregon."

"That is my intention." Spellman turned in the saddle and spoke to Breed in the guttural Comanche tongue. Breed stirred up the mules and steered the hidehunter's wagon toward the front of the line of prairie schooners. As he rolled past Lillian's wagon his inscrutable black eyes fastened on her, and Lillian felt cold dread trace an icy finger down her spine. She knew it was wrong to judge someone solely by their appearance, but this man Breed frightened her. He was a human predator, you could see it in his eyes.

They bade farewell to St. Joseph and turned their backs on civilization. Isolated outposts lay in their path, but for the most part it was the great unknown into which they were venturing, a wild and untamed frontier, on many a map still designated The Great American Desert because no one knew any better. Large portions of it had never been seen by a white man.

The countryside was pleasant enough at first, emerald green prairie scattered with boskies of trees. In the low places between the swells of the prairie lazy streams and little pools stood in rank marsh grass. The weather was good to them in the beginning; white clouds soared like a fleet of fast ships in the azure sky, and their blue shadows raced across the landscape.

One of the first obstacles to overcome was the Missouri River—St. Joseph lay to the east of the Big Muddy. The river was not quite so wild and wicked as it had appeared to Lillian near its confluence with the Mississippi, but it was still a dangerous crossing. A pair of flatboats were available, attached by pullies to stout ropes stretched between thick pilings on either bank. The wheels were removed from the wagons, which were unloaded and carried aboard the boats. They were then piled with goods, and canvas was securely lashed down over the entire load to protect provisions and furnishings from water damage. The boats could accommodate one prairie schooner at a time, so the task of getting the entire company across was a time-consuming one. Women and children clung to the bottom of the flatboats as the men hauled on the ropes—it was a wild ride, with the boats plunging like a bronco in the churning cauldron of the Missouri. As for the stock, they were secured by ropes and allowed to swim across, guided by men tugging on the lines from the western shore.

Eventually everyone got safely across, with no mishaps, not so much as a single mule lost to the river. This was considered a very auspicious beginning to the enterprise. But the very next day Lillian's horse, Ol' Blue, slipped its tether somehow and resolutely set off to the east, back toward St. Joseph.

"Seems you have a homesick horse," remarked Spellman. "Sometimes the stock are the first to become fed up with the prairie and make for home. I suppose it's all too new for them. Some say they are just showing good sense."

"It would simply break my heart to lose him," confessed Lillian.

Spellman nodded, and with a curt order in Comanche dispatched the half-breed, whose own saddle horse, a coyote dun, was tied to the back of the hidehunter's wagon. Breed took off in pursuit of the runaway. He tried to circle Blue and head him off, but Blue spotted him and realized what he was trying to do and broke into a gallop and kept the lead. Resorting to a different tactic, Breed held the dun to an easy trot and followed along behind Blue, by all appearances no longer attempting to catch up, but actually edging closer with every passing mile. Blue slowed down, too, but would not let Breed draw too near.

Soon they were completely out of sight of the wagon train. Spellman could tell Lillian was disconsolate, and assured her that the half-breed would recover the horse. They moved on. Late that night Breed returned with a disgruntled Blue in tow. Lillian took the lead rope from the half-breed with a heartfelt thanks. Breed said nothing, peering inscrutably into her eyes as though he could read the innermost secrets of her soul, and then he walked away, with a final "*Ho-shuh, ho-shuh,*" to Blue.

"That's Apache horse talk," Spellman told her. "Breed likes animals, especially horses, better than he likes people."

"I thought I would never see Ol' Blue again."

"The issue was never in doubt. Breed is the sneakiest character I've ever met. He could sneak up on God Almighty Himself. You tie that horse up good and tight. In a few days he will forget all about going home. I swear that sometimes a horse or a mule raised up back East just can't seem to abide this country, but your pony will get used to things after a while."

They reached the Platte River a fortnight later. This stream stood in stark contrast to the Missouri; the Platte was much better mannered, and shallow enough along much of its considerable length that a man could wade across on foot and never get his hair wet. But where the waters of the Missouri were so filled with silt as to be unfit for drinking, alkali rendered the Platte useless as a water supply.

The country had changed. It was rough and desolate

here, with only a few dusty trees scattered along the infrequent creeks, and sparse graze for the livestock. Barren sandstone ridges and deep gulches hindered their progress. The incessant wind howled across these badlands.

Here they met a few wagons rolling east—emigrants who had decided that a trek across this wasteland was too much for them. Here, too, they came across a piece of plank stuck into the ground alongside the trail, with a few black-edged words crudely etched upon it with a piece of iron heated in a fire.

LAURA MAY DAVIES
DIED APRIL 29, 1842
AGE 5 MONTHS

Lillian's heart was torn. Bad enough, she thought, to lose a child, but to be forced to leave the body in a dusty grave in the middle of this barren and merciless land! She didn't think she could have done it. "If anything happens to Johnny," she told Molly Wilkerson, "you may as well dig two graves. I shall not leave him alone in this land."

"There is no body in that grave any longer," remarked Tom Wilkerson. "The wolves come along and dig them up. Spellman told me."

"How awful," said Molly.

"This is a grim and savage land," said Lillian.

Two days later a storm came. A malignant black line of thunderclouds built up on the horizon, and as it loomed nearer, jagged bolts of lightning licked like the tongues of serpents at the earth, and the grumble of thunder shook the ground. A cool wind, fragrant with the scent of rain, struck them, and Lillian was glad of it at first, for the days had become hot and dusty, and the wind was refreshing. Moments later the clouds opened up and the rain came down hard and fast, silver sheets of it against the purple prairie. In no time at all everyone was drenched, and the trail was transformed into a morass of mud. Heads bowed, the animals in their harnesses plodded doggedly along with their hooves sinking into the viscous muck up to the fetlocks. Now the thunder crashed like a battery of cannon going off all at once right next to one's ear.

The storm pummeled them all afternoon, and Spellman called an early stop. Toward the end of the day a streak of red sky along the western sky promised eventual respite to the pioneers huddling under their canvas.

The night was chill and damp, and Lillian made room in the wagon for her and Johnny to sleep. Previously it had become their custom to make their bed beneath the prairie schooner. Spellman had suggested they lay a circle of rope around them if they wanted to sleep on the ground. "Rattlers and cottonmouths make poor bed partners," he had said. "They won't crawl over a rope." But tonight the ground was entirely too muddy.

In the early hours of the morning a tapping on the wagon's tailgate startled Lillian awake. It was Judd Pollock. He was on guard duty. His ruddy features were taut with excitement as he pulled back the tarp and peered in.

"Lay hold of your rifle, Miss Tasker, and keep alert."

"Why? What is it?"

"Sumpin out there," said Pollock gravely. "Mebbe injuns."

Before she could ask him anything more he was gone to waken the rest of the camp.

For the longest time Lillian lay there clutching the rifle, scarcely daring to breathe, much less move.

Johnny was still sound asleep beside her. Far off in the distance a wailing howl greeted the blood red moon as it crept above the black horizon of the prairie like a broad disk of molten lava leaking over the edge of the world. The sound made Lillian shudder violently. In the middle of the circled wagons the stock stirred restlessly.

She was so keyed up that when Spellman threw aside the tarp's flap an hour later she nearly shot his head off.

"You can go back to sleep, miss," he said. "False alarm."

"Are you quite certain?"

"Pretty sure. Breed's out there now. He won't let anything—or anyone—get close to the wagons."

"You put great faith in one man, Mr. Spellman."

"Sometimes one man is enough. Of course, that depends on the man, doesn't it? G'night, miss."

Lillian couldn't go back to sleep. Just before dawn she thought she heard someone slithering underneath the wagon, but she had no intention of venturing out to investigate. She had never been so happy to see the morning come.

But with the morning came a disturbing discovery. Someone had stolen a gingham dress and a Scotch plaid shawl Mrs. Blakemore had left out on the tongue of her wagon to dry.

That day the Pawnees showed up.

Chapter Five

The Pawnees made their winter villages along the Platte. During the summer they roamed the plains, searching for the great buffalo herds slowly grazing northward. Spellman declared them to be treacherous bandits without any redeeming virtues. If there was one consolation, he said, it was that they were inveterate cowards of the first order. If a Pawnee could slip up behind you and carve your spine out with a knife, he would, but he was unlikely to come at you straight on and risk getting his head blown off. Nowadays, with more and more emigrants following the Platte on their westerly trek, the Pawnees preferred to linger in the vicinity of the river, and what they could not beg from the pioneers they endeavored to steal.

Lillian wondered how anyone, even a Pawnee, could hope to prosper in this land. The great level plain extended countless leagues in every direction, broken here and there by a line of low, desolate sandhills, with the Platte, divided into a dozen threads of silver shallows, curling lazily through it. Apart from a few pronghorns, Lillian did not see another living creature—except for the ubiquitous turkey vultures and the equally numerous lizards which darted through the prickly pears.

That afternoon they came to a Pawnee village located beside the river. The Indian dwellings were made of mud and sticks, cone-shaped hovels, the entrances draped with threadbare blankets or animal skins. As they skirted the camp, women and children rushed out of the village and swarmed around the wagons like locusts. An Indian girl, perhaps twelve years old, walked alongside Lillian's prairie schooner and bawled inconsolably until Spellman rode by and tossed her a cheap trinket, a necklace of glass beads. The girl's tears disappeared. She beamed and scampered back to the village, protecting her shiny new possession from several other girls who tried to snatch it away from her. This contest degenerated into a cat fight, with much hair pulling and eye gouging, and in the struggle the necklace broke and scattered glass beads into the dust.

Spellman had a trunk filled with such fofarraw in the hidehunter's wagon, brought along for just this eventuality, and he distributed the cheap goods generously among the Pawnees, so that the majority of them went away happy. None too soon, in Lillian's opinion, they had put the village behind them, and pushed on another five miles before stopping for the night.

"I didn't see very many men in that village," Wilkerson remarked to Spellman.

"No. But you'll see them, soon enough. They'll be right along."

He was right. At dusk a party of a dozen mounted Pawnee braves rode up to the camp. Lillian noticed how their eyes seemed to gleam with avarice as they studied the company's livestock. They were short, square-built men, clad only in breechclouts and moccasins, their hair stiffened with gray river mud. They carried bows and quivers filled with arrows, and some of them had lances, but there wasn't a single rifle among the group. The Pawnees, decided Lillian, were a poor, dirty, dissolute lot who eked out a squalid existence in this inhospitable land, forced to try to survive in this region by the pressure of stronger, more advanced tribes. Even their small, shaggy ponies looked impoverished.

Sitting by the campfire, Spellman hardly paid their Indian callers any notice; he simply gave Breed a nod. Breed approached the Pawnees. It seemed to Lillian as though the Pawnees knew Breed. Or perhaps they could recognize a natural-born killer when they saw one. Whatever the reason, they were obviously leery of him. Breed spoke to them in their own tongue. He had slain a pronghorn that day—shooting from the wagon with his big Sharps Leadslinger, dropping the animal with a shot that impressed everyone who had witnessed it. Now he offered each of the Pawnee braves a choice cut of meat and told them to be on their way. They accepted the meat as though they had some kingly right to it, and with one last careful look around, as though they were taking an inventory, they vanished like ghosts in the gathering gloom.

"I have a hunch we haven't seen the last of that bunch," said Abney.

"Probably not," concurred Spellman. "We would be wise to double the guard tonight, just in case."

"Good idea," said Wilkerson. This was Daniel Blakemore's night; Wilkerson turned to him. "I'll stand with you tonight, Dan."

"Much obliged." The appearance of the Pawnee braves had rattled Blakemore, and he was doing a poor job of concealing that fact.

"I have another suggestion to make," said Spellman. "There is one wagon they won't go near, if they do happen to sneak back into camp tonight."

"You mean Breed's," said Wilkerson. "They didn't like the looks of him, did they?"

"He has a well-deserved reputation among the

Plains Indians," said Spellman. "And the Pawnees in particular have good reason to fear him. Some years back a band of Pawnee bucks stole Breed's favorite horse. Not the bunch we came upon today, but another. Breed tracked them back to their village. In the middle of the night he slipped into the lodge of the man who had laid claim to the stolen horse, cut his throat, lifted his hair. The man's wife awoke with her husband's blood in her face, and screamed. Breed killed her, too. Then he took his horse and was gone before the rest of the village knew what was happening. There wasn't a single man in that village brave enough to go after him."

"Good Lord," breathed Wilkerson. "That was pretty damned cold-blooded, if you ask me."

"Why? Don't you folks hang horse thieves? Breed used a knife instead of a rope, that's all."

"But the woman . . ."

Spellman shrugged his indifference. "Would it make you feel any better to know that he spared the lives of two children who also lay sleeping in the lodge that night?"

"I would think the Pawnees would want revenge."

"Not at all. They are cowards, and they fear Breed more than any other man alive."

"Then maybe they will leave us alone."

Spellman shrugged again. "Maybe. But why take unnecessary chances? My suggestion is this. Put whatever valuables you hold most dear in Breed's wagon. They will be as safe there as if they were locked up tight in a bank's vault."

"That's a suggestion, right?" asked Lomax. "Not an order?"

"In this case, only a suggestion. It is a matter of trust, of course. I would trust Breed with my life. Have done, as a matter of fact. But I would not expect you to trust him as I do. His appearance certainly does not inspire it, I'll grant you that. But he is not without honor, and he would not betray me. Which means, since he understands my commitment to this company, he would not betray you."

Wilkerson glanced at Blakemore, brows raised in a silent query. Blakemore nodded. "Makes sense to me, Tom. At least until we get out of Pawnee country."

"I'll ask the others," Wilkerson told Spellman. "But it will have to be completely voluntary."

Spellman was in full accord.

When Wilkerson broached the subject to Lillian she was skeptical at first.

"I've got about eighty dollars to my name," she said. "Not much, but it's all I have. It's my Oregon grubstake, Tom. Mine and Johnny's. Without it I couldn't buy seed, or food enough to make it through the first winter."

She didn't tell him about Warren Tasker—hadn't told anyone, for fear they might jump to the wrong conclusion. Warren, of course, would go out of his way to see to her needs, and Johnny's, but she did not want to be in a position where she had to oblige herself to him, since he might, being a mere mortal man, expect more from her in return for his kindness than she was willing to give.

"You don't have to do this if you don't feel comfortable with it," replied Wilkerson.

"What about you? What are you going to do?"

"I'm going along. I have a small chest with a little money in it, and some things that mean a lot to Molly and me. Things that we could never replace. I reckon they'll be safer in Breed's wagon. I saw the way the Pawnees looked at us and our belongings. And I saw the way they looked at the half-breed, too."

"Oh, very well, then." Lillian climbed into the back

of her wagon, returning a moment later with a small painted wooden box with brass hinges and a small brass clasp. She surrendered it to Wilkerson.

"What about your cow?" he asked. "Might be safer tied up to Breed's wagon."

"Yes. Take her along." As Wilkerson began to turn away, Lillian added, "Keep your eye on Breed, Tom. He is not a man to be trusted, no matter what Spellman says."

"I don't know that I trust him. But I think we can trust Spellman. He's done right by us so far, hasn't he? And the breed won't cross Spellman, of that I am sure."

Lillian didn't bother telling him that she didn't trust Amos Spellman any more than she did the breed. There was nothing tangible she could use to justify her opinion of their frontier guide. But she just couldn't bring herself to put any faith in the man.

The next day was hot and sultry until shortly after noon, when sudden darkness raced toward them from the west. Angry, swirling black-gray clouds blotted out the sun. A furious wind, cold and heavy with the scent of rain, struck them with a vengeance. Tied to the back of the Tasker overland wagon, Ol' Blue snorted and pulled desperately against his tether. Some of the mule teams stopped dead in their tracks, refusing to budge. Lillian was glad she had chosen oxen; they were too dumb to know what was coming.

When the storm hit them it was with hellish fury. An icy rain drenched everyone to the skin in a matter of seconds. The wind howled like a thousand starving wolves, blowing with such force that a person had to lean into it to keep from being knocked backward. It blew the canvas half off the Pollocks' wagon, and a mad scramble commenced as everyone jumped in to help rescue the canvas and lash it down. The mule teams came around before the storm to put their backs to it. To Lillian it seemed as though the wind was trying to tear her clothes off. She lost her bonnet. Not a moment too soon, she ordered Johnny into the wagon; an instant latter a barrage of hail hammered at the wagons. Lillian scrambled under cover. She felt sorry for the animals, but there was nothing she could do except cower in the prairie schooner and wait for the storm to pass.

Fortunately, the storm had soon blown past. The hail had knocked one of the Durant mules senseless. Other teams were tangled hopelessly in their traces. The dust of the trail had been transformed into mud. At Wilkerson's suggestion, Spellman ordered camp to be made on the spot.

An hour prior to sunset they saw a half-dozen black specks moving on the silver surface of the meandering Platte, a mile upriver. These turned out to be bullboats—tanned and treated hides pulled tautly over a frame of willow sticks, making a surprisingly resilient craft. They were laden with buffalo robes, and each was manned by two men clad in grimy buckskins or homespun. Their leader was a French Canadian named Jacques Pierre. Pierre's bullboat partner was a surly-looking young man of about eighteen years with scraggly, carrot-colored wisps of hair sticking out from under his woolen cap. His features were unpleasant to begin with, and not at all improved by unsightly scars which were the result of a childhood bout with the pox.

Spellman took Pierre off to one side to engage him in conversation. While Spellman did most of the talking, Pierre scanned the wagons as he listened, and laughed coarsely a time or two. His men waited in the bullboats, or stretched their cramped limbs on the bank, and none seemed inclined to have anything to do with the emigrants. That suited Lillian just fine, as they were a scoundrelous lot by the looks of them.

Eventually Spellman and Pierre shook hands and parted company. As the bullboats floated away downstream, Spellman returned to the camp to enlighten the others.

"Those boys used to be fur trappers, most of 'em," he said. "Now I reckon you'd call 'em hidehunters. Beaver's all but trapped out, but there's a strong market for buffalo skins back East these days. I warned them about those Pawnees. They say they've had no Indian trouble to speak of upstream, which is good news for us."

"Then I guess it will be all right for us to take back our valuables," said Lomax.

Spellman was startled. "Of course, you can do that any time you like. But we'll be leaving the Platte tomorrow."

"Leaving the river?" asked Wilkerson. "But why? Aren't we bound for Fort Laramie?"

"Yes, but I know of a shortcut that will save us several days getting there."

Wilkerson gazed dubiously at the great, desolate plain stretching away into the twilight distance. He hadn't realized how much he had depended on having the river close at hand. With the river at least a man knew that the Missouri lay somewhere to the east and Fort Laramie lay somewhere to the west; fifty miles out onto the plains and Wilkerson was quite certain he wouldn't know where anything was.

Spellman chuckled. "Don't worry. If it was only a matter of following a river to Oregon you and your kind wouldn't need the likes of me. I've traveled these plains many times, Mr. Wilkerson. I know my way around. We don't need a river to keep from getting lost."

* * *

The next morning Lillian awoke to the call "Rider coming in!" Parting the wagon's canvas flaps, she became aware that it was not yet dawn. The sky was overcast, and the black night seemed to begrudge the dull gray hint of a new day. She could see nothing from this vantage point, so she dressed hurriedly, picked up her rifle, and left Johnny sleeping the deep and dreamless sleep of the innocent.

The men were gathered across the wagon circle from her prairie schooner. She made her way around the livestock to join them. A solitary horseman was crossing the shallows of the river astride a tall gray Appaloosa. He checked the handsome horse a few yards shy of the wagons.

"Name's Falconer," he said. "Hugh Falconer. I've been smelling your coffee brewing for about a half hour now. Mind if I light?"

"Step down and welcome," said Wilkerson.

Falconer dismounted, a tall, broad-shouldered man with alert brown eyes and a full tawny beard. He wore a white capote adorned with broad red stripes over his buckskins. Drawing a Hawken mountain rifle from a saddlehorn strap, he ground-hitched the Appaloosa and stepped over a wagon tongue to stand before them. The Appaloosa nibbled at some sparse grass, but did not otherwise move; apparently Falconer was confident it would not stray far. Lillian could not recall ever having seen such a splendid horse. She was partial to Ol' Blue, of course, from long association, but she had to admit that Ol' Blue paled in comparison to Falconer's cayuse.

"You smelled our coffee," said Spellman. "How long you been out yonder?"

"Few hours. Didn't want to try coming in while it was slap dark." Falconer looked with faint amusement at the men, and at the way they gripped their firearms as though they were afraid he might try to disarm them. "You folks have had some trouble?"

"Thieving Pawnees back a ways," said Spellman.

"Ah. Well." That was all Falconer had to say on the subject of Pawnees. "Did you happen to see a party of hidehunters going down the river in bullboats?"

"Why yes," said Wilkerson. "Late yesterday."

Lillian could have sworn Spellman had started to shake his head in response to the stranger's query before Wilkerson cut in on him.

Falconer nodded. A savage gleam of anticipation enlivened his weathered features, and a faint Scottish brogue crept into his voice. "Good. Good. Was there a young one with them? Reddish hair, pocked face?"

"I saw him," said Lillian.

He looked at her and the smile hidden by his beard touched his eyes. "Thank you, ma'am."

"What do you want with those men?" asked Spellman.

"My quarrel is solely with the one I just described to you. His name is Dowd. He murdered an Arapaho boy about a fortnight ago."

"What does that have to do with you?"

"The Arapahos happen to be friends of mine. They've kept the peace with the white man, until now, but this deed has them up in arms. They've promised they won't put on their war paint if I bring Dowd to them."

"You mean you would turn a white man over to those heathens?" asked Norris Durant, aghast.

"If you'd seen what Dowd did to that boy, you'd wonder who the heathen was. He's a murderer, and must face the consequences of his act."

"But . . . but what will they do to him?"

"Unpleasant things, I'm sure. But if it's not done, your scalp, and those of your family, might end up hanging from an Arapaho lance."

"Hugh Falconer," murmured Wilkerson. "I believe I know that name." Remembering, he snapped his fingers. "That's it! I've read about you. Some fellow went with you to California some years back and wrote a book about his adventures there."

"Eben Nall," said Falconer. "He has a place ten days west of here, south of the river."

"They rate you right up there with Jim Bridger and John Colter," said Wilkerson. "You're a legend among the mountain men."

Falconer shook his head. "I'm a man like any other, and worse than some. Now, about that coffee . . ."

"I'll fetch you a cup," said Lillian.

"Much obliged, ma'am."

She hurried to the nearest campfire, at the Wilkerson wagon, and almost scorched her hands in her haste to fill a tin cup with the just-brewed coffee in the pot balanced on the stones that rimmed the fire.

"What's happening over there?" asked Molly. She was busy cooking flapjacks for breakfast and firmly believed that women should not interfere in the business of men, so she was fairly itching all over with curiosity.

"A man named Hugh Falconer," replied Lillian. "He's after those hidehunters we saw yesterday. One of them murdered an Indian boy. I knew they were no good the minute I laid eyes on them."

"How awful. I agree, they looked the type. But what can one man expect to do alone against that bunch?"

"I wouldn't want to be the one this man is hunting, even if I was traveling with a hundred friends."

Molly gave her a funny look, and a slow smile crept across her plump and pleasant face.

"Is that so? He must be quite a man, then."

"Yes, he must be."

Lillian returned to the knot of men talking to Falconer.

"Thanks, ma'am," said Falconer as he gratefully accepted the coffee. His hands, she noticed, were big and rough, bearing numerous scars, yet they took the cup from her own hands very gently, and his fingers brushed against hers, and she watched him as he sipped from the cup, and felt the blushing heat in her cheeks as his gaze, friendly and speculative, lingered on her face as though he found it pleasing. She could only hope her cheeks were ruddy from the blustery chill of the dawn.

Having tasted the coffee, Falconer gulped the rest of it down. One could not expect impeccable manners, thought Lillian, from a man who had lived most of his life wild as an Indian in the mountains. She figured him to be around forty years of age, but it was difficult to tell with Falconer; he had a younger man's trim agility, with an older man's wisdom inhabiting his eyes. Wisdom came from suffering. What privations and perils this man must have endured! There was always a price to pay for the advantage of being so strong, so bold, so unafraid, so sure of one's self. And Hugh Falconer was all of these things, Lillian was certain. A man would have to be, to have embarked on such a mission with such cool confidence.

The coffee gone, he returned the cup to her. "You folks headed up Oregon way?" He was looking at her as he posed the question, and she nodded, suddenly at a loss for words. "Far piece," he remarked. "Watch out for the Blackfeet when you get some closer to the high country. They are in a bad mood this year. As are the Sioux, or so I've been told."

"This is Amos Spellman," said Wilkerson. "Our guide. Maybe you've heard of him."

Falconer looked Spellman up and down. "Can't say as I have." His features were suddenly inscrutable, his tone of voice carefully noncommittal. Then he saw Breed for the first time, stepping away from his wagon, a stone's throw away, and Lillian watched Falconer's expression change into something almost predatory. "Who might that be?"

"His name is Breed," replied Spellman. "He rides with me."

"Is that so." Falconer turned abruptly to Wilkerson. "My advice would be to join up with another caravan, if possible. There's trouble on the high plains this summer, on account of the Indians, and you'll find it's true what they say about strength in numbers."

"I'll get them through," said Spellman, perturbed. He had taken Falconer's advice as a personal affront, as a questioning of his ability, and it did not sit well with him, which didn't surprise Lillian, who, from the start, had pegged Spellman as a man with a huge yet fragile ego.

"You do that," said Falconer, fixing a piercing gaze upon Spellman, and it seemed to Lillian as though he were giving a command, not making a comment.

"I'd best be on my way," said Falconer. "I wish you folks Godspeed." He glanced at them all, and at Lillian lastly, and again his gaze lingered upon her, and suddenly Lillian felt curiously sad to see him go.

But go he did, climbing aboard the Appaloosa and turning away to follow the river eastward, without another word, and without a backward glance, either. Lillian knew this because she watched him until he was out of sight in the gloomy threads of a slow-fading night.

"Get ready to move out," snapped Spellman, and walked away to have a word with Breed.

"Hugh Falconer," murmured Wilkerson, wearing a lopsided grin. "All the tall tales I've heard about him, I didn't think he was real."

"He's real," said Lillian. "And I wish that he was taking us to Oregon instead of Spellman."

Chapter Six

Hugh Falconer found the hidehunter's camp that night, but waited until dawn to make his move.

From the start he had been certain of catching up with his prey. The Platte was fast travel further downriver, but up here men who traveled her had to contend with sandbars and quicksand, and that slowed them down considerably.

When the sun came up he made certain he had it at his back, so that it would be in their eyes. He ground-hitched the Appaloosa on the backside of a high swell, out of sight of the camp, then positioned himself on the rim with his Hawken mountain rifle shoulder-racked, and haled the camp below.

The hidehunters were just beginning to stir. One man was down by the river, relieving himself. Another was trying to stir the coals of last night's fire into life. The rest were still in their blankets when Falconer called out from a hundred yards to the east. They scrambled for their weapons.

Falconer spotted Dowd immediately—that scraggly mop of reddish orange hair was hard to miss. He didn't have a stitch of clothing on, and he was a pale, scrawny piece of work. Falconer had to beat down a sudden surge of unreasoning anger, remembering what Dowd had done to that poor Arapaho boy. One quick shot would do the trick; at this range Falconer knew he could put a bullet right between Dowd's eyes, no problem. But justice would not be served that way. Not Arapaho justice. And that was what Dowd had to face for the crime he had committed.

"Jacques Pierre!"

The leader of the hidehunting crew shaded his eyes, trying to get a better look at Falconer, but the sun blinded him.

"Who are you? What do you want?"

"Name's Hugh Falconer."

Falconer could tell the name meant something to most of the twelve men down there on the riverbank. Generally, Falconer had found the legend constructed around his exploits to be a distinct liability. But on occasion it served him well. He was hoping this time it would make Pierre and his outfit think twice about tangling with him.

"Falconer? *Bonjour!* Come down, *mon ami.* You are welcome in our camp."

"I won't be when you know what I've come for."

"And what might that be, pray tell?"

"Dowd."

Pierre looked at Dowd, and Falconer wondered if he knew what his blanket partner had done. By all accounts Dowd had been alone when he had murdered the Arapaho boy. But he was the type to brag, and it wasn't something that would bother Jacques Pierre too much, anyway.

"I do not understand," said Pierre.

"He killed an Arapaho lad. He's coming back with me."

Pierre turned to Dowd. He didn't ask Dowd any questions. One look at Dowd's face told him all he needed to know.

"I only want Dowd," said Falconer, sensing that the

moment of truth was at hand. "The rest of you can be on your way."

Pierre made a quick decision.

He raised rifle to shoulder and fired at Falconer. The shot went wide—he really could not see his target clearly. But it served a purpose; Falconer ducked down below the rim of the swell.

"To the boats!" cried Pierre. *"Allez! Allez!"*

The hidehunters rushed to the bullboats, some leaving behind blankets and articles of clothing in their haste. The buffalo hides had been left in the boats overnight, as usual, and the hides, along with their lives, were all that really mattered to them. In no time at all they were on the river, and the current was sweeping them away from the campsite.

Falconer swung aboard the Appaloosa Indian-style and kicked it into a gallop, his demeanor one of stern resolve. He had tried to reason with them; now he would get the job done the hard way.

The Appaloosa could run like the wind, and Falconer was able to get well ahead of the bullboats without letting the hidehunters catch a glimpse of him, for knowing how to use the terrain like an Indian warrior was second nature to him—and you rarely saw an Indian unless and until he wanted you to see him.

Reaching a bend in the river, Falconer leaped off the Appaloosa, hid it away in a depression where it would be visible from the river, and took off running. He left the Hawken behind a log that lay along the bank and plunged into the Platte, swimming with strong strokes to the far side, where flotsam had caught in the roots of a scrawny tree growing on the brink of a ten-foot cutbank. Here he waited, only his head above water.

The bullboats soon hove into view. The hidehunters were watching the opposite bank, where they expected him to be. There were two men to a boat. While one worked the pole to keep the craft in the current, the other kept his rifle at the ready. Falconer was glad to see that Pierre and Dowd were in the last boat. Drawing a Green River knife from its belt sheath and putting the blade between his teeth to free his hands, he gauged time and distance and the speed of the bullboat and then submerged and struck out underwater. Here, even at its deepest, the Platte was only four or five feet to the bottom, but the murky water concealed him well. Falconer realized that if he made the mistake of surfacing too soon the hidehunters would see him, and he would be easy prey.

But when he did come up it was at the right time and place—all the bullboats had passed downstream except for the one manned by Pierre and Dowd. The French Canadian was poling. As Falconer grabbed the bullboat with both hands he raised his knees, lifting his feet off the riverbottom. His weight tipped the craft sharply over, and both of its occupants joined him in the river. Touching bottom again, Falconer let go of the bullboat and broke the surface again, to find himself bracketed between Pierre and Dowd. The latter was downstream, sputtering, arms flailing, having lost his grip on the rifle—and his nerve, for he could not swim a lick. Dodging a pack of buffalo hides, Falconer surrendered himself to the current, strong here in the middle of the river, and it carried him straight to Dowd. He locked an arm around Dowd's throat and turned to see what Pierre was doing.

A snarling curse on his lips, the French Canadian was reaching for Falconer with murder in his eyes. Falconer had one free hand—he used it to pluck the knife from between his teeth and slashed at Pierre's outstretched arms. Pierre howled in pain as the blade cut his forearm to the bone. The current carried him on by as his blood gave a pinkish cast to the water.

Dowd was clawing at Falconer's arm, making strangled, incoherent sounds. Falconer tightened the lock he had on the young killer's throat and struck out for the northern bank. The current had carried them a fair distance downstream from where the Appaloosa was hidden. When he reached the bank he let go of Dowd. Wheezing, spitting up a stomachful of river, Dowd got weakly to his feet. Falconer was waiting for him. His fist connected solidly with Dowd's jawbone and Dowd crumpled into an unconscious heap.

The bullboats were several hundred yards downriver by now. Nonetheless, one of the hidehunters tried a shot at Falconer, who didn't even flinch as hot lead sizzled past him. Pretty fair shooting, mused Falconer, from a boat being tossed about in a strong current.

Pierre was washed up on a spit of sand which split the main current into a pair of quickening chutes, some fifty yards down. Clambering soggily to his feet, he drew a pistol from his belt and aimed it at Falconer. The pistol misfired. Pierre hurled the pistol into the river in a fit of blind rage, and threw a string of livid curses across the river at Falconer.

"Keep going!" yelled Falconer. "He ain't worth dying for."

"You will have to kill me, Falconer!" Pierre plunged back into the river, fighting the current to reach the northern bank.

"Damn fool," muttered Falconer. He grabbed Dowd by the hair and dragged his limp body along the river's edge until he reached the place where he had first entered the Platte. Retrieving the Hawken from behind the log, he checked the load and turned as Pierre came into sight at a staggering run. Rivulets of blood dripped from one of the French Canadian's clenched fists. A knife was gripped in the other.

Falconer didn't waste his breath trying to warn the man a second time. He raised the Hawken to his shoulder and fired. At such close range the impact of the bullet, dead center in Pierre's chest, hurled the man backward. He twitched briefly on the ground and then lay forever still.

Drawing a long breath, Falconer reloaded the Hawken.

After tying Dowd's hands behind his back with a strip of rawhide, he rolled his still-unconscious prisoner into the shallows. Dowd came to and thought he was drowning, and began to thrash and sputter. Falconer retrieved him, dragging him back up onto the bank.

"Get on your feet," said Falconer.

Dowd managed to comply, no easy task with hands lashed behind his back. He glowered darkly at Falconer, then glanced at Pierre's corpse.

"I'm going to kill you," he announced, his voice flat and unemotional.

"It's been tried before. Most recently, by your friend there."

"When *I* try you'll be the one laid out for buzzard bait."

"You don't have much time to get the job done," said Falconer, thinking that it would be a grievous mistake to underestimate Dowd—the last mistake he would ever make. "You'll be with the Arapahoes in ten day's time."

"You know what they'll do to me."

"I know."

"You think you're better than me?" sneered Dowd. "You're no different."

"I'll answer for my sins when the time comes."

"That time is coming. Soon. Just who do you think you are, Falconer? This ain't none of your business. What gives you the right to hunt me down?"

"I had nothing better to do. Now come on. You've got a long walk ahead of you."

"At least let me have Pierre's clothes. He sure as hell don't need 'em no more."

"No."

"His moccasins, anyway."

"No. You might as well get used to pain."

Dowd smiled. That worried Falconer. Most men in Dowd's predicament, facing the future he faced, would have started to come apart at the seams by now. But Dowd could smile. He wasn't going to bemoan his fate, or beg for mercy. At least not yet. Even the bravest man would eventually break under an Arapaho knife. Falconer could muster no sympathy for Dowd, though. He couldn't get out of his mind what Dowd had done to that boy. Killing was one thing. But what Dowd had done qualified as butchery, pure and simple.

Falconer took a length of hemp rope from the Appaloosa's saddle and put the looped end around Dowd's neck. Dowd made no move, no protest, just watched Falconer with that wicked smile curling the corner of his mouth.

"I'm going to try to deliver you to the Arapahoes alive," said Falconer, "because that's the way they want you. But don't vex me too hard, boy, or I'll just kill you, skin you, and deliver your hide and head."

"You'll be waiting for me in hell, Falconer."

Falconer climbed into the saddle, looped the other end of the rope around the pommel, and nudged the Appaloosa into motion with his knees.

* * *

That same day Falconer reached the Pawnee village. He rode straight in and explained to the old headman what he was doing. The chief nodded his approval and invited Falconer to share a pipe with him. They sat on a blanket in front of the chief's hut. A short distance away, Dowd sat slumped over, taking advantage of the spot of shade cast by the tall Appaloosa, and spitting at a group of Pawnee urchins who were tormenting him. Falconer knew that a man who could work up enough saliva to spit like that wasn't too afraid—a man who was scared had a bad case of dry mouth.

"I am troubled," the old chief admitted to Falconer. "You are a friend of the Indian. Maybe you can help me."

"If I'm able."

"You can see that most of the young men of the village are nowhere to be found."

"Are they out looking for the buffalo?"

"They are hunting, but not the buffalo. They are going to kill some of your own people."

Falconer's eyes narrowed into muddy brown slits. "Why are you telling me this, ancient one?"

"I want no trouble with the white man. But it is a white man who is the cause of this."

"How do you mean?"

"Three moons ago a man named Spellman came here. He talked to the young men. They struck a bargain with him, against my wishes." Sadness deepened the creases around the old man's rheumy eyes. "The young men look to my own son for leadership. But he does not listen to his father anymore. He does not think about what is best for his people, only what satisfies him."

Falconer had hardly heard a word the old man was saying after Spellman's name reached his ears. What was that man up to, conspiring with Pawnee hotheads? It did not bode well for the emigrants he was guiding. Falconer's thoughts lingered on the woman who had brought him coffee during his brief visit with the Oregon-bound pioneers. He had a feeling she and her fellow travelers were in mortal danger—and from the very man in whom they had put their trust.

"What kind of bargain did Spellman make with your young men?" he asked the chief.

"Spellman will lead his people to a place north of here, in the sandhills. There he will steal what he wants from them and abandon them. Then my son and the other warriors will strike. They will kill all of Spellman's people. In return, they will have all the livestock, and any other possessions which Spellman has left behind."

Falconer was grimly silent. The moment he had seen Spellman's companion, the half-breed, he had suspected that the two of them were not to be trusted. He had never laid eyes on the breed until yesterday, but he knew the type well enough. The frontier was a lawless land, and fast filling up with all manner of cutthroats and scoundrels, men without honor, men whose allegiance was only to themselves. The breed was one such man. It was written all over him. Falconer had seen it in a glance. And Spellman, if only by association, was undoubtedly cut from the same rotten cloth.

"My people are hungry," sighed the Pawnee headman. "The buffalo have been scarce this spring. The young men have traveled far to find them, and many times they have returned with empty hands. The livestock which Spellman has promised will feed this village for a long time. That is why the young men are going to kill the whites, because they cannot hear my words over the crying of the hungry children."

"You must go further west to find the great herd this year," said Falconer. "In the valleys between the Platte and the Powder rivers."

"The mouths of my people will be filled with dirt, I fear, when the whites seek vengeance for what my foolish son and his followers are about to do."

Itching to be on his way, Falconer stood up. "I am grateful to you for telling me this. I will try to stop them."

The chief nodded. "If my son must die so that my people can live, I will understand."

"I hope no lives will be lost."

But Falconer knew in his heart that there was bound to be some killing done. It was a shame, because the only men who deserved to die were Spellman and the breed. He would show no mercy to that pair, who had conspired to rob and murder innocent people.

"I have a favor to ask of you," he told the chief. "I must travel fast if I am to stop your young warriors. My prisoner would only slow me down."

"Leave him with us."

"He is a dangerous man. I told the Arapahoes I would bring him back to them alive, but kill him if you find it is necessary."

The Pawnee nodded. "He will be here when you return."

Falconer went to the Appaloosa and came back with some tobacco, which he presented to the headman.

"This is all I have to give," he said, "as a token of our friendship. I give it in the hope that our people will learn to live together."

"It is good to have hope," replied the chief, his tone of voice revealing that he had none.

Chapter Seven

"Lillian, do you think they will find Spellman and the breed?"

Lillian Tasker reached out and put a hand over Molly Wilkerson's. They sat on the ground beside a campfire which was too feeble to throw back the deep gloom of gathering night.

"I think so, Molly."

"I am afraid of what will happen if they do," confessed Molly. "Tom is a brave man and all, but he is no match for the likes of Spellman and the breed. Oh, I almost wish he hadn't gone after them."

"He had to go."

"I know. What kind of man would he be if he didn't at least try? But I don't think I could go on without him."

"Don't talk that way. Tom will come back. They'll all come back."

With Dan Blakemore, Lee Donaghue, and Judd Pollock, Tom Wilkerson had set out to catch Spellman and Breed, who had skulked away like the thieving dogs they were in last night's black heart, having rendered Norris Durant, who was on guard duty, unconscious with a blow to the head that, according to Doc Holsberry, had caused a severe concussion. Durant was still out cold, and Lillian was beginning to wonder if he would pull through.

Every man in the company had wanted to go after Spellman, but Wilkerson had persuaded Abney and Lomax and Ted Norwood and his two sons that it would be unwise to leave the women and children undefended.

And so the four men had ridden out at first light, four or five hours behind Spellman and the breed, and Lillian suspected that by now the issue had been resolved, one way or the other, because Spellman would have been slowed by the hidehunter's wagon which carried everyone's purloined valuables—well, almost everyone's—while Tom and the others had been mounted on horses, the only four horses in the party; Lee Donaghue was riding Ol' Blue.

Lillian shared Molly's concerns, but she couldn't let on that she did, because Donaghue's daughter Lisle was staying in the Tasker wagon while her father was away, and the wagon was within earshot, and Lillian was fairly certain the poor, distraught girl wasn't sleeping—wasn't *able* to sleep. Lillian's heart went out to her. Having lost her mother, Lisle was now confronted by the terrifying prospect of losing her father, too. "If—if something happens," Donaghue had whispered to Lillian, "I'd be obliged if you'd look out for her." Lillian wondered why he had chosen her, but of course she had promised, and was prepared to treat Lisle as her own child from now on if the worst did happen.

Lee Donaghue's heart had not been in the mission to catch Spellman and the breed. Lillian was convinced of that, just as she was sure he had been the first to volunteer to ride with Tom Wilkerson in order to impress her with his courage. *God in heaven, I hope he doesn't get himself killed and leave sweet little Lisle an orphan just because he wanted to catch my eye.*

Jonathan Holsberry wandered over, slump-shouldered

and haggard. "I could use some coffee if you ladies have any to spare."

Lillian poured him a cup, and her thoughts wandered to the frontiersman named Hugh Falconer, for whom she had poured coffee three days ago. She found herself wishing Falconer were here. She knew next to nothing about the man, but for some reason felt all would be well if only he were with them now.

"What did you lose, Dr. Holsberry?" asked Molly.

"Oh, a little money, some letters, a daguerreotype of my dear wife, my father's watch. But, most of all, I lost my faith in my fellow man. And that is the greatest loss of all."

"How is Mr. Durant?" inquired Lillian.

"I am afraid he may lose his life."

"Dear God, no," breathed Molly.

Holsberry nodded gravely. "Head injuries are very tricky. We as yet know precious little about them. It is really in God's hands; there is nothing more that I can think to do for him."

Shuddering, Lillian gathered the shawl about her shoulders. Since leaving the Platte the day before yesterday they had traveled under overcast skies, with the constant threat of rain borne upon the chill winds which swept down from the north. They had no idea where they were, without the sun or the stars to give them guidance, and nothing but barren sandhills extending forever in every direction. The weather, then, had been Spellman's ally. He had used it to his own advantage, waiting for conditions such as these before robbing them and then abandoning them to their fate. They were truly lost in the wilderness.

"I find it difficult to believe," said Holsberry, "that Spellman would do such a dastardly deed as this. I mean, how can he hope to get away with it? Once we've told our story there will be no place—no civilized place, at any rate—that he could dare show his face. And all for what? A few hundred dollars in cash? A few mementos of value only to those to whom they belong?"

"Mr. Abney and Mr. Lomax between them had almost four hundred dollars," said Molly. "Tom and I had about two hundred ourselves. What about you, Lillian? You haven't said how much you lost."

Lillian had been dreading the question. But, regardless of the consequences, she wasn't going to lie.

"I didn't lose anything. Fortunately, I took my cow back the day before. And, well, the box I gave to your husband to give Spellman—it was empty. I took the money before I gave it up."

"But why on earth did you do that?"

"Because I never did trust Spellman."

"Perhaps you should have shared your suspicions about him with the rest of us, dear," said Holsberry.

"Maybe I should have. If so, I am sorry. But I had nothing to go on, no evidence against Spellman, and, well, it didn't seem right to question his integrity behind his back." She looked away from the others, into the flames of the campfire. "I do feel badly, like a sneak thief, somehow. All of you have lost your life savings . . ."

Molly laughed. "Don't be silly, dear. Do you think we would feel better if you had lost yours, too?"

"Pure nonsense," concurred Holsberry, manufacturing some gruff good cheer for Lillian's benefit. "At least one of us demonstrated enough good sense not to trust that devil Spellman. As I've said, I just can't fathom the whole business. Surely he doesn't expect to go scot free."

"It only makes sense," said Lillian, "if he doesn't expect any of us to survive."

They stared at her, slow to comprehend, but just then Abney emerged from the darkness and spoke up.

"Miss Tasker's got a good point. I keep thinking about them Pawnees. You saw how they seemed to know Spellman and the breed."

"They were afraid of Breed," said Molly.

"Sure. But that don't mean they're not in cahoots."

Abney's suspicions imbued the night with new menace, and for a moment all four of them were still, listening anxiously to the whisper of the wind and the lament of a distant coyote alone in the immensity of the trackless plains. But was it alone, wondered Lillian; and was it a genuine coyote? Perhaps the sound had issued from a Pawnee throat. Maybe a war party was creeping up on the wagons even now.

Lillian stood up, pulling the shawl closer about her. She felt too much like a target in the firelight. "I think I shall check on the children," she said. "Molly, please try to get some rest. Don't worry so about Tom. He'll come back, I just know he will."

"You ladies don't need to fret," said Abney with a degree of truculence. "Lomax and I are going to stand watch tonight. No thievin' redskin is going to get anywhere near one of the wagons."

Such brawny forcefulness was a bit out of character for Abney, mused Lillian, and she wondered if he had been sampling that liquid bravemaker of his. Turning toward her wagon, she could not share in Abney's confidence.

Climbing in under the canvas, she heard Lisle sniffling in the darkness. The poor girl had been crying.

"Everything will be fine," said Lillian wearily, suddenly tired of playing the role of the eternal optimist. "Your father will be back tomorrow, Lisle, or the next day. You'll see."

"Why did he have to go? I wish he hadn't. Doesn't he care about me?"

"Of course he cares. He is a very brave man, and what he's doing, he's doing for you."

"No he's not. He's not a brave man, either. He's doing this stupid thing to impress you. I've seen how he looks at you. I'm not blind."

The petulance in Lisle's voice took Lillian aback. She didn't know what to say. The girl's accusation confirmed her own secret fears.

"If anything happens to my father," said Lisle, "I'll never forgive you. Never."

The next morning, Lillian was first out of her wagon. It was still dark, still overcast, but she knew it was nearly dawn. She hadn't been able to sleep last night, thinking about Pawnees and Lee Donaghue and the man named Falconer—and when Falconer was the first sight to greet her eyes that morning she wondered if sheer exhaustion had made her delirious.

The mountain man was sitting on his heels at the fire, stirring up the embers. He nodded pleasantly at her. "Mornin', miss."

"How did . . . how long have you been here?"

"Couple hours, I reckon."

"You took a dreadful chance, with Mr. Abney and Mr. Lomax on guard and expecting a Pawnee attack at any moment."

"Not much of a chance, really," said Falconer. "One of them is yonder, underneath that wagon, more asleep than awake, and I can smell the whiskey on his breath from here. The other's stayed over on that side of the camp all night."

"You mean you just walked right in here without either one of them knowing?" Lillian was aghast.

"Yes, ma'am. I know what you're thinking. If I could do it, so could a Pawnee brave. And you're right."

Lillian's nerves were frayed after everything that had happened, and she almost jumped out of her skin as a startled shout came from Lomax beyond the wagons. Immediately the Norwoods, father and sons, boiled out of their wagons, half dressed and armed to the teeth. Lomax came running into the wagon circle, and the Norwoods were all shouting at once, trying to find out what was wrong. In the eye of the storm, Falconer squatted as calm as could be at the revived campfire.

"I reckon," he drawled, amused, "that they have discovered my horse."

Lillian had to smile. It wasn't really funny—that this man could ride up to camp, tether his horse, and make himself at home without a soul noticing, but she could scarcely refrain from laughing out loud at the whole ludicrous situation. *I am delirious,* she decided. *Delirious with relief that Falconer is here.* She was going to be safe. More importantly, Johnny was going to be safe. Falconer would see to that. She had had serious doubts about their safety last night, and hadn't wanted to admit it to herself, but she could admit it now. Now that it didn't matter anymore.

Lomax approached, wearing a belligerent scowl. "What the blazes are you doing here?"

"I heard you folks were having some trouble."

"Who told you?"

"A Pawnee."

"You a friend to the Pawnee as well as the Arapaho?"

"I know them. They know me."

Lomax relented. He was upset with Falconer for having shown him up in front of the others, but he had bigger problems than a bruised ego, and he could readily see the advantage to having the mountain man in the camp.

"That damned scoundrel—excuse me, miss—that fellow Spellman and his half-breed cutthroat stole us blind. Tom Wilkerson and three of the others are out looking for them."

"Better hope they don't find them."

The scowl reappeared. "What do you mean by that? I lost nearly five hundred dollars."

"You and Mr. Abney lost four hundred dollars," corrected Lillian. "He is your partner, remember?"

"Yes, I remember." Lomax didn't sound too enthusiastic.

"No offense," said Falconer, "But a few farmers are no match for the likes of Spellman, or the breed."

"What about you?" asked Lillian. "Could you help us? Could you get the money back?"

"Maybe. But first things first." Falconer checked the sky, black now, fading to gray. "We're going to have to deal with the Pawnees in a few minutes."

"Pawnees?" echoed Ted Norwood, walking up with his sons on either side.

"About twenty braves out yonder, waiting for enough light to see by. They've been out there half the night."

"I haven't seen anything," said Lomax uselessly.

"What are they waiting for?" asked Norwood. "Why haven't they attacked us?"

"A Pawnee doesn't care to die at night, in case his soul loses its way in the darkness."

"You actually saw them out yonder?"

Falconer nodded.

"And they didn't see you?"

"Wouldn't be here if they had."

"Thought you were a friend of the Pawnee," said Lomax.

"Didn't say friend. The old chief who told me about your predicament wants to keep the peace. But the young men of the village are out for blood and glory. They cut a deal with Amos Spellman. They kill you folks so nobody finds out what he's done, and they get the livestock and anything else that suits their fancy." Falconer glanced at Lillian, and she felt a cold chill travel up her spine. Clearly Falconer thought she would suit a Pawnee brave's fancy.

"Good God," breathed Norwood. "Twenty of the red bastards! I wish Wilkerson and them hadn't . . ."

"Wishing won't change things," snapped Lomax. "We've got five men who can fight," he told Falconer. "That's not counting Doc Holsberry."

"You're not counting me, either," said Lillian. "I can shoot a rifle."

"But can you hit anything? That's the question here."

Lillian's eyes flashed. "I have no doubt I can shoot as well as you can, Mr. Lomax. If not better."

"Everybody who can use a rifle better fetch one," said Falconer.

"Where will they come from?" asked Norwood. "Which direction?"

"Everywhere at once. They'll be on their ponies, riding low, so shoot the horses if you can't draw a bead on the rider."

The men headed for their respective wagons. Falconer turned his attention back to Lillian. "I'll stick with you, miss, if you don't mind."

In spite of the situation, Lillian smiled warmly. "I don't mind at all. But please call me Lillian."

He nodded. "You scared, Lillian?"

"A little."

"I think you're very brave."

"No I'm not."

"Being brave has nothing to do with being unafraid. It's a matter of how much being scared you can take."

Lillian wanted to tell him she wasn't nearly as afraid as she might have been if he hadn't been standing beside her.

But she didn't.

Chapter Eight

With Hugh Falconer's help, Lillian took some trunks and bags of flour out of the wagon and stacked them in a makeshift barricade beneath the prairie schooner, behind which they deposited Johnny and Lisle. When Johnny asked her what was happening, Lillian told him the truth, and was proud of the way he took it. Little fists tightly clenched, Johnny squared his shoulders and declared himself ready and able to help fight the wild Indians.

"Your job is to keep Lisle under the wagon and make sure no harm comes to her," said Lillian.

"I'll make sure," replied Johnny. "You can count on me."

"I know I can." Fighting back sudden tears, Lillian hugged him.

Taking Lisle by the hand, Johnny went under the wagon and settled in behind the barricade. Lillian joined Falconer, who stood at the rear of the wagon, the Hawken mountain rifle cradled in his arms. Several hundred yards from the circle of wagons, a lone Pawnee had suddenly appeared, as though he and his painted pony had sprouted from the ground. He rode the pony in a wide circle, and shouting at the wagons, held a lance high above his head before thrusting it into the earth.

Ted Norwood joined them, pointing with a belligerent chin at the warrior. "What's he up to? Some kind of challenge?"

"Not at all," replied Falconer. "Making the circle is a signal he's come in peace. He says he is a friend. Wants to come into our camp and parley."

"Peace? I thought you said they . . ."

Falconer brought the Hawken to his shoulder and squeezed off a shot.

The Pawnee somersaulted off the back of his pony, which darted away.

"What the hell are you doing?" cried Norwood.

"He was lying," said Falconer calmly, reloading the Hawken. "You'd best get back to your wagon."

Norwood took the advice.

Falconer turned to Lillian. "I know it doesn't seem fair, to kill an unarmed man without warning. But it was a ruse, all that talk about friendship. And that's one less Pawnee who could bring harm to you and yours."

"There is no need to explain yourself to me," she replied.

A bloodcurdling, ululating cry split asunder the dawn silence, and suddenly the other Pawnees appeared on galloping ponies, charging the wagons. They came from all directions, as Falconer had said they would. Most of them guided their ponies with their knees and fired their arrows at the wagons, so swiftly that they could loose a second shaft before the first one had struck its mark.

"Take the other end of the wagon, ma'am."

"Lillian. Remember?"

He smiled, impressed by her composure. Then the Hawken jumped to his shoulder and spoke, all in one quick, fluid, almost casual motion. Another riderless Indian pony veered off.

Taking up a position at the front of the prairie

schooner, Lillian gasped as an arrow thumped in the wagon's box, scant inches from her face. Undeterred, she brought the rifle up and fired at the most convenient target. Her bullet struck the Pawnee's horse and it collapsed, plowing a deep furrow in the dusty earth. The warrior tumbled head over heels. Hands shaking, Lillian poured gunpowder into the barrel from the horn hanging at her side by its sling, inserted the ball—a half ounce of St. Louis lead—and extracted the hickory ramrod from underneath the barrel. As she was tamping down the load she heard Johnny's voice, high and frantic, above the crackle of rifle fire and the war cries of the attacking Indians.

"Ma! Look out!"

Beneath the wagon, Johnny had risked a look above the trunks and flour sacks, and saw the Pawnee whose horse his mother had slain get to his feet and charge toward her with a snarl on his painted face and a knife in his hand.

Lillian just had time to affix a new percussion cap and squeeze the trigger, holding the rifle at hip level. She had left the ramrod in the barrel—at point-blank range it impaled the Pawnee. With a hideous scream the Indian stumbled forward into her. The impact jarred the rifle from her grasp. She fell, twisting away from the knife. Dying, the Pawnee collapsed, falling on the knife, and lay still in death.

Dazed, Lillian began to rise, heard Falconer shout something, and then he was bearing her back down to the ground, somehow shielding the fall with his body, rolling over on top of her. Suddenly the ground right next to their heads sprouted a Pawnee lance, and the earth beneath them trembled as the shadow of a mounted Indian passed briefly over them. Then the horse had carried its Pawnee rider on past, and Falconer, leaping to his feet, yanked the lance out of the ground and hurled it. As always, his aim was true. Lillian looked up in time to see the Indian topple from the pony with the lance jutting out of his back.

Falconer's strong arms brought her to her feet, and he spun her around against the side of the wagon. Still shielding her with his body, he drew the pistol from his belt. One shot, and another Pawnee fell dead. Lillian shut her eyes, overwhelmed by the violence of the scene.

"My God," she heard him say, his voice thick with emotion and that Scottish brogue, "you were almost killed."

"I'm sorry." It was all she could think to say, and she put her arms around him. Her whole slender frame was trembling now.

"It's all over, Lillian."

Belatedly, she realized that the shooting had stopped, the war cries ceased, but she didn't let go of him, because for once she felt safe.

"Are you hurt, Miss Tasker?"

This was Lomax, and she opened her eyes to see him running up to them through a dwindling haze of dust and powdersmoke.

"She's fine," said Falconer, and Lomax moved on, making the complete circle to see if any of the company had fallen.

Falconer made no move to extricate himself and, a little embarrassed, Lillian let go.

"I'm sorry," she said again, then made the mistake of looking at the man she had killed. Her stomach performed a slow and nauseating roll. Tasting bile, she mumbled, "Excuse me, I'm going to be sick." Turning away, she grabbed hold of a wagon wheel, bent over, and threw up. Johnny materialized beside her, concerned. "Get back under the wagon this instant," she snapped, a bit too harshly, she thought. But the world seemed a very perilous place at that moment, where life was cheap and death lurked all around. Johnny crawled back under the prairie schooner, rejoining the whimpering Lisle Donaghue, who cowered behind the trunks and flour sacks, looking like wild horses couldn't drag her out into the open. Lillian straightened, ladled water out of the big barrel strapped to the side of the wagon, and drank greedily.

Falconer had his back to her, out of deference to her condition, and she straightened and walked past him to retrieve her rifle from the ground. Then she remembered that the ramrod was still in the body of the Pawnee she had killed, though she carefully avoided looking at the corpse.

Holsberry rushed past, carrying his medical bag. "Ted Norwood took an arrow," he informed them brusquely, and was gone. Across the way, a woman's wail of grief set Lillian's teeth on edge. She knew somehow that it was Sadie Durant—knew, also, by the tenor of that tormented screech that someone had died. But she couldn't bring herself to go see, to try and comfort the poor woman. She had seen all the death she could stomach for one day.

Thirteen-year-old Billy Durant, in taking his ailing father's place on the line of battle, had been killed. A war lance had struck him in the chest, cracking open his rib cage and rupturing the heart within. Ted Norwood had taken an arrow through the arm, but Doc Holsberry deftly removed the shaft and arrowhead and had him patched up in no time.

Twelve Pawnees were dead or dying. From the one Lillian had killed, Falconer removed a breastplate decorated with hawk feathers. He also removed the hickory ramrod, cleaned it thoroughly so that no trace of blood remained, and placed it in the Tasker wagon.

The bodies of the Pawnee who had perished within the circle of wagons were carried out by the Norwood brothers. A mule, an ox, and Lillian's cow, Tessie, had been killed in the attack. Lillian almost wept at the sight of poor gentle Tessie lying there, riddled with arrows. But she shed no tears, thinking it too foolish to cry over a dead animal, when poor Sadie Durant was mourning the loss of her son.

They buried Billy Durant without delay, though his mother was reluctant to surrender him so quickly to the dust. But, despite Falconer's assurances that it would not happen, the other men in the company were concerned that the Pawnees might return in greater numbers to take issue with them again. Holsberry said a few words over Billy's grave, and, at Sadie Durant's behest, the Norwood boys fashioned a crude grave marker from a piece of planking removed from the Durant wagon. Lillian couldn't help thinking about Norris Durant. If and when the poor man regained consciousness he would be confronted by the fact that his son had been killed and lay in a shallow grave somewhere back there along the Oregon Trail.

The men began to dig other graves, these for the Indian dead, until Falconer called a halt to their efforts.

"In death there are no enemies," said Holsberry. "To bury them is the Christian thing to do."

"An admirable sentiment," replied Falconer. "But the Indians aren't Christians. They don't generally bury their dead. They believe the soul escapes the body through the mouth. If you fill the mouth with dirt, the soul is trapped in the corpse forever. So you see, it isn't a very Christian thing to do, after all."

"So we just leave them out here for the wolves and the buzzards?" asked Lomax.

"In time others will come along to retrieve the bodies."

"I think we ought to get a move on," said Jake Norwood, nervously scanning the horizon.

"But what about Tom Wilkerson and the others?" asked Abney.

"They can pick up our trail," said Lomax.

"Tom told us to wait right here." Abney pointed at the slate gray overcast. "Can you tell which way is west?"

"I think it's that way."

"You think."

"Perhaps Mr. Falconer would consent to guide us," said Holsberry.

The men looked at each other, then at Falconer. "How about it?" asked Lomax. "Are you game?"

Falconer glanced toward the wagons. He could see Lillian, who with Johnny's help was hitching the oxen to her wagon.

"Reckon I could," he said slowly. "But I have a couple of chores to do first."

"What kind of chores, if you don't mind us asking?"

"I'm riding back to the Pawnee village. With the permission of the men they belonged to, I'd like to butcher out the dead stock and give the meat to the women, children, and old people who are going hungry in that village."

"Feed the Pawnees?" Lomax was incredulous. "Didn't they just try to kill us? Or was I having a bad dream?"

"The women and children had nothing to do with that. Lillian . . . I mean, Miss Tasker has given me permission to give her cow to them. It is, after all, the Christian thing to do."

"You can have the ox," said Ted Norwood.

"The mule belonged to Donaghue," said Abney.

"I doubt very much if he would mind," said Holsberry.

"You said a couple of things," Lomax reminded Falconer.

"I have a prisoner to deliver to the Arapahoes," said the mountain man. "Arapaho country is due west of here. I could bring him along, but he's not what I'd call fit company for decent folks, and he's dangerous besides. You might not want his kind anywhere near your loved ones."

"But if we help you deliver him, the Arapahoes won't make trouble for us," said Norwood.

Falconer nodded. "That's a consideration. They would likely feel beholden to you. The Arapahoes are good friends to have—and very bad enemies."

"Worse than the Pawnees?" asked Abney.

"There are more of them, and they tend to be more experienced fighters."

"Well, it's okay with me," said Norwood.

"And me," said Abney.

"Wait a doggone minute," said Lomax. "You're talking about handing a white man over to red savages, aren't you? You men want to be a party to that?"

"I want to get me and mine safely through to Oregon," said Norwood. "That's what I want. He's a cold-blooded murderer, isn't he?"

"That makes it permissible to condemn him to a horrible death?" asked Holsberry. "What does that make us?"

"We're not back East, Doc," said Norwood. "This country ain't civilized. Out here it's dog eat dog. Survival of the fittest. Ain't that so, Mr. Falconer?"

"I reject that argument," replied the physician. "Are we to become savages because we live in a savage land? I won't have anything to do with it."

"We should vote," said Norwood. "We know where

Doc Holsberry stands. I say we help Mr. Falconer deliver his prisoner to the Arapahoes. You still go along with that, Abney?"

Abney nodded. He looked like he wished he was anywhere but here.

"What about you, Lomax?"

Lomax scanned their faces, ending up with Falconer. "I'll go along, too, I guess. It doesn't sit well with me, but we need a guide, and we need safe passage through Arapaho country."

"What about Wilkerson and the others?" asked Holsberry. "Shouldn't they have a say in this decision?"

"They may not have a say in anything, anymore," muttered Lomax.

"That's no way to talk," protested Abney.

"I have a suggestion," said Falconer. "We'll wait here a couple of hours. Maybe they'll show up. If not, we travel a half day west. There's good water ten miles in that direction. We'll wait there another day. If they're not back by tomorrow then chances are they won't be coming back at all."

"You think they'll catch up with those scoundrels?" asked Holsberry.

"No, sir. I don't. I think they'll give up."

"But they're mounted, and Spellman is slowed down with a wagon," said Lomax.

"Spellman will leave the wagon. So what do you say?"

It was agreed. If Tom Wilkerson and the others didn't return in time, one of Norwood's sons would drive Donaghue's wagon, while the wives of the other three missing men would have to manage on their own.

But they did return, just as Falconer's deadline expired, and everyone was greatly relieved to count four horsemen emerging from the haze of a cold, gray drizzle that had just begun to leak from the sky. Joy turned to concern, however, as the riders reached the circle of wagons and they could see that Judd Pollock was slumped in his saddle, a blood soaked tourniquet around his thigh, his pallor that of a dead man's. The others didn't look in much better condition. Their faces were dark with stubble, their eyes sunk deep in their sockets, their cheeks drawn and haggard. These were men so exhausted they could scarcely stand on their own two feet.

Holsberry had the Norwood brothers carry Pollock to his wagon. Wilkerson, Blakemore, and Donaghue were settled down by the campfire, blankets draped around their shoulders, and cups of coffee poured, which each man drank greedily. The rest of the company gathered round, eager to hear what had transpired. Finally, Wilkerson felt strong enough to oblige them.

"We came up on their wagon twenty miles south of here. Maybe they knew we were on their trail. We figured we would have to ride day and night after that if we wanted to catch them. So that's what we did. We lost their sign a time or two, but we were lucky enough to find it again."

"Yeah. Lucky," mumbled Donaghue dryly into his coffee cup.

Wilkerson continued, heaving a dejected sigh. He was a proud man, and he had been bested, and he didn't like to admit as much. Lillian admired him for what he had tried to do—what they had all tried to do. It had been very heroic, because they were farmers, and no match for the likes of Amos Spellman and the half-breed, and they had known it from the start and gone through with it just the same.

"The trail took us across the Platte River. They

kept on going south. At least I think it was south. Then, yesterday morning, we rode right into an ambush. Judd took the first bullet. We scrambled for cover. Two of our horses ran off. They kept us pinned down for an hour, and we never once caught a glimpse of either one of them. It was like being shot at by ghosts. Then they stopped shooting. I for one was too all-fired scared to stick my head up for another hour at least, until I was fairly certain they were long gone. Took a while to catch up with those two ponies. I made the decision to turn back. Figured next time somebody would get killed. We had been lucky. Push your luck and you might not live to regret it, especially when you're dealing with men like those. Sorry, folks."

"You made the decision?" Blakemore scoffed. "Why are you taking all the blame, Tom? I think I speak for Lee and Judd when I say we had gone as far as our nerves would take us. If Tom had wanted to keep after them he probably would have had to go on alone."

"You did your best," said Abney.

"But now what do we do?" snapped a disgruntled Lomax. "We've lost our whole grubstake, partner. Those thieving bastards took five hundred dollars that belonged to me."

"Belonged to us," corrected Abney. "And I wouldn't want anyone to have lost their life just to get it back."

"They did the best they could, Mr. Lomax," said Lillian sternly. She was aware of the fact that Lee Donaghue was looking up at her with those lonely eyes of his, pleading silently to notice him, maybe even grace him with a smile. She tried to ignore him.

"So they just get away with what they did?" asked Lomax. His gaze fastened on Hugh Falconer, who stood a little apart from the others, the Hawken mountain rifle cradled in his arms. "How about you? I bet you could track those two men down."

Everyone else looked around at Falconer. Lillian thought, *He is the one man here who could handle the likes of Spellman and the breed.* But she didn't want him to go, wouldn't have even if she had lost her savings along with the others. She was by now convinced that they would not make it to the promised land without Hugh Falconer to lead them.

Apparently she was not alone in that sentiment. Ted Norwood said, "He can't very well act as our guide while he's chasing Spellman halfway across the continent. They've got, what, a four- or five-day lead by now, and the Good Lord only knows where they're headed for."

"Comanchero country, most likely," said Falconer.

"Main thing for us is to get our families across the mountains before winter sets in," continued Norwood. "We can spread the word about Spellman, and he'll get his comeuppance sooner or later."

"After he's spent all our money," groused Lomax.

"At least we can see to it that he doesn't have the opportunity to prey on others," said Lillian.

"What do you say?" Lomax asked Falconer, still reluctant to let go of a slender hope of recovering his grubstake.

"I say forget the money. If it's any consolation, Mr. Norwood is right. Spellman will pay for his crimes, someday. The evil that men do always comes back to haunt them. Always."

Chapter Nine

Tom Wilkerson and Ted Norwood insisted on accompanying Falconer when he returned to the Pawnee camp, in spite of the fact that the former was exhausted from the futile pursuit of Spellman, and the latter suffered considerable pain from the wound in his arm. Both men felt greatly beholden to the mountain man, being certain that his presence during the Pawnee attack had averted disaster. And they were worried that Falconer might ride into trouble on account of the twelve dead Pawnee braves.

Lillian was worried about that, too—worried to the point of distraction as Falconer's departure became imminent. She hated to see the man go, for fear he would never return. So, as the men were mounting up to ride away, she rushed forward impulsively, to stand beside the frontiersman's tall Appaloosa, and she begged him to please be careful and come back safe.

"I will," he said. "You can count on that."

Falconer had calculated they would be gone for three, maybe four days, depending on the weather, and the rest had agreed to remain encamped on the banks of the creek to which he had led them the day of the Indian raid. Unlike the Platte, into which it flowed, this creek ran sweet and clean. Though Falconer had seemed confident that the Pawnees would not return, everyone was on edge, nerves still badly frayed from their recent harrowing ordeal.

In spite of the fact that she was afraid of seeing a Pawnee brave coming at her with a knife raised every time she turned around, Lillian was determined to have a bath in the creek. She hadn't had a decent bath since leaving Illinois, forced to resort to freshening up every morning out of one of the big water barrels attached to the overland wagon. Even so, she had felt guilty using the water supply for that purpose, and had done so judiciously, afterward feeling hardly cleaner than before. Her pores were clogged with the dust of the prairie. But now she had the creek, the best water she had seen in weeks, and it beckoned to her constantly. She could not long resist its siren song. The only problem lay in slipping away from the camp unnoticed.

Eventually she saw her chance and seized the opportunity. Fifty yards south of the wagon circle, a clump of dusty willows marked the spot where the creek described a dogleg turn to the east. Beyond the turn, a rise of ground provided here with the privacy she sought.

Out of sight and sound of the camp she felt suddenly alone and vulnerable, but she couldn't resist the creek, no matter what. Hastily shedding her dress and shoes, she waded out into the water in her undergarments. Then she chided herself for being so silly. With only God watching, why was she being so modest? Back out of the creek she came, and shed the wet undergarments.

The water was cold due to the recent rains, but she quickly became accustomed to it. She found a spot a bit downstream where the creek was deep enough that she could only just touch the gravelly bottom with her toes.

Keeping to the deepest part of the creek's channel, Lillian alternated between treading water and standing on her tiptoes, letting the gentle current lave her body. It was pure heaven. At that moment, for the first time in days, the sun found a seam in the overcast sky, and its warm light streamed through. Lillian was delighted, thinking that perhaps the Almighty was showing her a special kindness.

The memory of innocent and happier days came to her—of going with her sisters to the pond at the corner of the Birch homestead, those Sunday afternoons after church, grateful that their parents strongly conformed to the Bible's direction against working on the Sabbath. She wondered what her sisters would think of her now, cavorting naked in some nameless creek out in the middle of nowhere. One sister had married a career soldier and moved to Boston, while the other had wed a storekeeper. Both were now proper, conservative ladies, wives, and mothers, active in their communities, wanting for nothing, far removed from their rustic roots, and having cast off youth's spirit of adventure. They would be aghast, decided Lillian, smiling, and maybe, down deep inside, a little envious of her.

Returning to the bank, she retrieved the brick of soap she had thought to bring along. Shaking her mahogany brown hair undone, she found a place in the shallows where she could sit and give her tresses a good washing. Leaning on her elbows, she tilted her head back and let the current rinse the soap out of her hair. The sun was warm on her face, and the water began to chill her slightly. Reluctantly she left the creek, eschewed donning her wet undergarments, and put the dress on without them. The gingham clung to her wet body, and she tried to make herself as presentable as possible before gathering up her shoes and undergarments and turning back for camp. They would scold her for venturing off alone like this, but the deal was done and, frankly, she didn't care who knew, now that it was too late to prevent her.

One step—then she froze in place, a gasp escaping her lips.

Lee Donaghue stood there in the speckled shade of the willows at the bend in the creek. He moved as though to conceal himself, or run away, but realizing that Lillian had spotted him, he came forward, rifle racked nonchalantly on his shoulder.

"How long have you been spying on me?" she snapped, infuriated.

"I . . . well, I . . ." His eyes dropped away from her angry gaze, but he couldn't help staring at the way the wet gingham clung to her breasts and slender waist, and Lillian knew, with rising horror, that he had been there long enough to see all there was to see. She wanted to slap him, but tried to restrain herself, then gave in to the urge, and hit him so hard it sounded like a pistol shot.

Donaghue's face became a stony mask. "I saw you leave the camp. I was . . . worried about you. A woman ought not to go off alone out here."

Lillian only half believed him. "You should have made your presence known to me," she replied, her words daggers of cold steel stabbing at his conscience. "I thought you were a gentleman, Mr. Donaghue. Obviously I was mistaken."

The mask crumbled. "I'm sorry," he said with genuine remorse. "It's just that . . . you're so . . . I've been . . ." Frustration twisted his mouth. "I'm truly sorry. Please accept my apology."

Quick as it came, Lillian's anger subsided, and she felt the heat of embarrassment in her cheeks. Only one other man, her husband, had seen her completely naked. "That was a liberty you had no right to take," she protested.

"I honestly couldn't help myself. You're so . . . so beautiful."

"Nonsense. I'm not beautiful, and you're a grown man. You know right from wrong. You should be able to control your impulses, if you want to."

"My wife was pretty like you."

Dear God. "I am not your wife, Mr. Donaghue."

"I don't know what came over me."

"It's called loneliness. It's a wicked, horrible beast that eats your insides out. It won't let you sleep or eat. But you mustn't give in to it. You must fight against it every minute of the day. And night."

She was shocked to see tears in his eyes.

"Yes," he mumbled, trying to swallow the lump in his throat. "Yes, you're right, of course."

"You're a young man," she said with compassion now, the anger all gone, "and you've got your whole life ahead of you. You also have a beautiful daughter who needs you desperately. When the time comes, when the wounds have healed, you will find the companionship you need."

"I was thinking, perhaps, that you . . ."

"Don't say it. Don't even think it."

"But why not?" His voice had a raw edge of desperation. "You lost your husband. I've lost Emily. Seems to me we could . . ."

"It's really out of the question."

He looked away, then back at her, and a subtle transformation had occurred in him. "It's that man Falconer, isn't it?"

"I don't know what you're talking about."

"Yes you do. I've seen the way you look at him."

"Whether I look at him or not should be no concern

of yours," Lillian said, her temper on the rise again. "Now, if you'll excuse me . . ."

"You won't tell the others, will you?"

"Let go of my arm, Mr. Donaghue."

He let go. "You won't tell them."

"No." She walked on.

Anxiety gnawed at her as she followed the creek back to camp. How *had* she looked at Hugh Falconer? Had the others noticed what Lee Donaghue thought he had seen? How did she truly feel toward the mountain man? She tried to examine her soul, sort through her feelings, but she could make no sense of them.

Falconer, Wilkerson, and Norwood returned three days later. Lillian was so relieved she wanted to rush out to greet them, but, considering what Lee Donaghue had said about the way she was acting in Falconer's presence, she remained as aloof as possible. She knew how rumors could get out of hand and lead quickly to grave misunderstandings. It wasn't that she cared so much for her own sake what folks might say, but her foremost concern was Johnny and his tender sensibilities, and she had to make certain he heard no hurtful things.

Falconer said precious little about the visit to the Pawnee village, so the emigrants had to rely on Wilkerson and Norwood for the details.

Both men admitted they had been expecting trouble. Apparently, the survivors of the attack on the wagon train had arrived in the village before them. But no violence occurred. The Pawnees had been grateful for the meat. The old chief invited the trio of white men to share a pipe packed with a mixture of tobacco and *shongsasha*. Falconer had alerted his companions to the fact that the chief's son had died in the raid; after they had passed the pipe around, Falconer had presented the old man with the bone breastplate garnished with hawk feathers. "Your son was wearing this, wasn't he?" asked the mountain man. The old chief nodded gravely, taking the breastplate with the reverence one would expect a father to give the personal effects of a dead son. Wilkerson admired the old one's stoicism. The chief had survived many winters, endured many tragic moments, and they had served to prepare him, at least in some measure, for this, the most tragic moment of all.

"How did he die?" asked the chief, looking Falconer straight in the eye, a silent demand for the truth unvarnished.

"Bravely."

"That is all one can ask."

"I am sorry," said Falconer. "I did not have the chance to stop it."

"He would not have listened. There is nothing you could have done. Perhaps it is just as well. My people will have many sad days in the future. Things will never be as they once were. In a way, I am glad my son will not have to live through what is coming."

Wilkerson had pondered the old man's words as they rode west to rejoin the wagons. The faces of hungry Pawnee children haunted him.

"It's a crying shame," he told Falconer, over the next night's campfire, "That red man and white have to kill each other for this land. There is so much of it—more than enough, I would think, to go around."

"Won't be for long," replied the laconic frontiersman. "You and yours are just the beginning. Tens of thousands will come after you. The old man knows this. He knows what has happened to the tribes back east. What's left of those tribes is now just a handful of homeless wanderers who tell of a tribe more powerful than all the Indians put together, a tribe whose people are like the blades of grass. The hairy faces, the white eyes, the long knives. That's us, Mr. Wilkerson, and the old man knows the days of the Pawnees are numbered."

"You sound sorry. But you've killed more than a few Indians in your time, I would imagine."

"Too many. But they were all trying to kill me."

"I really can't blame them for trying to stop us. I guess we'd do the same, in their place."

"The old man is right about his son," said Falconer pensively. "He died a hero of his people. That's good. Better than living to see what will happen to his people in a few short years."

"It occurs to me that you must have come out here to get away from folks like us," said Ted Norwood.

"That's pretty close to the mark."

"Yet you've agreed to help us, even though you don't cotton to the idea of us settling out here any more than the Indians do."

"I know it's going to happen, and there is nothing I can do about it. But you should be warned—there are some men like me who want absolutely nothing at all to do with your kind, and they will not lift a hand to help you. A few may even raise their hand against you."

"What will you do when this land is all filled up?" asked Wilkerson.

"I won't live to see it," said Falconer bluntly. "And of that I am glad."

There was some discussion about what to do with Dowd, the young hidehunter Falconer was committed to delivering into the vengeful hands of the Arapaho. Dowd made the trip back from the Pawnee village at the end of a rope, stumbling along behind Falconer's Appaloosa, hands tightly lashed behind his back, the loop of braided hemp around his neck. As far as Falconer was concerned, Dowd could make the rest of the journey just like that, but Tom Wilkerson's conscience had nagged him mercilessly as he watched Dowd suffer silently for three days, and had to speak up against the mountain man.

"No matter what he's done," said the farmer, "you just can't treat him like this. Like an animal."

Falconer's expression was as inscrutable as a chunk of granite. "What do you suggest?"

"Hog-tie him and put him in the back of the wagon. At least let him ride to his execution."

"Whose wagon? Who wants to volunteer to carry a man who will slit the throats of man, woman, and child if he gets loose?"

"You can put him in my wagon," said Wilkerson.

"Or mine," said Blakemore.

Falconer shook his head in pure wonder. "You folks beat all I ever saw. But I'll go along with your wishes, even though it's against my better judgment. Just one request. If Dowd gets free somehow, kill him first, and feel sorry for him later."

The night before they were to embark on the next leg of their journey, Norris Durant regained consciousness. News of his son Billy's death hit him hard. The next morning, Wilkerson woke up to see the Durant wagons headed east, just about to dip below the horizon. He rushed up to Falconer to find out what had happened.

"They're quitting," said the mountain man. "Going to pick up the body of their son and go home. Worst of it is, there won't be a body to recover. Reckon the wolves have dug it up by now."

"They'll never make it back all alone."

"They might."

"You should have tried to stop them. Tried to talk them out of it."

"Wasn't *them.* It was *him.* Strikes me that what Mr. Durant says goes in the bunch."

"Poor Sadie."

"I have a few rules that I try to live by, Mr. Wilkerson. One of them is I don't tell somebody else what to do."

"Let them make their own mistakes, is that it? Even if it gets them killed?" Then, quickly, Wilkerson recanted. "My apologies. I shouldn't have said that."

"You're saying what you feel, so don't apologize. You want to ride out and try to talk some sense into Durant? Be my guest."

"No," said Wilkerson, turning toward his wagon. "It's a free country."

They got the prairie schooners straightened out and pointed west. Falconer climbed aboard the Appaloosa and rode up the line, checking the teams and the wagons and the people, missing nothing. He checked his horse at the Tasker wagon, third in line behind the Wilkersons and the Pollocks.

"Lillian."

He was curious, she could tell. Curious as to why she had been avoiding him since his return from the Pawnee village, and sensing that something had happened.

"The man I killed was the chief's son, wasn't he? The one wearing that . . . that whatever you call it."

Falconer nodded.

"I wish I hadn't killed him."

"I'm glad you did. Otherwise, he would have killed you."

"I hate to think I'm the cause of the old man's pain."

"Did you cause it? Or did his son?"

She gazed bleakly out across the barren plains. "I don't know that I'm going to like it out here after all, Mr. Falconer."

Sadly, silently, he rode on.

Chapter Ten

Fort Laramie was a trading post established by the American Fur Company, which for all intents and purposes held a monopoly on the Indian trade in the region marked by the Platte River north into Blackfoot country, and west to the Snake River. Originally formed in the thirties to compete with the Rocky Mountain Fur company in the acquisition of "brown gold"—beaver plews—the American Fur Company now held full sway, just as the Hudson's Bay Company did up in Canada.

Falconer called a halt at the crest of a string of barren hillocks. Down below, beyond a serpentine rust-colored creek, rose the red clay walls of the fort, on a tableland overlooking the chocolate brown Platte. Behind the fort were a series of arid ridges and bluffs, and in the far distance the dark blue heights of the Black Hills.

"You should know something about the men you are about to meet," Falconer told the emigrants. "Those who work for the American Fur Company are mostly *voyaguers*, French Canadians. You may have heard something about them back at St. Joe . . ."

"I heard they encourage the Indians to attack emigrant trains," said Blakemore. "That they bear us nothing but ill will."

"They are accustomed to trading with the Indians,"

said Falconer, "and the shortsighted among them don't realize the extent of the profits they could make by trading with pioneers like you folks. Then, too, they have had to answer to no one but themselves out here for the better part of ten years. This is their own private kingdom, you might say. The nearest U.S. Army outpost is six hundred miles east of here. But they know that eventually the army will come this way, just to protect the emigrants. Then the reign of the American Fur Company will be over."

"We are all short of something we would like to trade for," said Wilkerson. "But if there is going to be trouble, why don't we just swing wide around this place and continue on our way?"

"Because I'll be able to learn a great deal about what lies ahead from the traders in that fort. They will open their doors to you, if they see there is profit in it. But just keep your eyes open, be careful what you say, and if you run afoul of one of them, let me handle it."

Laramie Creek was easily forded—it was midsummer, and the water courses of the Great Plains, swollen by spring rains a couple of months earlier, had all greatly subsided. Since the Pawnee raid not a drop of rain had fallen upon the wagons. Every day a blazing sun had bleached the sky and scorched the earth. The rapidly dwindling contents of the water barrels had been cause for concern, since the water of the Platte and many of its tributaries was too alkaline for human consumption, but Falconer assured them that the Fort Laramie wells would remedy the situation.

Once across the creek they ascended a steep trail which gave them access to the plateau upon which the outpost was perched, and arrived at a gate flanked by a stout blockhouse. The walls, made of clay bricks dried in the sun, were fifteen feet high, ringed by a palisade. The walls were lined with men, women, and children—the denizens of the outpost, whose population exceeded a hundred souls.

Not far from the fort, the pioneers noticed rickety scaffolds of willow wood. Atop each of these odd structures were piles of bones mingled with the tattered remnants of blankets and buckskin clothing. Upon the ground, encircling the scaffolds, were buffalo skulls. Turkey vultures, at least thirty of them, were perched on the scaffolds, waiting for the next meal.

"Dakota Sioux burial ground," Falconer told Wilkerson as he rode alongside the first wagon in the train. "They like having the fort so close by. Figures it serves to keep their enemies, the Crows, from sneaking up and violating the remains, which is a favorite Crow pastime."

"These Crows sound like pretty unpleasant people," remarked Wilkerson.

"But for a few isolated incidents they've remained friendly. It's the Sioux you may find unpleasant. The Crows sure don't like them. The Sioux have been pushed west, and they stole a lot of Crow territory in order to make a home for themselves. Now the Sioux are as bad as the Blackfoot used to be. They war with many other tribes, particularly the Crows and the Snakes. And they don't like the *Meneaska,* either."

"*Meneaska?* I've never heard of that tribe."

"It's you, Mr. Wilkerson, you and your kind. They've tolerated trappers and traders, for we leave the land much as we found it. But the more wagons like yours the Sioux lay eyes on, the less they like it, for they have already discovered what damage a middle-buster can do to the bosom of Mother Earth."

They were met at Fort Laramie's gate by the outpost *bourgeois,* a burly, beetle-browed French Canadian by the name of Papin. Papin sported a pair of dragoon pistols jutting from a broad leathern belt. His incongruous outfit consisted of Indian moccasins and leggings, a red frock coat with the tails tied back, and a beaver hat set at a jaunty angle on top of his head. He had a fierce scowl on his face, which was transformed into a smile when he recognized Falconer. A smile, mused Lillian, that not even Papin's mother would trust. It reminded her of the way a fox grins on its way out of the chicken coop.

Papin assured Falconer that the emigrants were more than welcome to all the well water they could carry, and all the goods they could buy or trade for. Lillian was fairly certain their welcome would not have been nearly so warm had Falconer not been riding with them. The *bourgeois* obviously respected the mountain man, and was, perhaps, just a little afraid of him, too.

When Falconer told him about Dowd, Papin's smile became strained, and his bushy brows hooked into a frown.

"*Oui, oui.* I know Pierre and Dowd," he said. "They pass this way two moons ago, with their buffalo hides. Left their ponies here with me, and went down the river in bullboats."

Falconer carefully explained what lay in store for Dowd. "If you have any objections to what I'm doing," concluded the mountain man, "let's have it out right here and now."

"No, no. Makes me no never mind. What Dowd has done, it makes trouble for us, too."

"Then I'll have your word, as booshway of this post, that there will be no trouble over Dowd during our stay here."

Papin gave his word, but was clearly reluctant to do so, which led Falconer to suspect that Dowd might have a few friends among the inhabitants of Fort Laramie.

The next morning dawned on the arrival of a large band of Ogallalas, a branch of the Dakota Sioux.

A single brave galloped up to the fort on a fleet pony, thundering straight through the gate to shout a few words at Papin as the *bourgeois* emerged from his room—one of several that lined the walls of the stockade. Then, with a scowling glance at the wagons of the emigrants, which had been brought into the compound the night before for safety's sake, the Sioux warrior spun his nimble pony about and galloped away.

Papin immediately issued orders for the outpost's *cavallard,* a hundred-odd horses and mules which had been let out of their corrals to graze beyond the walls to be rounded up and brought back into the fort. Then he went hunting for Falconer. They spoke for a few minutes in earnest tones; then the mountain man joined Lillian and most of the other emigrants, who were gathered round the morning cookfire sharing a pot of coffee.

"Whirlwind and his Sioux are coming," was Falconer's grim announcement.

"I didn't like the way that Indian looked us over," confessed Blakemore.

"This is pretty bad timing," admitted Falconer. "Means we'll have to stay inside these walls until the Sioux move on."

"How long will that be?" asked Wilkerson.

Falconer shrugged. "No way of telling. Could be a few days. Could be a month. They've come to trade with Papin's bunch. Eventually they'll move on, to go after the buffalo and lay in some meat for the winter months. They probably won't make trouble here. They value their relationship with the American Fur Company, and the guns and whiskey that they trade their plews to get."

"Guns and whiskey!" exclaimed Lomax. "That sounds like a mighty dangerous combination."

"Could be, especially if they caught us out in the open. That's why we'll just have to wait them out. Stick close to your wagons when they come around. Given half a chance they'll rob you blind."

"We can hardly afford to lose a few days," said Wilkerson, "much less an entire month. I don't relish getting caught in the mountains when the snows come."

"No help for it. We're stuck here until the Sioux move on."

Within the hour the Indians had arrived, about two hundred men, women, and children. By Falconer's calculations that meant there were about sixty-seventy warriors they had to worry about. The Sioux had brought their lodges with them; the long poles were dragged by the horses, of which there were many—each male would possess four or five ponies at least, for horses meant wealth and prestige. Two or three of the poles were lashed to either side of the horse. The Indians' belongings were carried on the backs of the horses, or in baskets of woven reeds suspended between the lodge poles.

There were dogs, too, a lot of dogs, dogs everywhere, weaving through the legs of the horses. Dogs of every description, and most of them yelping or howling or whining, gaunt and half-wild creatures. Litters of puppies squirmed in reed baskets strapped to the horses. Seeing these beasts, Lillian was concerned for Johnny's safety. The Indian hounds looked perfectly capable of preying on small children.

It had seemed to Lillian rather arrogant, the way

that advance rider had galloped into the fort like he owned the place and shouted out that company was coming, whether Papin and the other traders liked it or not. Now the rest of the Sioux proceeded to set up their lodges in the very shadow of Fort Laramie's walls. Along with most of the emigrants—and a great many of the outpost's inhabitants—Lillian took Johnny up onto the parapets to get a better look at the Indians.

Lillian noticed that the Sioux women, helped by older children, were the ones who labored to erect the lodges. They were quick and efficient in their work; within a half hour more than fifty skin lodges stood, in no apparent order, to the west and south of the fort. The Indian ponies ranged far and wide across the plateau to graze, watched over by a half-dozen horse guards. Some of the Fort Laramie men grumbled about this, their horses were penned up in dusty corrals and would remain so for the duration of the Sioux visit, since the Indians were inveterate horse thieves.

While the Sioux women worked, a dozen or so warriors strode presumptuously up to the gate, which had been discreetly closed. They loudly demanded entry. Several of them had their faces painted black from chin to hairline. Johnny asked Lillian why this was so. A French Canadian standing nearby overheard the boy's question.

"Means they have just come back from a raid. Those who have killed an enemy are entitled to wear the black paint."

Papin ordered the gates opened to allow the warriors into the fort. He greeted Whirlwind effusively. The Sioux chieftain's regalia included buckskins adorned with splendid quillwork, a scarlet blanket draped over one shoulder, and a bonnet of eagle feathers upon his head. His pose was imperious, his attitude superior as he spoke with the Fort Laramie booshway. The other warriors dispersed throughout the compound.

Suddenly remembering that Falconer had warned them to stay close to their wagons when the Indians were on the prowl, Lillian took Johnny by the hand and descended from the wall. When she reached her wagon she noticed several of the warriors hovering around the prairie schooners. Wilkerson and the other men stood watchfully by, their weapons near at hand. The women and children had been put into the wagons, out of sight.

The Sioux glowered at the homespun-clad pioneers. They strutted about, muttering among themselves. Their hostility was a tangible thing. Falconer was present, walking up and down the line of prairie schooners, telling the men to stay calm and to make no aggressive moves. A rash act would result in bloody disaster. The Indians looked at him differently, without the contempt with which they eyed the emigrants.

When Lillian reached her wagon she found a Sioux warrior helping himself to the water in one of the barrels. His dark eyes were feral and cruel, like those of a lynx, and when they fastened upon Lillian she felt a chill travel up her spine. But she stood her ground nonetheless and defiantly returned his gaze.

"Help yourself," she said wryly.

He threw the ladle from which he had been drinking to the ground, brushed rudely past her, and proceeded to climb over the tailgate into her prairie schooner.

"Hey!" yelled Johnny. "Stay out of our wagon!"

The warrior snarled something that Lillian was certain was a Sioux profanity, then threw aside the canvas flaps to peer into the wagon.

"Hush, Johnny," said Lillian, holding her son close. She cast a glance about her. The others were too busy trying to protect their own possessions from pillage to notice her plight, and she realized she was powerless to prevent the Indian from ransacking her wagon. Johnny struggled to escape her grasp, but she held on to him, fearing for his life if he tried to stop the warrior, yet proud of him, too, for being so brave.

Then Hugh Falconer appeared, coming around the wagon. With the sweep of a brawny arm he sent the Sioux sprawling to the ground. The warrior pounced to his feet, features a portrait of cold fury. Falconer barked at him in his own tongue. The Sioux had gripped the hilt of a knife sheathed at the small of his back. Recognizing Falconer, he removed his hand from the weapon. Surly, he backed away, gave Lillian one last malignant glance, and was gone.

"Are you okay?" Falconer asked her.

"Yes. Fine." She knew her expression betrayed her. She was, in fact, quite shaken.

"He thought you didn't have a man around. That's why he took such liberties." Falconer smiled at Johnny. "He didn't realize he was taking a big chance with you here, son."

"What did you tell him?" asked Lillian.

"That this was my wagon."

"You mean that I was your woman."

"I meant no offense. But it is fairly certain to cause them to keep their distance from now on."

"Why? What makes them so afraid of you?"

"Not afraid. Just careful. I have not seen much fear among the Sioux. They are a special breed among the tribes of the plains."

With that he left her and continued on his rounds.

Watching him go, Lillian caught herself speculating on what it would be like to actually be Hugh Falconer's woman.

* * *

Several days went by, and the emigrants grew increasingly restless, trapped inside the walls of Fort Laramie. Papin sent word down the trail that the outpost was invested by Dakota Sioux and warning off any other wagon trains that might be headed that way; he had enough trouble on his hands without more pioneers showing up on his doorstep. A reluctant host, he would have preferred that Falconer's party take their chances and move on, but he realized he could not be so callous as to force them to leave. Were he to throw these people to Whirlwind's red wolves lurking just outside the gate, he could expect to answer to the United States Army for the deed. As for the Sioux, they seemed inclined to wait, if necessary, until hell froze over to get their hands on the settlers.

In spite of all this, Hugh Falconer appeared unconcerned. His boundless patience, his fatalistic acceptance of the situation, grated on Tom Wilkerson's nerves. With each passing day Wilkerson became more and more agitated; of all the emigrants he was endowed with the clearest perception of the risk they were running if they delayed their westward trek. They had come less than a third of the way to the Oregon Territory, and had at best only three more months to make the mountain crossings before winter snows closed most of the passes. Finally he could stand it no longer, and confronted Falconer. He knew right where to find the frontiersman. It had become Falconer's custom to spend most of the day near the gate, smoking his pipe and watching the goings-on in the Ogallala encampment.

"We've got to do something," he told the mountain man. "We can't just sit holed up in here forever. Most of the others agree we should try to make a break for it. Take our chances on the trail. We drove off the Pawnees, and that with four of us off on a wild goose chase. If the Sioux attack us we'll give them a heck of a fight."

"Pawnees are one thing," replied Falconer. "Sioux another."

"I know you think highly of them, but . . ."

"I think highly of my own scalp, too. Listen, Tom. Whirlwind and his warriors might be inclined to dally here for a chance at our hides, but they'll eventually change their minds."

"How can you be so sure?"

"The longer they linger here the emptier become the bellies of their children. Sure, their hunters bring in an occasional elk, but they've got to get after those buffalo herds, and soon, or they'll be starving come winter, and they know it. They want glory, but in the end they'll have to put glory aside and provide for their families."

The next day Papin came to Falconer with news that several of the Ogallala women and children were suffering from a painful inflammation of the eyes. The band's medicine man had been unable to remedy the situation with all his chants and potions.

"You have a physician in your company," said the Fort Laramie booshway. "If he could help those women and children—one of the women is Whirlwind's daughter, by the way—you might find Whirlwind obliged to you. He is not without honor."

Falconer nodded. "We might. I'll speak to Doc Holsberry."

"Good!" Papin was delighted, seeing an opportunity to rid himself of his worrisome guests. "I will arrange it with Whirlwind."

Holsberry was inclined to take the chance. That people were suffering concerned him, and if they were Indians hostile to him and his own kind he could not be seduced to lay aside the Hippocratic oath to which he had been unswervingly faithful for thirty years.

"If the treatment fails," said Falconer, "we may not come out of the Sioux camp alive."

"I understand. You said 'we'?"

"I'm going with you, of course."

"I am not surprised."

Holsberry gathered what he needed from his medical stores, while Falconer explained to Tom Wilkerson what they were about to do. Wilkerson didn't like it.

"It's too big a risk."

"You want to get out of here, don't you?"

Wilkerson could not deny that was so.

On their way out of the gate, Falconer asked Holsberry if he thought he could cure the malady afflicting the Ogallalas.

"I have a salve that might do the trick."

Falconer smiled. "Eye of newt and toe of frog, wool of bat and tongue of dog?"

Holsberry was delighted. "*Macbeth*! You are acquainted with Shakespeare?"

"Some," said the mountain man modestly.

"Outstanding," said Holsberry. "When this is over you and I shall have to discuss our favorite works." Beyond the gate, the good doctor eyed the nearby Sioux camp and squared his shoulders. "But now we have a job to do. 'Be bloody, bold and resolute,' my boy. 'Laugh to scorn the power of man.' "

Chapter Eleven

When finally they emerged from Whirlwind's lodge, the day had nearly run its course. The lodges stood like dark pyramids against a scarlet-and-orange western sky. It seemed as though most of the camp's population was standing in front of their chief's abode, and when Falconer and Holsberry stepped into sight the crowd fell ominously silent.

"I don't see any smiling faces," remarked the doctor, wincing as he kneaded the small of his back, where a persistent ache had lodged itself.

Whirlwind came out of his lodge. Standing between the white men and the Sioux congregation, he spoke briefly to his people. Immediately their faces lightened, and Falconer heaved an audible sigh of relief. Fort Laramie's gate was only two hundred yards away—but that was a very long distance to cover if you had to fight the Sioux every step of the way.

"What did he tell them?" whispered Holsberry.

"That he was satisfied with your work, Doctor."

"I have to admit, it was touch and go there for a while."

"Because you didn't put on a big show."

"Beg pardon?"

"You didn't chant, or dance around the lodge, or pretend to be locked in mortal combat with the evil spirit inhabiting the bodies of your patients. That's what the Indians expect from a medicine man."

"I see," said Holsberry. "Well, I'm afraid I don't dance at all well, and I can't carry a tune in a bucket, but I shall try to put on a better performance next time. If, God forbid, there *is* a next time."

Falconer smiled. Holsberry's courage impressed him. The good doctor had appeared completely unconcerned about the danger they had been in all afternoon.

Whirlwind had looked positively grim when they arrived, and was merely perfunctory in his courtesy. His daughter, however, proved more amiable than Falconer had expected from a person in such obvious pain. Her eyes were swollen almost completely shut. Pus mixed with tears leaked from the red crusty corners of her eyelids. Holsberry engaged in a brief examination, nodded to himself, and applied a creamy salve to the girl's eyes. Through Falconer, who served as interpreter, he told her to keep her eyes closed, and to make sure she would not be tempted to open them, he put in place a clean white dressing like a blindfold. Whirlwind's daughter cried out in joy moments later, declaring that the pain had already been diminished. Only then was Whirlwind's scowling, suspicious demeanor transformed into something more pleasant.

A dozen other women and children, as well as one old man, were summoned. The majority of them suffered the same affliction as Whirlwind's daughter, and received the same treatment. After hours of sitting cross-legged on a buffalo robe in the dim and smoky confines of the skin lodge, Holsberry was overjoyed when the last patient had been attended to.

"You acquitted yourself well," Falconer complimented him as they started back to the fort.

"I am glad to be of help. Overexposure to the sun,

some dirt, and an abysmal grasp of personal hygiene caused the affliction. The salve should solve the problem. We shall know for certain in a day or two. Do you think that by this good deed we have secured safe passage through Sioux territory, Mr. Falconer?"

"We'll know soon enough."

Two days later, Whirlwind entered the fort and invited Papin to a feast that night in the Sioux encampment. The Fort Laramie booshway, however, was not to be the guest of honor—that honor was bestowed upon Dr. Holsberry. Apparently all the Ogallalas afflicted by the eye malady had reported marked improvement in their condition.

"Oh, that's not at all necessary, really," protested Holsberry, when informed that the feast was being laid on in his honor.

"It is, however, necessary for you to attend," replied Papin.

"He's right," said Falconer. "To decline would be dangerous. They'd consider it an insult."

"Dangerous, yes," added Papin. "Perhaps fatal, even. Whirlwind is a very prideful man, *comprendez-vous*?"

"Yes," said an unenthusiastic Holsberry with a sigh. "I understand. I would much rather stay here in my wagon and read, but . . ." He glanced at Falconer. "Are you going along, as well?"

"My presence is also required."

"Then I shall not suffer alone. My daughter will probably want to come along."

Grace Holsberry had become quite a terror the past few days, bored to the point of distraction with confinement in the outpost.

"Talk her out of it," advised Falconer.

"But why? Surely there could be no harm in her

coming with us. Apparently the Sioux are our friends now."

"No, they're not. You helped Whirlwind's daughter. He is obliged to do something for you in return. That's the extent of it. Don't read more into this, Doctor. As for your daughter, every buck in that camp has his eye on her."

"They do?" Holsberry had been blissfully ignorant of this fact.

"They do. If she waltzes into their camp there will be trouble, sure as shooting."

"Well, since you put it that way . . ."

"I insist." Falconer had long ago decided that sooner or later trouble would erupt on account of the doctor's beautiful and flirtatious daughter. The most likely source had appeared to be the Norwood brothers, Clete and Jake. Falconer figured he could handle them when the time came. But a passel of romantically inclined Sioux warriors was something else again.

That evening, Falconer, with Papin and Holsberry, entered the Sioux camp. Around a great blazing bonfire in the center of the encampment sat Whirlwind and most of the band's warriors. A dozen young maidens performed a provocative dance around the fire, and then they were joined by some of the unmarried men, strutting about, in Holsberry's opinion, like roosters as they tried to grab the laughing, elusive, willowy girls. The spectacle embarrassed Holsberry a little, and he was glad now that he had not brought Grace along. She had pouted and fumed just like her mother used to do, but he had been firm. He would not have wanted her innocent eyes to gaze upon such lewd and unwholesome conduct.

This dance was followed by a solo performance put on by the band's wizened old medicine man. He chanted and shuffled about the fire while the rest of the Ogallalas watched raptly. Then a fellow disguised as a buffalo, wearing the hide and headgear of a bison, appeared suddenly out of the darkness and galloped about the fire to the joyous whoops of the Sioux audience. A warrior leapt to his feet and pretended to pursue the buffalo man, finally "slaying" it with a lance, to the lusty shouts of approbation from his fellow warriors.

"What in heaven's name was all that about?" Holsberry asked Falconer.

"It's a good sign for us," replied the mountain man. "The shaman predicts they will be successful in their upcoming buffalo hunt."

"They will leave soon," added Papin, "to find the great herd."

Whirlwind's daughter personally waited on Falconer and Holsberry. The doctor had removed the bandages that evening, and her eyes appeared to be almost healed. Holsberry did not fail to notice that she was very attractive, her figure slender yet shapely, accentuated by her soft deerskin dress. Her blue-black hair was long and lustrous, framing a heart-shaped face. But Holsberry soon became uncomfortably aware that she was paying him an inordinate amount of attention.

"She's flirting with you, Doc," said Falconer, amused. "Looks like you've got an admirer."

"Me?" Holsberry chuckled nervously. "You must be mistaken. Good heavens, I'm old enough to be her father."

"Doesn't matter. Love is blind. You're the great healer. You've got big medicine. She's yours for the asking."

"You're having your fun with me, Mr. Falconer."

"Maybe a little. But, if you did marry her, you'd sure solve our Sioux problem."

The doctor gaped at him. Falconer's expression was

deadpan, and Holsberry wasn't quite sure how serious the mountain man really was.

Whirlwind's daughter disappeared into her father's skin lodge, returning a moment later holding a plump brown puppy by its hind legs. Right in front of Holsberry's horrified eyes she smashed the puppy's head with a club, then swung the bleeding carcass back and forth through the fire until all the hair was singed off. She butchered it out and dropped chunks of puppy meat into a kettle of hot water. Bloody-handed, she turned and beamed at Holsberry.

"That's your dinner, Doc," said Falconer. "She picked the fattest puppy out of the litter just for you."

"I think I'm going to be sick," muttered Holsberry. "Surely you don't expect me to . . . to . . ."

"A dog feast is the greatest compliment a Sioux can offer his guest."

"You're kidding me still, Mr. Falconer . . . aren't you?"

"Dead serious. If you refuse, our lives won't be worth a plugged nickel."

Holsberry swallowed the bile rising in his throat. Suddenly, Whirlwind's daughter did not look at all attractive to him. He prayed for divine intervention before the poor puppy came out of that kettle and was placed before him.

Intervention, divine or not, came in the form of one of Papin's lieutenants. He wore a look of urgency on his face. He whispered in the booshway's ear. Then Papin turned grimly to Falconer.

"It is Dowd. Somehow he has freed himself . . ."

Falconer was on his feet, running in the direction of the fort.

As Falconer raced through the gates of Fort Laramie with Papin and Holsberry hot on his heels, he heard a moaning wail that froze the blood in his veins. An inhuman cry, like the cry of a tortured animal welling up from a soul in anguish, but he knew it issued from a human throat, and knew also what it must signify—that someone was dead or dying. *I should have killed Dowd,* he thought. *I should have ended his miserable life at the first opportunity.* The recriminations echoed hotly in his brain.

Reaching the overland wagons, he found most of the emigrants and some of the outpost's inhabitants clustered together. Some of them held lanterns aloft to throw back the shadows of night. The wailing came from within a clutch of grim, rigid people, and the mountain man bulled his way through—to find Daniel Blakemore curled up in a twitching, bleeding ball, his whitened face twisted in the agony of death throes. Blakemore's wife Lena was on her knees beside him, rocking back and forth, her face and hands streaked with her husband's blood, and tears mingling with the blood on her cheeks.

Falconer became aware of Tom Wilkerson standing beside him.

"It was Dowd. He got loose. Had a knife. Don't know where he got it. Daniel happened to be the first one he saw when he came out of my wagon. He cut Daniel with the knife. Just . . . just gutted him like a fish. I saw it all. I wasn't fifty paces away. But I couldn't move. I couldn't believe what I was seeing was real. I just . . . I just stood there and watched . . ."

"Get on with it," snapped Falconer angrily, staring at Blakemore and at Blakemore's wife.

"He ran. Dowd, I mean. Grabbed a young boy. Not one of ours. One of those that lives here at the fort. Now he's in one of those rooms yonder. Some of Papin's men are about to go in after him."

Falconer blinked, tore his gaze away from the dying

man and the soon-to-be widow, turning bleakly to find Papin.

"Take charge of your men," he told the Fort Laramie booshway. "Don't let them go in after Dowd. He'll kill the boy."

Papin left without a word. Kneeling briefly beside Blakemore, Doc Holsberry rose and turned away, sickened.

"There is nothing I can do for him. He's dying."

"Are you sure?" This was Wilkerson, unwilling to accept the cold, hard truth.

"He's holding his intestines in his arms," rasped Holsberry. "Yes, I am quite certain."

Falconer saw Lillian appear at Lena Blakemore's side, trying to console her. Lillian looked up at him and he quickly averted his eyes, not wanting to see the reproach there, knowing it had to be there because he knew he was to blame for what had happened and assumed everyone else knew it, too.

"What are we going to do?" Wilkerson asked him.

"You're not going to do anything. I'm going to do it."

"What? What are you going to do, Falconer?"

The mountain man did not respond. Passing by Holsberry's wagon to retrieve his Hawken—he had deemed it prudent not to carry the weapon into the Sioux camp that night—he crossed the compound to the row of rooms beneath the western wall, dwellings of the outpost's denizens. A dozen or so of Papin's men stood about, their rifles aimed at the door and single shuttered window behind which Dowd had taken refuge with his hostage.

"Tell your men to fall back," Falconer told Papin.

Papin was accustomed to giving orders, not taking them, but there was something about the look on Hugh Falconer's face that prompted the booshway to obey without question. He barked at his men in the French patois, and they backed away reluctantly, like wolves driven off from a recent kill. Not far, but far enough to suit Falconer as he approached the door to the room.

"Dowd."

"That you, Falconer?"

"Is the boy still alive?"

A yelp of pain was his answer.

"Yeah, he's still above snakes." Dowd chuckled. "But he won't be if you or anybody else tries to come through this door."

"It's me you want. Remember? You said you were going to kill me. Here's your chance. Let the boy go."

"Oh, I remember. I told you you'd be waiting in hell for me. Yeah, I don't forget. But not now, Falconer. Tonight I'm going to ride right out of here. I'll square things with you some other time. One morning you'll wake up strangling on your own blood, and the last thing you'll see is my pretty face. What do you think about that?"

"I think I should have killed you a long time ago."

Again Dowd chuckled—a sound that set Falconer's teeth on edge.

"You missed your chance. You stupid bastard. Did you really think I'd let you take me back to the Arapahoes alive? You know what they would have done to me. Put my eyes out with burning sticks. Skinned every inch of flesh off my bones. And that's just for openers. Nossir, I wasn't going back."

"What do you want?"

"A fast horse. Me and the boy are going to take a little ride."

"Not the boy."

"I'm telling you the way it's going to be!" shouted

Dowd, furious. "I want a horse, and I want it right now, or so help me the boy dies."

Falconer walked back to where Papin was standing. "Bring up a horse for Dowd."

"*Mon Dieu!* You cannot let him go free! I heard what he said. He must not be allowed to take the boy away from here. Dowd will kill him for sure."

"Bring up a horse. Dowd won't reach the gate alive."

"What will you do? How can you be sure?"

"Damn you, Papin . . ."

Papin backed away from the cold fury etched on Falconer's features and ordered one of his men to fetch a horse.

It was Falconer who took the pony to the door. "I've got what you asked for, Dowd," he said quietly.

The door opened a crack. It was too dark inside for Falconer to see anything.

"Step away," said Dowd. "Try anything, and the boy's blood will be on your hands, Falconer."

"I won't try anything," lied Falconer, backstepping.

"Put your rifle on the ground and keep moving back."

Falconer did as he was told. Dowd slipped out through the door and grabbed the horse's dangling reins with one hand—he had the boy by the hair and dragged him out of the room, threw him bodily across the saddle. Falconer saw the rawhide thongs on Dowd's wrists, the knife in Dowd's teeth, and he figured one of Papin's men had smuggled the knife to Dowd somehow. But none of that mattered. It was no use trying to shift the blame to someone else. He had to carry that burden alone.

Dowd swung aboard the pony Indian fashion and with one last ugly grin at Falconer kicked the horse into a gallop, bending low over the body of his struggling hostage, reins in one hand, the knife now in the other and held at the boy's neck.

Falconer strode with grim purpose to where the Hawken lay on the hardpack. Picking up the rifle, he brought it to his shoulder and fired before Papin could shout a protest.

The booshway thought Falconer's intention was to shoot Dowd, and he didn't think even a man of Falconer's prowess with a rifle could be certain of hitting Dowd and not the boy in the dark.

But Falconer killed the horse instead.

The pony nosedived into the dirt, throwing Dowd and the boy forward.

Falconer dropped the rifle, drew his Green River knife, and began to run.

Stunned by the fall, Dowd struggled groggily to his feet. Swaying unsteadily, he saw the mountain man coming at him. A strangled cry of pure fear escaped him as he realized that he had lost his knife in the fall. A few feet away, the boy was getting up, dazed but unhurt. Dowd lunged at him, but Falconer plowed into him before he could reach his hostage. Locked in a fatal embrace with Dowd, Falconer drove the knife home to the hilt. Dowd's body went rigid. Then he fell away. On his back, he gave Falconer a weak grin. "I'll see you . . ." he gasped. Coughing up blood, he died.

Wiping the blade of the knife on his buckskin leggings, Falconer walked over to Papin, bringing the boy along with him. "No harm has come to him," said the mountain man.

Papin nodded, looking past Falconer at Dowd's body sprawled in the dust.

"What about him?"

"I want you to take care of that for me. I've got to

get these people over the mountains before winter comes."

"I will do it. I will take his head to the Arapahoes, and leave the rest of him for the buzzards."

"Suits me," said Falconer, and he walked on.

Chapter Twelve

They buried Daniel Blakemore at Fort Laramie the next morning at dawn. Less than an hour later they were rolling out through the gate. The Sioux were striking their skin lodges and loading down their ponies. Abney was afraid the Indians planned to follow them until they were out of sight of Fort Laramie before attacking, but Falconer assured him that this was not the case. These Ogallalas were looking for buffalo, not scalps, and would be for weeks to come.

In the days that followed they passed through an arid, broken country of hills and hollows, covered with wild sage and cactus. Infrequent creeks rambled through gorges choked with cottonwood and ash. The going was not easy. This country was tailormade for breaking down prairie schooners and exhausting livestock. Every delay only served to heighten a sense of anxiety which pervaded the company. Would they make it through the mountains before the snows came and closed the passes? This was the question first and foremost on everyone's mind.

Try as she might to maintain good cheer, Lillian Tasker couldn't help but subscribe to the same concern. Mr. Abney's words, spoken the night prior to their departure from St. Joseph, kept haunting her. *I think we are all going to come to grief,* he had said. The theft of their money and valuables by Amos

Spellman and the half-breed had struck everybody as the worst sort of catastrophe at the time, but it paled now almost to insignificance compared to the violent ends met by Billy Durant and Daniel Blakemore. What next? What new disaster lurked somewhere up the trail? Maybe Abney had been right, after all.

Something else bothered Lillian. Hugh Falconer had been acting strangely ever since the incident with Dowd at Fort Laramie. He was keeping to himself now. Days would pass without his uttering a single word to her. She tried to persuade herself not to take it personally, because he was giving everyone else the same treatment, but her feelings were hurt nonetheless. He kept well ahead of the wagons most of the time, guiding them through the rough country. Whenever possible he would point Tom Wilkerson, who drove the lead wagon, in the right direction, and then he would ride off, north or south or west, and was usually gone for the rest of the day. He almost always returned with fresh meat—a black-tailed deer, some sage hens, or rabbits—to augment their usual supper rations of beans, coffee, and bread.

Finally Lillian could stand it no longer. She waited until she could catch Tom Wilkerson alone and asked the farmer if he knew what was bothering their guide.

"So you've noticed it, too?" Wilkerson shrugged shoulders bulky with muscles from a lifetime of plow-wrestling. "He hasn't talked to me about it, and I'm guessing it has something to do with Daniel's death. I think Falconer blames himself. He knew Dowd was a dangerous and desperate man who would try to make a break for freedom sooner or later."

Lena Blakemore had retreated into herself. Lillian could sympathize with her plight; she knew what it took to make a go of life with a family to provide for and her man snatched away from her. *At least I had a home and some land to work,* thought Lillian. Poor Lena had none of these things. Dowd had taken her husband and Spellman had taken what little money she had, and she faced a bleak prospect if she even made it to the Oregon Territory. Her two children, a boy and a girl, aged five and three respectively, were too young to be of any real help to her. All they could do was console her by their very presence. Lillian could remember how much it had helped just having Johnny to hold. In fact, it still helped.

But Lena did not seem to want consoling. She spoke to no one, not even, as far as Lillian knew, her own children. Sometimes, when the going was especially rough, one of the Norwood brothers would take over the reins and drive the Blakemore wagon through the bad spot. She accepted this help in stony silence, sitting there stiff and ashen and staring out at nothing. She could not be enticed to eat for days following her husband's death, and later, when she did finally take some nourishment, it was without enthusiasm. That was normal, Lillian assured a concerned Molly Wilkerson, and she was speaking from experience. Poor Lena Blakemore had misplaced her will to live. In time, God willing, she would rediscover it.

But then, one night, while most of them sat around a fire, Lena Blakemore snapped. Hugh Falconer rode in with a deer draped over his saddle, and as he dismounted and stepped into the firelight, Lena rose suddenly and launched herself at him with a shriek that scared everybody half out of their wits. Lomax fell backward off his three-legged stool, and Judd Pollock jostled his tin cup recently filled with hot coffee, scalding his hand.

"You bastard!" screamed Lena, pounding her fists into Falconer's face and chest, tears cascading from her eyes. "My husband's dead on account of you!

You're to blame! My Daniel is gone, and it is all your fault, you bastard!"

Falconer just stood there, making no move to defend himself, a stricken look on his face, but Lillian knew the pain he felt came from his own tortured soul, and not from Lena's blows.

Tom Wilkerson recovered from his shock and grabbed Lena and pulled her off the mountain man. Only then did Falconer move. Blood trickled from a nostril. He wiped it off his upper lip, looked at it on the back of his hand, and then without a word turned and walked away, disappearing as night wrapped its cloak of shadows around him.

Lena struggled fruitlessly to escape Wilkerson's grasp. "You bastard!" she screamed after Falconer. "You bastard! You bastard!"

Suddenly she went limp, fainting dead away. Clete Norwood helped Wilkerson carry her to her wagon. Lillian tried to comfort the Blakemore children, who were scared and sobbing witnesses to the scene, but they were inconsolable.

The next day Falconer went hunting again. He returned with another deer for the company as a whole. He also had a couple of rabbits dangling from the horn of his saddle. These he brought to Lena Blakemore. She refused to accept them. Falconer left them hanging on her wagon and walked silently away.

In the days and weeks to come, Falconer continued to provide Lena and her children with extra game. The others did not complain about the special attention he bestowed upon the Blakemore family; after all, he never failed to keep their bellies full. Slowly but surely Lena's attitude toward the mountain man changed. Spurning him cruelly at first, she began to tolerate him, and then, finally, accept his special favors as though they were her due. Still, she seldom spoke to him, but Hugh Falconer would not be deterred.

One evening a few weeks out from Fort Laramie, Lillian saw Falconer over by the Blakemore wagon, with Lena's girl on his knee and the boy, laughing, running circles around them, pretending he was a Sioux warrior out for their scalps. Lena emerged from the wagon, and when Falconer spoke to her she nodded and smiled. This was the first time Lillian had seen her smile at him.

The scene, indelibly stamped upon her mind's eye, would not leave Lillian alone. It was painfully clear to her what had happened. Feeling responsible for Daniel Blakemore's death, Falconer had made up his mind that it was his solemn duty to look after Lena and the children, and he was going to do so whether she wanted him to or not. On her part, Lena had gradually come around to accepting Falconer's help as though she deserved it. An odd situation on the face of it, but under the circumstances, perhaps understandable.

Yet how long would it go on? Until they reached Oregon? Lena would still need a provider and protector even then. Lillian surmised that Hugh Falconer was not the kind of man who would set a time limit on the service he felt obliged to render the young widow; he would consider his debt one that would take a very long time indeed to repay in full—if it ever could be repaid. As for Lena, Lillian was afraid she might come to depend too much on the mountain man, perhaps even care for him, in spite of herself.

The prospect troubled Lillian deeply. It was silly, of course, but it felt as though she had lost Falconer. She had liked him and he had liked her—she could admit all of this to herself now, now that it was too late—but the bond forming between them Falconer had torn asunder the moment he had committed himself to the care and keeping of the Blakemores. Lillian experienced a bitter sense of loss, a profound sense that the opportunity to find the happiness which had eluded her for so long had slipped through her careless fingers.

A few days west of Fort Laramie they could see the mountains clearly—a jagged blue line along the western horizon, a barrier of granite and snow beyond which lay the promised land.

Passing Independence Rock, some of the men carved their names in the stone for posterity, as had hundreds before them—trappers, traders, pioneers—perhaps as a hedge against the fate of an anonymous grave, which had befallen so many who had ventured into the untamed frontier. As she helped Johnny scratch his name and the date into the rock, Lillian Tasker wondered what had become of all the people whose names were etched here. Had they come to grief, or did they prosper now in their new beginning? Which would it be for her? She felt very much alone and uninspired.

Past Devil's Gate—a deep and narrow gorge through which a sweetwater river plunged in wild abandon—they found good graze, abundant water, extensive woodlands. They were glad to have put the plains behind them. This country was rich and pleasing to the eye. But South Pass, through which they passed ten days later, was much less so; the arid sagebrush valley was the gateway to the far western frontier.

Fort Bridger lay to the south, but Falconer turned them north by west instead, bound for the headwaters of the mighty Snake River. The mountain ranges loomed on all sides of them now, ranges of soaring granite peaks cloaked in snow. The steep foothills were thick with aspen and other hardwoods, giving way at higher elevations to the conifers. The rivers ran clear and sweet over their rocky courses and were positively jumping with fish. The valleys were lush with grass.

The days were warm, but the nights began to turn quite cold. It was late August, yet one morning Lillian woke to a very unpleasant sight. There was a film of ice in the water barrels.

On the last day of August they reached the Snake River. Lillian had the feeling they were coming to the end of their journey, after four and a half months on the trail. Perhaps it was because the Snake was the first major river they had come to that flowed in a westerly direction. She knew it would lead them north to the Columbia and the Oregon Territory. Understandably, she was dismayed when Falconer called them together and fed them some unvarnished truth about their situation.

"You folks got a pretty late start out of St. Joseph," he said, "and you've had some delays along the way. You're about halfway to your destination at this point."

"Halfway!" exclaimed Lillian.

He nodded gravely. "The going gets much rougher from here on."

"What are you trying to tell us?" asked Ted Norwood.

"We'll probably have snow in a fortnight. I reckon we're in for a hard winter. It will come early and stay late. By my calculations, you won't make it to Oregon this year."

A stunned silence greeted this frank pronouncement.

"You can't be sure of that," protested Judd Pollock, the first to recover enough to speak.

"The signs are everywhere. I know what I'm talking

about. I've spent the better part of twenty years in these mountains. In two weeks' time there will be plenty of snow on the ground. In a month's time many of the passes will be closed until spring. I doubt we'll be able to find passage over the Blue Mountains."

"What do you suggest we do, then?" asked Tom Wilkerson, almost choking on his disappointment.

"Now's the time to be thinking of permanent shelters for the winter. We need to start soon laying in provisions, cutting firewood, gathering fodder for the livestock. We'll have to work hard and fast to beat the snows. No time to waste. If we try for Oregon, we'll end up a couple hundred miles north of here, snowbound, and our time run out. I was born in the highlands of Scotland, and although I remember very little about my childhood, the one thing I do recall were the hard winters. Yet Scottish winters are nothing like what I've seen in this country. And you've lived through nothing that could possibly prepare you for it, either. It's difficult to describe. Rivers freeze from bank to bank and clear to the bottom. Trees split right open from the cold. I've seen animals literally frozen in their tracks. And, like I said before, this will be an early winter, and a very harsh one."

"Well," said Wilkerson, "I suppose we could make a winter camp, wait until spring to move on." He nodded grimly at the masks of chagrin on the faces of the others. "I know, I know. We've all had our hearts set on reaching Oregon this year. But some things are just beyond our control."

"The plans of men are subject to the whims of God," murmured Doc Holsberry.

"But where?" asked Norwood, bleakly surveying the windswept crags that pierced the sky on every side. "Where do we spend the winter?"

"I know of a place," said Falconer. "A valley a long

day's travel north of here. We won't be troubled by Indians there. Plenty of wood, water, and graze."

The others talked it over, and Falconer stepped aside to let them hash it out among themselves. He intended to say no more on the subject. If they took his advice, all well and good. If they chose not to, and decided to risk everything and press on, he would be with them to the end, even though it would be against his better judgment. Better judgment played no role in this. He was committed to this group and he would not abandon them, no matter what. Lena Blakemore was one reason, but not the only one.

He knew it was wiser not to press the issue with these people. They would have to battle it out amongst themselves, a contest between self-interest and common sense. Since leaving St. Joseph they had been confronted by one mishap after another. Falconer was an excellent judge of character, and he could sense that they would not allow themselves to be pushed into something. Even if it was the smart thing to do. They had been pushed around enough. Press a reasonable man too hard and he will become obstinate on principle; he will cut off his nose to spite his face, on account of injured pride.

Lillian Tasker and Tom Wilkerson were the most sensible, patient, and farsighted of the lot, and they were inclined to take Falconer's advice, and Falconer admired them for it, because they were no different from the others in one respect; both of them had been suffering from a bad case of Oregon Fever for many months now, if not years, and their hearts had been set on getting to the promised land, and they didn't want to give in now, especially after having endured so much. But they were clearheaded enough to realize that lives—theirs and their children's—took precedence. Sometimes people were so consumed by their dreams that they forgot this, until it was too late. The mountains, Falconer knew, would claim many lives in the years to come because a lot of people had a tendency to try to do the impractical even if it killed them.

Judd Pollock and Lee Donaghue were inclined to go along with Lillian and Wilkerson, as was Abney, who seemed to Falconer to regret having ever stepped foot west of the Mississippi River. But Abney's partner Lomax was mule-headed stubborn. All he could think about was getting to Oregon and opening up his store and selling the merchandise he and Abney had hauled halfway across the continent and making a profit. He lived for profit, had little else to live for, and it blinded him to the risks. Ted Norwood suffered from the same disease, to a slightly lesser extent; he had been dreaming about that sawmill and blacksmith shop for so long now that the dream had begun to consume him. As for Holsberry, the good doctor was indifferent. His situation was similar to Falconer's in that he considered himself a servant of these people, and was committed to sticking with the company no matter what. He had his daughter's well-being to consider, of course, but he was the oldest of the men, and had survived many hardships and tragedies, and figured he and Grace would survive no matter what the decision. He did not, could not, fully appreciate the dangers of going on any more than the others could. He was a bookish man, not a man of the soil; he understood the human body as well as anyone, but knew precious little about nature.

Only Falconer had lived through what was coming. But the mountain man had a few hard and fast rules by which he lived and, as he had informed Tom Wilkerson upon the abrupt departure of Norris Durant and his family, he never tried to tell others what to do. Often in life a person came to a fork in the trail, with one path leading to redemption, and the other to destruction, and he would try to guide others down the right path, if he knew with certainty which one was right, but he would not *force* others to follow him if they were bound and determined to destroy themselves. He did not want anyone else telling him what to do, so it was "do unto others" for him, and always would be.

Finally Wilkerson broke away from the others and approached the mountain man, who was smoking his clay pipe and contemplating the stars while the emigrants debated life or death.

"We've decided to do what you suggest," said Wilkerson. "Will you take us to this valley you told us about?"

Falconer nodded.

"But it occurs to me," said Wilkerson, "that maybe we should ask Lena Blakemore for her opinion. She has a right to be a part of this decision."

"Not necessary, in her case."

"And why not?"

"She would leave that decision to me."

Wilkerson was struck by the peculiarity of the situation as it had developed between Falconer and the widow woman. But he had better sense than to make any comment in Falconer's presence.

"Well," he mumbled, "if you say so."

"What did Lillian Tasker say?" asked Falconer as Wilkerson began to turn away.

"She says she agrees with whatever you think is best. She puts a great deal of faith in you, Mr. Falconer. I guess we all do."

Falconer did not respond.

Chapter Thirteen

Late that same day they reached the valley which Falconer had recommended, with just enough light lingering in the purple sky to provide them with a tantalizing glimpse of their surroundings. They liked what they saw. The valley was about eight miles long, approximately two miles wide except at the northern extremity, where it narrowed considerably between brooding granite cliffs. It opened onto the Snake River valley to the south, with snow-clad peaks to the east and west, and a high pass to the north which, said Falconer, would be closed until "green up" as soon as the first heavy snows fell. The foothills were cloaked with fine stands of aspen and other hardwoods mingled with fir. The leaves of the hardwoods had begun to turn, splashes of gold and red against the darker green of the conifers. The floor of the valley was gently rolling grassland, interspersed with copses of willow and hackberry. Two creeks plunged down the mountain slopes at the northern tip of the valley, joining a couple of miles south of the high pass to curl through the valley like a crooked snake. The creeks were fairly jumping with trout; they hooked a dozen in less than half an hour and had a fine supper.

Lillian awoke the next morning to the sound of galloping horses. She was relieved that for the first time in almost five months she was not going to have to wrestle the team of oxen into their traces and then spend all day on a hard wooden bench being jarred and jounced for one agonizing hour after another, her eyes and nose and mouth clogged with the dust kicked up by the wheels and hooves of the wagons and teams in front of her. The morning was quite cool, and she felt suddenly very lazy. All she wanted to do was stay under the blankets and the old star pattern quilt her mother had made, where it was warm and cozy. But then Tom Wilkerson was calling out her name. Reluctantly she threw the blankets and quilt aside, pulled her frayed flannel wrapper closed, and parted the canvas flaps to peer out over the prairie schooner's tailgate.

Wilkerson was mounted and armed, and for a disconcerting instant Lillian thought there must be trouble.

"What is it, Tom? Indians?"

"No, nothing like that. We're all riding out to scout up places to build our cabins."

"Oh, I see."

"You know, when it's all said and done we'll probably be spread out from one end of the valley to the other. After all these months of being together, I guess most of us hanker for some elbow room. I was thinking you might want to ride out, too. Find a good spot for your own place. Be sure to take your rifle along. Falconer says he doubts if there are any Injuns about, but none of us want to sit around waiting for him to go out and make sure. If you come across anything you don't like just fire a shot and the rest of us will come running.

"Yes, all right. I will."

"As for your cabin, Lillian, don't you worry. Since you don't have a man around, we've all decided to pitch in and build yours first. All of us working together, it won't take long."

"What about Lena Blakemore?"

It was a leading question, of sorts, and Wilkerson knew it. The sharp edge to Lillian's words gave her away.

"We were aiming to do the same for her, but Falconer said we needn't concern ourselves on that score. He aims to build her cabin on his own."

"Of course he does."

"Lillian, it's none of my business, but I figure it's a matter of atonement with him, the reason he's been helping Lena out the way he has. He feels obliged to take Daniel's place. That's all there is to it."

He was trying to console her, and the fact that he could tell she was hurt and thought she needed consolation embarrassed Lillian, for it meant she was permitting him to see into that very private corner of her soul where she cached her innermost thoughts and desires.

"What Hugh Falconer does is certainly of no consequence to me, Tom."

Wilkerson just looked at her, not knowing what to say, and Lillian chided herself for making such an idiotic and counterfeit statement, for of course the denial was patently false—she had never been a very good liar.

Realizing that anything he might say would just make matters worse, Tom Wilkerson touched the brim of his hat and heel-tapped his horse into motion. Lillian turned back into the wagon and felt bitter tears burn the corners of her eyes, but she fiercely fought them back, because Johnny was stirring, slowly awakening to the new day.

Although Johnny protested hotly and then threw a fit, Lillian left her son in the care of Molly Wilkerson and rode out on Ol' Blue, taking the rifle with her. She tried to apply herself to the task at hand, finding the place she wanted to spend the winter. But she just couldn't seem to muster up the enthusiasm to do so. She rode aimlessly, and the only thing she sought was solitude. All morning she roamed. Once, emerging from a stand of aspen trees, she saw Judd Pollock, quartering across a meadow, and she pulled Blue back into cover, hiding until Pollock was gone. She didn't want to see anyone or be seen. Didn't want to talk, or have to force a smile.

After a few hours she grew weary of riding, having come to the northern end of the valley. A pervasive misery leeched the energy right out of her. She hitched Blue to the log upon which she sat, on the edge of a pleasant meadow terminating fifty yards away at a cutbank below which one of the creeks danced to its own sweet music. Above her, a waterfall plunged hundreds of feet down a perpendicular granite face, disappearing with a roar into the blue shadows of a deep gorge. High overhead an eagle soared with effortless grace, and way up on a shale slope near the top of the waterfall she saw something move. Staring at the creature for a while, she decided it must be a bear, perhaps a grizzly. Finally it vanished into a jumble of boulders at the top of the barren gray scree.

Lost in her own thoughts, she did not hear the horseman's approach until he was almost upon her—then Blue whickered a warning and she snapped out of her reverie and grabbed the rifle and had it aimed before she recognized Falconer, astride his lanky Appaloosa.

"Oh, I'm sorry," she said, mortified, and quickly lowered the weapon.

He smiled. "Don't be. That's exactly the right reaction out here. I'm sorry if I startled you."

"I thought you might be an Indian. But, of course, you told us there weren't any Indians in this valley."

"Shouldn't be. But I've been wrong before." He sat in his saddle and scanned the timberline, as though he were searching for something in particular, and the silence between them lengthened until it became uncomfortable, and Lillian cast about for something, anything, to say to break it.

"I thought I saw a bear way up on that mountain," she said, pointing. "Could it be a grizzly?"

"Could be."

"I've heard they are ferocious creatures."

"They've killed many a man that I know of. When the first snows come we'll have to be careful of them, as they may come down into the valley looking for food."

"What do they eat?" The only bears Lillian knew anything about were those that inhabited the eastern forests and whose diet consisted primarily of fish and insects.

"They'll be after dogs or cows or even horses. If you have to shoot one, aim for the head. One bullet to the body won't generally stop a grizzly unless it's a lucky shot. If you get caught out in the open, afoot, don't think you can outrun him, because you can't."

"Well," she said, gazing up at the mountain, "maybe it wasn't a grizzly, after all."

He didn't respond, and she turned her head to look at him and noticed that he was watching her with a curious expression on his bearded face, an expression she could not quite fathom.

"Are you looking for a place to put your cabin?" he asked.

"Yes. I think this meadow will do nicely. What do you think?"

Falconer was alarmed. "You'll be well away from the others."

"That is my intention."

"But . . ." He shook his head, cutting off further protest.

"Tom Wilkerson says the other men will raise my cabin first," she said.

"They're good people."

"What about you? Where will your cabin stand?"

"I'll not have one. When the snows come I'll find shelter."

Under Lena Blakemore's roof? Lillian wanted to say it, but refrained from doing so. Hugh Falconer, she decided, was a fool. Couldn't he see what Lena was up to? Clearly she was taking advantage of this man's guilt, and she was going to milk it for all it was worth. Quick as it came, the anger in her receded, and she felt sorry for Falconer.

"Have you never had a home?" she asked.

"Once. A cabin, high above the timberline. I lived there for several years."

"Alone?"

"No. With my Shoshone wife."

"You were married?"

"In a manner of speaking. There was no preacher, no vows exchanged, but then those things don't make a marriage."

"What was her name?"

"Touches The Moon." Anticipating the next question, he added, "She's dead."

"I'm so sorry."

"Nothing lasts forever."

"That's not true. Your love for her will last forever, won't it?"

Surprised, he nodded. "Why, yes. You're right about that." He straightened in the saddle. Lillian realized that for many weeks now she had seen him in the saddle from dawn to dusk, constantly on the move, and yet he never seemed to tire. The Appaloosa was grazing, and he gave the reins a tug to lift its head. "Well, I'd best be moving on." Still, he hesitated, reluctant to leave, watching her with a sorrowful light in his eyes.

"Lillian?"

"Yes?"

Falconer grimaced, shook his head. "Be careful. I could be wrong about the Indians."

Pulling sharply on the reins, he turned the Appaloosa and rode away.

Before the day was out the trees began to fall, as the ringing of axes enlivened the hush of the purple twilight. The emigrants took the canvas from the overland wagons and used it to make temporary shelters on the land they had chosen. The second day was spent getting settled in. On the morning of the third day every man but for Doc Holsberry—and Hugh Falconer—showed up at the meadow on the northern tip of the valley where Lillian Tasker had decided to have her cabin. They came in one wagon, with their axes and, in the Norwoods' case, a crosscut saw. Molly Wilkerson and Mrs. Pollock and the Holsberrys came later, on about noon, to help Lillian feed the hungry men.

Wilkerson took charge of the operation, handing out assignments. While he and Judd Pollock and Lee Donaghue took their axes up into the trees to begin felling full-grown firs, hauling them back to the building site chained behind a pair of lumbering oxen, Lomax and Abney trimmed saplings for rafters, and the Norwood brothers dropped a big cedar and proceeded to saw it into bolts from which they would rive shakes for the cabin roof. Ted Norwood's wound had fully healed, and he was able to square and notch the logs that Wilkerson and his coworkers were bringing in.

By noontime the first tier of logs, the base of the cabin walls, had been notched and fitted into place. For the midday meal they enjoyed trout harvested from the nearby creek, along with cornbread, blackstrap, and plenty of good, strong coffee. At dusk the walls were up, the rafters set, and the door and one window framed.

The next day, as agreed, Wilkerson and Lee Donaghue returned to finish the cabin while the rest of the company turned their attention to putting up the Pollock cabin. It had been decided that the families would come first: the Pollocks and the Wilkersons—Falconer had made himself solely responsible for providing the Blakemores with shelter. Then the Holsberry and Donaghue cabins would go up. Bachelors Lomax and Abney, and the three Norwoods, would come last.

While Donaghue split shakes off the cedar bolts, Wilkerson chopped and shaped clay bricks out of the cutbank with which was mixed hay that Lillian scythed out of the meadow, and water from the creek. These bricks were used for the construction of the cabin's fireplace and chimney. That afternoon, while a slow fire served to harden the chimney bricks, the men laid the cedar shakes. Johnny insisted on doing something to help, and they gave him the task of keeping them supplied with shakes, transporting them from the pile on the ground to the men on the roof. When the roof was finished, Wilkerson and Donaghue threw together a stout door and heavy shutters for the window. Lillian assured them she could find some leather and hinge the door and shutters to their frames.

"I'll be by sometime tomorrow and help you move your belongings inside," said Donaghue. He glanced at Wilkerson, who nodded permission; Tom was the boss when it came to putting up the cabins. Wilkerson figured they would be finishing up the Pollock cabin tomorrow, and could do without Donaghue's sweat for half a day.

"That really won't be necessary," said Lillian. "Johnny and I can manage just fine."

"No bother," insisted Donaghue. "I reckon we'll be neighbors, Lillian. My place will be a couple miles down the creek. I'll be closer to you than any of the others."

What a happy coincidence, thought Lillian.

"Your first concern," said Wilkerson, "should be laying in enough meat to last you through the winter months. Won't take long for us to fish the creek out, and though there are plenty of deer in the valley now, once we start hunting in earnest they'll clear out right quick."

"I can manage, thank you," said Lillian.

"I'll shoot a couple of deer for you," offered Donaghue.

"Mr. Donaghue, I appreciate your kindness, but I am able to do my own shooting. You have Lisle to look out for, remember? Tom, I will see you tomorrow at the Pollock's."

That evening she collected a bucketful of serviceberries from a nearby thicket and spent the night making two pies, which she and Johnny, riding double on Ol' Blue, carried down to the spot where the finishing touches were being put on the Pollock cabin. Darkness fell as they returned to their own cabin. Lillian sharply checked Ol' Blue some distance away.

"What is it, Ma?" asked Johnny, trying to get the words out over a yawn. He had spent all day playing with the other children, something Lillian was happy to see.

Slipping off the horse, Lillian drew the rifle from the leathern loops which held it to the saddle.

"Probably nothing. You just stay put, Johnny, you hear me? I'll be right back."

She didn't want to frighten him, but there was growing concern on his face, so she smiled reassuringly and put a comforting hand on his leg.

Approaching the cabin, she tried to peer into the darkened interior through the open door—the door being slightly ajar was what troubled her. She was absolutely certain she had closed it and lifted the string latch into place. Who could have opened it? As best she could recollect, everyone had been at the Pollocks' all day—everyone except Hugh Falconer and the Blakemores, and she thought it unlikely they were responsible.

Maybe Falconer had been wrong. Maybe there were Indians lurking in this valley . . .

Her heart was pounding frantically against her rib cage as she ventured into the cabin, rifle held ready in a white-knuckled grip. The cabin's one room was small, and she was quickly able to confirm that no one was here. Nothing appeared to have been disturbed; she and Johnny had carried most of their belongings in from the prairie schooner last night.

Breathing a sigh of relief, Lillian set the rifle aside to light a lantern. Then she saw it—and gasped.

Someone had crudely carved two words on the inside of the door. Two words that drove a spike of cold dread into Lillian's heart.

GIT OUT.

Chapter Fourteen

Early the next morning she rode down the creek to the place where she knew Hugh Falconer was building the Blakemore cabin, dropping Johnny off with the Wilkersons so that he could play with Edna and Phoebe. Tom had fashioned a temporary shelter for his family, using the canvas tarpaulin from the prairie schooner. He had already left that morning to join the other men in finishing the Pollock cabin. Molly expected all the men back by noon at the latest to begin on their own place.

Lillian had spent a harrowing, sleepless night; Molly Wilkerson took one look at her and knew all was not well. But Lillian refused to admit that anything was wrong. She had made up her mind to tell only Falconer, at first.

In three days Falconer had made tremendous progress on the Blakemore cabin. The walls were up, and when Lillian arrived he was preparing to put up the rafters. Lena Blakemore was cooking breakfast over a fire in front of her own canvas shelter. She greeted Lillian with cool civility, offering her a cup of coffee. Lillian declined. She asked Falconer if she could speak to him privately. At that moment Lena's attitude took a turn for the worse. Lillian discerned a glimmer of jealous hostility in the woman's eyes.

Falconer walked with Lillian down to the creek.

When they were well out of earshot of the shelter, she told him about her frightening discovery.

"I haven't told anyone else," she concluded. "I wanted to talk to you first. You always seem to know the right thing to do."

"You think it might be one of them?"

"I don't know what to think, frankly."

"You're not telling me everything."

Her first impulse was to flatly deny the accusation, but she thought better of it. "Well, I . . . I have no proof, but . . ."

"Just say it straight out, Lillian. That's always the best way."

Lillian sighed. "It occurred to me that Lee Donaghue might have done it."

She paused, watching his face, and was struck by the fact that he didn't appear at all surprised.

"It's clear he's fond of you." The mountain man nodded. "Anyone could see it."

"He's not, really. He just thinks he is. He's a very lonely, heartbroken man, and he doesn't know how to deal with loneliness or heartbreak. He made advances once, and I spurned him and, well, he might be trying to scare me. I don't know. I'm probably wrong. But of all the people in this company, he is the only one who would have any reason that I know of to do something like this."

Falconer brooded over it for a moment. "You mean to scare you into wanting to have a man around."

"Sounds far-fetched, doesn't it? And it probably is."

"I'd like to have a look around your cabin."

"I was hoping you would."

Falconer returned to the shelter, spoke briefly to Lena, then went off to fetch the Appaloosa, which was grazing on a long tether in the meadow behind the unfinished cabin. Lillian waited beside Ol' Blue, trying to ignore the ugly looks Lena was throwing her way. *She thinks I am trying to steal him away from her,* realized Lillian, shocked. *She has staked her claim.*

Falconer spent more than an hour circling the Tasker cabin on foot, studying the ground for any clue to the identity of the person who had left the ominous warning on the cabin door. Eventually he rejoined her in the cabin, shaking his head grimly.

"Nothing?" she asked.

"Not a trace. I don't think Lee Donaghue could have done this."

"Why do you say that?"

"He's not good enough not to leave at least some sign of his passage."

"Who is? Indians?"

"No. An Indian would not have left such a message."

"Then who?"

Standing in the doorway, he slowly scanned the timberline. "I have been acquainted with some men who could manage it."

"You mean . . . men like you? Mountain men?"

Falconer nodded, preoccupied with thoughts he was careful to keep to himself. *He's worried,* thought Lillian, and that, more than any other aspect of the situation, frightened her. And being frightened made her angry.

"I will not be run out of my home," she said.

She spoke with such vehemence that Falconer turned, startled, a smile twitching at the corners of his mouth. He looked at her the way he had that very first day, when he had showed up at the camp alongside the Platte River, asking about the hide hunters. It gave her the same strange feeling, like butterflies trapped against her ribs, and she felt suddenly very envious of Lena Blakemore, because she wanted Falconer to stay here with her, not with Lena. Lillian knew she would feel unsafe as soon as this man took his leave, and she almost, impetuously, asked him straight out to stay, wondering what he would do then, whom he would choose, her or Lena, desire or obligation. She knew he cared for her. Maybe even loved her. But she regained her senses just in time. For one thing, it would not be fair to ask him to make such a choice, to impale him upon the horns of such an impossible dilemma; besides, she was afraid he would put aside his own wishes and choose obligation. He believed very strongly in his duty, his debt, to Lena Blakemore, and he was the kind of man who would forsake everything, even his own life, and certainly his own happiness, to fulfill the obligation and repay the debt.

"I don't believe whoever did this means you any harm personally," said Falconer. "He is just trying to run you off."

"But why? What have I done?"

"You're here. That may be enough."

"I don't think I understand."

"You're trespassing, Lillian."

"Do you know who did this?"

"No. But I think I know the kind of man he is. And if I'm right, he considers this valley his own private reserve, especially when it comes to folks like you."

"Folks like me? What's wrong with folks like me?"

Falconer shrugged. "Everything, as far as he's concerned. You cut down the trees, you plow up the ground, you fence off the land, drive off the game, and dirty up the creeks. All those things this man came out here to escape."

"Civilization," summarized Lillian.

"In a manner of speaking."

"We're talking about a man a lot like you, aren't we?"

"In some ways. But I've come to realize that nothing good lasts forever, that times change and you've got to change with them if you want to survive. Some men like me refuse to accept that. The fur trade that brought them out here is dead, but they linger on, looking for a place to live where they won't be bothered."

Lillian drew a deep breath. "But you don't think I am in any danger?"

"This man we're talking about may be half wild, but I don't see him killing a woman and a boy."

"Well, I will surely kill him if he comes around, and if I have the chance, because I won't risk any harm coming to my son." She thought he might be speaking, not out conviction, but merely to reassure her. "I hope you're right."

The look on his face made her regret having said it.

"I'm sorry," she said. "That wasn't fair. My safety, and my son's, is not your responsibility. I'm staying of my own free will, and if anything happens to us it most certainly will not be any fault of yours."

Falconer looked no more comforted than he had seemed before. "I will come by and check on you whenever I'm able," he said, and left so suddenly that she did not have the chance to say anything more.

That same day, on about sundown, Tom Wilkerson and Lee Donaghue rode up to the Tasker cabin. They looked bone-tired, and had every reason to be, having labored to erect two cabins in the span of four days. They looked concerned, too, and as Lillian poured them some coffee Wilkerson explained the reason for their visit.

"Falconer came by the Pollocks' today, told us

about *that.*" He pointed to the message carved into Lillian's door. "We've all agreed—we'll take turns spending one day up here to watch out for you and your boy."

"*You* agreed? Don't I have anything to say about it?"

Wilkerson was dumbfounded. "Well, we . . . I just thought that . . ."

"Tom, I appreciate what you're trying to do, really I do." Lillian's smile was wan. "I'm having to do a lot of apologizing today. It's just that this incident has rattled me a little, I guess. But you men have other responsibilities, people of your own to look out for. The man who did that might visit your place next."

"Whoever did it probably knows you're alone," said Donaghue.

"Perhaps so." Lillian recalled the Sioux warrior, back at Fort Laramie, who would have ransacked her wagon but for the timely arrival of Hugh Falconer. "Not having a man around does have its drawbacks."

"Yes," agreed Donaghue enthusiastically. "But you know you don't have to . . ."

Lillian didn't want to hear what he was going to say; she had a pretty good idea what it would be and she was in no mood. "But," she interrupted, "I am not defenseless, and if anyone thinks I am, then they are gravely mistaken." She looked Donaghue straight in the eye as she spoke, personalizing the statement.

Wilkerson could tell sparks were about to fly between Lillian and Donaghue, and he tried to steer a new course for the conversation.

"Falconer says he thinks it might be another mountain man, living alone somewhere up near the timberline, someone who considers us trespassers."

Lillian decided not to share her own suspicions regarding the author of the message, since he was present.

"We just can't in good conscience leave you to your own devices," continued Wilkerson. "I hope you understand, Lillian. It's not that we think you're unable to take care of yourself and Johnny. We all know better than that. But there's no telling what a man like that might do. Living half wild and all by your lonesome in this country could do something to your mind, I reckon. I know you don't want our families put in jeopardy on your account, but Lomax and Abney and all three of the Norwoods don't have to worry about that. As for the rest of us, when it's my turn I can take Molly and the girls over to Judd's place, and when it's his turn he can bring his family over to me. Please, Lillian. We want to help, and we'd all feel better if you'd let us do this."

"What about Falconer?"

Wilkerson winced. "He says as soon as he can finish the Blakemore cabin he's going up into the mountains to find the man who left that message."

"Oh, I see."

"He'll find him, too. So you see, this will be a temporary arrangement, that's all."

Lillian nodded. Thinking of Johnny's welfare, she set aside foolish pride. Fact was, she didn't want other men guarding her—she wanted Falconer, and only Falconer. But Falconer had instigated this "arrangement," as Wilkerson called it, since he could not do the job himself, and Lillian realized that just because she couldn't have what she wanted didn't mean it was a bad idea.

"I'm obliged to all of you for thinking about my son and me," she said.

Relieved, a big grin stretched across Wilkerson's

face. "Good," he said. "We'll start tomorrow morning. Lee here volunteered to take the first day."

Why am I not surprised? thought Lillian.

Finishing his coffee, Wilkerson headed out the door. He was eager to get back to his own family. But Donaghue lingered on the threshold, hat rolled up in his hands.

"Tomorrow I'll get started making you a new door."

"That isn't necessary . . ."

"No trouble. I'll bring Lisle along, if that's okay with you."

"Of course, you must bring her."

"You sure you'll be okay tonight, Lillian? I mean, Lisle and I could come back this evening."

"No, thank you."

"I don't mind . . ."

"No, Lee."

A quick flash of resentment came and went in Donaghue's eyes.

"I'll see you first thing in the morning, then," he said.

She nodded and with some effort fixed a smile on her face as she firmly shut the door. GIT OUT—she stared bleakly at the crudely carved words as she leaned heavily against the door, waiting until she heard the sound of the two men riding away. *Maybe I should never have left Illinois.* But then she scolded herself for the thought. *I'm just tired, and disappointed, because things are not working out like I want them to. Nothing new in that. It doesn't matter. I'll make do. I always have. . . .*

The day that Lee Donaghue stood guard at the Tasker cabin was one of the longest days of Lillian's life. Not because of anything Donaghue did, ironically enough, but rather because Lillian kept waiting for him to do some foolheaded thing that would infuriate or embarrass her, or both. Yet Donaghue spent the entire day in a standoffish mood. Lillian thought that maybe he was playing some kind of game, hoping perhaps that she would think he was suddenly no longer the least bit interested in her, in the hopes that she would reconsider and warm to him as a consequence. That likelihood in itself angered Lillian, since if it were true, it would mean that Donaghue thought she was no different from Grace Holsberry, a flirt whose method, typically, was to lead a man on one day and turn a cold shoulder to him the next, just to keep him on tenterhooks. Lillian simply could not invest much hope in the possibility that Donaghue had genuinely given up on the notion of their having a relationship. She just didn't think he had enough sense, in his present state. It wasn't really his fault; she knew precisely what the anguish of loneliness could do to a person.

He helped her carry the few heavy pieces of furniture from the prairie schooner into the cabin, and she spent the day putting her house in order, while Lisle and Johnny played together—it was so good to see Johnny act like a child once more. Donaghue spent the day outside, keeping alert, doing what he had come to do. Lillian talked him out of working on a new door. She didn't think it wise to let him do anything of that nature for her. That evening they all sat down to dinner like one big happy family, a situation fraught with peril from Lillian's point of view, and yet Donaghue hardly seemed to notice. After dinner he posted himself outside the door. Lisle and Johnny slept on blankets in front of the fire. It got pretty cold, and Lillian, against her better judgment, felt compelled by simple human compassion to invite Donaghue inside. But, to her surprise, he declined the offer out of hand, and remained at his post, huddled obstinately in his blanket, until dawn, when Jake Norwood arrived to take over for him, at which time he and a sleepy-eyed Lisle took their leave.

By morning Lillian was beginning to indulge in guilt for having treated Donaghue in such a way that he preferred remaining out in the cold to spending a night under her roof. That was a silly way to feel, Lillian knew, because if there was a wall between them it was of his making, not hers, but she couldn't help herself—until Johnny informed her that Lisle had told him that one day they might become brother and sister.

"She said her pa told her you and him might get married someday," muttered Johnny. He glowered at her for a moment, then blurted out, "I don't want a new pa. You're not really going to marry Mr. Donaghue, are you?"

That took care of the guilt in a hurry. "Absolutely not," she replied, fuming.

"He was just making it all up?"

"Yes."

"You're not looking for someone to take Pa's place, are you?"

"No one could take your father's place, Johnny."

He nodded vigorously. "That's right. Nobody. I don't want you to marry anybody else, Ma. You won't, will you?"

"Well, Johnny . . ."

"Promise me you won't ever marry."

She promised. Promising was the easy way out, and she took it.

Late that day she went out to ask Jake Norwood if he would like some tea or coffee, and found him down by the creek. He had scraped away some of the bark on a cottonwood tree, creating a target of sorts about the size of a man's head. At ten paces he was practicing throwing a knife at the target. He was very grim and businesslike. Lillian, watching from the crest of the cutbank for a moment, unbeknownst to Jake, took note of the fact that he hit the target more often than not.

When, finally, he became aware of her presence, she smiled and said, "You're very good at that, Jake. I doubt very much if anyone will dare try to bother me while you're here."

Jake glared at the tree. "I just pretend it's Clete," he said darkly.

"Your brother? Why on earth would you do that?"

"Yes, he's my brother. But I hate him, just the same."

"Why do you hate him?"

"Because he knows how I feel about Grace, and he's gone ahead and tried to steal her away from me."

Lillian was shocked. She hadn't realized that the situation with Grace Holsberry and the Norwood boys had progressed so far. But of course she had been preoccupied with her own problems. After a moment of reflection she realized that she really wasn't too surprised by this disturbing revelation; back in St. Joe she had seen the way Jake and Clete had looked at Grace, vying for her smiles, and she had predicted then and there that something like this would happen. Amazing how a woman like Grace Holsberry could tear a lifetime's fraternal bonds asunder with such ease.

"Think what you're saying, Jake," she said. "You can't mean it."

"But I do. I do mean it. Grace loves me, and Clete had better back off if he knows what's good for him."

"Grace doesn't love anybody, except herself."

"Don't talk about her that way. You got no call. You don't know her."

With a shrug, Lillian turned and went back to the cabin. There was nothing she could say that would bring Jake Norwood to his senses. He was too firmly caught in Grace Holsberry's web to extricate himself.

Later that day Lena Blakemore arrived, riding Falconer's Appaloosa. Standing in the cabin doorway, Lillian watched her approach with a sense of foreboding. She had a hunch this was no social call.

Nonetheless, she put a pleasant smile on her face and invited Lena inside. Lena declined and did not even bother to dismount.

"I know what you're trying to do," she said, her tone accusatory. "But it won't work. I won't let you take him away from me."

"I'm sure I don't have the slightest idea what you're talking about, Lena."

Lena scoffed at that. "Don't try to act so innocent. You want Falconer for yourself. Everybody knows you do. All this business about a mysterious man coming down out of the mountains to threaten you . . ."

"Would you like to see what's carved in my door?"

"Who's to say you didn't put it there yourself? You made the whole thing up, to get Falconer in your bed."

Lillian tried hard to tamp down fast-rising anger. "You're wrong," she said stiffly.

"You love him. I'm not wrong about that. Tell me the truth. Am I wrong about that?"

"No," said Lillian. "I do love him. And you don't."

"Of course I don't. But I need him. My children need him most of all. My husband is dead, and he's to blame, and he owes me."

"That's insane. How can you do this to him?"

"I can do it. Watch me and see. You just keep away

from him. He belongs to me now. It's bad enough he's going up into the mountains tomorrow to find this mysterious man who doesn't even exist, just because he thinks you might be in danger."

"The man does exist, Lena, and we *all* could be in danger."

"You won't have Falconer. I've lost one man, I don't intend to lose another. Love has nothing to do with this. I have to look out for my children, and for myself. And I'll do whatever I have to do."

Lillian knew when she was being threatened, and she didn't cotton to it one bit, but she caught the sharp retort before it slipped off her tongue. A kind of madness was a lurid light in Lena Blakemore's eyes, and Lillian was convinced the woman had become unbalanced. She reminded herself that Lena was actually powerless to keep Hugh Falconer corralled if he didn't want to be. After all, it wasn't really Lena keeping Falconer to herself, but rather Falconer's commitment to paying a debt he had convinced himself that he owed, and once she had this clear in her mind Lillian felt the anger subside, and she began to pity Lena Blakemore.

"Hugh Falconer will do what he wants to do, Lena," she replied, "and there is nothing either you or I can do about that."

"Don't be too sure." Lena wheeled the Appaloosa sharply and rode away.

Chapter Fifteen

The same day that Lena Blakemore delivered her warning to Lillian, Falconer finished the cabin. Next morning before dawn—and before Lena awoke—he took his leave. When she awakened a short time later and saw that he was not beneath the canvas shelter where he had slept the night before, Lena rushed out in her nightclothes, unmindful of the morning chill, to look for the Appaloosa, which was customarily on a long tether in the meadow. The horse was gone, too, and Lena wept hot, bitter tears. She knew Falconer had headed up into the mountains on a fool's errand, motivated by his concern—or was it more than concern?—for Lillian Tasker, in search of a phantom that only existed in the conniving mind of that Tasker bitch.

Falconer had decided not to spend days scouring the high reaches of the mountains which encompassed the valley. He thought he knew a better way to flush from hiding the man he was seeking. Up at the north end of the valley, a high windswept granite shoulder jutted out from a snowclad peak. A difficult and sometimes dangerous climb was required to reach it, but the Appaloosa was a surefooted mountain horse, and by midafternoon Falconer had arrived at his destination.

There, in the midst of a small bunch of wind-twisted

junipers, stunted by exposure to harsh elements at this elevation, he made his camp. On three sides there was a sheer drop of boulder-strewn slopes a thousand feet below. If anyone approached the campsite they would have to do so along the shoulder which, for most of its length, was no more than thirty paces wide. Here, on this remote eyrie at the top of the world, Hugh Falconer settled down to wait.

He built a fire, larger than was necessary for warmth, and kept it burning the rest of the day and long into the night. An abundance of firewood was readily available, so he kept the blaze well stoked. He figured most of the folks down below could see the fire, a speck of brilliant yellow light piercing the black cloak that night threw across the valley, and he wondered what they would make of it. Such idle speculation on the subject of the emigrants inevitably steered his thoughts to one pioneer in particular—Lillian Tasker. Lillian, and her long mahogany brown hair, her warm hazel eyes, the way her mouth curled so fetchingly at the corners when she smiled, and as he sat huddled in his woolen capote, buffeted by cold blasts of wind, he thought of her safe and warm in her bed in that cabin thousands of feet below. He confessed to himself that only once before in all his life had he been so drawn to a woman.

On about midnight he let the fire die down, took his blankets and horse deeper into the trees, and made his bed, sleeping with the Appaloosa's reins tied around his left wrist, while his right hand rested on the Hawken mountain rifle.

An hour or so before daybreak he awoke from a light sleep. No telltale sound had roused him, yet he knew with complete certainty that he was no longer alone on the granite spur. The Appaloosa's head was turned, its ears pivoting quickly this way and that, its nostrils flaring as it tested the thin, cold air for a scent. The wind had died down during the night, and it was quite still. Hearing nothing, Falconer lay there, unmoving as the stone upon which his lean body reposed, and eventually the scent reached him, too—the unmistakable scent of a bear. Yet he knew this was no bear. A bear was incapable of such stealth.

Though he did not see or hear anything, Falconer was sure that at one point the intruder was only a few strides away. The Appaloosa whickered a soft warning. The presence faded noiselessly back into the junipers. A moment later, Falconer heard him over by the dead fire. Soon he could hear the flames crackling as they began to consume the kindling. Falconer sat up, peering though the scrub. As the flames gained strength he detected a bulky shape hunched over in silhouette against the uncertain firelight. He waited a while longer before throwing aside the blankets and getting to his feet. Tying the Appaloosa to one of the trees, he took up the Hawken and walked over to the fire.

The man's back was to Falconer. He wore a long coat made from the hide of a grizzly. Shaggy hair fell upon his shoulder. The bear smell was very strong now. Grime-blackened hands reached out to capture the heat escaping from the fire as the man turned his head slightly and drawled, "Long time, Hugh."

It was a deep and gravelly voice, vaguely familiar, stirring the dust of distant memory. Falconer moved sideways for a better view of the man's firelit face.

"Don't you remember me?"

"Yes," said Falconer. "I remember. Been a long time, Bearclaw."

Bearclaw Johnson grunted, turning his attention back to the fire.

Like Falconer, Bearclaw Johnson was a legend

among the mountain men. The centerpiece of that legend was Johnson's lifelong feud with bears. Any kind of bear qualified for Johnson's animus, but the grizzly was his arch foe. No one knew the reason behind this obsession—Johnson was an extremely taciturn man when his past became the subject of conversation and conjecture. But the fact remained that Johnson's main purpose in life seemed to be killing bears. It was said that on one occasion a rock slide had trapped Johnson in a cave with a she-grizzly; Johnson killed the bear with a knife, lived for weeks on its meat and the water available from a slow-dripping seep, warmed himself with the grizzly's uncured hide, and used its bones to dig himself out of his mountain tomb.

Johnson had been one of the thirty men Falconer had handpicked six years ago to accompany him on an expedition to California—an adventure of epic proportions which had since become well known back East, thanks in large part to the publication of the journal faithfully kept by Eben Nall, another of Falconer's companions on that expedition. When the brigade crossed the Sierra Nevadas, Johnson had wandered off in search of bear and had not, to Falconer's knowledge, been seen since by a white man. Most folks had come to the conclusion that Bearclaw had finally crossed paths with a grizzly he couldn't handle.

Falconer moved closer now, seating himself cross-legged on the opposite side of the fire from Johnson, laying the Hawken across his knees, as Johnson had done with his own Sharps percussion. Falconer didn't know what to expect; he knew Johnson, but they had never been friends. No one was Bearclaw Johnson's friend. Johnson had usually kept to himself, steadfastly refusing to join a fur-trapping brigade in all his years in the high country, and it had surprised some that he had even agreed to be a participant in Falconer's

California expedition. Falconer had chosen him because he was a crack shot and a hard fighter and Falconer had been fairly certain there would be a strong need for such a man on that occasion. Social graces had not been a prerequisite.

"Thought I was dead, didn't you?" rumbled Johnson, smirking behind his tangled beard.

Falconer shook his head. Unlike others, Falconer had never written Bearclaw Johnson off. This man was extremely hard to kill—and Falconer hoped he wouldn't be called upon to try to get the job done now.

"Reckon I shouldn't have run off on you boys the way I did," continued Johnson, "but I smelt bear spoor, and when I get that smell in my nostrils I cain't think about nothin' else. Something comes over me. Can't help myself. You ain't changed much, Hugh. The years have been easy on you."

"You've changed, though. Those are the most words I've ever heard you string together at one sitting."

Johnson chuckled, a sound akin to that made by a herd of shaggies on the run and heard from way off.

"I haven't parlayed with another white man in six years. Kept to myself mostly, except summer 'fore last I got squawed up. Ute gal. She keeps my blankets warm, and my belly full, and my buckskins mended, and she don't vex me too much. Never has much to say, and that suits me. Guess it's all pent up inside, you know, all these words. I see you've got yoreself a squaw, too. A white gal."

"No. Her husband was killed back at Fort Laramie. I'm just trying to help her and her children out."

It didn't surprise Falconer that Johnson knew about Lena Blakemore. No doubt Bearclaw knew all there was to know about every person in the valley. He was certain, as well, that Johnson had left the warning on Lillian Tasker's door, coming and going without leaving any trace at all came easy as drawing breath to a man like Bearclaw Johnson.

"You shouldn't have done it," said Johnson with a mournful shake of his head.

"Done what?"

"Brought them plowpushers out here. There ain't no place for the likes of them in these mountains."

"No use trying to scare them off. I want no harm to come to them, Bearclaw."

Johnson stared into the fire for a long time. Falconer watched him like a hawk. There was no reading this man, but it was certain he didn't cotton to being threatened, and there was a clearly implied threat in what Falconer had said. Johnson didn't move an inch, didn't even blink; he was as animate as the high granite crags just now illuminated by the soft golden pink light of a newborn day.

"Reckon we need to talk some more," said Johnson, rising suddenly in a fluid motion.

Falconer saw no need for further discussion. He had said what he came to say. On the other hand, he wanted to avoid a confrontation with Bearclaw Johnson if it was at all possible to do so. He wasn't afraid of Johnson—Falconer was afraid of no man, having prevailed against all manner of men—but he respected Johnson's prowess and, contrary to the legend surrounding him, was not by preference a violent man.

Bearclaw Johnson stood there, looking down at Falconer with perfect impassivity, providing no clue by stance or demeanor what he would do if Falconer refused his unspoken invite to go with him and continue the discussion elsewhere. But Falconer nodded and got to his feet, kicking the fire to death. Retrieving the Appaloosa, and with one last look at the valley below, he followed Johnson off the narrow rock outcropping.

Bearclaw Johnson had deposited his horse in some trees on the mountain slope. Both men forked their saddles and negotiated a narrow trail through conifers clinging sparsely to the rocky and precipitous incline. Johnson, of course, led the way. He never once looked back. They rode for the better part of an hour, roughly northward, in the direction of the high pass. This brought them eventually to Johnson's home in a stand of timber wedged between a rocky spine draped with snow and a boulder-strewn slope of shale angling steeply to the rim of a deep gorge carved into the mountainside. Snowmelt nourished a cascade which tumbled pell-mell through the trees and down the shale to plummet over the rim of the gorge. From the trees one could see the upper half of the valley.

Johnson had utilized a shallow cave in building his cabin, erecting three walls on the shelf of stone jutting like a petulant lip from the mouth of the cave. The roof, like the walls, was constructed of whole logs. There were no windows, and the single doorway was draped with buffalo hides. Falconer noticed a wisp of gray smoke rising through the hole cut into the roof. By a lowlander's standards the dwelling was primitive indeed, but to a mountain man's eyes it appeared quite substantial.

With the exception of the few years of his idyllic high country sojourn with Touches The Moon, the Shoshone girl he had loved so much and who had died ten years ago, Falconer had never had a roof over his head that he could call his own, and it was odd to find Bearclaw Johnson with one; Johnson had never been one to put down roots, but by the amount of work he had invested in this place it was clear he intended to remain for quite some time.

Johnson seemed to read Falconer's thoughts. As they dismounted in front of the cabin, he said, "I'm gettin' soft in my old age, Hugh. Used to be I'd swear I never needed nothin' but this big sky over my head at night. But then, I said I'd never get squawed up, too. Now all I want to do is live up here with my woman and not be pestered by man nor beast. You can understand that, I reckon."

Falconer nodded. Once he had felt the very same way, when he had taken up with Touches The Moon, and he felt bad for having invaded Johnson's privacy. But there was no undoing what he had done. Lillian Tasker and the rest of the emigrants were settled into the valley for the winter and he wasn't about to uproot them just to please Bearclaw Johnson.

"Come on in," said Johnson as he passed through the door, "and meet my wife."

Falconer followed him inside. The interior of the cabin was dim and smoky. The log walls were lined with pelts of bear and buffalo and deer, and the stone floor was similarly covered. The cave portion was strewn with hay cut from some high mountain meadow before the first snow; obviously Johnson kept his horse there when foul weather made it necessary to do so. In the center of the cabin, a small, hot fire crackled inside a ring of stones. Meat cooked on a wooden spit, fat grease sizzling as it dripped into the leaping flames. By the smell Falconer could tell it was bear meat.

She had been standing near the fire as the men entered, but upon seeing Falconer she shrank back into a dark corner, like a wild animal trapped in its own den. Johnson chuckled.

"We don't get too many visitors," he explained to Falconer. "She's a mite shy."

"Her Indian name?"

"Sun Falling."

Falconer spoke to her in fluent Ute. "Sun Falling, I am honored to be a guest in your lodge."

His words had the effect of calming her fears. She ventured closer, a timid smile on her lips. "You are welcome in our lodge," she replied.

"Wagh!" exclaimed Johnson. "You have a way with wimmin, Hugh, I must admit. Why, you could charm the fur right off a beaver if you set your mind to it. Want to sink your teeth into a bear steak?"

Falconer thought it best not to refuse. He sat with Johnson at the fire while Sun Falling cut chunks off the spitted slab of meat, impaling the chunks on sharpened sticks and handing them to the mountain men. They ate Indian style, without conversation, and only when they were finished and their bellies full did Bearclaw speak.

"Wanted you to see what I got," he said, wiping his mouth with the back of his grime-blackened buckskin sleeve. "About as close to heaven as I'm ever likely to get. Figure you of all people can understand."

Again Falconer nodded, with a glance at Sun Falling, and powerful, poignant memories assailed him, memories of the happiest years of his life, living with Touches The Moon in idyllic solitude. Sun Falling was not as pretty as his Shoshone bride had been; her features were plain, her build less willowy than that of the Indian girl Falconer had loved—still loved—with such fierce ardor.

"I do understand," he replied, "and I'm glad for you, Bearclaw."

"I'll fight to keep it."

"You don't need to worry about those folks down

yonder. They're bound for Oregon Territory. But they got a late start, and ran into trouble along the way. We'll winter down below, and be on our way come green-up."

"I hate 'em," muttered Johnson darkly. "I hate the smell of them. I hate the sound of their axes. I don't blame the Injuns for fightin' to keep 'em out of their lands. I love this country, Hugh, and I don't want to see it destroyed. That's what they do. Destroy the land and everything on it."

Falconer laughed softly. "We showed them the way, Bearclaw. You and me and our kind. That's the irony of it all. They're coming, because we filled in the empty spaces on the maps and loudly sang the praises of this land. They're coming and there will be no stopping them."

"We could stop 'em. Yes we could. Them plowpushers are weak-kneed cowards. No match for the likes of us."

"That's where you're dead wrong. They are the bravest people I've ever met, bar none."

Johnson grunted his skepticism.

Falconer leaned forward. "Hear me, Bearclaw. Those folks mean you no harm. Come spring, they'll be gone. The scars they leave on the land will heal. Let's have a truce. If you want to keep what you've got, leave them alone, because if it's war you hanker after you won't win it."

"You makin' a threat, Hugh?"

"You know I don't make threats. Just telling it straight." Falconer made the Indian sign for Truth, holding his right hand, closed into a fist, under his chin and extending the forefinger, then moving the whole hand forward away from his face. This meant that what he said came straight from the heart by way of the tongue. "You threaten the wives and children of those men and they will hunt you down and kill you."

"That'll be the day." Johnson squinted suspiciously at Falconer. "I reckon you'd help 'em get the job done, too, wouldn't you?"

"I've floated my stick with theirs," said Falconer solemnly. He put out his hand. "But I'd rather give you my hand in peace than raise it against you in war."

For what seemed an eternity to Falconer, Bearclaw Johnson glowered darkly at the proffered hand. Then he glanced at Sun Falling sitting silently inscrutable on the other side of the fire, and Falconer saw in Bearclaw's rugged countenance something he had never thought to see there. *He'll do it, but only for her sake,* realized Falconer.

Johnson clasped Falconer's hand in his own.

"Were it not for Sun Falling," he said, "I'd tell you to go straight to hell, Hugh. But a woman's like likker. A man can get too attached to both, and both will make him weak. I want no harm to come to Sun Falling, so I'll make peace. Until green-up, that is. Take them away from here in the spring, and don't tarry, hoss. And warn them to stay off my mountain, or there'll be blood spilled, sure as shootin'."

"I'll tell them," said Falconer.

Chapter Sixteen

A week later, Lillian Tasker stepped out of her cabin and knew that the heavy snow was about to fall. She could tell by the appearance of the clouds that obscured the tops of the peaks on the west side of the valley. It was certainly cold enough, of late the days had not been warming up, as they had previously. She pulled the shawl closer about her shoulders and turned her thoughts to the things she would have to do in the days to come to prepare for the winter.

She and Johnny had just finished making a stick corral for the oxen. They would have to work hard to stock in enough firewood, and more meat would be nice, too. In a matter of weeks they would be snowed in. They still had some flour and bacon and rice, and at Fort Laramie she had purchased some coffee and sugar to replenish her dwindling supply of these staples—even though the "mountain prices," as they called them at the American Fur Company outpost, had been exorbitant. But this would be a long winter, and would call for strict rationing just to make it through to spring without having to do without, much less to have anything left over for the completion of the journey to the Oregon Territory.

Then, too, there was the lean-to shelter for Ol' Blue she and her son were putting up on the back side of the cabin. In the past couple of days she had cut and trimmed two dozen saplings, and the axe handle had made new calluses on her work-roughened hands. Once the shelter was finished they would need to go up into the meadow and cut some hay before deep snow blanketed the ground. So much yet to be done, and so little time.

A rider was coming, and long before he reached the creek Lillian recognized Hugh Falconer. Her heart performed a funny flop in her chest. Why was he coming to visit her? Maybe to tell her he had extricated himself from Lena Blakemore's web. Lillian smiled wryly at herself; that was certainly taking the art of wishful thinking to a new level.

Then, as the Appaloosa splashed across the creek, she saw the deer, a big buck with a magnificent rack, draped across the mountain man's saddlehorn.

Checking the Appaloosa in front of the cabin, Falconer let the deer slide off to the ground. *They grow them big out here*, thought Lillian. This buck was almost twice the size of the largest deer she had ever seen in Illinois. Johnny emerged from the cabin, having heard the horse. Now he stepped close to the carcass and admired the sixteen-point rack.

"Thought you and the boy could use some fresh meat," said Falconer.

"Thank you," said Lillian, "but you needn't have gone to all the trouble on our account. I happen to be a fair hand with a rifle."

Falconer looked perplexed, and Lillian silently chastised herself for such foolish and ungrateful talk.

"No trouble," he replied, at length. "I figured you were plenty busy with other things, and this big feller just walked right out of the woods in front of me this morning."

So why didn't he take it to Lena Blakemore? Lillian shook her head. She was being plumb childish. Only a fool would look a gift horse in the mouth, especially in her situation.

"I apologize," she said. "I didn't mean to come across as ungrateful. Please come inside. I've got some hot coffee. It's awfully cold today, isn't it?"

"It's brisk." Falconer dismounted, ground-hitched the Appaloosa and followed her inside, pausing to tousle Johnny's hair. Johnny lingered outside, still admiring the buck.

Seating himself at the table Lillian had hauled halfway across the continent, Falconer admired the smoothness of the dark varnished wood under his hands and said, "I can help you out with butchering that deer if you like."

"Oh no," she said, bringing him the coffee. "I can manage."

He took the cup from her and sipped the steaming hot brew, and the memory of that day when they had first met came back strong to her, and he looked up, his eyes filled with a kind of wistful amusement, and she realized he was remembering the same moment. Lillian had to smile, and he answered with a smile of his own. Then he looked away, and his gaze swung idly to the door, where Bearclaw Johnson's menacing message was etched.

"Haven't had any more trouble, have you?" he asked.

"None. Tom Wilkerson came out to tell me what you had done. You know, I think I might have seen him, this man Bearclaw Johnson, way up on a mountainside, the day before he left that on my door. I thought it was a bear, maybe a grizzly. Remember? I told you about it."

"There are a few grizzly up there, but it very well could have been Bearclaw."

"You're sure he'll leave us be?"

"Pretty sure. Long as he's left alone. If I thought otherwise I wouldn't be leaving."

"Leaving?" Lillian realized she was looking crestfallen, and tried to mask it with a facade of casual interest. "Where are you going?"

"After Spellman and the half-breed."

"But I thought you told us to forget the money they stole. You gave the impression there was little or no hope of ever finding them."

"I can find them. This is a big country, but you can find a man in it, even if he doesn't want to be found, so long as you've got the time and know where to look. Whether they've still got any of that money they stole is another matter."

"Sounds like you don't believe they do."

"Men like that generally spend their ill-gotten gains in a hurry."

"If you think that is the case, then why go after them? This hardly seems the time to be making such a trip, with winter almost upon us."

Falconer rang down a curtain of brooding silence between them. It seemed to Lillian that at least a full minute crept by before he responded.

"Lena Blakemore asked me to go."

For some reason that pricked Lillian's temper. She did not pause to ponder why. "And you simply must do everything she asks of you, is that it?" Naturally, she immediately regretted the outburst. "Oh, I don't know why I can't learn to keep my big mouth shut," she said, miserably. "I keep having to apologize to you, don't I?"

Falconer smiled. "That's one of the things I admire about you, Lillian. You always say what you think."

"Don't go just because she wants you to. I haven't told anyone about this, but, well, Lena came to see me the day before you went up into the mountains.

She's determined to keep you for herself. Not because she loves you. Quite the contrary. She hates you. She blames you for her husband's death, and she would rather see you dead than see you happy."

"Happy?"

"Yes, happy. Being here with me and Johnny."

Falconer stared at her, his features betraying nothing, and Lillian tried to swallow the lump lodged firmly in her throat. She had mustered enough courage to blurt out her true feelings and there just wasn't enough left over to sustain her as she waited breathlessly for Falconer's slow-coming reply. She just sat there across the table from him, petrified with fear.

"I'm not going just because she told me to," he said. "It's just that, if I get her money back I think I'll feel as though I've done all I need to do for her. If she gets to Oregon with a grubstake she'll be fine on her own."

"Really?" gasped Lillian, delighted. "Do you mean it?"

"Sure. I said it, didn't I?"

"But you don't think you'll recover the money, even if by some miracle you find Spellman and the breed."

"But I've got to try." Falconer finished the coffee.

"And when you're free? Fulfilled your obligation to Lena? What then?"

Falconer did not look up from his coffee cup, and Lillian was glad, because she was certain she would have melted under his gaze at that moment. Her skin tingled, her heart raced, her breathing was high and fast. Never had she been so bold in affairs of the heart, but she was compelled to press the issue, knowing that this would be her last chance, and tired, too, exceedingly tired of living in uncertainty where Hugh Falconer was concerned. Tired of being the proper young lady, of playing the game the way she was supposed to. A woman wasn't supposed to throw herself at a man, to pursue him the way she was pursuing Falconer at this moment, trying to drag the truth out of him, the truth about his feelings for her, and if they had a future together. The not knowing was a real burden on her, and she couldn't bear it for much longer. She *knew* she couldn't wait until he came back from his search for Spellman and Breed—*if* he came back at all. She had to know *now*.

So Lillian wasn't going to play by the rules this time, couldn't afford to emotionally, even though she ran the risk of Falconer thinking less of her because she was so forthright. She had put him in a very uncomfortable situation with her last question, and she realized that, because he wasn't the kind of man to whom the ability to articulate his innermost desires came easy. It would be completely out of character for him to come right out and tell her what she wanted to hear, or to sweep her into his arms and kiss her with a passion that would say more than words ever could about the way he felt.

"It isn't just for Mrs. Blakemore," he said. "It will be a true hardship for all the others once they get to Oregon if they don't have at least a little money. You were the only one smart enough not to trust Spellman."

Lillian's heart sank. He had deftly skirted the issue, and wasn't going to say what she wanted so desperately to hear; she tried to tell herself it didn't mean he didn't love her, but she was hurt, all the same. It occurred to her that perhaps she had been too vague. *Maybe I should come right out and tell him that I love him with all my heart.* But she couldn't bring herself to do it. She couldn't step that far over the line.

"How long will you be gone?" she asked, as though it were merely idle curiosity.

"Might take all winter. One thing, though—I'm fairly sure Spellman and the breed will settle in somewhere, at least until spring. All I've got to do is find out where they're holed up."

"I see. Would you like some more coffee?"

"No thanks." He sat there a moment, the empty cup gripped in both hands, unwilling to take his leave, with the feeling that there was unfinished business between them. But he had no idea how to finish it, so he finally stood up to go.

"Are you leaving today?" asked Lillian in anguish.

Falconer nodded. "Sooner I leave, the sooner I'll be back. We've still got to get to Oregon, you know."

"I'll miss you, Hugh. We'll miss you. We wouldn't have made it this far without your help."

"You sell yourself short, Lillian."

She shook her head, and felt tears burning in her eyes. She couldn't help herself. "I have this horrible feeling I won't see you again."

Falconer cleared his throat. "You and the boy will be safe enough. Bearclaw Johnson will keep his end of the bargain. There's little chance of seeing any Indians, and none at all once the snow lies heavy on the ground. But game will be scarce, and the wolves may come down into the valley in search of food."

"Wolves?"

He nodded. "A pack of them. But they won't bother you. Those stories about wolves trying to claw their way through doors to get to people on the other side are just tall tales. They'll not harm you, though they might try for your horse or the oxen if they're starving. Be sure to lay in plenty more firewood. It's going to be a long, cold winter."

"Yes. Very long, and very cold."

He turned away and went to the door.

"Hugh?"

He swung back around and she came to him, into his arms, holding him tightly, and laying her head against his chest.

"Please come back," she whispered, unable to restrain the tears.

He held her for a while, stroking her mahogany brown hair, marveling at its softness, and at the way her body felt pressed against his. It was a memory in the making, a memory he would cherish in the months to come, that would warm him during the many cold nights which lay down the trail. It was a promise, too, a promise of the future that was his for the asking, and which would sustain him until his return.

But Falconer was not one to make a vow he did not know he could keep. He had no illusions about the dangers of the task he had accepted, and he would provide Lillian no comforting but empty guarantees. So he simply held her for a time, then gently freed himself and left the cabin, swinging aboard the Appaloosa, giving Johnny a wave, and riding off without a backward glance.

Lillian watched him go until the forest swallowed him up.

Chapter Seventeen

She felt both good and bad, full and yet empty, happy but sad at the same time, and sometimes it became so confusing, and so emotionally exhausting that all she could do was sit there in a daze, until Johnny noticed something was wrong and asked her if she was feeling okay, concern digging little furrows between his eyebrows. Then she would snap out of it and manufacture a smile and try to act as though nothing was the matter.

At least she knew that Falconer cared, as she cared for him. He hadn't put it into words, but then he wasn't the kind who would do that, or perhaps even could do it—it wasn't his nature. But he felt the same way as she did, and she no longer harbored any doubts whatsoever on that score. It was as though his love had been communicated through the arms that had held her, so strong and yet so gentle, in the cabin doorway. *God has made a man just for you,* her mother used to tell her, *and he is out there somewhere, and in time you will find him.* Lillian had thought that Will Tasker was that man. She had made a mistake there, but she was certain now that Hugh Falconer was no mistake. He was that man her mother had told her about. While she had shared Will's bed in Illinois, Falconer had been up here in these mountains, in the snow with the grizzlies and the wolves and the elk, in this splendid isolation, alone but not lonely, becoming the man for her, and wasn't it odd and magnificent how God worked His will? It was God's handiwork that the two of them had met in all this immensity. It had to be. Lillian had at last found the man she was meant to find, and that made her happy, happier than she had ever been.

And yet this true happiness was tempered by his leaving. He was gone, perhaps for months. Maybe even gone forever. He was, after all, a mortal man—stronger, smarter, tougher, harder to kill than most men because the iron in his body and soul had been forged within the crucible of these mountains where only the fittest survived. Still, all it would take was one bullet. Lillian worried most of all about the breed. The breed was a particularly dangerous man. She had sensed this from the very first. Amos Spellman, for all his big talk about his fabulous and daring exploits on the wild frontier, did not measure up to Hugh Falconer. But the half-breed did.

Falconer was gone. She had found honest love, true happiness, and then she had had to watch it go, and although she was happy she was also sad for this reason. That terrible beast called loneliness was clawing at the door to her heart once more, the beast she had tried to leave behind in Illinois. The beast had followed her trail, all the way across the prairie, across the high plains, into the mountains, and she had been too busy and too tired to notice, and now it was with her again, more fiercely ravenous than ever before, and sometimes during the day, most unexpectedly, in the middle of a chore, it would leap out of the shadows at her and she would have to fight back the hot tears. Of course at night, while she lay awake, weary yet unable to sleep, thinking about Falconer, picturing him huddled near a small fire in the middle of the big lonesome, the beast lurked beneath her bed, and she would shudder and pull the star pattern quilt her mother had made to her chin, and she would try to keep the beast at bay with the memory of how Falconer had held her with those strong yet gentle arms. When Falconer returned he would banish the beast forever, but until then the beast remained.

There were plenty of things to do to keep busy. She and Johnny smoked the venison, finished the lean-to for Ol' Blue, brought in the hay, stocked up on firewood. Lillian tried to push herself into that level of exhaustion where the mind gives up trying to function, in order to escape the beast, but if it worked it was never for very long.

Four weeks after Falconer's departure the snow lay heavy on the ground. At first it came like a thief in the night, transforming the land. In the days that followed the temperature dropped, and ice formed on the edges of the creek, and sometimes it snowed from dawn until dusk and beyond. Lillian saw the tracks of the wolf pack, and heard them howl in the evening stillness, but she wasn't afraid. Two weeks after first hearing them she saw them, crossing open ground between two stands of snow-clad trees, on the far side of the creek. They traveled single file, seven of them, one big black male in the lead, the smaller females in the middle. They looked at her as she stood in the doorway, then disappeared like ghosts into the forest.

Even with Johnny she craved human companionship more than she had ever craved it before, and often she and her son would saddle Ol' Blue and ride south along the creek. She always skirted the cabin of her nearest neighbor, Lee Donaghue, for fear that if she called on him even once he would misconstrue the visit and read more into it than he should. Besides, she felt a little guilty for having suspected him of carving the words on her door.

The Pollocks were the next nearest, and she visited them occasionally, but often she felt compelled by her friendship with Tom and Molly Wilkerson to go even further down the valley. The Wilkersons were always glad to see her, and sometimes she spent the better part of the day with Molly while Johnny played with Edna and Phoebe. And when it was time to go home, Molly never failed to warn her to beware of the wolves, as by then everyone knew the pack had ventured down into the valley. Lillian would tell her not to worry, the wolves would not bother her, and she made Tom promise not to go out and try to hunt them down. He promised, amused by the fervor of her plea. The wolves reminded Lillian of Falconer in a way. They had the same spirit, the same nobility, the same wild strength. They had been forged in the same crucible as he, and she wanted no harm to come to them.

As the weeks passed, Lillian ceased to be concerned by the presence of Bearclaw Johnson. Apparently the man was going to abide by the bargain he had struck with Falconer. No one saw him, or any sign of him.

But one day the tranquillity which had settled like the deep snow in the valley was shattered. When Lillian and Johnny arrived at the Wilkersons', Tom was grimly saddling his horse while a distraught Molly stood in the cabin doorway, her two daughters clinging to her skirt.

"Ted Norwood just rode by," Tom told Lillian. "On his way to fetch Doc Holsberry. Clete is bad hurt."

"What happened?"

Tom shook his head. "Ted didn't waste the time to tell me. I'm riding on up to the Norwood cabin."

"I'll leave Johnny here and ride with you."

They reached the Norwood cabin in advance of Ted and Doc Holsberry, to find a bloody trail across the snow leading up to the door of the cabin. Inside, Jake stood over his brother, his features ashen. Clete lay on the floor, covered with blankets. His face was a milky shade of white, his lips blue. His left foot was a mangled, bloody mess. The jaws of a heavy steel trap were still clamped to his ankle, and in places white pieces of shattered bone could be seen protruding from the torn flesh.

"Good God in heaven!" breathed Wilkerson. "What . . . ?"

"He went down to the crik to fetch some water," mumbled Jake, as though in a trance. "We heard a shout, ran down to find he had fallen into the crik. The current carried him under the ice. We almost didn't find him. He stepped into the trap on the bank, I reckon, and fell in."

Wilkerson bent down. "We've got to get this trap off his leg."

"I couldn't do it," said Jake, backing away, horror in his eyes. "Pa told me to get it off while he went for the doctor but I just couldn't do it, every time I tried Clete made this godawful sound . . ."

Wilkerson judged that Jake would be of no help to him, and he turned to Lillian. "Fetch me a stick of that kindling yonder."

Lillian did as he had asked.

"Now, you've got to try and hold him still," said Wilkerson, "while I pry these jaws open."

Lillian nodded and dropped to her knees beside Clete. She thought Clete was unconscious, but as soon as Wilkerson touched the trap Clete's eyes snapped open, his breathing became harsh and rapid, his body arched, and the most inhuman and horrible sound Lillian had ever heard welled up from his throat.

"Keep him down!" snapped Wilkerson.

Lillian flung herself bodily across Clete's chest, pinning him to the ground as Wilkerson, grunting with exertion, used the stick of wood to pry the jaws of the trap open. Pieces of bloody flesh clung to the iron teeth, and Lillian shut her eyes tightly against the sight. Clete writhed and flopped beneath her, but he was in a weakened state, and could not throw her off. Wilkerson kept one knee on Clete's good leg. He soon had the trap removed. Working swiftly, he removed his leather belt and used it for a tourniquet just above the knee. Then he drew his knife and cut away Clete's blood-filled boot, which the trap had almost cut in two.

Moments later, Lillian heard horses outside. Ted Norwood burst into the room, his features a picture of anguish as he saw his son's condition. Doc Holsberry followed him inside. Kneeling beside Wilkerson, he examined Clete's ankle, his own features carefully impassive.

"He's lost a lot of blood," said Wilkerson needlessly.

Lillian raised herself off Clete, certain now that he was unconscious. His head lolled to one side, spittle mixed with creekwater leaking from the corner of his mouth.

"The foot will have to come off," said Holsberry.

"What did you say?" This was Ted Norwood, not wanting to believe his own ears.

"You heard me," said Holsberry curtly.

"You're not cutting my son's foot off," said Norwood.

"He's right, Ted," said Wilkerson. "There'll be no saving it. The bones have been crushed."

"No."

Rising, Wilkerson took Norwood by the shoulders.

"Use your head. Gangrene will set in if it isn't done, and Clete will surely die."

"You don't understand, Tom," said Norwood, glaring at Holsberry. "He's doing this on account of Grace. He doesn't think my boy is good enough for his daughter. He doesn't like them hanging around. He's getting back at Clete. That foot doesn't have to come off. He *wants* to cut it off."

"That's crazy," said Wilkerson. "Doc's trying to save your son's life. If he wanted Clete dead he could leave the foot on and let nature take its course . . ."

Holsberry was standing now, glaring right back at Norwood. "I have devoted my entire life to saving others. How dare you imply that I would permit personal considerations . . ."

"You see?" cried Norwood. "He admits it."

"I admit nothing of the kind. I have no quarrel with your son. I am half inclined to leave the decision to you, but then Clete would die. That foot must be amputated, and that is what I am going to do."

"Let him do it, Pa," muttered Jake.

Norwood's whole body seemed to deflate in resignation.

"Very well, then," said Holsberry, sensing that there was no more resistance in Norwood. "Tom, Lillian, will the two of you assist me? Good. We need hot water and clean bandages. And we shall have to strap him down. I will need a hot iron or the blade of a knife heated in the fire with which to cauterize the cut and close the arteries. We must work swiftly. There is no time to waste."

When the surgery was finished Lillian stepped out of the cabin, weak in the knees and in desperate need of fresh air. The horror of what she had witnessed lingered like the after-effects of a vivid nightmare. Her hands shook and her stomach felt as though it were tied up in knots. A bitter taste like copper was on her tongue.

Ted and Jake Norwood were outside in the snow, for they had been unable to watch the gruesome goings-on within the cabin, and Tom Wilkerson came out right behind Lillian, because he had heard the sounds of Lee Donaghue, with Abney and Lomax, arriving, all three of them astride shaggy mules and all three of them armed.

"What happened here?" asked Lomax.

Wilkerson glanced at Ted Norwood, but Norwood seemed not to have heard the query, being lost in morose thoughts, so Tom spoke up, telling the newcomers everything he knew.

"Will he pull through?" asked Abney.

"Doc thinks there's a good chance. We'll know for sure in a day or two."

"Where did that trap come from?" asked Lomax.

Lillian noticed that Donaghue seemed completely disinterested in the conversation. He was watching her, and she studiously ignored him.

"Somebody must have put it in the creek a long time ago, for beaver," offered Wilkerson.

"Let's see it," said Lomax.

Wilkerson went inside to fetch the trap. Coming back out, he dropped the steel device in the muddy snow. Lomax slid off his mule and knelt to take a closer look. He didn't touch the trap; it was covered with Clete's blood and flesh.

"This is no beaver trap," he said.

"Are you sure?" asked Wilkerson.

"Sure I'm sure. It's a bear trap."

"Whatever it is," said Wilkerson, "it's probably been there for a long while. You can see all the rust on it. It was just Clete's bad luck to find it the way he did."

"Didn't Falconer say that man Johnson hunts bear?" asked Lomax. "Maybe he put it there."

"Maybe he did."

"I mean maybe he put it there to catch something besides bear."

Wilkerson stared at him. "I don't think so. For one thing, Johnson gave Falconer his word."

"Yeah, like Amos Spellman gave us his word? You can't trust these damned mountain men, Tom. Their word isn't worth a bucket of warm spit, if you want my opinion."

"What about Falconer's word? Now that he's gone you suddenly get brave enough to say these things."

"I say now that Falconer is gone this man Johnson is up to his old tricks again."

"By God, Lomax, I think you must be right," said Ted Norwood. "One of us goes down to the crik every day to fetch water. We always stick to an old game trail. If that trap had been there long we would have found it before now. Somebody put it there. Somebody who knew we went down that trail every day at least once."

"Wait a minute," said Wilkerson. "You're jumping to conclusions, Ted."

"All I know is, my boy ain't a whole man on account of whoever set that damned trap. And it must have been Bearclaw Johnson. Who else would've done such a thing?"

Lillian glanced at Jake. He caught her looking at him and turned his face away.

"What do you think, Jake?" she asked. "Who else might have wanted harm to come to your brother?"

Jake shrugged. "Must have been Johnson."

"I'm going to track that son of a bitch down and

kill him for what he's done," said Ted Norwood, a kind of madness gleaming in his eyes.

"I'm with you, Ted," said Lomax. "I never liked the idea of sitting around waiting for Johnson to make his move against us. We should have done something about him the day he left his mark on Miss Tasker's door. What do you say, Lee?"

Donaghue nodded. "I agree. As long as he's up there in those mountains I have to worry about what might happen to Lisle."

"I know Judd Pollock will see it our way, too." Lomax turned to Abney. "What about you? Got the stomach for this kind of work?"

"Of course," said Abney, defensively, believing that Lomax was implying he didn't have the nerve to go along.

"Hold up," protested Wilkerson. "You all can't do this . . ."

"The hell we can't," growled Norwood.

"You'll stand no chance against a man like Johnson. You don't know the mountains, for one thing. For another, you're all farmers, not manhunters."

"There'll be six of us," said Norwood, "against only one of him. I'm assuming you won't be coming along, Tom."

"You're right. I'm not going."

"Funny. I never took you for a coward."

"Think what you like. Fact remains, you don't know if Johnson set that trap or not. You're just scared, and hurt, and you feel the need to strike back, and he's the best target. So you think. But *he'll* be the hunter up in those mountains, Ted. Not you."

"Stay down here with the women and children, then." Norwood sneered. "Jake, go fetch Judd Pollock. We're gonna get the son of a bitch who did this to your brother."

Chapter Eighteen

Falconer had not told them exactly where Bearclaw Johnson lived. All they knew for certain was that their prey could be found somewhere up near the timberline. They climbed all that day, keeping to treacherous game trails made more treacherous by the fact that their mules and horses were unaccustomed to mountain travel.

Ted Norwood took the lead. His son had been the one to suffer at the hands of the man they were seeking, and that gave him the right to make the decisions. The others had grown used to looking for leadership from Tom Wilkerson and felt more comfortable in the role of follower. Besides, Norwood had the drive, the passion, the obsession for vengeance which the others, after the first grueling day, found they lacked.

As they climbed ever higher, the bitter cold invaded their bodies and made their bones ache. In their haste to get started they had failed to take into consideration the need for additional blankets and adequate food supplies. But no one said a word about giving up and turning back that first day, afraid of what Ted Norwood might say or do in response to their lack of commitment. Even Abney, who of them all was perhaps the least committed, kept his doubts to himself. The flask of John Barleycorn was a comforting weight in the pocket of his coat.

Scarcely a word was spoken all day. The men were too busy trying to keep their mounts on the steep, narrow trails. And too busy keeping their eyes peeled for Bearclaw Johnson. When they passed through the forests they expected the mountain man to be lurking in the shadows, and when they crossed the high snow-clad mountain meadows they expected a rifle shot from the wooded fringe. No one harbored any hope of actually sneaking up on Johnson. By the end of that first day their nerves were thoroughly frayed.

When night came, the bone-biting cold grew more severe, and all they could think about was a nice warm fire, but when Ted Norwood ignited moss and kindling with sparks enticed from stone and flint, Judd Pollock was the first to give voice to second thoughts.

"Maybe we ought not to have a fire," he mumbled through jaws locked tight to still his chattering teeth. "Might lead him right to us."

"Let it," growled Norwood. He alone seemed impervious to cold and hunger and dread. "I want him to find us. Be easier that way."

"We've broken the peace he made with Falconer," said Lomax. "We've come up into the mountains."

Norwood nodded, blowing on the newborn fire to give it strength. In moments the flames were licking at the pile of sticks, and Norwood quickly added larger pieces of wood.

"He'll come, and when he does I'm going to kill him. He'll learn the hard way that it don't pay to tangle with me or mine."

"We better keep watch tonight," said Pollock. "Two men every two hours. Who'll stand the first watch with me?"

"I will," said Abney.

"You?" scoffed Lomax. "I don't care to wake up dead, or trust my scalp to a drunken fool."

"I don't have to take that from you," snapped Abney, leaping to his feet.

His vehemence startled the others, who were accustomed to seeing Abney adopt a submissive attitude in the presence of his business partner.

Lomax chuckled. "Sit down before you fall down. You've emptied that flask of yours today."

"I have not, and stop telling me what to do. You're always talking down to me, like I'm your nigger slave. Next time you try to tell me what to do I'm going to break your teeth."

Lomax was stunned. He didn't know whether to be angry or amused, because he couldn't quite tell whether this was Abney or the liquor talking.

"And you two are going into business together?" mused Donaghue aloud, trying to make a joke of it and defuse the situation.

"I've been meaning to talk to you about that," Abney told Lomax. "When we get to Oregon I'm taking my share of the goods and going my own way. I'd rather be partners with Lucifer himself than with you."

Now Abney was furious. He didn't cotton to the idea of having competition, and he had come to think of all the merchandise in their wagons as belonging to him, even though Abney had invested an equal share of the funds. "We had a deal, and you're not backing out of it now."

"Watch and see if I don't."

"Quiet!" rasped Norwood. "I thought I heard something."

Everyone froze, listening intently. All Donaghue could hear was the whisper of the northern wind and, far below, the blood-chilling howls of the wolf pack. *Even the wolves have better sense than to be up here in the dead of winter,* he thought. Glancing speculatively at Norwood, he wondered if Ted had really heard something or had just devised a surefire way to silence the quarreling Abney and Lomax.

Finally Norwood relaxed and said, "Judd, you and Lee take the first watch. Jake and I will spell you in a couple of hours. Better try to get some sleep, boys. Long day ahead of us tomorrow."

Abney bundled himself up as best he could in his single blanket and tried to get comfortable on the hard, cold ground with his feet as close to the fire as he could get them. He couldn't feel his toes. For that matter his fingers, nose, and ears were numb, too. Worst of all, his stomach was growling like a riled grizzly bear. Miserable in body and soul, he lay awake for a long time, curled up in a fetal ball, silently cursing himself for a damned fool. He had that feeling they were all going to come to grief. Had felt that way since leaving St. Joseph. He had always been afraid of what awaited them out here, in the dark expanses of wilderness. Now he *knew* what was out there. Death and destruction. He felt very lonely and useless—and doomed.

Lillian Tasker spent most of the next day at the Norwood cabin. Doc Holsberry was there watching over his patient. Today, said the physician, would tell the tale where Clete's recovery was concerned. Either he would get much better or take a turn for the worse and, ultimately, perish. Nothing more could be done for him. The issue was really whether he had the will to live.

Grace was present also, though she didn't want to be. Holsberry had refused to let her stay home alone, in case Bearclaw Johnson was on a rampage in the valley. She was bored and wouldn't lift a finger when it came to nursing Clete. *So much for love and ro-*

mance, mused Lillian. Grace was interested in Clete Norwood the big strapping young man full of life and passion. But Clete the invalid, the cripple, was of no use to her.

Tom Wilkerson came by about noon. He told Lillian that Lee Donaghue had brought his daughter to stay with him and his family, and as he relayed this information he gave Lillian a curious look. Lillian knew why—Tom was wondering why Donaghue had not asked Lillian, his nearest neighbor, to look after Lisle, as he had done on a previous occasion. Lillian was wondering the same thing herself. Had Donaghue finally realized that he had no future with her? She could only hope that was the case.

Lillian could tell something was bothering Wilkerson, and it didn't take a lot of coaxing to extract the truth from him. He felt as though he ought to have gone with Ted Norwood and the others, even though he was convinced that what they were doing was wrong—and foolhardy to boot.

She tried to persuade him he shouldn't feel that way. "There was just no reasoning with them," she said.

"I realize that. But maybe I could have talked some sense into them later."

"You would have been wasting your breath, Tom. They wouldn't listen. Like children, they've got to learn the hard way. I just hope nobody gets killed during the lesson."

"They're scared. That's all. They've been scared ever since Johnson carved his message on your door. They've been waiting for Johnson to strike again, and waiting has worn their nerves down."

They were sitting at the table in the Norwood cabin, warming themselves by the fire. Doc Holsberry sat wearily in a chair beside the rope-slat bed upon which lay the ailing Clete. Grace stood over in the corner, pouting. Johnny was out playing in the snow in front of the cabin. Lillian marveled that her son seemed impervious to the cold.

Leaning over the table, she pitched her voice in a low whisper so that neither Grace nor her father could hear. "I don't think Bearclaw Johnson set that trap, Tom."

Wilkerson just looked at her, furrows deepening between his eyebrows.

"If anybody was out to get Clete it was Jake," she continued.

"His own brother?" exclaimed Wilkerson.

Lillian put a finger to her lips. Grace was watching them now.

Wilkerson lowered his voice. "But why would Jake . . . ?"

"Because of her."

Wilkerson glanced over his shoulder at Grace, and Lillian told him what Jake had said that day at her cabin, when she had caught him polishing up on his knife throwing.

"I can't believe he would do such a thing to his own brother," said Wilkerson.

Lillian knew better. It wasn't that Tom *couldn't* believe it, but rather that he didn't *want* to.

"Supposing you're right," he said. "Where did he get the trap?"

"Found it, I guess. No telling where, or how long it had been lying about. The point is, if Jake did set the trap for his brother, Bearclaw Johnson didn't break his promise to stay out of the valley and leave us alone."

"But we'll have broken ours," said Wilkerson.

Lillian nodded. "With a man like Johnson, that could mean all-out war."

"God help us." Wilkerson sighed. "All the things that have happened to us since we put St. Joe behind us, I almost wish sometimes we hadn't come."

"I'm not sorry. No matter what happens."

Wilkerson had to smile. "You're got the kind of spirit it takes to survive out here, Lillian. Some people don't."

"Thank you. And I'm glad you didn't go with the others, Tom, because we might as well face it, they're no match for a man like Johnson, especially not up there in the mountains he knows so well."

"What are you trying to say?"

"That they might not come back."

"Good God, Lillian, don't say such things."

"You know it's a very real possibility. And if they don't come back, we'll have to be ready for a visit from Johnson."

Wilkerson exhaled slowly through thinned lips as he pondered this unpleasant prospect. "Yes, we'd better turn our thoughts to that. You know, I kind of wish Falconer was here."

"So do I," said Lillian, with feeling. "But we'll manage without him. We must. If we can't handle this on our own then we don't deserve this land."

Wilkerson gave her a sly look. "You know, Falconer is a lucky devil."

"What?"

"To have a woman like you in love with him."

Lillian blushed.

"Oh, don't bother to deny it," said Wilkerson. "It's plain as the nose on your face. You love him, and he loves you. But I feel sorry for you, at the same time. Falconer is a wild spirit. You'll have a heck of a time trying to tame a man like that. I don't know that you could, any more than you could capture the wind. He's not cut out to be a farmer, Lillian. So what will you do?"

"I don't know." A vague sense of dread invaded Lillian's soul.

"It's none of my business," said Wilkerson, "and maybe I shouldn't be talking my way into the middle of it. But I like you, Lillian. We're friends, aren't we?"

"Yes, you're the best friend I ever had, Tom."

"I feel likewise. So I care about what happens to you. And it seems to me that Falconer is born to wander. I can't see him settling down in one place for very long. Some men are like that. They've got to see what lies on the other side of the mountain. That's in his blood, and you'll not be able to rid him of it easily."

Lillian knew Wilkerson was right, and a deep sadness overwhelmed her. It was enough for today to know that she loved Falconer and he loved her in return. But she would have to consider tomorrow someday. If not for her sake, then for Johnny's.

That day, Ted Norwood led them higher and deeper into the mountains. Cold and hungry, the others followed without enthusiasm. They no longer gave much thought to finding Bearclaw Johnson; they were too miserable to even worry very much about an ambush. But Norwood's obsession with revenge still burned like a red hot flame. No one wanted to be the first to look him in the eye and suggest turning back. So they rode wretchedly on, shoulders slumped, heads bowed.

Late in the afternoon they came to a stretch of forest where a fire had stripped the trees bare. The blackened trunks pointed like hundreds of accusing fingers at the sky from whence the lightning, the instigator of the fire, had come. In the spring the forest would begin the long but inevitable process of regeneration.

For now, though, covered with a blanket of snow, there was no life here, and the eerie silence of the scene was accentuated by a heavy mist as winter clouds crept over the divide and down the other side, clinging to the slopes.

Suddenly a rifle shot shattered the stillness.

Ted Norwood's mule made a huffing sound and crumpled into blood-splattered snow. Jake cried out in panic as he saw his father go down, thinking he had been hit, but Norwood was unhurt. Scrambling to his feet, he looked at the dying mule, slow to comprehend what had happened to him. This odd paralysis gripped the others, as well.

A second shot rang out, and from Judd Pollock's horse issued a shrill whinny as it staggered sideways and then fell dead, pinning Pollock's leg beneath it.

"Take cover!" yelped Lomax.

Dismounting in a hurry, they sought the protection of the nearest tree trunks. The mule Jake Norwood had been riding took off, crow-hopping and displaying much more energy than Jake could remember ever having seen in that particular knobhead. Lomax's mule followed, and in no time at all both animals had vanished into the mist.

A third shot, and Donaghue's mule jumped, brayed, fell, thrashed a moment in the snow, then lay still.

"He's killing our animals!" shouted Lomax, uselessly, his voice shaky with rage and fear combined.

Judd Pollock was struggling to get out from under his horse and yelled for help.

"Keep your head down, Judd!" Norwood shouted back. "Lie still!"

It was sound advice, and Pollock took it, lying half buried in the snow, as motionless as the nine hundred pounds of horse that lay across his leg.

As the echo of the last shot faded, the others

searched the trees for any sign of their attacker. But there was nothing to see, or to hear.

"Think it's Johnson?" whispered Abney.

"Who the hell else would it be, you idiot," sniped Lomax.

"I'm not an idiot," replied Abney, truculent. "Damn your eyes."

"Then stop acting like one."

"Shut the hell up, both of you," snarled Norwood. "See anything, Jake?"

"Not a blasted thing, Pa."

They waited for half an hour, hardly daring to move. Lying in the snow, they were soon soaking wet and shivering with cold.

"He must have gone," said Abney, fervently wishing for a drink. The flask was in his pocket, and there was a little whiskey left in it, but he dared not sneak a drink because Lomax was lying only a few feet away and he didn't care for any more snide remarks from his sharp-tongued partner regarding his fondness for strong spirits.

"Stand up and walk out there and we'll find out," suggested Lomax.

"Hey!" yelped Pollock. "I can't feel my leg!"

"Just hold on, Judd," shouted Lomax. "Your leg's still attached to your damned body. What would you like us to do? Come out there and get our heads shot off?"

"Johnson!" bellowed Ted Norwood, so loudly and unexpectedly that everyone else nearly jumped out of their skins. "Bearclaw Johnson, you yellow-bellied coward! Show yourself! Fight like a man!"

Lee Donaghue smirked. That was funny, coming from a man who, like the rest of them, was bellydown in the snow trying to hide themselves behind trees. Donaghue knew one thing for certain. *He* wasn't going anywhere. He hadn't let on to the others, and they were too preoccupied to notice, but his rifle was lying in the snow over there on the other side of his dead mule where, in his panic to seek cover, he had dropped it. All he had was a flintlock pistol, and he wasn't even sure it would fire.

What I want to know, he thought, *is why Johnson killed our mounts and not us?*

With a curse, Ted Norwood got to his feet and stepped brazenly out into the open. "Come on, Johnson! You and me, man to man! What do you say?"

"Pa!" yelled Jake. "Pa, get down!"

"For the love of God, Ted," shouted Lomax. "Take cover."

"He's gone," said Norwood bitterly. "The son of a bitch is long gone."

Donaghue distinctly heard a sharp, ugly smacking sound, and Ted Norwood jackknifed. The gunshot rolled through the dead forest as Norwood toppled forward to lay facedown in the snow. Making incoherent noises, his son rushed to his side and rolled him over. Norwood's lifeless eyes looked up at nothing through clots of bloody snow, surprise captured forever in them. A third eye, this one black and bleeding, right between the other two, gaped at Jake. With a strangled cry of pure horror Jake fell backward.

A bloodcurdling war cry froze Lee Donaghue in place. He saw a huge bearded man in buckskins and a bearskin coat appear suddenly out of the white haze, moving extremely fast for someone of his bulk. He leaped upon Jake Norwood and struck savagely with the butt of his rifle. Jake collapsed, knocked cold. Lomax got to his knees and fired wildly, but the shot went wide and Bearclaw Johnson, with a snarling laugh, closed on him. Lomax tried to run, but Johnson pounced on him like a big cat on a rabbit, bearing him to the ground. Lomax screamed for mercy—a scream cut short as Bearclaw hit him with a fist at the base of the neck.

Johnson looked up to see Lee Donaghue running away as though the hounds of hell were after him. Then the mountain man rose, whirling into a crouch, as Abney charged forward, rifle at hip level. Abney squeezed the trigger. The rifle misfired. Bearclaw laughed again. "This is my lucky day!" he roared with delight as he struck Abney's rifle aside with the barrel of his own long gun, then slammed the stock of his weapon into Abney's face. Abney went down, blood spewing from his mouth and nose.

Bearclaw looked again for Donaghue, but saw no sign of him. With a disappointed shrug the mountain man walked over to the place where Judd Pollock was pinned beneath his dead horse.

"Sweet Jesus," breathed Pollock, looking up at Bearclaw's face.

Sitting on the dead animal, Bearclaw Johnson chuckled, an unpleasant leer on his face.

"Not even close, hoss," he said.

Chapter Nineteen

Abney woke up in a world of pain. It didn't help that Bearclaw Johnson was kicking him in the ribs. Spitting out a mouthful of blood and tooth fragments, Abney tried to reach for his nose, which was the part of his body giving him the most pain of all. Only then did he realize that his hands were tightly—and, of course, painfully—lashed together behind his back.

Bearclaw leaned over him, grinning. "You been holdin' up the show, pilgrim. This ain't no time to sleep. You can sleep when you're in the grave."

Looking around, Abney saw Lomax, Judd Pollock, and Jake Norwood. They were sitting up against dead tree trunks, and their hands were also tied behind their backs. Jake was crying silent tears. They made channels in the dirt on his cheeks, and it all came back to Abney in a terrifying rush. Ted Norwood was dead. *I knew something like this would happen,* he thought. *We're all going to die in this godforsaken wilderness.* But there was no panic in him, curiously enough. He was possessed of the fatalistic calm of a man who is resigned to his fate.

"Where's Lee?" he asked.

"That must be the one that got away," drawled Bearclaw.

With a glimmer of hope, Abney searched the obscuring haze. If Lee Donaghue was free, then maybe . . . just maybe . . .

Bearclaw chuckled. "Last time I seen him he was runnin' so fast I figure he's halfway to St. Joe by now. You don't honestly think he'll give a single thought to savin' your lousy hide, do you, boy?"

Abney shook his head, that glimmer of foolish hope extinguished.

"So here we are," chatted Bearclaw, resting his bones on the stiff-legged carcass of Judd Pollock's horse. Producing a plug of shag tobacco, he bit off a chew with yellowed teeth, looking with amusement at each of his prisoners in turn. Then he shook his head. "You boys are a sorry-lookin' lot, I tell you. Cain't hardly believe you had the gumption to come up here on my mountain. I told Falconer what would happen. Long as you stayed down yonder in the valley you were safe."

"And you promised to stay up here and leave us alone," snapped Lomax, truculent.

Abney hated to entertain any complimentary thoughts about Lomax, but he had to admire his partner's courage. Took a lot of nerve, under these circumstances, to talk back to Bearclaw Johnson.

"I kept my word," said Bearclaw. "I always have. Will, till the day I die."

"You set a bear trap down by the Norwood cabin that cost Clete Norwood his foot," retorted Lomax.

Bearclaw stared at him, chewing methodically on the tobacco. Finally he spit a stream of brown juice to stain the churned snow between his feet and said, "Pilgrim, I don't know what the blue blazes you're talkin' about."

"You mean you . . . you didn't set a trap?" asked Lomax.

"Nope."

"You're lying."

"Bold talk from a man in your predicament," observed Bearclaw.

"Why would he lie?" asked Abney. "If he'd done it he'd be bragging about it."

Johnson nodded. "Most likely. But I didn't do the deed. Reckon you'll have to look amongst yourselves for the culprit."

Lomax glanced at Abney. He was perplexed, and so was Abney, because both men were fairly certain the mountain man was telling the truth. *Which means,* thought Abney, *our coming up here was a mistake in more ways than one. Ted Norwood died for nothing, and I guess we will, too.*

"Now you boys perk up your ears and listen good," said Bearclaw. "I ain't gonna kill you, on account of Hugh Falconer seems to like you, though why God only knows."

"Then why did you kill Ted Norwood?" asked Lomax.

" 'Cause he was in a bad mood, and I don't fool around with folks like that. Too dangerous. Now you boys get back down yonder where you belong. Take your dead with you. You've got one mule left, so I guess you'll all have to walk, lessen you want to carry a corpse all the way down the mountain."

"I can't walk," said Pollock. "My leg . . ."

Bearclaw stood up and walked over to Pollock and for a dreadful instant Abney thought Judd was doomed. Leaning over, the mountain man put his face close to Pollock's and Pollock shrank back from his fierce demeanor.

"I'm giving you a chance to live, pilgrim. You gonna take it?"

"I'll walk," said Pollock, gulping at the lump in his throat.

Bearclaw nodded. "That's the spirit." He took a knife from a sheath on his belt and with a flick of the wrist buried it blade first in the snow between Pollock's legs. "Cut yourselves loose and git," he said. "And don't never come back up here. You hear? I won't be so kindhearted next time I see your ugly faces."

With that he turned and loped away, disappearing into the haze.

In headlong flight, Lee Donaghue headed downslope. At first he ran in blind panic, falling countless times, careening out of control off trees and rocks, so that in a matter of minutes he was a bruised and bloody mess. Exhaustion quickly overtook him, and he sat for a time, sucking air into his tortured lungs, listening for sounds of pursuit. He heard nothing. In a short while the daylight would abandon him, and a fresh dose of panic began to rise in him again as he contemplated spending a night up here in Bearclaw Johnson's inhospitable domain. He tried to calm himself, tried to think, but it was hard to think when you could scarcely even breathe. The air was very thin at this high elevation, especially for a lowlander, and Donaghue wheezed for a long time, his heart pounding like a runaway stallion in his chest. Eventually he could summon the strength to stand up. His knees felt like jelly. His clothes were torn in a dozen places, and so was his flesh. The bitter cold cut through him like a knife.

Another impediment to clear thinking was the nightmarish image of Bearclaw Johnson charging out of the haze with that nerve-jangling war whoop on his lips, dispatching Jake Norwood with one stroke, Lomax with the second, and then Abney. *What chance do I have against such a man on my own*? The answer was simple and unassailably true. No chance whatsoever. Donaghue figured that by now the others were dead, and he wasn't long for this world, either, unless he got down off this mountain in a hurry.

He continued downslope. He wasn't running any longer. For one thing he was too tired to run, and for another he didn't think it would do much good. If Bearclaw had it in mind to catch him, then he was as good as caught. His thoughts turned to Lisle. His poor daughter, to lose both parents one so soon after the other. What would become of her? *I should have stayed with her, instead of coming on this insane venture. Why did I do it*? Another simple answer. To show Lillian Tasker what a brave man he was, so that she would regret spurning him. *She must have known all along what a fool I was.* Lisle's well-being was the important thing. He realized that now. Now that it was too late.

Self-evaluation so brutally frank plunged him into self-reproach. Bitter tears burned in his eyes as he thought of his daughter and how selfish he had been these past months since Emily's death, worried only about himself, indulging in self-pity, giving in to loneliness. Lillian had tried to warn him. He said a prayer, not knowing if the Almighty was even listening. He had not been on speaking terms with God of late, because God had taken Emily away from him and he had deeply resented that. In the depths of his grief he had even cursed God. But now he prayed anyway, a silent prayer, not for him, because he did not deserve it, but rather for Lisle. Because he knew Lisle wasn't safe, either. There was nothing to stop Bearclaw Johnson from going down into the valley and killing everyone else, even the women and children.

He was so wrapped up in these grim deliberations that he stumbled to the very brink of the cliff and nearly blundered right over into destruction. The wooded slope abruptly ended at a thousand-foot drop into a rocky gorge. Fortunately for him the cloud haze thinned a bit at the rimrock. Battling hopelessness, he stood there a moment, giving the chasm that blocked his escape a bleak perusal. No way down. He would have to go around. Left or right? The gorge appeared to narrow to the left, while it definitely widened and deepened to the right. Perhaps he should go left—he had no idea what direction left was—and look for a way around the gorge.

After two hours of hard going, Donaghue reached a trail that angled across a barren scree slope. It was dark now, the last shreds of light fading from the sky. At least he was out of the haze, and the first stars twinkled in the black velvet of the heavens. By now he had come to the conclusion that he was somewhere in the vicinity of the north end of the valley, not too far from the high snowbound pass. The trail was distinct, guiding him through a stand of conifers. It was so very cold! Spittle froze on his chin. He gave some thought to finding shelter. His stomach was a hard, hungry knot and he didn't have much strength left. His fear had brought him this far, but he was beginning to think he had escaped Bearclaw, at least for the time being. Resigned to the fact that he would have to spend the night in the mountains, he tried to convince himself that tomorrow he would find his way down to the valley. *By this time tomorrow I'll be sitting by my own fireplace, warm and fed and holding my darling Lisle.*

To his growing consternation he noticed that the wind was picking up, sweeping the snow on the ground and swirling it about him. He had long since lost all sensation in his hands and feet, and he wondered if he was suffering from frostbite. Wondered, too, if he would freeze to death before morning. He had some powder and flint in his pouch, and the pistol, so it was conceivable that he could build a fire. But a fire up here might be seen for miles. It might guide Bearclaw Johnson right to him.

Then, as he began to succumb to despair, he saw a speck of yellow light dead ahead. Drawing cautiously closer, he was eventually able to distinguish the cabin, well hidden in a stand of timber wedged between a rocky spine draped with snow and a boulder-strewn slope of shale angling steeply to the rim of the gorge. The three-sided cabin was nestled against a stone shelf. There were no windows; the light leaked out past hides which draped the doorway.

He stood there for a while, shivering uncontrollably, staring at the cabin. His thought processes were working well enough for him to deduce that in all likelihood this was Bearclaw Johnson's den. Who else would be living up here? Who else would Bearclaw *let* live up here? Donaghue's first impulse was to run away. But suddenly a spark of anger flared into an inferno of unreasonable rage in his soul. He was through with running. He should not have run away in the first place. Now he had to live with the terrible guilt which came from knowing he had abandoned his companions to their horrible fate. That he would have met the same end as they was no consolation. He should have at least stood his ground and for once acted like the man he so desperately wanted to be.

Besides, he was too tired and cold and hungry to run away. It boiled down to this: If he was going to have any chance of survival, any hope of seeing Lisle again, he had to find shelter—and that cabin was the only shelter to be had up here. If he ran away he would surely perish. If he went forward he would probably die. The difference between surely and probably was all he had. He was armed, and Bearclaw Johnson was just a mortal man, after all. The anger grew inside him, born of guilt and carried on a tidal wave of desperation, and before he was even aware of making a conscious decision, Lee Donaghue had drawn the pistol from his belt and was staggering toward the cabin.

Reaching the cabin doorway he swept aside the hides with one last thought frozen in his mind—I'm not even sure this pistol will fire. But it didn't matter anymore. Whether he killed Johnson or Johnson killed him was not the issue anymore. He was, at last, going to stand his ground.

The interior of the cabin was illuminated by a small fire in a circle of stones. The walls and floor were covered with pelts of every description. The cabin proper was only slightly larger than the cave which had been formed beneath the shelf of stone and which the log walls of the cabin now enclosed. Shadows retreating from the firelight gathered there and at first, with vast relief, Lee Donaghue thought the place was uninhabited—until something moved at the rear of the cave. Donaghue's breath caught in his throat. He swung the pistol in that direction, straining his eyes to pierce the shadows.

"Come out of there," he rasped. He had one shot—if the damned weapon fired—and he wanted a clear target.

The shadows moved again. Donaghue could scarcely refrain from taking a wild shot. He was shaking, so he doubted that he would be able to hit anything even at point-blank range.

A woman took shape before him, emerging into the flickering firelight. She was clad in a fringed deerskin dress with a little beadwork on the shoulders. Her dark eyes gleamed with the wild light of a cornered animal.

"Where's Johnson?" asked Donaghue. His voice startled him. It was a croaking travesty of its usual self.

She made no move, no sound. Her features were inscrutable, betraying no fear, betraying nothing, but Donaghue could sense she was afraid. Of course she had to be, and he felt a little ridiculous menacing her with the pistol. *She probably doesn't understand a word of English,* he thought. Bearclaw Johnson obviously wasn't here. He wasn't the kind of man who would cower in the shadows. *Especially from me,* thought Donaghue. Perhaps, after doing away with Ted Norwood and the others he had headed on down into the valley to continue his killing spree. The possibility turned Donaghue's blood into ice. If anything happened to Lisle . . .

He was nearly compelled to rush out into the night in an attempt to reach his daughter's side come what may, but reason overcame impulse this time. He would not be able to descend the slopes until daylight and, besides, he was too weakened from hunger and exposure to the cold to travel another mile.

"I need food," he told the Indian woman, making a gesture with his free hand which he hoped approximated the movement of a person putting food to his mouth.

The woman just stood there.

"Damn it," muttered Donaghue. Lowering the pistol, he began to cast about the cabin for something to eat.

No sound betrayed the woman, but rather an animal instinct for survival made Donaghue whirl to face her as she lunged at him. All along she had been concealing a knife behind her back. Now she brandished the blade overhead, striving to plunge it into his back.

With a strangled cry Donaghue fell back before the swift and savage onslaught. The pistol in his hand jumped and spat flame; he was not even aware of pulling the trigger. The bullet struck her in the chest. Her expressionless mask shattered, and the look of surprise and fear—the fear of death, of the great unknown—on her face filled Donaghue with immediate remorse. That she would have killed him, or tried to, made little difference. She was not responsible for what Bearclaw Johnson had done; in fact, he could see that all she had been trying to do was defend herself from a stranger who had forced his way unbidden into her home and menaced her with a pistol.

She fell quietly, almost gently, to the fur-carpeted ground, the knife slipping from her fingers. Donaghue went to her, knelt beside her, and as he watched in mortification the life flicker out of her eyes he mumbled a broken "I'm sorry."

Rising, he backed away from the corpse, completely unaware that he had left the discharged flintlock pistol beside her body. The night wind whimpered and moaned as though in mourning for her needless death. Suddenly unable to bear being in her presence, Donaghue turned and fled, stumbling blindly out into the snowy darkness.

Instinctively he took the path of least resistance, downslope. He fell many times. Emerging from the trees, he arrived at the barren scree slope. Crossing it diagonally, with no concept of where he was going in his confused mind, with only the image of the woman's face as the life went out of her, he slipped and fell one last time, where in warmer months snowmelt had fashioned a tumbling creek that terminated in a spectacular waterfall at the rim of the gorge.

Now the draw which the creek had formed was slick

with ice, and Lee Donaghue found himself sliding down a precipitous incline, faster and faster, unable to stop himself. The black maw of the gorge opened up beneath him and he screamed once, his daughter's name, as he was hurled into eternity.

When Bearclaw Johnson arrived at his cabin, the body of his squaw Sun Falling was still warm.

After releasing the four men who had come up into his mountains to kill him for something he had not done, Bearclaw had followed them for a couple of hours as they made their descent into the valley. He was fairly certain he had succeeded in putting the fear of God—or, more precisely, the fear of Bearclaw Johnson—into them, but one thing he had learned about the human species was that you never could tell what a person would do. This inherent unpredictability, this knack for doing all kinds of foolishness without rhyme or reason, had motivated Bearclaw to go to great lengths to divorce himself from the human race. Only when he had been satisfied that the four men had no intention of doubling back did he strike out for home.

Now, standing in mute shock over the body of his woman, Bearclaw chided himself mercilessly for ever having squawed up. He had never before allowed himself to become attached to anyone or anything for just this reason—a lesson he should have learned on that black day thirty-five years ago when a mad-as-hell she-bear had killed his father, literally tearing him limb from bloody limb right in front of Bearclaw's eight-year-old eyes.

Bearclaw did not weep for Sun Falling. Eventually he stirred himself and lovingly wrapped the corpse in a buffalo hide. The remainder of the night he lay close beside her, watching the dying fire with unblinking eyes. The next morning he collected all the powder and shot in his possession, a pistol, two knives, and a tomahawk. Then he set fire to the cabin and watched it burn, with Sun Falling's body inside. The morning haze slowly dissipated, and under an azure sky Bear-claw Johnson started down the mountain.

It was a good day for killing.

Chapter Twenty

On the same day that Bearclaw Johnson started down the mountain to seek vengeance, Judd Pollock, Jake Norwood, Lomax, and Abney reached the valley, with Ted Norwood's corpse draped over the one mule. By chance they emerged from the forested slope near the Wilkerson cabin. Tom was saddling his horse when he saw the men stumbling through the snow drifts into the open. It was midmorning, and he was on his way to the Norwood place to check on Clete's condition—not to mention the condition of Doc Holsberry, who had kept a constant vigil over his patient since the amputation.

Alarmed, Wilkerson ran out to meet the ragged, starving, exhausted party. "Good God!" he exclaimed, identifying Ted Norwood as the dead man. "What has happened?"

"As you can see," replied Lomax bitterly, "we found Johnson."

He proceeded to give Wilkerson the bare details of their disastrous excursion into the mountains. When they reached the cabin all four men collapsed like rag dolls on the floor. Molly plied them with hot stew and coffee. Judd Pollock passed out, and Wilkerson had Abney help him carry the man to the bed. Jake Norwood sat huddled by the blaze in the fireplace, staring morosely into the flames; he ate little, and said not a word.

When Wilkerson asked what had become of Lee Donaghue, Lomax shook his head.

"Can't say, Tom. Reckon he must have run off. When Bearclaw Johnson came charging at us out of nowhere Lee just disappeared."

"Tom!" This was Molly, her tone stern, and when Wilkerson glanced her way she nodded sideways at Lisle Donaghue, who stood like a pale statue across the room.

"Don't worry, Lisle," said Wilkerson. "I'm sure your father is fine."

"Yeah," said Abney. The stricken expression on the girl's face touched his heart. "We just got separated. He'll be along." But his words lacked conviction.

"It's a wonder Johnson didn't kill you all," said Wilkerson.

"He said he didn't have nothing to do with what happened to Clete," said Abney.

"Do you believe him?"

Abney nodded. Wilkerson glanced at Jake, remembering what Lillian Tasker had told him. Could it be possible that Jake had devised such a diabolical scheme to maim, or perhaps even kill his brother, and all on account of that young vixen Grace Holsberry? His first impulse was to pry the truth out of Jake right then and there. But time enough for that later, he told himself.

"Johnson could have done us all in," said Lomax. "Yet he let us live. I'm inclined to agree with Ab. Must've been like you said, Tom. That damned old bear trap could've been there for years, and it was just Clete's bad luck to find it the way he did. Ted Norwood died for nothing."

"I've got to get over to Donaghue's cabin," said

Wilkerson. "Maybe he made it back alive. You boys stay put and get some rest. Molly will take good care of you."

Lying back with a long and laborious groan, Lomax said, "I don't think I could stand up even if I wanted to."

Wilkerson finished saddling his horse and rode as fast as he could to the Donaghue cabin. The place was empty. Poor Lisle, he thought, a bad feeling in the pit of his stomach. He had a strong hunch that no one would ever see Lee Donaghue alive again.

Since he was in the proximity of the Tasker cabin he rode on over to tell Lillian what had happened. Lillian Tasker was smart, and her heart was strong, and Wilkerson realized how much he depended on her for well-thought-out opinions and sound advice.

"I'm wondering," he told her, "if we shouldn't load up our wagons and try to get out of this valley while the getting's good."

"We wouldn't get far," said Lillian. "No, Tom, I think we should stay put. Stand our ground. We have shelter here, and stout walls to protect us should more trouble come our way."

Wilkerson nodded. "You're right, of course. Guess I'm just rattled by all this. God, one man dead, maybe two!"

Lillian was over by the window. "Tom, come take a look at this."

What now? wondered Wilkerson as he joined her. The heavy wooden shutters were open just a crack, and as he peered outside Lillian said calmly, "See that smoke way up near the north pass?"

Wilkerson saw it, a thin black plume against the clear blue sky.

"What could it be? Indians? That's all we need."

"I don't know what it means," said Lillian.

"Maybe you and Johnny should come stay with us until we're sure there's no danger."

Lillian agreed. Sending Johnny out to saddle Ol' Blue, she hastily gathered some provisions and put them in an empty flour sack. These, her Bible, a couple of blankets, the star pattern quilt, and her rifle was all she would take, even though she had no idea how long she would be away.

It was afternoon by the time they arrived at the Wilkerson cabin. Molly informed them that Jake Norwood had gone home, taking his father's corpse with him, and ignoring her suggestion that he stay and rest and try to eat something. "He never said a word to me," she concluded. "Didn't even seem to hear me. Poor lad, to see his father killed, and his brother crippled that way."

Wilkerson glanced at Lillian. They had agreed not to share their suspicions about Jake Norwood with the others—not until they were sure.

"I'd better get over there," said Wilkerson.

As he neared the Norwood place, the next cabin up-valley from his own, he saw more smoke. This came from the vicinity of the Tasker and Donaghue cabins. He surmised that one or the other was on fire, and that started him worrying about Indians again. But Falconer had said they should not have Indian trouble here. Could the mountain man have been wrong? Wilkerson shook his head, confused and afraid. This was one of those days when the whole world seemed to be turned upside down.

Arriving at his destination, Wilkerson saw the mule which had brought Ted Norwood's remains down from the mountain standing wearily in front of the cabin. Doc Holsberry stood in the doorway, anxiety deepening the lines on his face.

"Where's Jake?" asked Wilkerson.

Holsberry pointed a shaky finger. "Over there, in the trees. My daughter is with him."

Wilkerson looked in the direction the troubled physician was pointing and saw Jake digging furiously in the snow with a pick. Grace stood nearby. Urging his tired horse into motion, Wilkerson rode on over. Jake was so busy digging and Grace so busy talking that neither noticed Wilkerson's approach.

"You *must* take me away from here," Grace was saying. "I simply cannot stand it any longer. *Please,* Jake. Just you and me. You won't be sorry. I promise."

Jake kept digging. The bent body of his father lay nearby, partially covered with a blanket.

"Jake!" Her voice was shrill with desperation. "Don't you want me? I'm yours, all yours, if you will just take me out of here. Oh, I am simply going to die if I have to spend one more day in this valley!"

Jake drove the pick deep into the frozen ground as though he were plunging it into the heart of his most hated enemy. He turned on Grace with such violence in his expression and posture that she shrank away from him in fear.

"Want you? *Want you?* By God, don't you know what I've done for you? My own brother, for God's sake . . ."

It was then that he first saw Wilkerson, sitting on his horse not twenty paces away.

Grace turned and, seeing Wilkerson, burst into tears.

"Nobody will take me away from here!" she screamed at Wilkerson, as though he were solely to blame for all of her tribulations. Then, sobbing, she ran for the cabin, stumbling in the heavy piles of virgin white snow agleam in the afternoon sunlight.

Neither man watched her go. Jake stared at Wilkerson, who gravely and unflinchingly returned his gaze. For a long moment no word passed between them. Finally, Wilkerson dismounted.

"I'll help you bury your pa," he said, taking the pick from Jake's unresisting hand.

Jake's shoulders suddenly sagged as he glanced at his father's body.

"He's frozen stiff. I can't . . . I can't even straighten him out. We'll have to dig a crooked grave." He laughed, only it wasn't really a laugh, and silent tears began to fall from his eyes.

"It's all my fault. I set that trap. I found it, and set it where I knew Clete would go when he fetched water from the crik. That was Clete's chore that day. I should have owned up to it before my pa went up into the mountains."

"Yes," said Wilkerson quietly. "You should have."

Jake dropped to his knees beside Ted Norwood's corpse. "I'm so sorry, Pa. So sorry . . ."

"What's done is done, boy. Get hold of yourself. Let's get your father buried. There's no time to waste. We've got trouble. One of the cabins to the north is burning. Either the Donaghue place or the Tasker, I can't tell which."

Jake looked blankly at him, as though he had suddenly lost the ability to comprehend the English language.

"Snap out of it, Jake! Go fetch the rifle from my saddle and keep an eye peeled while I dig."

Jake nodded and did as he was told. Wilkerson attacked the ground. It was hard work, but he was used to that, and kept at it until the job was done, sternly ignoring the protests of the muscles in his arms and back. They laid Ted Norwood to final rest and covered him up, and Wilkerson took it upon himself to mumble a few words.

"Dust to dust, ashes to ashes. We commit Ted Norwood, a loving father and faithful friend, to the ground in the sure and certain hope of his resurrection. Amen."

"Amen," muttered Jake.

"Let's get back to the cabin," said Wilkerson, scanning his surroundings. He had the feeling that someone was watching them from deeper in the snow-draped woods. But he saw nothing out of the ordinary. Taking his rifle from Jake, he gathered up his pony's reins and started back. Jake lingered miserably at the grave site until a stern command from Wilkerson prompted him to move.

They were only a few steps from the cabin when something hit Wilkerson high in the back of the shoulder and drove him to the ground, wincing at the white hot pain that shot through his body. The gunshot shattered the winter silence an instant later.

Wilkerson fought rising panic as he realized he had been shot. After the initial lancing pain a cold numbness swept through his shoulder, and he groped with fingers to find the exit hole. Yes, there it was; the bullet had gone clean through. His fingers came away sticky with warm blood. Not to worry, he told himself. He had been hit high and it was not necessarily a mortal wound. An odd calmness and clarity of mind seized him then. He was vividly aware of several things at once—a bearded, buckskin-clad demon loping out of the nearby woods with a bloodcurdling war cry on his lips; Doc Holsberry appearing in the cabin doorway, only six feet from where he lay, and freezing in horror at the scene; and Jake Norwood, white as a sheet, lunging for Wilkerson's rifle lying in the snow.

"It's Johnson!" cried Jake. "He's come to kill us all!"

"Get me inside, Jake."

Jake seemed not to hear. He fumbled with the rifle. Johnson was a hundred yards away and closing fast, not a bad range for a fair shot, but Jake was shaking violently, and he fired with too much haste to have any hope of hitting his mark. Bearclaw Johnson roared his contempt as the bullet whistled by and kept coming.

"Jake," said Wilkerson, trying to stand on his own accord. "Get inside."

Jake Norwood made a funny sound and ran straight at Bearclaw Johnson, wielding the empty rifle like a club.

"Jake! No!" This was Grace, trying to push past her father in the doorway. Doc Holsberry shoved her back inside and came to Wilkerson's assistance. He reached Wilkerson just as Bearclaw closed in on Jake Norwood. Jake swung the rifle, but Johnson ducked under and plowed into Jake, sending him sprawling. Casting aside his own long gun, Bearclaw brandished a knife. Jake was back on his feet in an instant. He had the strength and agility of youth, and he had often fought with his brother, but none of that was going to help him now. Again he tried to club Johnson with the rifle. The mountain man batted the weapon away, closed in for the kill, and gutted Jake Norwood as he would a fresh-killed deer, from sternum to groin.

Witness to this butchery, Tom Wilkerson was momentarily paralyzed with shock. Most shocking of all was the disdainful ease with which Bearclaw Johnson took Jake's life, with no more effort or remorse than if he had swatted a fly.

Jake fell backward, dropping the rifle, clutching spasmodically at his terrible wound. When he hit the ground a geyser of blood spewed forth to spatter Bearclaw and the pristine white snow. Bearclaw passed a hand over his own face, smearing the hot blood of his victim across his fearsome visage and, turning, he fastened a mad gaze upon Wilkerson and Holsberry.

That got Wilkerson moving again. He made it into the cabin with Holsberry's help. Leaning heavily against the wall, he watched the physician slam the door shut and drop the stout wooden bar into its sturdy slots. Grace Holsberry was huddled in a corner, sobbing into her hands.

"Why did he do it?" gasped Holsberry, a stricken look on his ashen face. "He didn't have a prayer."

Wilkerson knew he was talking about Jake Norwood. "He knew he didn't."

"But why, then? Why did he do it?"

Wilkerson shook his head. He thought he had the answer—something to do with atonement, vengeance, loss of the will to live—but he didn't believe this was the time or the place to discuss Jake's motives for committing suicide.

"A gun," said Wilkerson, wincing. The numbness was beginning to wear off, and the pain came back strong. He felt dizzy, light-headed, nauseous. "I need a gun, Doc."

"Clete's rifle," said Holsberry, and fetched the weapon. In the bed at the back of the one-room cabin, Clete lay sleeping, oblivious to what was going on. *Poor Clete,* thought Wilkerson. His father and his brother were both dead now at the hands of that savage lunatic.

Checking the rifle's load and priming, Wilkerson shuffled over to the single window. A lateral gunshot had been carved into the pair of heavy shutters. He could see Jake lying stiff in the pink snow. But Bearclaw Johnson had vanished.

"Let me look at that wound," said Holsberry.

"Just slap hot iron to it, Doc. The bullet went clean through."

With Holsberry's help, Wilkerson shrugged out of his blanket coat. The physician used a knife to cut away the blood-soaked shirt. Wilkerson kept a lookout for Bearclaw through the gunslot. What was the man up to now? Perhaps he had moved on. Wilkerson was sure now who had set those fires in the north end of the valley. Maybe Johnson was working his way down the valley. If that was the case . . .

Dear merciful God in heaven. Molly and the children.

The next cabin south was Wilkerson's own.

Lillian was there, with Lomax and Abney. But that was small consolation, because they could not know that Bearclaw Johnson was on a murderous rampage.

Chapter Twenty-one

Tom Wilkerson was right to be concerned that the occupants of his cabin would be perilously unaware of Bearclaw Johnson's coming until it was too late. The contours of the valley, which hooked slightly west by north at its upper end, prevented Lillian and the others from seeing the smoke from the fires which the vengeance-seeking mountain man had started—fires that quickly consumed both the Tasker and Donaghue cabins and everything in them. Had they listened very hard from outside the Wilkerson cabin they might have heard, very faintly on the cold, still air, the gunfire from the vicinity of the Norwood place, but none of them were out of doors at that time. The fire was crackling fiercely in the fireplace and Abney and Lomax, sprawled on the floor near it, were snoring heavily, sleeping the deep and exhausted sleep of men who had had little or no rest for more than forty-eight hours, so Lillian did not hear the shooting.

Bearclaw Johnson lingered for a spell around the Norwood cabin, keeping undercover and contemplating how he might best get the people cowering within its walls in his grasp. Having spent some time prowling the valley when the emigrants had first arrived, he knew that this cabin had been occupied by the Norwoods. The father and son were now dead by his own hand, and good riddance since, in Johnson's opinion, all settlers were vermin, and every last living soul in this valley was to be held accountable for the death of his squaw Sun Falling. The third Norwood, apparently, had blundered into some old bear trap and lost his foot. That meant the current occupants of the cabin consisted of a wounded farmer, an old man, a young woman, and a cripple. Bearclaw figured he could make short work of the whole bunch—if only he could get inside, or smoke them out.

In the end he decided to save such pleasant work for later. He had to assume they had guns, and there was little hope of setting fire to the place from the outside. He had started the fires at the Tasker and Donaghue cabins from the inside, smashing furniture into so much kindling and then dousing the wreckage with coal oil from convenient lanterns. No, he would continue his bloody way down the valley, kill the others, and come back for this group.

Less than a mile from the Wilkerson cabin, as he traipsed through a stand of trees, Bearclaw Johnson spotted the wolf pack silently loping in single file on a course roughly parallel to his own. They were no danger to him, and Johnson had been in the mountains long enough to know this. He could recollect no case where a wolf had attacked a man, unless the beast was sick. But he was in a killing mood—if Sun Falling could not live then nothing else deserved to, either—and without thinking he raised his rifle and squeezed off a shot. But the wolves were too far away and moving too fast, and he missed, something that rarely happened. Cursing a blue streak, Johnson quickly reloaded, but before he could take aim a second time the wolves had vanished as though into thin air.

This time Lillian Tasker heard the gunshot. She opened the door of the cabin and stepped out to survey the line of trees to the north.

"What is it, Lillian?" This was Molly, standing in the doorway behind her.

Turning, Lillian saw by the expression on Molly's face that Molly was very nearly overcome with anxiety. The nightmarish events of the past few days had taken their toll on her, and Lillian wasn't sure she could take another shock.

"I heard a rifle," she said, saying it with a smile and trying to sound as casual as possible.

"Maybe Tom saw a deer. Game has gotten to be so scarce . . ."

She doesn't really believe that, any more than I do, thought Lillian. Hunting would be the last thing on Tom Wilkerson's mind today. The whole company was very likely in jeopardy; they had reason to suspect that perhaps hostile Indians lurked in the vicinity, and they knew a half-mad old mountain man was prowling nearby, a man who had already killed one of them and might at any moment decide to finish off the rest of them. No, Tom wouldn't be so foolish as to risk a shot at a deer under such circumstances.

Lillian took Molly inside. She closed and barred the door. Panic glittered in Molly's eyes when Lillian dropped the bar into place, but she thought of the children, as Lillian had hoped she would, and kept her mouth shut. Johnny was playing marbles with Edna and Phoebe. Lisle sat by herself, an expression on her pale and frozen face that tore at Lillian's heart every time she saw it.

Kneeling between Lomax and Abney, Lillian shook them awake. It was nearly as hard as trying to bestir dead men. They were groggy and inattentive until she told them she had just heard a gunshot. Abney's eyes popped wide open.

"Maybe it's Bearclaw Johnson!" he exclaimed.

"Ssh! Don't let the children hear you," said Lillian sternly.

"He kept our guns," said Lomax. "We have nothing to fight with."

"I have a rifle," said Lillian. She looked at Molly.

"Tom has the rifle," said Molly, "but I do have my father's old fowling piece."

Lillian nodded, and Molly fetched the long-barreled shotgun from where it stood in a corner with a straw broom and an axe. Abney was at the shuttered window, looking through the gunslot, fumbling in the pocket of his coat for the flask of whiskey.

"I don't see anything," he said hopefully.

Lomax took the fowling piece from Molly, looked it over. It was loaded, of course; on the frontier people got in the habit of keeping their weapons ready to use at a moment's notice.

"We have no shot," said Molly, striving to keep her voice from trembling. "It's loaded with horseshoe nails and small stones."

Lillian joined Abney at the window as Abney took a sip from the flask. He grinned sheepishly at her. "A little antifogmatic, as they say. Smooths out the nerves."

"I don't think there is anything wrong with your nerves."

"Really?" Abney was pleased, but self-assessment quickly sobered him. "I'm not a brave man, by any means."

"Oh, I think you sell yourself short, Ab."

"Bad habit for a would-be merchant, don't you think? But seriously, I'm just not cut out for living in this country, Lillian. Never should have come out here. A man must come to terms with his own limitations, and live his life accordingly."

"Nonsense. Do you suppose Hugh Falconer was

born bearded and wearing buckskins and tough enough to fight a grizzly bear with one hand tied behind his back?"

Abney chuckled. "You do have a way with words."

"I'm just saying a person can always adapt. There is nothing you can't do if you dedicate yourself to the doing."

Lomax came up. "See anything?"

"No," said Lillian. "I'm going out there."

"Are you insane?"

She shook her head. "There was only one shot. Maybe Tom or Jake is in trouble. Maybe it was a signal."

"If they're in trouble then it's just too damned bad for them," said Lomax.

Lillian and Abney just stared at him. Realizing that Molly had heard him, Lomax was ashamed.

"Hell," he grumbled, "I didn't mean that. If you're going out there, Lillian, then I guess I'll be going with you."

"And me, too," said Abney.

"You don't have a gun," Lomax reminded him.

Abney went to the corner and hefted the axe. "This will do nicely, thanks."

"One of us needs to stay here," said Lillian.

"Give us the rifle and you stay," suggested Lomax.

"I most certainly will not stay. This is my rifle, and if anybody is going to use it I will."

"But . . . well, you're a woman."

Lillian's lips thinned in exasperation. "You men don't seem to have done too well for yourselves. Frankly, I am sick and tired of people assuming that I am somehow at a disadvantage because I don't happen to have a husband."

"It isn't that at all," fumbled Lomax, flustered. "I just . . . well, men are supposed to . . ."

"That's very chivalrous of you, Mr. Lomax, but I am poorly suited to play the role of the helpless damsel in distress."

Abney had to smile. "You're just plain whipped this time," he told his partner.

Lomax nodded. "I can see that is true. Very well, then. Ab, you stay here. I'll go with Lillian."

"Why do I have to stay? Look here, if you're trying to say . . ."

It was Lomax's turn to be exasperated. "I'm not implying you're a coward, if that's what you think. I know better than that now. Guess I was wrong about you, Ab. You've got as much grit as anybody I know. But you're hurt worse than I am."

"Who says?"

"All anybody would have to do is look at your face. Lord, Bearclaw Johnson didn't do much to help your looks. You've got half your teeth knocked out and I'm betting your nose is broke."

"It is. But I don't need my nose, or my teeth, for this. I don't aim to *bite* anybody."

"Listen to us," said Lomax, shaking his head in disbelief. "Arguing over who's going out there to get himself killed."

"Ab," said Lillian, "would you please stay and look out for the children?"

Abney grimaced. "If you insist, ma'am."

As she and Lomax left the cabin, Lillian reminded Abney and Molly Wilkerson to bar the door behind them. Handing the rifle to Lomax, she climbed into the saddle strapped on Ol' Blue's back, clenching her teeth to prevent them from chattering, and not entirely from the cold, either.

"I want you to know I think this is a damnfool thing we're doing," Lomax informed her as he handed back the rifle.

"Probably," replied Lillian. "Come along."

She held Ol' Blue to a walk, so that Lomax could keep up as he high-stepped through the deep snow toward the line of trees. She searched the blue woodland shadows but saw nothing to alarm her. Maybe Lomax was right; maybe this was utter madness. But she was sick and tired of being holed up in a cabin waiting for disaster to strike, afraid to even venture out of doors. She had been afraid ever since finding Bearclaw Johnson's menacing message carved in her door and she wasn't going to cower a moment longer.

Reaching the edge of the woods, they paused and listened, but only heard the rasping of breath in their frozen throats.

"There's nobody out here," declared Lomax, eager to return to the warmth and relative security of the Wilkerson cabin.

"Something," said Lillian. "There *is* something. Look at Blue."

The horse was sniffing the air, whickering nervously, and beginning to fiddlefoot.

With a roar Bearclaw Johnson charged.

He seemed to appear out of thin air, and it so startled Ol' Blue that the horse reared, something he had never done. Caught completely off guard, Lillian came out of the saddle, rolled over Ol' Blue's haunches and hit the ground. The snow made for a soft landing, and she was unhurt. Somehow she held on to the rifle. Standing over her, Lomax brought the old shotgun to his shoulder and fired both barrels. Bearclaw was only ten paces away, and the full brunt of the shotgun's loads hit him in the chest and face. The mountain man fell backward, writhing in the snow, clutching at his ruined face.

"I got him!" cried Lomax, in disbelief. "By God, I got him!"

But his exultation turned into stark terror as Bear-claw rolled over and got slowly to his feet. The sound that issued from his snarling mouth, a sound of pure, guttural hate, froze Lomax where he stood. Johnson swung his rifle around and triggered it. The weapon misfired. Bearclaw threw the rifle down in disgust and plucked the tomahawk from his belt, hurling it at Lomax just as Lillian's rifle spoke.

The impact of the bullet striking him in the groin knocked Bearclaw down again. Lomax fell, too, the tomahawk buried deep in his shoulder.

Johnson lay still, and Lillian turned her attention to Lomax, who was thrashing about in the blood-spattered snow.

"I'm killed," he gasped. "Oh Lord, I'm killed."

"No you're not," said Lillian. Taking firm hold of the tomahawk, she pulled it free. Lomax groaned and lapsed into unconsciousness.

Brandishing the tomahawk, Lillian whirled, prepared in spite of her fear to approach the body of Bearclaw Johnson and finish him off if that half-ounce ball of St. Louis lead from her rifle hadn't killed him.

But the mountain man was gone.

She stared in disbelief and rising panic at the spot where Bearclaw had fallen. There were his tracks in the snow, moving away. It hardly seemed credible that a mere mortal man could be wounded so gravely and still get up and walk away. And how could a mere mortal disappear like that?

He could not have gone far. This she knew. He was hiding, somewhere nearby, probably watching her.

Lillian was brave—but not brave enough to reload her rifle and venture deeper into the woods to find and finish him. A wounded animal was the most dangerous prey to hunt—and the same applied to a wounded man.

Ol' Blue stood faithfully near at hand. Lillian knew she had to get Lomax on the horse and back to the cabin. But, try as she might, she couldn't lift the unconscious man, or rouse him, either. Repeated efforts to do so quickly exhausted her, and she sank into the snow beside him, gasping for breath, afraid that Bearclaw might reappear and yet determined not to leave Lomax—and only then did she see Abney running across the open ground from the cabin, coming to help.

"I saw it all," gasped Abney. "He went down twice, but he didn't stay down."

They got Lomax across the saddle. As Abney led Ol' Blue back to the cabin, Lillian reloaded her rifle and brought up the rear, watching the woods for any sign of Bearclaw Johnson. She didn't see him. *I hope he dies,* she thought. *I hope he bleeds to death.* She had never wished a man dead before, but she felt no remorse for her thoughts. She knew she would never feel safe again until she saw Johnson in his grave.

His cabin burned by his own hand, Bearclaw Johnson had to go elsewhere to find shelter, and he knew right where to go. Intimate with every square foot of these mountains, he made his way to a cave where once, many years ago, he had looked for bear to kill.

Like a mountain lion that is wounded and hunted, he instinctively sought high ground. It took him all night and most of the following day to reach his destination. He could not avoid leaving a trail of blood, and expected his enemies to come looking for him. To his astonishment, he saw no evidence of pursuit. They were, he decided, complete and utter fools. *They ought to finish me now, while they've got the chance.* They would not get another.

He was in a bad way, but he had been so before,

and he gave no thought to dying. There was unfinished business to tend to. Sun Falling's murdered soul cried out for vengeance, and would not be at peace until every last one of the emigrants was dead. Bearclaw had no intention of dying before justice was done.

It vexed him sorely that for all his effort he had managed only to kill the one, Jake Norwood. Two more wounded, but they might live, which did not suit Bearclaw one bit. Worse still, a woman had come damned close to curling his toes. A woman! Now, didn't that beat all? When he had seen her and that man Lomax coming toward the woods from the Wilkerson cabin he had not reckoned on the woman proving herself to be such a cool-headed and tough-minded adversary. She had courage, and Bearclaw admired that, and it was just too bad she would have to die right along with the rest.

Lomax's shotgun blast had done its fair share of damage—apart from a dozen minor wounds, a bent nail had put out Bearclaw's left eye. But the ball from the woman's rifle had caused the most life-threatening wound of all, striking him in the groin above the right leg. The bullet was lodged deep, and Bearclaw could not remove it. When he tried to dig it out with his knife the pain was so excruciating that he passed out.

That wound and several others became infected, and for several days Bearclaw Johnson lingered at death's door. The fever that wracked his body made him delirious. Swimming in and out of consciousness, he lost track of time, and could not have said how long he languished in that dark, cold tomb of stone. He slaked a constantly raging thirst with icicles which formed like fangs of crystal at the entrance to the cave.

When, finally, the fever broke, he awakened to a gnawing hunger. Still unable to move, his only nourishment was derived from a few strips of dried venison which he discovered in his hunting pouch. When that was gone he chewed on fringe cut from his buckskin leggings. In time he found the strength to stand and emerged from the cave in search of something to eat, unable to know until night fell and he saw the moon that about three weeks had passed since first he had crawled, more dead than alive, into the cave. His face was a hideous mask of scars, his eye socket covered with a crusty scab. His clothing hung loose on a gaunt frame.

The bullet from Lillian's rifle was lodged against his pelvic bone and caused him severe pain with every step. Bearclaw figured he would suffer from that wound until the day he died. Not that he expected to live all that much longer. Because one day Hugh Falconer would return, and when he found all the emigrants he cared so much about laid out for buzzard bait he would seek his own vengeance, and know right where to lay the blame. As a one-eyed cripple, Bearclaw didn't give much for his chances in a man-to-man fight to the death with Falconer. Falconer could be meaner than hell with the hide off when he got riled. Best he could hope for was to take Falconer to hell with him. It would be good, mused Bearclaw, to have a man of ol' Hugh's caliber along on that particular trip, because they said the devil was one mean son of a bitch.

Finding game in the high country in the dead of winter was no easy task, one made more difficult for Bearclaw since he was not very mobile and was also reluctant to use his rifle. It occurred to him that the folks down below in the valley might have talked themselves into believing he was dead and, if that was so, he sure didn't want to disabuse them of the notion.

With his mobility so severely impaired, it took Bearclaw two days to scout the immediate vicinity of the cave. When he discovered the marmot's den in a pile of rocks he laid up in waiting for a whole day before the varmint stuck his nose out and got caught in the snare Bearclaw had made by splicing together about six feet of long fringe. Dragging the thirty-pound critter back to his own den, Bearclaw didn't bother making a fire; he skinned the marmot and ate it raw.

The next day he ate what was left and felt much better. Now he could contemplate the future and look forward to the time when he could return to the valley and finish what he had started. Before, he had underestimated the emigrants. He wouldn't make the same mistake twice.

One month—by the next full moon he figured he would be as healthy as he was ever going to be again. Then he would steal down into the valley as silent and unseen as the shadow of death and exorcise the demons raging in his soul. Then, finally, maybe the world would learn to leave Bearclaw Johnson the hell alone.

After several days of cowering in their cabins, Lillian and the others allowed themselves to hope that they had seen the last of Bearclaw Johnson. "He has crawled off somewhere to die," said Abney, and he kept saying it, each day with a little more conviction.

They buried Jake Norwood next to his father. Both Tom Wilkerson and Lomax began to travel the road to recovery, thanks in no small measure to the medical skills of Doc Holsberry. Clete Norwood's condition improved, too. He took the news of the deaths of his father and brother better than anyone expected him to. The fact that Grace Holsberry would have nothing to do with him seemed to bother him more.

Her cabin and belongings destroyed by the fire Bearclaw Johnson had set, Lillian and Johnny moved into the Norwood cabin. That suited Clete just fine—he was lonely and needed someone to look out for him. Lillian's oxen had broken out of their corral and she had to track them down; with the help of Abney and Judd Pollock all but one was recovered. The loss of her belongings was a severe blow to Lillian, but she was heartened by the discovery of the box, in which she had kept all her money, relatively undamaged in the charred wreckage of the cabin. It wasn't much of a grubstake, but how could one quibble over a miracle? She still had the prairie schooner, a team of oxen less one, Ol' Blue, and, most importantly, she and Johnny were still alive. This was just one more setback, one more tribulation, and she obstinately refused to be daunted by it. She was determined not to let the frontier conquer her. No, she would conquer the frontier, if it was the last thing she ever did.

Not knowing if Bearclaw was alive or dead, they tried to talk Lena Blakemore into abandoning her cabin, which was rather isolated from the rest. Abney and Lomax offered to share their Spartan accommodations with her and her children. At first she refused, then abruptly changed her mind. That put them all in four cabins which were relatively close to one another. Lisle stayed with the Wilkersons. By now everyone had accepted the fact that Lee Donaghue was never going to return.

Days turned into weeks, and their apprehension regarding Bearclaw Johnson continued to wane. They longed for spring, knowing it was yet two or three months away, but it gave them something to look forward to, to plan for. Come spring they would go on to Oregon. They all agreed it would be good to settle down in the same place. After everything they had endured together, a strong bond had formed. Even Lomax and Abney had all but ceased their bickering.

It was as though they were one big family, mused Lillian—with the exception of Lena Blakemore, who remained emotionally distant.

Lillian wondered about Hugh Falconer. In fact, hardly an hour went by that she didn't think about him. Would he ever return? They could make it to Oregon Territory without him. Nothing was going to stop them now. Still, she longed to see him again, if only to know he was safe. Even if he did not come back to her, but rather to Lena. Lillian wasn't worried so much about Amos Spellman. Falconer could handle him, of that she had not a doubt in the world. It was the half-breed. The breed was a killer. . . .

Chapter Twenty-two

Keeping to the eastern side of the mountain, Hugh Falconer rode due south, crossing the high sagebrush plains cut through with deep barrancas. As the weeks passed and he continued on his course the land became more arid, the monotony of sweeping deserts broken by towering sandstone buttes, sculpted by time and the elements. When he crossed the Purgatoire he knew he was in Comanche country.

The Comanches were the terror of the southern plains. They had always been stubborn adversaries of foreign encroachment, fighting the Anglo-American expansion westward as ferociously as they had contested Spanish exploration two centuries earlier. They were the bitter foe of other Indian tribes as well, tolerating only their Kiowa neighbors. The Utes called them Komantcia—the enemy—and the Spaniards had corrupted the name to Comanche. The Comanches called themselves The People.

The tribe was composed of several bands. The largest was the Penatekas, or Honey Eaters. There were the Quohadi, or Antelopes, who dominated the Llano Estacado and, further north, the very warlike Buffalo Eaters. In one way or another every aspect of Comanche life focused on the art of war. Their territory incorporated much of the range of the great southern herd of bison, and since the buffalo was the life's blood of Comanche society, they zealously defended their territory against all intruders. Master horsemen, they struck swiftly, often raiding very far from home, sometimes venturing deep into Mexico, and making life exceedingly perilous for the inhabitants of the young Republic of Texas. They looted, raped, and killed with extraordinary efficiency. When pursued by a hostile and superior force, a Comanche raiding party would split up into small groups; if the pursuers divided themselves in order to continue the chase they would discover, usually when it was too late to save themselves, that the Comanches had reunited at some prearranged rendezvous to turn on their enemy and defeat him piecemeal.

There were no Comanche war chiefs—any warrior could don the feathered war bonnet and lead a raiding party, assuming he could acquire a shaman's blessing and persuade other young men that if they followed him they would return heaped with loot and glory. A Comanche foray usually consisted of twenty or thirty warriors. Occasionally, though, the different bands would unite and hundreds of Comanches would engage in an expedition against an enemy. Falconer was aware of the great raid of a few years earlier, when nearly a thousand Comanches, led by Buffalo Hump, had struck deep into the heart of Texas, cutting a swath of death and destruction clear from the Staked Plains to the Gulf Coast. After sacking the town of Victoria and obliterating the port of Linnville on Lavaca Bay, the Comanches had turned north for home, driving thousands of stolen horses before them and towing mule trains laden with booty. Thirty Texians lay dead in their wake, and more than a dozen were taken prisoner, most to be ransomed or used as slaves. One prisoner was found dead by the Texians who swarmed from all over the Republic like angry hornets to give chase; the soles of the poor man's feet had been sliced off and he had been forced to walk for several excruciating miles in this condition before his captors put him out of his misery and took his scalp.

The raid ended poorly for the Comanches, as they turned to fight their pursuers at Plum Creek, abandoning their traditional tactics because they had a clear superiority in numbers. But fighting Texians toe to toe, even with superior numbers, was not a smart thing to do. When the smoke cleared, eighty Comanche warriors lay dead, and only one Texian had lost his life. Many stolen horses were recovered, in addition to a good portion of the stolen loot. But no one could deny the audacity of the great raid—very few Indians could claim to have captured a white community like Linnville, lock, stock, and barrel.

Comanche raiders accumulated a great deal of loot. Horses and whiskey and guns they appropriated for their own use, but there were many items seized from ransacked farms and villages for which they had no practical use. Such things were usually traded to the Comancheros in exchange for more horses, whiskey, and guns—commodities of which the Comanches could never seem to get enough.

The Comancheros were Mexicans mostly, with a few white renegades thrown in for bad measure. Texians despised them one and all because they acted as quartermasters for their arch enemies, the Comanches. Some were mustangers, while others were traders who brought the guns and whiskey east from the entrepot of Santa Fe. There were several Comanchero posts on the Staked Plains. Chief among them was a place called Helltown. It was an appropriate name. In Helltown life was the cheapest commodity. This was not to say that Helltown existed in a state of complete anarchy, as some believed—no community could so exist. The law of Helltown came from one man, the so-called Lord of the Comancheros, Rodrigo Shay.

Falconer knew for a fact that Amos Spellman and the half-breed had traveled south after robbing the emigrants and leaving them to face the Pawnees near the Platte River. He figured they had headed for one of three possible destinations Santa Fe, the Texas Republic, or Helltown. In none of these places would many, if any, questions be asked that might require Spellman to explain by what means he had acquired his ill-gotten loot. Falconer surmised that in time Spellman might reappear in St. Joseph or St. Louis; if the coast was clear he might even try to pull the same trick again on a new bunch of unsuspecting pioneers. But it made sense that he would hightail it out of the United States, beyond the reach of American justice, just in case the Pawnees had failed to wipe out the wagon train and news of his skullduggery reached the authorities. Such an eventuality might even make Texas untenable for him—though they had forged a separate republic out of the frontier, most Texians had once been United States citizens and wanted to be again. So Falconer decided to try Santa Fe first before running the risks that a visit to Helltown entailed.

Some years earlier Falconer would have met with a warmer welcome than that which greeted him now in Santa Fe. Americans were viewed with suspicion these days, thanks in large measure to several recent expeditions undertaken by Texians to lay claim to land along the Pecos River and the upper reaches of the Rio Grande, and even beyond. The Texas Republic claimed this land, along with Santa Fe, but the Santa Feans weren't buying into it. In addition, the Texians had been quarreling with Mexico about their southern border; the Mexicans did not recognize the Texian claim to the territory which lay between the Nueces and the

Rio Grande. Anyone in Santa Fe who gave thought to the future realized that a clash with the land-hungry *Yanquis* was inevitable. Texas President Mirabeau B. Lamar had talked long and loud about creating a Lone Star empire that incorporated the entire Southwest, and Santa Feans did not bother trying to draw fine distinctions between Texians and Americans.

Falconer's reception would have been even colder had he made the mistake of giving his true identity. His expedition into California six years earlier was perceived by the Mexican government as a reconnaissance sponsored by the United States. That was untrue, but Falconer surmised that it would be a complete waste of time trying to convince the Mexicans of that.

Still, Falconer was not the only American in Santa Fe. The flow of commerce begun twenty years ago between Santa Fe and Missouri still thrived. Now the mule trains were protected by United States troops. Where profit was concerned, politics always played second fiddle.

Falconer had visited Santa Fe twice before; he knew where to look and who to talk to. In no time at all he learned that Spellman and the half-breed had indeed until recently graced the town with their presence. As Falconer had feared, Spellman had spent a great deal of money in the *cantinas,* drinking strong spirits in Homeric quantities and dallying with the women who made their living working in those dens. Then the breed had killed a man; apparently his victim had been unknown to him, but the breed had witnessed him cruelly abusing a horse. In a busy plaza thronged with witnesses, Breed had murdered the man with a knife, cutting him so savagely that the undertaker had worked through the night trying to sew the corpse up and make it as least halfway presentable for the next day's funeral.

The half-breed fled into the desert; Spellman tried to disassociate himself from the murder, but to no avail. He was the breed's partner, and as such was confronted by a suddenly hostile populace that believed in guilt by association. He, too, slipped away in the night. The family of the murdered man offered a handsome reward, the equivalent of one thousand dollars American in gold for the return of the breed, dead or alive, and another five hundred dollars in gold for his friend Amos Spellman.

Thus far, no one had tried to collect the bounty, because it was believed that both fugitives had sought refuge among the Comancheros.

Falconer did not hesitate. The next day he reprovisioned and put Santa Fe behind him, riding east onto the Staked Plains. His mind was made up. He would try to bring both Spellman and the breed to justice, collect the rewards, and give the money to Lena Blakemore and the other emigrants. He had no use for gold, and they would need grubstakes when they arrived in the Oregon Territory next spring. It struck him as ironic that he had been on a similar mission—tracking the hidehunter Dowd for the murder of the Arapaho boy—when first he had met Lillian Tasker and the other emigrants.

He could only hope he would meet with more success in this new and even more dangerous manhunt.

Falconer nurtured no illusions about his prospects for getting in and out of Helltown in one piece, and as he neared the remote Comanchero stronghold he thought more and more about Lillian Tasker, wondering if he would live to see her again. He had made it a point not to promise her that he would return, but only death could prevent him from doing so.

Lillian was a distraction, and more often than not

he was trying—usually with a notable lack of success—to get her off his mind. Sometimes, as the Appaloosa plodded across endless miles of barren, monotonous, desert plains, he would catch himself daydreaming about her. And at night, as he sat with a blanket draped around him, cross-legged before the fire he had built in a foot-deep hole and then covered with dirt, his mind would wander back to her, in that cabin in a remote valley a thousand miles away. He knew this was very dangerous; he traveled now in what the Mexicans called *despoblado,* or no-man's-land. The country was thinly populated, and the Mexican government, chronically strapped for funds, did not possess the resources to control or tame it. It had, therefore, become a haven for lawless elements. Bands of Apache and Comanche raiders roamed this wasteland. So did the *mesteneros*—the mustangers—and the hidehunters. Tough customers every one. They had to be, to survive here. Jedediah Smith had died not far to the east; the legendary mountain man had been waylaid by Comanches on the banks of the Cimarron and riddled with arrows. The bones of countless others lay bleached and scattered across this land. Falconer kept telling himself he needed to pay attention to his surroundings if he wanted to take his bones back to the high country where they belonged.

But it was exceedingly difficult—nigh on impossible—to keep from thinking about Lillian. When Touches The Moon had died Falconer had sworn over her grave that he would never love another, and he had meant to keep that promise. Years of lonely wandering followed, but he had managed eventually to come to terms with loneliness, and he always had the memories to keep him company. He had been convinced that he would never find a woman who could measure up to Touches The Moon, who was even half as good or half as brave as his beloved Shoshone maiden.

Now he realized how badly he had been off the mark in that respect. Lillian reminded him a great deal of Touches The Moon. They weren't at all alike on the outside, but many were the similarities between them when it came to what was inside. And that, after all, was what really mattered. Lillian was intelligent, courageous, and compassionate. She spoke her mind and had a level head on her shoulders. She did not think only of herself but was unfailingly considerate of others. She was a good mother, and Falconer knew she would make a good wife. Best of all, she loved him. God only knew why, or what she saw in him, but there could be denying the depth of her feelings for him.

Question was whether he was ready to get hitched. A family was an awesome responsibility, and he wasn't exactly cut out to be a sodbuster. Therein lay the reason he had ventured west in the first place, a callow boy at the tender age of fifteen, running away from his father's farm to live a life of adventure. Even though the life of adventure had very nearly cost him his life a dozen times before he turned twenty, he never once longed to return to the civilized world where drudgery was his certain fate. He might have found work at his uncle's gristmill, or applied himself diligently to his studies and perhaps in time become a lawyer, a species much in demand in the early days of the Republic, and a position used by many as a stepping stone to political office.

But none of those careers had appealed to Falconer. Besides, he had never been one to apply himself with anything remotely resembling diligence to his studies. He had much preferred traipsing through the woods, learning to read animal sign, to sitting on a hard wooden bench struggling through a primer. Only later had he acquired an appetite for Shakespeare and the Roman poets. He was very much the self-educated man, which meant his knowledge had great gaping holes in it; his education had been pursued in an entirely self-indulgent manner, strictly according to his interests, and so could not by any stretch of the imagination be termed well-rounded.

So if he could not or would not remold himself into a farmer, would Lillian be willing to live his kind of life? Touches The Moon, as it turned out, had been content to live in mountain solitude, happy to visit her tribe perhaps once or twice during the year. Could Lillian endure that kind of isolation? Falconer tried to look at the situation from her point of view and grimly concluded that it would be right arduous to be the wife of a frontiersman who had no visible means of support and bleak prospects for the future.

Of course, there was Johnny to consider, too—and Lillian would most assuredly give a lot of thought to what was best for her son. Would she want him to grow up to be a self-educated, buckskin-clad nomad of the high country? Soon there would be no place left for the mountain man. The world was shrinking fast. Falconer had to concede that he would want better for his own son.

So there were problems he could anticipate when he ruminated about the future he and Lillian could make for themselves. But that did not quell his desire for her. Perhaps he could find something to do in Oregon that was not too onerous. Perhaps it *was* time to try and put down some roots, to give up the life of the wanderer. To get something you wanted you always had to give up something else. It was always so.

But first he had to pay his debt to Lena Blakemore. He had to get into Helltown and get out again with

Spellman and the half-breed so that he could collect the reward offered for them in Santa Fe. When he gave Lena her share of that gold he would effectively emancipate himself. He would no longer feel obligated to her. Lillian had been wrong about one thing. He *was* responsible for Daniel Blakemore's death because he had known all along how dangerous Dowd could be, and he had been the one to put Blakemore, and all the other emigrants, at risk by bringing the hide-hunter into their midst. He had to pay his debts.

So he had to get that gold for Lena and the emigrants. There was no other way. Only then could he free himself to love Lillian Tasker.

He crossed paths with a band of mustangers who told him how to find Helltown. In fact, they said, they were headed there themselves and would he care to ride along with them? Falconer declined the offer. They were riding south, and Falconer had harvested enough information in Santa Fe to know that Helltown did not lie to the south, but rather somewhere to the east. The covetous way the *mesteneros* eyed the Appaloosa gave him a clue as to their true intentions. He was pretty sure that if he made the mistake of riding with this hardcase lot he would wake up dead and his horse and possibles purloined.

Seven days out of Santa Fe he finally found what he was looking for, a squalid collection of miserable adobe and picket houses surrounding the ruins of what appeared to be an old mission. He had heard that long ago Jesuit missionaries had tried to Christianize and civilize the Apaches and Padoucas who lived on the Staked Plains. They enjoyed a modest success with those Indians, but when the Comanches came, ousting the other tribes, the Jesuits found out the hard way that the new warlords of this trackless wasteland were not interested in their proselytizing. The massacre of a half-dozen priests resulted in the abandonment of the mission, which then stood abandoned and forgotten for decades, ravaged by the passage of time—until the Comancheros came.

They found the place eminently suited to their needs—a rendezvous point for mustangers, traders, and Comanche raiders, somewhere far removed from the roads and towns of the law-abiding. A place too remote for the Mexican soldiers of even the far-reaching Texas Rangers to bother.

From a distance Falconer studied Helltown for a long time. Then he wheeled the Appaloosa and rode due west until sundown. By his calculations he was ten miles away when he stopped to bed down for the night on the rim of a dry wash. He dug his hole, made his fire of buffalo chips, let it burn for a spell, then covered it with dirt. Over this he spread a blanket and sat cross-legged with another blanket over his head. The winter wind howled its frozen message across the plains. He ate a bit of venison jerky and drank a little water from a cork-stoppered gourd. After that he went to sleep. He had taught himself how to do that a long time ago; no matter what the situation, or how troubled his thoughts might be, he could sleep, because he knew his body and mind needed the rest. He slept sitting up for four solid hours, the Appaloosa's reins tied to his wrist, the Hawken rifle across his lap.

Before dawn broke he roused himself and ground-hitched the horse, tying a knot in the reins and burying the knot a foot deep in the rocky soil. He gave the Appaloosa some water. Removing the saddle, he threw it over a shoulder and started walking. A quarter mile later he glanced back and saw that the Appaloosa was still watching him. *Wondering,* mused Falconer, *if I've gone* loco, *leaving him out here like this.* Falconer calculated on being back, with any luck, before the day was out.

Shrugging the saddle into a better position on his back, he continued on his way.

By midday he had reached the Comanchero stronghold.

Chapter Twenty-three

They let him walk right into Helltown because he was one man on foot and there were dozens of them, maybe a hundred armed men all told, and he posed no threat. Men, women, and children came out of their huts or stopped what they were doing in the streets to stare at him. Not that the streets were laid out in any kind or order; Falconer steered the straightest course possible for the old mission which marked the center of the Comanchero community. He gave the impression that he owned the place. There was no hesitation in his stride, not so much as a glimmer of trepidation on his face. Instinct warned him that if he demonstrated even a smidgen of fear or uncertainty he was doomed.

These people were a rough-looking bunch. The men wore buckskin and homespun and were generally armed to the teeth with a wide variety of weapons. Some of the women were Indian, the rest Mexican. Dirty children and mangy dogs were in abundance.

Finally two men stepped forward to stand, legs braced, shoulders squared, side by side to block his path. Falconer was expecting them. He didn't try to go around them. He stood there and looked them in the eye and waited, his expression perfectly inscrutable.

"*¿Quien esta usted?*" asked one of the men.

"Speak English if you want to talk to me," said Falconer.

"He wants to know who you are," said the other man, in English. His pale skin and yellow hair marked him as one of the few *Yanqui* denizens of Helltown.

"Name's Falconer."

"Where's your horse?"

"Snakebit, some miles back."

"Bad luck."

"I get my share."

"What are you doing way out here?"

"Looking for somebody."

"Who might that be?"

"Man named Spellman. Know him?"

"I might. He a friend of yours?"

"We've met."

The American spoke to the Mexican in the latter's tongue. Falconer was not well enough acquainted with the language to follow what passed between them. He dropped the saddle and cradled the Hawken mountain rifle in his left arm, his right hand resting over the hammer. The two men confronting him did not fail to notice this. Falconer was not threatening them outright, but it was clear he was ready for trouble and would not shy away from it.

"I know Spellman," said the American. "Matter of fact, he's right here in Helltown. What do you want with him?"

"He owes me some money."

The American's smile was crooked. "Well now, that don't surprise me none."

A horseman arrived from the direction of the old mission. He wore a red sash around his head; the ends dangled long down his back. He was a young Mexican, and again Falconer could not understand him when he spoke, but his tone was authoritarian as he addressed the two men who stood in the mountain man's path. The American answered readily, and with respect. The horseman glanced at Falconer and snapped a curt command before wheeling his horse around and returning whence he came.

"Rodrigo Shay will want to see you," said the American. "He runs things around here."

Falconer nodded. So far so good. He was at least going to have an audience with the Lord of the Comancheros. He had not been killed outright. That was something. The two men acted as his escort, the American leading the way, the Mexican bringing up the rear.

Rodrigo Shay awaited him in the remains of the chapel, sitting in a horsehair chair on the dais where once an alter had stood. Part of the roof had collapsed long ago—shattered beams and adobe rubble lay in heaps upon the floor. Off to one side, the nave had been transformed into private quarters, the furnishings consisting of a narrow four-poster bed, a cabinet filled with books, a long maple table with four high-backed chairs, and an iron stove in which a fire burned hot. But out here, in the main part of the chapel, open to the sky, it was quite cold.

Shay was sprawled in the chair like a king on his throne, afflicted with ennui, with no more worlds to conquer. He was a burly man, with brawny shoulders and powerful legs. Square-jawed and bull-necked, his roan beard was dusted with gray. His attire consisted of Wellington boots, yellow nankeen trousers, a cougar-skin vest, and a long gray wool greatcoat.

The only other person in the chapel was the horseman who wore the red sash. He was still mounted, having ridden the coyote dun that wore his saddle straight through the doorway and up to the dais.

"This here's Rodrigo Shay," said the American needlessly, indicating the man in the chair.

Shay tilted his head forward an inch. "My friend, I cannot as yet welcome you to Helltown. First you must state your business. Leave nothing out. The penalty for deception is severe." He pointed over his shoulder at the cross secured to the wall behind him. It consisted of two heavy, squared beams and stood fifteen feet high. Falconer could see bloodstains on it. "We crucify those who violate our laws."

Falconer had never been a churchgoing man. He found God in the splendor of the high country. But he still considered a church to be sacred ground, and it provided him with a keen insight into the kind of people these Comancheros were to know that they performed their executions here in God's house.

"I've come to see a man named Spellman," he replied. "He owes me money."

"How did you know to look for him here?"

"Spellman is a thief. What better place to look?"

Rodrigo Shay smiled. "How did it come to pass that he owes you this money?"

"He stole it from some friends of mine. They sent me to get it back."

Shay leaned forward in his chair. "Spellman has no money with which to repay your friends. He gave all he had left to me. It was the price of sanctuary here. With it he purchased my protection. Do you understand what I am telling you?"

Falconer did, and he didn't like the sound of it one bit. This was a complication he had not foreseen.

"Maybe we can strike a bargain."

"I am always willing to discuss such matters, if there may be a profit in it." Shay glanced at the two men who had served as Falconer's escort. He didn't have to say anything—they knew what he wanted from them, and they promptly left the chapel without a word. The man on the coyote dun remained. Falconer pegged him as Shay's lieutenant, perhaps the only man here that Shay could trust. If there could be any trust at all in a place like Helltown.

"I always like to know a little something about the people with whom I conduct business," said Shay. "So I will begin by telling you some things about myself. My father was an Irish mariner. He sailed the seven seas. One day he jumped ship in California. A self-educated man, my father, with a keen business sense. He prospered as a trader among the Spanish, and married the daughter of a grandee. I was their only progeny. They sent me to the best schools. Gave me the very best of everything that money could buy. But I inherited my father's love of adventure. As a young man I struck out on my own, to make my own fortune in Santa Fe. I was one of the first to trade with the Comanches. Some said I was a traitor to my own kind for doing so. After all, the Comanches were everyone's enemies. But there was profit in it, tremendous profit, and I could not resist. I am the one who found this place, and those who reside here do so at my whim. There. You now know the barest bones of the story of my life."

Falconer said, "There isn't much to tell about mine. I came West to live in the mountains, and that is what I've done for almost twenty years."

"You are entirely too modest. Did you think I had not heard of you? Many people come here for many reasons. I hear a great many things from all corners of the frontier. Were you not the man who led his brigade across the Sierra Nevada into California six or seven years ago?"

Falconer nodded. "No great feat. Jedediah Smith

had gone before us. And we didn't stay in California long. Had a spot of trouble."

Shay laughed. "So I am told. Now, as to this man Spellman. As I said, he is under my protection. I have a responsibility, which would include, I suspect, protecting him from you, if my instincts are right. What could you offer me that would bring me to forget my obligation?"

"Spellman is a wanted man in Santa Fe. So is the half-breed who rides with him. Let me take them back and collect the reward, and I will give you half."

"This I did not know. They should have told me themselves."

"Maybe they didn't trust you. It's a nice reward."

"Many of the men in Helltown are wanted somewhere for something. How would it appear to them if I became a party to your scheme?"

"Spellman isn't one of you, is he?"

"You are a perceptive man. No, Spellman is not a Comanchero. But Breed—Breed is a different matter altogether. He *is* one of us. Was long before he began to ride with Spellman. You cannot have Breed."

"Then I'll settle for Spellman," lied Falconer.

Rodrigo Shay sat very still for what seemed to Falconer a small eternity, his shamrock green eyes fixed on the mountain man. This was the moment of truth; Falconer was well aware of the fact that if Shay decided not to go along, then he was a dead man—his chances of getting out of Helltown, of ever seeing Lillian or his beloved mountains again—were slim and none. He was betting his life that Shay's avarice exceeded his sense of responsibility, that greed meant more to him than his word, and that honor was less important than profit to the Lord of the Comancheros. Falconer thought it was a bet worth making. After all, it had been avarice that had compelled Rodrigo Shay to forsake the comforts of life as a member of the California aristocracy and risk his life to trade with the Comanches. Was there such a thing as honor among thieves? If so, Falconer knew he was doomed.

Finally, Shay glanced at the man on the coyote dun. "Bring Amos Spellman to me, Angelo."

Without a word the man turned his horse and rode out of the ruined chapel.

By an effort of will Falconer remained inscrutable, disguising his great relief. He had Spellman. Now all he had to do was get the breed.

When Amos Spellman was brought before Rodrigo Shay and began to protest the deal struck by Falconer and the Comanchero leader, Shay listened for a moment and then nodded to Angelo. The latter silenced Spellman by laying the butt of his pistol across the man's skull.

Falconer informed Shay that he wanted to leave right away and would need a pair of horses. Apparently, in addition to squandering almost all the money and valuables he had stolen from the emigrants—giving what remained to Shay in payment for sanctuary in Helltown following the difficulties in Santa Fe—Spellman had also lost his horse in one final, desperate wager in which he hoped, forlornly, to recoup his losses. But Shay agreed to provide two grass ponies, hardy mustangs accustomed to the Staked Plains. He also insisted on sending one of his own men along with Falconer.

"Angelo will go with you," said Shay. "He is unknown in Santa Fe. You may give him my share of the reward you collect for our friend Spellman."

Falconer gave Angelo a speculative glance and the dark, slender Mexican youth smiled, but there was no humor in the smile, no friendliness—on the contrary, there was something distinctly predatory about it. Angelo carried a brace of pistols in his belt and a sheathed Bowie knife strapped to one leg and there could be no doubt that he was adept at the use of these weapons. Angelo did not look very trustworthy as far as Falconer was concerned, but obviously Shay trusted him explicitly.

Also obvious was the fact that Angelo was going along to make certain Falconer did not harbor any aspirations to cheat Shay out of his share of the reward, or, if he did, that he would deem it wiser not to act on them. Falconer had expected some such arrangement. He hadn't ever dared hope that Rodrigo Shay would be so naive as to trust him. The Lord of the Comancheros had not attained his present exalted position, or held on to it, by being ingenuous.

What it boiled down to was this: Falconer knew he would probably have to kill Angelo, because he had no intention of keeping his end of the bargain struck with Shay. And Angelo didn't look like he would be all that easy to kill.

"What about the breed?" asked Falconer. "For some reason he is true to Spellman."

"He is being searched for as we speak," replied Shay. "When he is found he will be detained for several days."

"He won't like it when he finds out you betrayed his partner."

Rodrigo Shay shrugged. "Risks are often run in the pursuit of profit. But your concern," he added wryly, "is touching. Permit me to reciprocate. When you have your share of the gold, my friend, I suggest you put this part of the country behind you as quickly as you can."

"Good advice, and I'll gladly take it. One more

question, Shay. Am I going to have any trouble riding out of here with Spellman draped across a saddle?"

"Angelo will be with you."

"Is that supposed to make me feel better?"

"If you knew Angelo it would. As for Spellman, I will think of something to tell them."

Falconer was willing to wager that Shay *wouldn't* tell the Comancheros about the gold he thought he was getting in exchange for betraying Spellman. As Shay had indicated, many of the denizens of Helltown were probably wanted somewhere, and they would cease to feel secure under Shay's aegis if they knew he was capable of turning them in for the bounty on their heads.

Less than an hour later they were riding out of Helltown, Falconer riding a wiry chestnut and leading the horse across which the still unconscious Spellman was draped, tied to the saddle beneath him, with Angelo bringing up the rear. They were the object of considerable Comanchero curiosity, but no one ventured to contest their departure. Though he still had Angelo to worry about, Falconer was pleased with the way things were going so far. He had successfully preyed on Rodrigo Shay's avarice. He had won the game, or at least the first round. As for Breed, he had a hunch he would see the man again long before they arrived in Santa Fe.

In this he was right on the mark. They were only a couple of miles out of Helltown when Falconer, checking their backtrail for the dozenth time, saw a plume of dust marking the progress of a rider coming after them. The horseman was a mere speck of black on the dun-colored plain, at least a mile away, but Falconer knew who he was.

"Rider coming," he told Angelo.

Shay's young lieutenant turned in his saddle and looked.

"It's the half-breed," remarked Falconer. "Has to be."

"Yes." Angelo was very calm. In addition to his other weapons, he now carried a Sharps-Borschardt .45 buffalo gun. This he drew from the fringed buckskin sheath tied to his saddle and riding beneath his right leg.

"We better kill him now," said Angelo.

Falconer nodded. They checked their horses. Falconer remained in the saddle while Angelo dismounted. Holding rein leather in one hand, he laid the long barrel of the Sharps across the bow of his saddle for support, lifted the hinged sight, and drew a bead on the still-distant rider. Falconer figured the range at three-quarters of a mile now. The Sharps could throw a bullet a very long way—folks said you could shoot the gun today and kill tomorrow—but Angelo was going to have to be quite a marksman unless he waited for the breed to come closer.

He did not wait too long. At a range of half a mile, Angelo squeezed the trigger. The Sharps boomed like a cannon, the hard recoil kicking the Comanchero's shoulder back. Angelo's horse tried to bolt, but he held on, peering through the dust kicked up by the coyote dun's drumming hooves.

Falconer saw the rider topple sideways off his horse. *At least,* he thought, *that reward is payable dead or alive.*

"I got him," said Angelo matter-of-factly, watching Breed's horse take flight across the dusty plain.

"Fine shooting," said Falconer. His Hawken lay across the front of his saddle, and he turned it slightly so that it was aimed at Angelo's back. "Now you can get shed of that buffalo gun, and the rest of your weapons, too."

Angelo did not appear angry or afraid, and Falconer wondered what kind of life the young Comanchero had led that he could stand here now and look down the barrel of the Hawken with such unshakable composure. But he had not survived in *Comancheria* by being stupid or foolhardy—he cast the empty Sharps-Borschardt away. The pistols and the Bowie knife followed. He could assume that Falconer hoped to avoid killing him, else the mountain man would have already triggered the Hawken.

"This is what we'll do," said Falconer once Angelo had dispensed with his killing tools. "We'll go back and make sure the breed is dead. Then you'll have to walk back to Helltown, because I'll be needing your horse."

Angelo turned and was about to climb into his saddle when Falconer said no, he would walk, leading the horse. The Comanchero complied. Falconer rode alongside and a little to the rear, keeping the Hawken trained on Angelo's back. Comancheros were not to be trifled with, and just because Angelo was unarmed didn't mean he wasn't still as dangerous as a sackfull of rattlesnakes.

They had gone but a hundred yards when a rifle spoke and Angelo fell, shot dead.

The reins slipped out of the Comanchero's lifeless hand, and his horse, snorting and wild-eyed, veered away. Falconer cursed as he saw Breed rise up from the sage a few hundred yards away. He came at a loping run, reloading his single-shot percussion rifle on the move, and Falconer considered trying to plug him with the Hawken, but the chestnut mustang beneath him was not the Appaloosa—the Appaloosa was trained to stand in the midst of gunfire. This cayuse was pivoting, provoked by the shooting and the smell of blood and wanting badly to follow Angelo's fugitive horse as it galloped to freedom. Falconer was shrewd enough not to risk a shot from the hurricane deck of this animal. If he dismounted he would have the devil of a time trying to get off a good shot while holding on to two horses. So he reluctantly turned the pony and gave it free rein. The horse took off, and Falconer dragged the pony carrying Amos Spellman along behind. He hated to run from a fight, especially from a fight with a man worth a thousand American dollars in gold, but he did want to see Lillian Tasker again . . .

Breed's second shot killed Falconer's horse.

Falconer was not caught completely unaware as the animal collapsed in midstride. He landed on his feet, losing the reins of Spellman's horse in the process but managing to keep possession of the Hawken. Spellman's horse, confused, paused a moment before taking off—that brief hesitation gave Falconer the time he needed to grab the reins and loop them around the pommel of the saddle he had recently and precipitously evacuated. Spellman's horse didn't cotton to being tethered to a dead pony, and balked, but the rein leather held.

Looking east, Falconer saw the half-breed coming resolutely on, reloading again, still a few hundred yards away. Testing the wind that gusted icily down from the north, from left to right across his line of fire, the mountain man brought the Hawken to his shoulder and fired. Breed somersaulted and disappeared into the sage. *I hit him low,* realized Falconer. Reloading, he moved warily forward, fairly certain that the breed was still above snakes.

He was right. Breed popped up out of the sage when Falconer was a scant fifty yards away. Both men fired simultaneously at what amounted to point-blank range with long guns. Breed's bullet hit Falconer just below the rib cage on the left side and exited out the back, staggering the mountain man. This time Falconer's aim was true, and the half-breed sprawled dead.

Falconer clutched at his side. Warm blood was sticky between his clawing fingers. He felt dizzy, and shook his head to clear the cobwebs. Having been shot twice before, he knew the wound was not a mortal one, and he counted himself fortunate indeed. Reloading the Hawken, he moved to Breed's side. The man had been hit three times. Angelo's bullet had caught him in the shoulder. Falconer's first shot had struck him in the thigh. The killing shot had entered at the base of the throat. *This man,* mused Falconer, *took a lot of killing.*

Scanning the desert plain, Falconer saw no sign of Angelo's runaway horse, or the breed's either. He retraced his steps and fetched Spellman's pony. Spellman was conscious now, struggling in futility against the ties that bound him to the saddle. Drawing his Green River knife, Falconer cut him loose and pitched him over onto the ground.

"Your half-breed friend is lying yonder," said the mountain man.

"You take me back to Santa Fe they'll like as not kill me for something I didn't do."

"You should be more careful about the company you keep."

"You're a cold-blooded bastard, Falconer."

Falconer's laugh had a raw edge. "When I have to be. Now get up."

He had Spellman drape Breed's body across the saddle.

"We're going to walk all the way to Santa Fe?"

asked Spellman. "I don't think you'll make the trip, Falconer. You're bleeding bad."

"Don't worry about me. I'll go as far as I need to."

He pointed Spellman west and ordered him to start walking. Spellman led the horse, while Falconer brought up the rear. Every step was pure agony, but the mountain man did not falter. The Appaloosa was only seven or eight miles away—*if* it was where he had left it. Would it be? Falconer refused to contemplate otherwise. He kept telling himself that an eight-mile walk with a hole in his side was no hill for a stepper when it meant getting back to Lillian.

The thought of her made the pain easier to bear.

Chapter Twenty-four

Grace Holsberry knew that if something didn't happen soon she was simply going to die. Her boredom was reaching fatal levels.

For weeks now she had been cooped up in this miserable cabin with nothing to do and nobody to talk to. Oh, her father tried to engage her in conversation, usually on the subject of the books he loved so much and was trying, without much success, to coax her into reading. But she didn't want to talk to her father at all, much less about the silly old ideas contained in dusty old books. She greatly resented her father for bringing her out here into this godforsaken wilderness, even at times despised him for being such a doddering old fool that he thought it had been necessary in the first place.

Of course she realized that there were some who would say it was all her fault, that Doc Holsberry had given up the practice which he had built thirty years earlier and nurtured into prosperity because of his daughter's shocking indiscretions. But Grace was not one to accept blame, as the concept of an individual being responsible for his or her own actions was, if not alien to her, extremely inconvenient, considering all the things she had done which society would not approve of.

Was it her fault that James Ramseur, that handsome

devil, had fallen head over heels in love with her? And was she to blame because she was endowed with more than her fair share of feminine charms, not to mention feminine wiles? Was she guilty because Ramseur had been unhappily married to a shrill, unattractive harridan to whom the very thought of being intimate with a man, even her husband, was repugnant? Was she to blame because James had been so indiscreet in his desire for her that the whole town had become aware of his indiscretions. Most assuredly not guilty, on all counts.

James had married his wife not for love but rather to gain access to the upper crust of local society. Grace didn't blame him for that. She herself had long ago decided that were she ever to marry it would be to improve her standing in the community, and for no other reason. What was the point of subjecting yourself to the tribulations of wedlock if there was to be no profit in it? But James had been foolish in his passion for her, not caring if the whole world knew he lusted after her. What embittered Grace most of all about the whole affair was that the town had blamed her for *everything*. As though James had been powerless to defend himself against her alluring spells.

Thank God they don't burn people at the stake anymore, thought Grace, 'else those high and mighty, holier than thou, Christian folk would have cooked her for sure. But they had done the next best thing—they had run her out of town. The powers that be had come calling one day to have a long and earnest talk with her father. Grace hadn't been privy to their conversation, but she had a pretty good idea what had been said, because a few weeks later her father had sold the house, turned the practice over to a younger doctor fresh out of some eastern medical school, and moved.

Often Grace chided her father for bowing to pressure like that, assuring him that the unkind things that people said about her, the names they called her behind her back—names like vixen, Jezebel, and worse—did not bother her in the least. That was a lie; such words did hurt, but she would never in a million years have given them the satisfaction of seeing that they hurt her.

Her father, though, had adamantly refused to listen to her pleas, and Grace decided *he* was the one hurt by the idle talk of the good Christians, that *he* was the one running away, not her. With youthful resilience, Grace had talked herself into looking forward to the Oregon Territory, since it was inevitable that she was going there, and because everyone said women were in such short supply in that new country. That meant she ought to have her pick of any number of eligible young bachelors. They also said fortunes were going to be made in Oregon, which meant some of those eligible young bachelors would be rich and successful, too.

The journey itself across the Great Plains and the Stony Mountains, as folks back in eastern Ohio were still wont to call them, had been a daunting prospect from the first because Grace was averse to discomfort, but she had tried to make the best of a bad situation. The presence of the Norwood boys had been a pleasant surprise, too. She had never seriously contemplated marrying either one of them. How foolish that would be, before she even had a chance to survey the field in Oregon! No, they had served as mere distractions. And what big, handsome distractions they had been!

The terrible things that had happened were no fault of hers. If either Clete or Jake had for one minute thought she was the least bit interested in marriage it had certainly not been on account of anything she had said. That a man felt obliged to make a respectable woman out of a girl he dallied with was a fatuous male misconception if ever there was one. And to think that Jake had intentionally crippled his brother out of blind jealousy—it was all simply too horrible to contemplate.

Poor Jake! If only he had waited his turn. It wasn't easy to slip away and find a little privacy, just a few minutes without anyone missing them. She and Clete had managed on only one occasion, but they had taken full advantage of that golden opportunity. Just thinking about that time—Clete's hard, lean body pressing down on top of hers, his hot breath against her skin as he hungrily explored every soft curve and each sweet valley of her body—the memory of it made her squirm. But then silly old Clete had gone and bragged to his brother about what he had done, a very ill-considered move, but then men were like that.

Just as before, everyone blamed her for what had happened. Even her own father held her accountable. He hadn't actually come out and said so, but she could tell. Life just wasn't fair.

Weeks had passed—crawled by with excruciating slowness—since that hideous man Bearclaw Johnson had come down into the valley and killed Jake. Grace was convinced, along with almost everyone else, that Bearclaw was dead, that he had crawled off to die from the wounds Lomax and Lillian Tasker had inflicted on him. Since then the snow had been falling almost constantly from depressing overcast skies, with only a handful of days when the sun had made an appearance, and it had gotten so that the drifts were so deep they made travel from one cabin to another, though the distance might be only a mile or two, more trouble than it was worth. This was especially true for

Grace. She couldn't stand the way others looked at her or, as was often the case, *avoided* looking at her. So she was condemned to remain in this miserable one-room cabin, where she sulked the whole day long and made life perfectly miserable for her father.

As bad as things were today, she almost went out of her mind contemplating tomorrow, for it was not even Christmas yet, and there would be another eight weeks of this infernal snow in the new year before any hope of spring, and finally departing this accursed valley, bound for the promised land of the Oregon Territory. Grace honestly didn't think she could keep her sanity until spring.

Her father had erected a curtain, a couple of blankets on a sapling pole, to give her a modicum of privacy, sectioning off a corner of the cabin just large enough to hold her bed and trunk and a chair. Now, sitting in the chair, an unread book open on her lap, drowning in self-pity, Grace heard her father stirring on the other side of the curtain. The day was growing old, and she assumed he was about to warm up the stew Mrs. Pollock had sent over by Tom Wilkerson the day before yesterday. Grace seldom cooked—she almost never found herself in the mood to work that hard, and it was quite impossible anyway without a proper stove.

"Grace, dear," said Holsberry, standing just beyond the curtain, "I am going out to get a little more firewood. We're running low."

Peeved, she did not even answer, and she listened as he shuffled out the door. She felt a twinge of remorse, just a twinge. Was it really fair to make his life miserable just because she was in a wretchedly poor state of mind? Part of her knew that if she only made a small effort to make the best of this situation, as she had done during the trek across the plains, she would not only feel better, but time would pass much more quickly. But then another part of her countered with the argument that if she had to suffer, sequestered in this wretched hovel like a nun, then everybody else ought to suffer as well.

She tried to focus her attention on the book, a volume of Byron's verses. Byron was such a romantic rebel, and this was one of the few books her father owned that she could stomach. Shakespeare was just so much gibberish as far as she was concerned.

The door creaked open on its leather hinges, and she heard a loud thump.

"Father?"

No answer. Perhaps he had dropped some firewood on the floor and gone out for another armload. A cold blast of winter air made her shudder. The old fool had left the door open! Vexed, she tossed Byron on the bed and rose to lift apart the two blankets.

Her father lay facedown on the floor, and Bearclaw Johnson stood over him.

"Well, ain't you a purty thing?" leered the mountain man.

Grace screamed.

Bearclaw threw back his head and laughed. His face was an appalling sight, with numerous scars and one black, encrusted, empty eye socket.

Grace shrank back into the corner as he reached for her, wading through her flailing arms as she tried to fend him off, and then she fainted from the horror of it all as his rough, dirty hands clawed at her dress . . . .

Tom Wilkerson healed quickly from the gunshot wound, and as soon as he felt able he began to visit the other cabins on a regular basis. At first Molly objected, not out of fear of being left alone with Edna and Phoebe and Lisle Donaghue, but rather out of concern for her husband's well-being. In the past Wilkerson had always bent over backward to accommodate his wife's wishes, or at least reach a satisfactory middle ground of compromise when her wishes were diametrically opposed to his own. But every now and then he felt so strongly about something that no amount of cajolery on Molly's part could dissuade him from pursuing the course he thought was right. This was one of those times.

He knew she was under a terrible strain, and the last thing he wanted to do was add to her concerns, so he tried to explain to her that it was his responsibility to occasionally check on the others. It had never been formally agreed upon by all concerned, but he was the de facto leader of the company now—or what was left of the company. This had been so even before Hugh Falconer's departure in search of Amos Spellman and the half-breed. Unlike Spellman, Falconer had never sought authority over the emigrants. He had merely served as their guide, subordinating himself to their will, as when he had suggested wintering in this valley. Had they decided to press on for the Oregon Territory he would have tried his level best to get them there even though he knew the risks were great and the chances of successfully crossing the high mountain passes dismally small.

Wilkerson had not sought the mantle of leadership. It had evolved slowly during the company's westward trek, and was well established by the time they reached St. Joe. Every group needed a leader—it gave the group cohesion, and no group, he told Molly, needed cohesiveness more than theirs, especially after everything that had happened. The long and short of it, then, was that he was duty-bound to check on the others from time to time, if for no other reason than to keep them from feeling isolated. They all had to stick together if they hoped to make it to the promised land.

He developed a routine. One day he would call on Lillian Tasker and Clete Norwood at the Norwood cabin, as well as the Pollocks, whose cabin was a couple of miles south. The next day he would strike out further south, to visit the cabin occupied by Lomax, Abney, and Lena Blakemore and her children. Finally he would swing by the Holsberry place. On the third day he would stay home, and on the fourth he would set out for the Norwood and Pollock cabins again, and so on. He rode horseback at first, but the snow became so deep in parts of the valley that before long he had to resort to using a pair of snowshoes he had made.

Though nearly two months had passed since Lillian and Lomax had gotten the best of Bearclaw Johnson, Wilkerson kept a wary eye peeled for the mountain man. Everyone agreed that the man was probably dead, and Wilkerson always appeared to concur, but in his heart he knew they were just indulging in a lot of wishful thinking. The possibility remained that Johnson had crawled off not to die but to recuperate from his wounds. These mountain men were extremely hard to kill. The others desperately wanted to believe that Johnson was dead, so he never shared his doubts with anyone but Lillian, because Lillian had come out and confessed to him that she would not rest easy unless she actually laid eyes on Bearclaw's lifeless corpse. Wilkerson felt the same way.

But he never saw any sign of Bearclaw Johnson, or of anyone else, for that matter. Weeks ago he had given up any hope of seeing Lee Donaghue ever again. The man was dead. Had to be. How or where he died would probably forever remain a mystery. Wilkerson had already begun to think of Lisle as his own daughter. So had Molly. They did not need to talk about it; they both loved children, and their hearts went out to the orphaned girl. They would raise Lisle as their own, with no preference shown to their natural offspring. Edna and Phoebe seemed to be adjusting well to the situation.

In fact, Wilkerson saw very few living things at all as he made his rounds, traipsing from cabin to cabin. Once he saw a deer and killed it with a single shot, butchering it out on the spot and leaving very little for the wolves to quarrel over. The meat he distributed equally among all the others provided a welcome change from a monotonous fare which consisted primarily of biscuits, beans, blackstrap, and smoked meat.

Occasionally he saw the wolf pack, but they never bothered him, and he returned the favor. When he saw them or crossed their trail, he always recalled with amusement Lillian's impassioned defense of the animals, begging him not to shoot at them. As usual, Lillian had been right; the wolves had not been a problem. They hadn't attacked a single mule or ox.

Christmas was coming, and Wilkerson had been urging everyone to congregate at his cabin for the occasion. They would celebrate the birth of their Savior and give humble thanks to Almighty God. Despite their many trials and tribulations, or perhaps because of them, they had much to be grateful for. Bearing in mind the difficulty of getting about out of doors, the Wilkerson cabin, being the most centrally located of the dwellings still inhabited, would be the most logical location.

Having delivered the invitation to the occupants of the Lomax-Abney cabin, Wilkerson was on his way to the Holsberry place when he saw fresh footprints in the snow. An invisible hand clutched his heart and squeezed it. He tried to tell himself that they might have been made by one of the others, but no amount of calm and collected reasoning could temper the dread rising within him. He quickened his pace, and when he saw from a distance that the door to the Holsberry cabin was standing open he abandoned calm reason altogether and rushed forward with his rifle ready.

Doc Holsberry was sprawled just inside the door, and when he saw the blood matting the physician's gray hair and crimson rivulets on the man's face he thought at first that Holsberry was dead. But when he knelt to feel for a pulse, Holsberry groaned and stirred, and Wilkerson praised God. Rising from Holsberry's side, he swept aside the blanket curtain which gave Grace a private corner of the room. Grace was gone. There was clear evidence of a struggle. Worst of all, the girl's dress lay in shreds across the bed.

Wilkerson saw the places on the cabin's hardpack floor where snow from the intruder's feet had melted. This was the only sign left by the man, yet Wilkerson knew without a doubt that Bearclaw Johnson was back.

Chapter Twenty-five

"We'll have to go after him," said Abney.

"He left a trail a blind man could follow," said Wilkerson. "Means he wants us to follow him. That's why he took Grace, too. You see, I think he learned his lesson last time. This way he gets us out of the cabins and up into the mountains."

Taking Doc Holsberry back to his cabin, Tom Wilkerson had paused to tell Lomax and Abney what had happened. Neither man had wanted to believe it was true, but then Holsberry had spoken up for the first time since regaining consciousness. "It's him. I saw him. He came out of nowhere. Seemed to materialize out of thin air like a ghost. But he is flesh and blood, and he took . . . he took my darling Grace . . ." The physician's voice wavered and broke.

"It's a wonder he didn't kill you, Doc," said Lomax.

"I wish he had," muttered Holsberry.

"No," said Wilkerson, "he left you alive for a reason. He let you see him for the same reason. So you could tell us he was back, in case we all believed he was dead."

It was at that point, with manifest reluctance, that Abney said they would have to go after the mountain man. This was the last thing in the world Abney wanted to do, and he was absolutely convinced that neither he nor anyone else would survive the attempt, but one look at poor Doc Holsberry and a man was left in no doubt as to what he had to do, if he was any kind of man at all. Now here was Wilkerson telling them it was a trap.

That bothered Lomax particularly, because he resented Wilkerson for having had the good sense not to go into the mountains with them that first time. Of course, Lomax knew it wouldn't have changed the outcome—Bearclaw Johnson would still have gotten the best of them even with Wilkerson along. And, of course, Wilkerson had been right not to jump to conclusions regarding the identity of the person who had set the bear trap that had cost Clete his foot, and nearly his life. Since then, Wilkerson and Lillian Tasker had informed everyone of what Jake Norwood had done and said, and the evidence was incontrovertible. Jake had done the terrible deed out of jealousy. Still, Lomax was resentful, and it seemed to him now that Wilkerson's caveat might be the man's opening salvo in an attempt to wriggle out of going into the mountains this time, too. As a result, Lomax was thinking very uncomplimentary things about Tom Wilkerson—like maybe the man was an out and out coward.

"What choice do we have?" he asked sharply. "If we don't go up after him, Bearclaw will just come back down here and finish us off. I don't like the idea of chasing after him any more than anybody else does, but somehow we've got to kill that son of a bitch cold stone dead, or we're all doomed."

"We're doomed anyway," muttered Abney. "I've known it all along . . ."

"This is a decision all of us should have a hand in

making," said Wilkerson. "Bring Lena and the children to my cabin. We had better stick together until this is resolved."

No one argued with that bit of reasoning. No sooner had Wilkerson safely deposited Holsberry, Lomax, Abney, and the Blakemores at his place than he was off again to fetch the Pollock's, Lillian and Johnny Tasker, and Clete Norwood. He stopped at the Pollocks' place first and gave them the news, then pushed on to the Norwood cabin. When he informed Lillian that Bearclaw Johnson had kidnapped Grace Holsberry, she did not appear too surprised.

"So, he is alive after all," she said. "I was never truly convinced . . ."

"Lomax and Abney are talking about going up into the mountains again," said Wilkerson. "It's a trap, I'm certain. What are we going to do, Lillian?" He relied on her for common sense advice. She had a way of seeing a matter clearly, of stepping away from it and observing it from all angles and rendering an objective verdict, and he was praying she could come up with a solution this time.

"We need Falconer," she said.

Wilkerson was dismayed. Wishful thinking would avail them nothing. She detected the disappointment on his face and managed a smile.

"Not very helpful, am I, Tom? You know, I had just about decided, after everything we've been through, that there wasn't any crisis we couldn't handle, as long as we stuck together. You, me, and the others, just on our own, even if we never saw Falconer again. I'd convinced myself that if he did not return by spring we could reach the Oregon Territory without him, and I still think that's true, but this . . . this is altogether different. Bearclaw Johnson is no ordinary obstacle to our progress."

"He is a madman," declared Wilkerson. "Why is he doing this? Just because we broke the peace and invaded his precious mountain? My God, Lillian, do we all have to die because we made a mistake? If Johnson is so unbalanced, then I must fault Falconer for having been so foolish as to believe he could strike a deal with such a man, a deal that would stick."

"Maybe Falconer did make a mistake," conceded Lillian.

"Well, it's no good wishing he were here. He's not. Johnson is our problem. Either we deal with him or die." Clearly, by his tone of voice, Wilkerson believed the latter would be the case.

Lillian got her rifle, powderhorn, and shot pouch. She also took a flour sack outside and dug around in the snow behind the cabin until she found the old bear trap where it had been discarded weeks ago. She put the trap in the flour sack.

They placed Clete and Johnny on Ol' Blue's back and headed for the Wilkerson cabin. Clete could get around some indoors, using a crutch fashioned from a forked sapling, but he could not have made much progress in the deep snow. He had not said a word, and did not, until they were nearly to their destination. Then, out of the blue, he said, "I say we just let him have her, and good riddance."

Lillian was leading Ol' Blue—Wilkerson had forged a little ahead and was too far away to hear Clete's muttered remark.

"What did you say?" asked Lillian, certain she had heard him wrong.

"I said we should just let Bearclaw Johnson have her. She ain't worth dying over."

"That's no way to talk, Clete."

"But it's true."

"I thought you were in love with Grace Holsberry."

"I thought so, too. But I've had a lot of time to sit around and think things through, haven't I? She's evil, that one. Pure evil. She's to blame for my pa and Jake being dead. I don't blame Jake for what he did. He was under her spell, same as me."

"Well, you *should* blame him," she replied sternly. "He was responsible for his actions. So are you, Clete. If you did something to turn your own brother against you, you can't very well lay the blame on Grace, not all of it, anyway."

Clete was silent for a long time. Finally, crestfallen, he said, "I did. I bragged about me and Grace, right there in front of him. I wanted him to know. Wanted him to hurt, knowing we'd . . . we'd . . ."

"You'd what?" asked Johnny, riding behind Clete and holding on to him with both arms wrapped around his middle.

"Never you mind, Johnny Tasker," said Lillian. "Listen to me, Clete. Whatever Grace has done, and whatever we might think of her, she doesn't deserve this. And she is one of us, Clete. One of us, for better or worse. Don't you forget that."

Clete drew a long, ragged breath and nodded. "You're right, ma'am. I was wrong. I'll do whatever is in my power to do to get her back."

"We all will," said Lillian.

But would everything in their power be enough this time? Lillian had to wonder. Could they save Grace, or even themselves?

"It has come down to this," was Judd Pollock's grim assessment. "Either we kill Bearclaw Johnson or we're all as good as dead."

They sat or stood around the table in Tom Wilkerson's cabin. Mrs. Pollock and Molly Wilkerson were trying to keep the children entertained, but the anxiety of the adults was a raging contagion within these walls, and the worried expressions on the faces of the young ones deeply troubled Lillian. They also made her angry.

"That man has terrorized us all quite long enough," she declared. "Time we put a stop to it."

"Easier said than done," remarked Lomax. He was remembering his last excursion into Bearclaw's mountains and shuddered at the memories. The fire was blazing in the nearby hearth, but he could not feel its warmth. An icy dread had invaded his bones.

Glancing at Doc Holsberry, who sat at one end of the table with his head in his hands, Wilkerson said, "Our first priority should be getting Grace back safe and sound."

"Which we can't do without killing Johnson," said Lomax.

"God only knows what horrible things he has done to my daughter already," mumbled Holsberry.

Wilkerson knew the torn remnants of Grace's dress were preying mercilessly on Holsberry's mind. Was it true that there were fates worse than death? Wilkerson had a hunch that Bearclaw had left the dress as a kind of motivation, to prey upon a father's darkest fears, and spur the rest of them to rush into his trap, blinded by rage. Perhaps his only interest in Grace was as bait to set that trap. Wilkerson very much wanted to believe this was so, but one could never be sure when dealing with a man so obviously deranged as Bearclaw Johnson. And there was no point in trying to persuade Doc Holsberry that his daughter had not already been brutally ravaged. No amount of reassuring or supposition would counter the image of that torn dress.

"Well," said Pollock, glancing pensively across the

room at his wife and children, "we've got to go, haven't we? No use putting it off."

Lomax looked at Wilkerson. "Are you coming with us this time, Tom?"

Wilkerson nodded. He turned to Clete. "We'll leave everything down here in your hands, Clete."

"I wish I could go with you," said Clete earnestly. "But I know I would just slow you down. You can rely on me, Tom. No harm will come to your family, as long as I'm alive. Or yours, Judd."

Wilkerson put a hand on the young man's shoulder. "I know we can count on you. And Lillian here can outshoot us all, so you'll have help."

"I'm going with you," said Lillian.

"Now listen, Lillian . . ."

"No, Tom. You listen to me. You'll need all the help you can get if you want to win this fight."

Wilkerson shook his head. "Hugh Falconer would have my scalp if I let you go into harm's way." He glanced at Lena Blakemore, who quickly glanced away.

"If he'll be wanting your scalp," said Lomax wryly, "he'll have to take it away from Bearclaw Johnson."

Wilkerson smirked. "Now is this really the time and place for gallow's humor?"

"How do you intend to keep me from going?" Lillian asked.

"She's come closer to killing Johnson than any of the rest of us," said Abney. "One more rifle sure wouldn't hurt, if you ask me."

Wilkerson looked to Judd Pollock for support, but Judd just shrugged. "What are you going to do, Tom? Tie her up and leave Clete stand guard over her until we get back?"

"I ought to. It's not right that a . . ."

"If you say it, Tom, so help me," warned Lillian.

"I may be a woman, but that doesn't mean I can't fight for my son and my friends. So if you say anything about this being no job for a woman, Bearclaw Johnson will be the last of your worries."

Wilkerson had to smile. "To be honest, I'd feel better with you along."

"Let's get if we're going," Judd Pollock sighed. "We've got a few hours of daylight left, and if it snows during the night we could lose the trail."

"This time," said Abney, "we're taking enough provisions for several days."

"We won't be gone too long," predicted Wilkerson. "Clete, if we're not back by the day after tomorrow, you hitch a team of the strongest oxen to the stoutest wagon and get everybody the hell out of this valley, if you can. Head south until you reach the Snake River. Might find some help down there."

Clete nodded grimly. Getting a wagonload of women and children through these mountains in the dead of winter, much less finding help, was a desperate proposition fraught with peril. Even so, it was better than remaining in the valley and waiting on certain death.

Lillian put a hand on Doc Holsberry's arm as Wilkerson and Pollock left the table to say their goodbyes to their families. "You should stay here, Doc," she told him. "You're in no condition to go."

"I'll go," said the physician. "You may need my services before this is done. I would be obliged for the loan of a pistol. I am sure to prove a dismal shot, but I want a weapon, nonetheless. I have dedicated the past thirty years to saving lives, Lillian, but I am going to take a life this time, if I get the chance. Bearclaw Johnson's life. It was Bacon who said that revenge is a kind of wild justice which the law ought to weed out. But there is no law out here, is there? Not even

God's law, so I think I can ignore Romans, Chapter 12, Verse 19, and opt for wild justice."

"I still believe that good will prevail over evil," said Lillian.

"That is what we are going to find out, my dear."

Chapter Twenty-six

Grace Holsberry regained consciousness, shivering violently, in the cave where Bearclaw Johnson had spent weeks of agony recovering from his wounds. The bitter cold cut right through her. Her thin unmentionables, camisole and petticoat, once pretty silk things, were now dirty and torn, and perfectly useless for warmth. Her father had tried to talk her into wearing flannel undergarments, but of course she had rigorously refused. Now she wished she had taken his advice.

She found herself suddenly wishing for many things—now that it was too late. Wishing she had not been so insolent and disrespectful to her father these past weeks, even months. Oh, what was the use? She might as well admit it—she had been sulky and impudent for years, taking perverse pleasure in hurting her father's feelings, and all along he had tried to do only what was best for her, even going to the extreme of forsaking his practice back East to remove her from the scorn of their neighbors, to provide her with a fresh start in the Oregon Territory. Most folks went to Oregon to make a new start for themselves. But not her father. He was making the move entirely for her benefit. *I shall never see Oregon now. I shall never see my poor, sweet father again, either.*

Bearclaw Johnson sat cross-legged near the cave entrance, paying no attention to her, gazing outside, a rifle resting across his knees. *Please let this be a nightmare,* prayed Grace, *and let me wake up safe and sound in my own bed, and I promise I won't be so mean and spiteful and selfish anymore . . .*

But the prayer would avail her nothing, she knew. This was no nightmare, but rather a living hell, and she was paying the price for her innumerable sins. There would be no second chances, never were. A person always reaped what she sowed. She would pay for all the pain and suffering she had inflicted on others with her own pain and suffering, now, and pay tenfold. The fire and brimstone preachers at whose dire warnings she had always scoffed were right after all, except that hell was not somewhere below in the molten bowels of the earth, but here, right here in this dark, cold, smelly cave.

Grace tried to pretend she was still unconscious, trying not to move, but something gave her away—without even turning his head to look at her, Bearclaw grumbled, "Don't even think about tryin' to run off, girly. I'll take a knife to you. Skin the soles of your feet plumb off. Then you won't be goin' nowhere for a long spell."

She sat up, hugging herself, shaking not just from the cold but also because she was afraid. She had never been more afraid.

"I won't try to run away. I'm so c-cold. I just want to g-go home. Please let me go."

He turned his head and leered at her and she looked quickly away, repulsed by the sight of his ruined face.

"Your people will be coming to fetch you home right soon."

She realized then why he had taken her, and shook her head. "No. They won't come. They hate me. All of them. They think I am the cause of all the trouble they've had. And they're right. They won't try to save me and I don't blame them."

"They'll come," insisted Bearclaw. "Ain't got nothin' to do with whether they like you or not."

"Why?" Grace sobbed. "Why are you doing these awful things?"

"No tears, girl. I cain't abide tears. They're a pure waste. One good thing about Injun wimmin. They don't feel sorry for themselves."

"I won't cry," she said, wiping at her cheeks.

Bearclaw nodded. "Good. You know, you're a right purty gal."

Oh dear God. The idea that this man might get a notion to have his way with her made her nauseated, and she almost started crying as his one good eye roamed slowly over her body.

"But you're a mite thin for my taste," he continued. "And I don't care much for white wimmin. That pale skin—they look like dead people. I'll take an Injun gal any day of the week. They know how to take care of a man. You wouldn't last a week up here."

Grace lifted her chin in defiance, his contempt stinging her pride. "Yes I would. I'll . . . I'll make a deal with you, Mr. Johnson. I'll take care of you, I'll do anything you want me to do, if you'll just . . . if you'll just let the others alone."

Bearclaw threw back his head and barked a sharp, ugly laugh. "Now ain't you sumpin! You'd give yourself up for the worthless lives of them that hates you?"

"Yes," said Grace. "At least that way I will have done something right once in my life."

"Huh!" Bearclaw resumed his intense scrutiny of the snow-covered slopes below the cave. For a moment he said nothing more, and Grace thought that perhaps he was giving her proposition serious consideration. Then, gruffly, he said, "No deal. You could never take Sun Falling's place. Never."

"Sun Falling?"

"My wife," snarled Bearclaw with such vehemence that Grace shrank back. "She's dead, thanks to you and yourn."

"I . . . I don't understand."

"She's dead, I tell you. What's to understand? And you're all gonna die, too. Won't be no going home for you, gal."

The bones of the marmot Bearclaw had trapped and eaten raw weeks ago littered the floor of the cave along with those of other small creatures, all picked clean. Snatching up a splintered rib, Grace lunged at the mountain man, intent on driving the sharp-pointed bone into his cruel heart. She didn't come close—with a vicious backhand swipe he sent her sprawling, and before she could recover he was on her, straddling her, and she fought him with a helpless fury. He tore at the camisole, ripping it open, and when his rough hands mauled her breasts she tried to scream. Laughing, Bearclaw cuffed her with a fist, driving her head back against stone, and she slipped gratefully into unconsciousness again.

He stripped her bare. Using fragments of the petticoat, he tied her hand and foot. Returning to the cave entrance, he sat down and used what was left of her undergarments to braid a silken rope, all the while hopefully scanning the slopes below.

Leaving Johnny was the hardest thing Lillian had ever had to do. Harder, even, than watching Hugh Falconer ride away in his search for Spellman and the half-breed just moments after confirming, by merely holding her in his arms, that he reciprocated the feelings she had for him. She wasn't at all sure she would ever see her son again, but she knew she had to do this. The only way to insure Johnny's safety was to kill Bearclaw Johnson, and she was committed to doing just that.

Tom Wilkerson gave her some of his clothes, a woolen shirt, stroud trousers, and a pair of boots she had to stuff with strips of cloth just so her feet didn't come right out of them. Over this she donned her old blanket coat. Actually, it had belonged to Will—the dead husband of another world that seemed so far away, and so different from the one in which she now found herself.

They struck out on foot, she and Tom Wilkerson, Judd Pollock, Doc Holsberry, Lomax, and Abney. She and Tom carried percussion rifles. The others had lost their long guns in their first excursion into the mountains. Now Pollock carried an old smoothbore musket that, he claimed, his father had used fighting right along with old William Henry Harrison during the 1812 war. Doc Holsberry carried a pistol in his medical bag. Abney had a couple of horse pistols, while Lomax brandished the fowling piece provided by Molly Wilkerson. His shooting pouch was filled with bent nails and small pebbles. "I once drew Bearclaw Johnson's blood with this thing," he said, "so maybe I'll get lucky with it again."

Lillian thought they were so brave, and she was immensely proud to have them for friends. None of them honestly believed they had a prayer of prevailing over Bearclaw Johnson, but here they were, just the same. What's more, they were determined to rescue Grace Holsberry, willing to lay down their lives if necessary for the sake of the person they now knew was responsible for much of the tragedy that had befallen them since their arrival in the valley. Truly, these men were cut from heroic cloth. Silly though it seemed to her, Lillian was resolved to do all within her power to make certain no harm came to these men, and she was comforted at the same time by the sure and certain knowledge that they felt likewise where she was concerned. Indeed, she decided, they *were* a family, bonded together by the trials they had endured on the Oregon Trail. They had lost so many members of that family—Ted and Jake Norwood, Lee Donaghue and, God forgive her for even thinking this way, perhaps even Grace Holsberry. Lillian could not bear the thought of losing one more.

They were going on foot; the deep snow, and ice at higher elevations, would make travel by horse and mule not only impractical but dangerous. In addition to their weapons and blankets and all the powder and shot available to them, Wilkerson, Pollock, Lomax, and Abney took turns carrying a burlap sack filled with hastily collected provisions—biscuits, smoked venison, some coffee, a pot and pan, and some sulphur matches in a watertight tin. Doc Holsberry carried his medical bag, while Lillian toted the sack that contained the rusty, bloodstained bear trap.

When they stopped to rest for a few minutes about an hour before sunset, Wilkerson asked her what she was carrying. He had been too preoccupied until now to even notice. Lillian showed them all the trap.

"Now just what do you aim to do with that?" queried Judd Pollock.

"I don't know. I thought it might come in handy, though."

"You never know," said Wilkerson, humoring her.

Pollock shook his head, but said nothing more on the subject. He didn't need to; clearly he could foresee no useful purpose in hauling the bear trap all over the mountains.

As darkness gathered in the valley and enveloped

the lower slopes, Lillian marveled at the sunset colors painting the high snows in shades of red and gold. Indigo blue shadows filled the spaces where the sun's dying rays could not reach. This land, she mused, was one of spectacular beauty, as well as grim brutality. Born of a farmer, and a farmer herself, she valued the land for the bounty her nurturing could produce from it. But she could also appreciate the inherent value of its primitive state, and could understand why men like Hugh Falconer loved this high country so dearly. Or why a man like Bearclaw Johnson would want to keep these mountains all to himself.

They built a fire for warmth and thawed their frozen limbs. No one argued that this might be folly, that it could betray their exact location to Bearclaw Johnson. They wanted to settle accounts with the mountain man once and for all. They were tired of being scared, of not knowing what to expect next, and nothing could be served by delaying the final confrontation.

Tom Wilkerson suggested that the others try to sleep while he stood watch. Though tired, no one could sleep. All night they sat around the fire, huddled in their blankets, half expecting Bearclaw Johnson to come charging out of the darkness at any moment. Yet the mountain man failed to make an appearance. Finally, the long and nerve-wracking night was over. By dawn's first light they cooked some coffee. Lillian forced herself to eat a little something. She didn't have much of an appetite, nor did the others by the looks of it, but she realized her body needed nourishment.

That morning they climber higher. A few hours from their campsite they came to the edge of a mountain meadow. In the middle of the snow-blanketed opening stood the trunk of a lightning-struck tree. And to this dead column of blackened wood was tied by means of a silken rope the nude body of Grace Holsberry.

Doc Holsberry uttered a strangled cry of sheer horror. Dropping the medical bag, he lurched forward, but Wilkerson restrained him.

"Let me go!" cried Holsberry. "Oh dear God, my precious Grace . . ."

"Don't go out there, Doc," said Wilkerson.

"What is it, Tom?" asked Lomax.

Wilkerson was scanning a steep, boulder-strewn slope looming above the meadow.

"I think he wants to draw us out into the open. That way he can pick us off, one by one."

"Must be so," concurred Pollock. "That explains why he's staked her out like she is."

"The bastard," muttered Lomax.

"Look!" exclaimed Abney. "She's still alive!"

Briefly, Grace Holsberry struggled in vain against her bindings. Then she was once more still.

"She hasn't seen us," muttered Pollock. "That's good." He did not want her to see them standing helplessly by while she struggled for her life.

"I must go to her," said Holsberry, still in Wilkerson's strong grasp. "For the love of mercy, Tom, let me go to her."

"It's certain death, Doc, if Bearclaw's up in those rocks."

"I don't care. I can't just stand by while my daughter suffers."

Wilkerson's features clearly betrayed his own anguish. He glanced beseechingly at Lillian.

"We'll be of no use to her dead," said Lillian, her voice hollow, for she thought she might be sentencing Grace Holsberry to die by these words. "We should wait until dark."

"What?" gasped Holsberry. "She is clinging to life as we speak. I doubt she could survive until nightfall."

"Lillian's right," said Wilkerson. "I'm certain Bear-claw Johnson is somewhere up in those rocks yonder, just waiting for us to break cover. I will try to get up there and flush him out before dark."

"Not alone you won't," said Pollock.

Doc Holsberry slumped to the ground, a picture of dejection, and finally Wilkerson released his hold on him and took Lillian aside. "I'm glad you're not insisting on going this time. I would have to do everything in my power to stop you. Not because you're a woman. Because you are a friend."

"Be careful, Tom."

He nodded, and looked away so that she might not see the hopelessness in his eyes. "When night comes maybe you will have a chance of reaching Grace. I pray to God she will still be alive. If so, I know you will get her safely down the mountain. And, Lillian . . . when you see Molly, tell her . . . tell her I love her . . ."

"You will tell her yourself, Tom."

"Yes. Of course." Wilkerson turned away. "Ready, Judd?"

Pollock nodded grimly.

They plunged deeper into the woods, to circle around the high mountain meadow.

Lomax was standing over Doc Holsberry, ready to restrain the physician if he tried again to run to his daughter's side. "We'd better keep a close watch on the doc, Lillian. No telling what he might do."

"You do that," she said, carefully scrutinizing the trees on the far side of the meadow. Abney moved to stand beside her. He was gazing up at the rocky slope.

"You think they have any chance?" he asked. "Tom and Judd, I mean. Any chance of killing Johnson."

"Not up there they won't."

Slow to comprehend, Abney stared at her.

"The one thing Bearclaw Johnson *isn't* is predictable," said Lillian. "I don't think he's up in those rocks at all, Ab, because that's where we expect him to be."

"If not, then . . ."

She recognized the dawning horror in his eyes, and nodded.

"Yes, Ab, I think he's right close."

"Then why in heaven's name did you let Tom and Judd go off on a wild-goose chase?"

Lillian sighed. "Because they have families, Ab. Children who need their fathers. I don't want them to get killed."

Chapter Twenty-seven

Clete Norwood also spent a sleepless night, seated in a chair between the door and window of the Wilkerson cabin, his back to the wall, the rifle laid across his lap. Molly, Lena Blakemore, and Mrs. Pollock and the children got some rest, most of them in blankets on the cold hardpack floor. Gazing at all the women and children in his charge, the burden of responsibility lay heavily on Clete's young shoulders, and that was the reason he could not get a wink of sleep.

He wondered if maybe Bearclaw Johnson hadn't managed to lure Lillian and all the men off into the mountains so that he could slip down into the valley and massacre the women and children. That would be something Johnson, with his twisted, diabolical mind, might well think of. If true, Clete was resolved that harm would come to these people only over his dead body.

So Clete spent the long night with his ears cocked for any telltale sound that would betray someone lurking just beyond the cabin walls. He heard nothing, except the howling of distant wolves, until just before dawn. By then he was so keyed up that he had to wonder if he wasn't hearing things. It sounded like someone walking through deep snow, out front of the cabin. Minutes crawled, and he heard nothing more.

Rising, he went to the shuttered window, removed the wooden plug from the gunslot, and peered outside. He watched until the gray threads of dawn began to pierce the darkness, but in this half light he could make nothing out except an expanse of snow and a distant dark line of trees across the frozen creek.

Molly got up and brewed some coffee, trying to be quiet so as not to wake the others. She smiled wanly at Clete, and he managed a smile in return. Poor Molly, he thought, so afraid she will never see her husband again. A hollow pain swelled up inside Clete as his thoughts turned to his father and brother, cold in their graves. He resolved right then and there to never allow himself to care for another human being as long as he lived. Better, he decided, to live with loneliness than to risk suffering this kind of pain again, the pain of losing a loved one.

It was as Molly brought him a cup of fragrant, just-brewed coffee that Clete heard Ol' Blue whicker. The horse was stabled in the lean-to with Tom Wilkerson's blood bay, out behind the cabin. But that was definitely Ol' Blue whickering. Lillian's horse had a keen nose for trouble. Clete went rigid in his chair, gripping the rifle so hard his knuckles turned white.

"What is it, Clete?" asked Molly.

He shook his head, scarcely daring to breathe, much less speak. Then he heard a thump against the cabin's back wall. The sound nearly made him jump right out of his skin. Molly was unnerved, too. She jostled the coffee, spilling some on her hand. But she dared make no sound, either.

"The horses," whispered Clete, finally. "Somebody's around back near the horses."

"Maybe it's the wolves."

He shook his head. "I heard them a while back. They're at the north end of the valley."

"Who, then? Who could it be?"

Clete heard the edge of panic in her voice, saw the glimmer of it in her eyes, and he fought down his own panic in order to allay her fears, or try to.

"Don't fret, Mrs. Wilkerson. I won't let anything happen to you or yours."

"I know you won't, Clete." Molly tried her best to act reassured. "I know."

There came a tapping on the door.

Clete shot up out of the chair. With a gasp, Molly took a step backward. Across the room Lena Blakemore sat up and, with one glance at Clete and Molly, assumed the worst.

"Oh dear God!" she cried, her voice shrill.

"Quiet!" rasped Clete.

"Is that you, Clete?"

Clete couldn't believe his ears. He knew that soft-spoken voice, with its faint Scottish burr.

"Falconer!"

Clete removed the bar and threw open the door.

Falconer stood there, Hawken mountain rifle cradled in his arm, in his long, trail-grimed, blood-stained capote.

"You've been hurt!" exclaimed Molly.

"Some ways back," replied Falconer, stepping across the threshold. "It healed up on the trail." His dark, concerned gaze swept the cabin and its occupants. Then he noticed the way Clete was leaning on his rifle for support, and his eyes traveled downward, to where the bottom of Clete's stroud trouser leg had been tied in a knot.

"I see you've had some trouble while I've been away," said the mountain man. Coming into the valley, he had been alarmed to find the southernmost cabins empty.

Lena was on her feet. She came to Falconer and

threw her arms around his neck. "Falconer! You've come back!"

"I said I would." He gently but firmly disengaged himself. "Where's Lillian?"

Lena Blakemore took a step back as though he had slapped her.

"She's gone," said Clete. "Gone with Tom and Judd, Lomax and Abney, and the doc."

"Gone where?"

"To kill Bearclaw Johnson. He kidnapped Grace Holsberry."

"So much has happened," sobbed Molly. She was crying softly now, because her relief at seeing the mountain man again had released the floodgates of pent-up emotions. Now everything would turn out all right. She no longer had to be brave. "Clete's father and brother are dead. So is Lee Donaghue," she added with a pitying glance across the room at Lisle, who sat with Edna and Phoebe clinging to her on either side.

"It started not long after you left," said Clete.

"Tell me later," said Falconer. He took a pouch from his belt and handed it to Lena Blakemore. He said not a word. Nor did she as she took it. The gold coins contained in the pouch rang richly together.

Then he was gone.

At first Bearclaw Johnson was pleased with the way things were working out.

On the other side of the high mountain meadow he saw the six from the valley pause at the verge of the opening when they spotted Grace Holsberry tied to the lightning-struck tree. He was a little disappointed that they did not rush out into the meadow to save her; he figured he could have killed most if not all of them right then and there, had they done so. But he hadn't really expected them to be so rash. Sodbusters were stupid, but not *that* stupid.

When he saw two of the men leave the others to skirt the meadow he knew where they were going—up into the rocks, where they thought he must be hiding. That was what he *had* expected of them. With only one eye he could not identify the two brave souls, and that bothered him some. Not that it mattered in the long run. The fools had split up, just as he had hoped they would. *I'll kill these four down here first,* he thought. *Then I'll get rid of the other two. And then, if she ain't already dead, I'll cut the girl's throat and head on down into the valley to finish up.*

What did bother Bearclaw was that he couldn't figure out who the sixth man was. He had counted on there being only five capable of making the climb. Surely that Norwood boy, the one who had lost his foot in the bear trap, couldn't be part of this group. So who the blue blazes was the sixth man? *Damn but I must be getting old. Used to be I could see better'n most with both eyes closed.*

Lying half buried in the snow, Bearclaw Johnson watched the four who remained on the other side of the meadow. After a couple of hours he began to grow impatient. He fairly itched to shed blood. Sun Falling's anguished soul was crying out to him, a lonely wanderer lost in limbo. He could hear those cries plain as day. In fact, they had been getting louder and louder. Gotten so he couldn't even sleep. The only way to free Sun Falling's soul from dark purgatory, thereby stilling her cries for vengeance, was to kill these people. *Then I will rest from my labors and wait for Hugh Falconer, who will seek his own terrible vengeance at my expense.*

He couldn't believe these people were going to leave that poor little half-dead naked girl hanging out there on that tree all day. Sure, it made sense to wait until dark before trying to rescue her. Only they ought to know better than to think he was going to let any of them live that long. And the girl's father had to be one of them. How could he refrain from rushing to save her, regardless of the risks? Only one possible answer. They were cowards, every last one of them. Bearclaw hated them all the more for being yellow. *Maybe they should have brought that woman along. The one that shot me and nearly sent me to hell. Now that one had grit.*

Bearclaw decided to slip around the rim of the meadow and get closer, so he could better see what those four lowlanders were up to. He didn't want to wait too long. By now those other two were up in the rocks, and eventually they would realize he wasn't up there, where he belonged.

He got within a hundred yards of them and, of course, the fools had no idea he was so close. Such men, mused Bearclaw contemptuously, were unsuited to life on the frontier. *If I don't kill them now something else will before another year is out.* Hugh Falconer had said they were the bravest folks he had ever known. Obviously ol' Hugh was not the judge of character he had once been.

Three of the men were close together in a dense clump of trees. The fourth had found a good spot between two more trees, some distance from the others. Bearclaw could not see much of the fourth man—part of a blanket coat, the brim of a hat, the barrel of a gun. They all seemed to be watching the girl tied to the lightning-struck tree. Watching her die from exposure to the cold. Bearclaw shook his head. Such cowardly men did not deserve to live.

Wincing, he put a hand to his head, palm against temple, and pressed as hard as he could. Sun Falling's murdered soul was screaming now. *I can't wait any longer,* thought Bearclaw. *I just can't.*

He moved closer. At fifty yards he stopped again, brought the rifle stock to his shoulder, and drew a bead on the fourth man, the one stationed apart from the others. He aimed dead center at the blanket coat, squeezed the trigger. Bearclaw knew he had hit his mark before the powdersmoke cleared. As the rifle's report shattered the wintry stillness, he broke into a run, a Ute war cry on his lips.

Running full tilt, he weaved through the trees, and even though two of the other three men fired at him they could not hit him, and the war cry became a laugh of pure exultation welling up from the depths of Bearclaw's own tortured soul to ring against the stern granite crags piercing the azure sky, a sound as primeval as the howl of the wolf and the scream of the eagle.

With reloaded rifle in one hand and pistol in the other he closed in on the sodbusters, firing at almost point-blank range—at the one called Lomax with the long gun, at the one named Abney with the short. Both men went down. Spinning, Bearclaw saw the girl's father, the old man, his face very drawn and pale, standing like a duelist in the snow, aiming a pistol at him. The pistol spat flame. Bearclaw accepted the bullet into his body with a bloodcurdling growl that didn't sound at all human. The bullet hit him high in the chest, but what was a little more pain? *They can't stop me. No one can stop me until I have finished what I set out to do.*

He swung the rifle like a club. The stock shattered against the old man and knocked him to the ground. Facedown in the snow, he lay still. Bearclaw moved on in great loping strides for the two trees close together where the fourth man was located. He hadn't stirred, so Bearclaw figured him for dead, but wanted to make sure. He grabbed the man, threw him violently to the ground, and just as his startled mind registered that the hat and blanket coat were being worn by a length of rotten log, the steel jaws of the bear trap came leaping out of the snow and closed around his leg.

Bearclaw's roar of rage and pain seemed to shake the very mountains.

He fell writhing in the snow, snarling like a wild animal. Groping at the trap, trying without success to separate the jaws that tore so deeply into his flesh that he could feel them gnawing at the bone, he saw a figure darting across the meadow toward the lightning-struck tree.

Spittle leaked from his gaping mouth as he stared. It was the woman—the Tasker woman.

Lillian Tasker had been crouched in the snow fifty yards from where the others had bravely waited for Bearclaw Johnson. All she had on now were Tom's woolen shirt and stroud trousers and the too-big boots, and the cold cut right through her. The cold and the fear had her shivering uncontrollably. She had seen it all and now, as she raced for the tree and Grace Holsberry with a knife in one hand and a blanket in the other, the tears came to her eyes. Abney, Lomax, Doc Holsberry—all had fallen before Bearclaw Johnson's terrible onslaught. Were any of them still alive? She had had some slim hope that they might somehow kill the mountain man. After all, they had known he was coming. But he had dealt with them in a matter of seconds, in a whirlwind of shocking violence.

She heard Bearclaw's snarling roar of outrage, but she dared not look back. As soon as the trap snapped shut she had broken cover and begun to run for all she was worth. She didn't know how many guns Bearclaw carried or whether, if he had one loaded and ready to fire, he could shoot her down even with those steel jaws chewing at his leg. Most men would be rendered completely helpless in Bearclaw's situation. But he was no ordinary man.

She reached the lightning-struck tree. The knife's blade severed the braided silk, and Grace pitched limply forward into the snow. For an awful moment Lillian thought she must be dead. Her lips were blue, and her skin had a strange, translucent quality, like milkglass. But the shock of falling into the snow revived Grace. Half conscious, she seemed not to recognize Lillian at first. But as Lillian knelt beside her, Grace uttered a small cry of joy. Sobbing, she threw her arms around Lillian's neck.

"No time for tears now," Lillian said sternly. "Can you walk?"

"I—I don't know."

"You must try." Lillian put the blanket around Grace's shoulders. "If we're to live we must hurry."

She helped Grace to her feet. Only then did she dare look back toward the trees where Bearclaw Johnson had been wrestling with the trap.

The breath caught in her throat.

Bearclaw was coming toward her across the meadow, dragging his leg, trap and all, leaving a trail of blood in the snow.

Could nothing stop this man?

"Damn you!" screamed Lillian, furious even though she was scared out of her wits. "Damn you to hell!"

Bearclaw kept coming, slowly, inexorably.

"Run, Grace. Run!" With a firm grip on the girl's hand, Lillian headed in the direction of the boulder-strewn slope. Tom Wilkerson and Judd Pollock were up there somewhere. Perhaps they could see down into the meadow. Surely they had heard the gunfire. They were bound to be coming to help.

When they reached the trees, Lillian looked back a second time. Bearclaw was passing the lightning-struck tree, halfway across the meadow by now. He wasn't moving very fast—at least the trap was slowing him down. Lillian realized they could probably outdistance him. Even as she allowed herself to hope, she watched in horror as Bearclaw raised the pistol, aiming it at them. She hurled Grace to the ground and covered the girl's body with her own. The bullet passing over them made a loud and unnerving crackling noise.

"Come on, Grace," said Lillian, a sudden and deliberate calm overtaking her, "we must keep going."

"I can't . . . I can't go any further . . ."

"You must!"

"Lillian, save yourself."

"No!" Lillian wrenched Grace to her feet. But Grace could no longer stand on her own accord. Realizing this, Lillian positioned herself so that as Grace slumped helplessly forward she fell across her shoulder. Carrying Grace in this manner, Lillian plunged deeper into the trees.

She didn't manage to get very far before her knees began to buckle. Grace weighed as much or more than she did, and the snow was even deeper here, having collected in drifts beneath the trees. *Dear God give me strength!* When she thought she could go not a step further, she did so anyway by a supreme exercise of will. Straight ahead she could see a jumble of large rocks at the base of the slope. She staggered toward them, the breath wheezing in her throat.

But she just couldn't make it. Falling, she scarcely had the strength to lift her face out of the snow. Grace was unconscious. *I won't give up. I won't!* Crawling now, she tried to drag Grace along behind her. If they could only reach the rocks. Maybe they could find a place to hide where Bearclaw couldn't find them. She knew in her heart this wasn't likely; there seemed to be no escaping Bearclaw Johnson. He was the devil incarnate. He was the grim reaper in human form. He would find them, and kill them, but still it seemed vitally important to reach those rocks, as though just getting there was a victory in and of itself.

"Lillian."

She looked up to see Hugh Falconer standing there.

He dropped to one knee and set aside the Hawken rifle and she tried to get up but couldn't manage and just fell into his arms. His arms—those strong, wonderful arms she had missed so much—went around her, and she knew no harm would befall her here, in these arms.

"I love you," he said, saying what he had not been able to say the last time they were together, and he felt her warm tears on his face.

Chapter Twenty-eight

Bearclaw Johnson had vanished again.

Tom Wilkerson and Judd Pollock reached the base of the slope to find Lillian holding Grace close, trying to share her body's warmth with the half-dead girl. Grace was wrapped snugly in Falconer's woolen capote. Falconer stood over them, the Hawken cradled in his arms, apparently impervious to the cold, clad now only in his buckskins. His expression was grave, as in response to their anxious queries he informed them that Bearclaw was nowhere to be found. Their hearts sank at the news.

"He must be killed," said Wilkerson. "Never in my life have I ever wished anyone dead, but no one is safe as long as that man is alive."

Falconer nodded. "This time he can't help but leave a trail."

Wilkerson glanced wearily at Pollock. "We're going to have to track him down, Judd, and finish this."

Pollock agreed. "Let's get it done," He sighed.

"No," said Falconer. "I'll go alone."

He glanced at Lillian, and saw the concern in her eyes.

"He's badly hurt, Lillian. The outcome is not in doubt. But I should be the one to do this. He and I are . . . old acquaintances." Falconer turned to Wilkerson. "I'll rely on you to get them back down to the valley, Tom. I'll join you there shortly."

"What about Lomax and the others?" Pollock asked Lillian. "We heard shooting, but couldn't see what was happening in the trees from way up yonder." He tilted his head in the direction of the rocky slope. "Then we saw you running across the meadow, and Johnson after you."

"I fear they may all be dead," said Lillian.

"We better go find out," said Wilkerson grimly.

He handed his rifle to Pollock and lifted Grace in his arms. Falconer helped Lillian to her feet.

"I can walk," she said with a smile.

He let her go, knowing it was a matter of pride. She put an arm around his waist, and side by side they crossed the high meadow, following Wilkerson, with Pollock bringing up the rear.

They were nearly to the trees when Doc Holsberry and Abney came stumbling out into the open, supporting one another. Abney's shirt and coat were soaked with blood.

"Is she . . . ?" Holsberry stared in horror at his daughter's limp form in Wilkerson's strong arms.

"She's alive, Doc. Just unconscious."

Holsberry took her hand with both of his and squeezed it, too moved to speak.

"What about Lomax?" asked Pollock bluntly, fearful of the truth.

Abney shook his head. He also could not bring himself to say a word.

They moved back into the trees. A fire was built, snow melted in the pot, and coffee boiled. Holsberry wanted to get some warm fluids into his daughter as quickly as possible. A blanket was cut into pieces, and these were wrapped about her hands and feet. Then Holsberry turned his attention to Abney, though the latter insisted he did not need to be fussed over. Bear-claw's bullet had put a nasty hole in his side, but it had passed clean through, and Holsberry, working out of his medical grip, applied sulphur powder and then a tight, clean dressing.

Hunkered down near the fire, they drank the coffee. Lillian and Falconer shared a cup. There were so many things she wanted to tell him—how much she loved him, and how much she had missed him, and how she never wanted to be apart from him for one more day. Instead, she sat close beside him and silently relished every minute of their being together. It was enough that she had him now, at this very moment, loving her the way she loved him, with a love perhaps too deep and abiding for mere words.

"Reckon we'd best bury Lomax right here," said Pollock. "We'll have our hands full getting down the mountain as it is." He glanced compassionately at Grace.

"I'm so terribly sorry, Ab," said Lillian.

Abney nodded his appreciation. Stricken, he murmured, "I'm going to open that store in the Oregon Territory, come hell or high water. That's what he wanted. For years that was all he dreamed about. And he'll have it, I swear. Lomax & Abney—that's how the place will be known."

"We're burning daylight," said Pollock. "Let's get a move on."

He and Wilkerson used knives and rifle butts to excavate a hole in the snow, down to the frozen ground. Much effort was required from that point on, but at length they had managed to dig a shallow grave. Wrapped in a blanket, Lomax was laid to final rest. Wilkerson said a few words and then Abney stepped forward to say a few more.

"George Lomax was my good friend. That was his

first name. George. He didn't much care for it, and never used it unless he had to, I don't know why. Maybe because George was his father's name, too, and they did not get along. He told me his father used to drink too much, and would beat his wife and children without mercy when he was under the influence. So I will call him Lomax, as I always did, out of deference to his wishes.

"Might have seemed like, at times, that Lomax and I hated each other's guts. He was a forthright and outspoken man, a man of strong opinions, and powerful likes and dislikes. He was always strong in his opposition to my drinking even a little, on account of he had seen the damage whiskey can do to a man. We were equal partners, but he always gave the orders, and I let him, because for one thing he was usually right, and for another he did not want to entrust his future to a man who relies as I do on John Barleycorn, and who can blame him for that? But when times got bad you could always count on him. He would never let you down. I reckon that's plain by what's happened here today. Here he lies, having given his life to save another's. I'm sure he was right proud to do it, as I am right proud of him for having done it. I only hope I can run our store half as well as he could have. That's all I've got to say."

Falconer walked over to Abney and put a hand on his shoulder. "That was well said. No man had a better eulogy. I for one have no doubt you will prosper in the Oregon Territory, Ab."

"I'll second that," said Judd Pollock.

As they began to disperse, Wilkerson turned to Falconer. "I just remembered why you've been away for so long. Did you . . . did you find Amos Spellman?"

"I did. The breed, as well. He's dead. Amos Spellman is in a Santa Fe jail. I suspect it will be a good long while before he breathes free air again. And there's fifteen hundred dollars in gold waiting for you down below. I left it with Lena Blakemore. I'll trust you to divvy it up amongst yourselves in accordance with your losses."

"Fifteen hundred dollars!" exclaimed Wilkerson. "In gold! But how . . . ?"

"A long story. I'd rather wait until later to tell it. Right now I'd best go attend to Bearclaw."

With a glance at Lillian, who stood at Falconer's side, Wilkerson nodded and turned away.

"You were very brave today," Falconer told her when the others were out of earshot.

"I was very scared."

"That's what I mean. Scared, but still able to do what had to be done."

She put her arms around him and laid her head against his chest. She could hear the slow, measured beats of his strong and noble heart. "But I'm tired of being brave, or scared," she sighed. "I just want to be safe, for a change."

"You will be safe."

"Do you have to go? Oh, I shouldn't have asked. I know you must. But please be careful."

"He's almost done for, Lillian."

"Don't underestimate him."

Reluctantly, he freed himself from her embrace. "I'll be back in a day or two."

"I'll be waiting," she said as he turned away, and she watched him go, loving him with all her heart and soul while knowing there would be no holding him. Truly happy, and yet deeply saddened. Perhaps there was no way to separate happiness from melancholy—a person could not have one without the other.

* * *

The deep snows forced Falconer to leave the Appaloosa a quarter-mile downslope from the mountain meadow. He pressed on afoot, following Bearclaw Johnson's trail—a trail easy to follow, as Bearclaw was losing a lot of blood. Falconer doubted he would be long in catching up. But in this he was mistaken. Bearclaw's resilience surprised him. Higher into the mountains Bearclaw climbed, even higher toward the timberline. When darkness fell, Falconer had still not found his prey.

He saw the fire from some distance away and realized that it blazed like a beacon from the granite spur where, months ago, he had built his own fire to summon Bearclaw. Now Bearclaw was summoning him. Falconer climbed resolutely higher, aided by the light of an early moon in the star-spangled sky. The temperature plummeted, and without his capote he began to suffer from the bitter cold.

Reaching the stone outcropping, he advanced cautiously through the stunted junipers, making no more sound than a ghost. Eventually he could see the fire, and the bulky shape of Bearclaw Johnson sprawled next to it. Falconer moved cautiously closer. Still, Bearclaw did not move, though Falconer was sure that if he yet lived he knew by now that he was not alone. Then, abruptly, Bearclaw sat up. Falconer swung the Hawken around to bear, aiming the rifle at him, and Bearclaw chuckled, coughed, and hawked up some blood, which he spat into the flames.

"No, I ain't dead yet," said Bearclaw. "Now don't be bashful, Hugh. Warm your bones at my fire."

Falconer sat on his heels across the blaze from Bearclaw, glancing at the trap still clamped to Johnson's mangled leg.

"Need some help getting that thing off?" he queried.

"Leave it be."

Falconer's gaze swung to Bearclaw's ruined face. Johnson grinned.

"I ain't as purty as I once was, am I, Hugh?"

"You've done some damage yourself, Bearclaw."

"They come up here to spill my blood, Hugh. Accused me of sumpin I didn't do. I kilt one of 'em. Had to. He warnt gettin' down off my mountain till one of us was dead. But I did let the rest of 'em go, on account you spoke so highly of their worthless hides. That was my mistake. 'Cause when I got home I found Sun Falling dead. One of your sodbusters did the deed. Didn't know which one, so I decided I had to kill 'em all."

"Even the women and children?"

Bearclaw nodded. "I know what you want, Hugh. You want to shoot me. You're mad as hell. I can tell. You get real quiet when you're mad. Go ahead. I'm a gone beaver anyhow. But then you might ought to save your powder."

"You should blame me, not them. I was the one who brought them here."

"Mebbe. But you warn't here to blame." Bearclaw looked about him at the silver blue moonlight on the snow-covered slopes. "God, but I do love this country, Hugh. Mebbe I love it too damned much. I'm right glad I ain't gonna live to see it overrun by them vermin."

"They have as much right to the land as we do."

Bearclaw grunted, a skeptical sound. "What you gonna do? Take up plow-pushing?"

"I don't know."

"Soon there won't be a place for you in this world, hoss." With a heavy sigh Bearclaw lay back down. "Put another log on the fire. It's a mite cold tonight."

Falconer went back into the trees, returning a moment later with an armful of wood. He added a few stout sticks to the fire. Bearclaw Johnson's one good eye was shut. His breathing was ragged. Falconer knew he was nearly gone. He sat down to await the end.

An hour or so later Bearclaw stirred. "Quit your bawlin'," he muttered, his eye still closed. "I done the best I could, and it was the worst I ever done. I'm comin' . . . I'm right with you . . ."

Those were Bearclaw Johnson's last words, for sometime in the early hours of the morning he died. When dawn began to roll back the night shadows, Falconer rose from beside the ashes of the dead fire. He checked Bearclaw for a pulse and, finding none, left the man where he lay.

Late that afternoon he knocked on the door to the Norwood cabin. Johnny answered, opening the door just enough to peek outside.

"Hello, boy," said Falconer. "Mind if I winter here?"

Johnny looked solemnly at his mother, who stood in the middle of the cabin, watching him with a strange intensity. Then he swung the door open wide.

"I don't mind," he said.

Lillian smiled as Falconer crossed the threshold.

Epilogue

Clete Norwood gathered up his belongings and moved in with the Wilkerson's, claiming that the memories were too strong and painful for him to remain in the place where he had spent the last hours with his father and brother, buried now, side by side, beneath the trees down along the creek. Lillian knew there was another reason; Clete felt like he was in the way, with Hugh Falconer having moved in. Like all the others, save Lena Blakemore, Clete accepted the fact that Lillian and the mountain man were a "couple," and even approved of the arrangement.

Johnny accepted this, too, though his approval was slow in coming. With Johnny there were good days and not-so-good days, but through it all Falconer handled an extremely difficult—and, for him, novel—situation with tact and patience. Occasionally he took Johnny out hunting or exploring, beginning the long process of teaching the boy everything he knew about survival in the wilderness—which was everything there was to know. Sometimes, at night, as they gathered around the fireplace after dinner, and after Lillian had read aloud a chapter or two from the Bible, or a little out of the well-worn volume of Shakespeare that Falconer owned, the mountain man would tell Johnny a story culled from his many adventures in the high country, or relate to the boy what he knew of legendary figures like Jim Bridger and "Broken Hand" Fitzpatrick.

Lillian knew how difficult the adjustment would be for her son. Johnny still missed his father and, of course, would always love him very much. He was afraid that if his mother loved another she would forget his pa. It took time, but Lillian eventually convinced him that this was not so, and Johnny, seeing that she was happier than she had ever been in his memory, finally came around.

Falconer remained the perfect gentleman. He had moved into the cabin, but not into Lillian's bed. Even though Lillian wanted him so much it hurt, she knew this was the only way, for Johnny's sake if for no other reason. It would make no difference to Tom and Molly and Judd and the others. They were like family. But Lillian had to wonder about the future. They couldn't go on like this forever. Yet Falconer never broached the subject of marriage, and Lillian was afraid to. The future was uncertain and worrisome, not just for that reason, but because she and Falconer came from two entirely different worlds, and one of them would have to give up the life they knew and adjust to living in the other's world. Lillian preferred to postpone the day of reckoning for as long as possible. Happiness and sadness being two sides of the same coin, she did not have the courage to flip that coin and let it fall where it may.

Romance blossomed in another part of the valley, as well. A change had come over Grace Holsberry since her harrowing ordeal as Bearclaw Johnson's captive. No more did she sulk about the cabin, or strive to make her father's life a living hell. Now she did her level best to make Doc Holsberry as happy as she could. And she spent a lot of time nursing Abney back to health. As the weeks went by, and Abney recovered from the gunshot wound, Grace virtually set up house in the cabin he had once shared with Lomax. Lena Blakemore and her children had moved back to the cabin Falconer had built for them, and it got so that Holsberry began to concern himself with the propriety of his daughter spending so many hours in the abode of a bachelor. Abney never made any untoward advances, of course, but still . . . Considering what had happened in the past, it was a subject about which Holsberry was very sensitive.

Finally he turned to Lillian for advice. Lillian had made up her mind to attend to her own business and stay out of Abney's, but she informed the physician that she could make no comment regarding the situation until she had seen it with her own eyes. So, one day in early February, she paid a call on Abney. She was not surprised to find Grace there. She *was* surprised to see how clean and orderly the cabin was. She knew Abney well enough to realize this could not be his doing. Visiting for a couple hours, she took her leave and reported back to Holsberry.

"Ab and your daughter are deeply in love, Doc. I shouldn't be surprised if they don't marry as soon as they reach the Oregon Territory."

Doc Holsberry was flabbergasted. Grace had never been in love with anyone but herself. Could this be true? Lillian was sure that it was. There could be no mistaking the way Grace had looked at Abney. Convinced of Grace Holsberry's conversion, Lillian was glad for Abney, who deserved the happiness a good woman could bring a man. She was confident he and Grace would prosper in Oregon.

Oregon. That was all the others ever talked about as winter drew finally to a close. The going would not be easy, but they were sure they would make it to their destination with no further mishaps. Even Abney was optimistic, for a change. The nightmare was over, the worst behind them. The frontier has tested them. It had bled them, and they had lost some of their number, but as always the strong survived.

The promised land called to them with its siren song, and as the days slowly but inexorably warmed, and the snow gradually withdrew from the lowlands, and the creeks gamboled down their stony courses and, full of snowmelt, occasionally jumped their banks. The game returned to the valley. Bearing witness to all of this, the emigrants felt the blood in their veins quicken with anticipation. Repairs were made to the overland wagons, harnesses and canvas tarpaulins. A makeshift smitty was built, and Clete brought out his blacksmithing tools; new braces and rims and shoes for some of the livestock were fashioned from the old. Everyone worked with enthusiasm, eager to be on their way. Tom Wilkerson kept asking Falconer when it would be time to go. The mountain man judged when the high passes which lay ahead of them would be clear of snow sufficiently to permit wagon passage. Six weeks, he said. Four weeks. A fortnight.

Unlike the others, who could barely restrain themselves to wait for the nod from Falconer that would mean they were leaving the valley at long last, Lillian wished that she could make time stand still. In the past, spring had always been her favorite time of the year, when the world blossomed with new life and promise. But now she hated to see the ice and snow depart the valley, for their going marked the coming of the moment of truth she had hoped to postpone forever, the moment she and the man she loved would have to consider their future plans.

Lillian awoke one morning to find Falconer saddling the Appaloosa. Fear struck deep like a dagger in her heart. She could not bring herself to ask him where he was going or when—if—he would return. She looked so forlorn, standing there in the cabin doorway, that he took her in his arms and held her close.

"I'll be back, Lillian," he said. "I've just got some thinking to do, and I think best when I'm in the saddle."

She nodded mutely, put on a brave face, and waved to him as he steered the Appaloosa across the creek and into the woods.

Later that day Tom Wilkerson showed up. He was disappointed in having missed Falconer, for he had wanted to confirm that the mountain man was going to lead them west the day after tomorrow. But when he saw the mask of silent misery on Lillian's face he forgot all about himself.

"That long face has something to do with Falconer, doesn't it?" he asked, trying to coax the truth out of her.

She nodded. "I am afraid that I shall lose him, Tom. You told me once he was a wild spirit, as impossible to catch as the wind. That he wasn't cut out to be a farmer. Well, you're right. He knows it, too."

"I shouldn't worry, if I were you. You love him, don't you?"

"With all my heart. I would be lost without him. I think that somehow I knew he was the man for me the moment I first saw him."

"The mistake people make," said Wilkerson, "is that they try to change the people they love. Don't try to change him, Lillian. For one thing, you won't succeed. If you love him, change yourself. Do what you must to keep him."

Deep in thought, Lillian got up and poured them some coffee. When she sat back down at the table across from him, Wilkerson saw that the troubled frown was gone from her face. Her hazel eyes sparkled with a firm resolve.

"You're right, Tom. I will do as you suggest. But it will mean I cannot go on to the Oregon Territory."

"What? But I thought . . . You had your heart set on Oregon, Lillian."

"I thought that was what I wanted. But I see now that it isn't. I've found what I want, right here in these mountains."

"But what about Johnny?"

"He will have a father again. That is something every child desperately needs. Johnny will have the best of both worlds. Hugh will teach him all about the land and how to survive in it. I will make sure he gets the book learning he requires."

"Will you stay here, in this valley?"

Lillian shook her head. "I think of all our friends who are buried here, and in a way I hate to leave them behind. But no, I will find a more likely place, perhaps on the Snake River. In the years to come many thousands more will be coming this way. They will need a safe place to rest and reprovision. I will give them such a place."

"And you will make a great success of it, I have no doubt."

She put her hand over his. "You've been a true friend, Tom. The truest I've ever had. I will miss you. All of you."

"And I you." Deeply moved, Wilkerson gulped down the rest of his coffee and got up from the table. "I'd best be getting back."

"I'll come say good-bye to Molly and the children tomorrow."

"Oh, I almost forgot." At the door he turned and took a leather pouch from his coat pocket. "This is for you."

"What is it?"

"Some of the gold Falconer brought back."

"No, Tom, I couldn't. I didn't lose any money . . ."

"We don't want any more than we lost, and after we divvied it up there was some left over. We all agreed, we want you and Falconer to have it. I knew he wouldn't take it. I hope you will. Please."

Lillian took the pouch. "Thank you."

He nodded and beat a hasty retreat while he could still cling to the tattered shreds of his composure.

Late that afternoon Falconer returned. Lillian met him as he swung down off the Appaloosa. "I have something to tell you," she said, taking him by the hand with the sweetest smile he had ever seen and leading him inside.

Lillian's decision presented Falconer with a fresh dilemma. He did not want to leave her and Johnny alone, but he had set out to take the others to the Oregon Territory and he was obliged to finish what he had started. She told him to go on, and not to worry.

"But I'll be gone until midsummer, at least," he said.

"And we'll be waiting for you when you get back."

In the end he did not have to leave them alone. Hearing of Lillian's decision, Clete Norwood decided to stay, too. He would set up a blacksmith shop at the outpost Lillian had it in mind to establish. In that way he would not be so far from the graves of his father and brother. Falconer felt better knowing Clete would remain behind. Though crippled, the young man had a valiant heart.

The day of departure dawned with five overland wagons ready to roll, the Wilkersons in one, the Pollocks in another, Lena Blakemore and her children in a third, the Holsberrys in a fourth, and Abney driving the fifth loaded to the gills with merchandise for his store.

"There is a missionary up in the Flathead country," Falconer told Lillian as he took his leave. "Reverend Gray. I met him some years ago at rendezvous. I will bring him back with me."

Lillian laughed with joy. "Are you proposing, Hugh Falconer?"

"Reckon I am." He grinned. "Fact is, I've been sleeping on hard ground for twenty years now, and I'm suddenly getting right tired of it."

She gave him a long, lingering kiss full of passion and promise.

"You'll have a nice soft bed waiting for you when you get back," she said.

He rode away, turning once to wave. Lillian waved back. So did little Johnny, standing beside her. This time Lillian knew she would see him again. Of that she had no doubt. And that night, sitting by the fireplace, with the star pattern quilt her mother had made over her legs to fend off the evening chill, she listened to the howling of the wolf pack on the moonlit slopes, and her smile was one of rare contentment, for she knew she had found at last the promised land.

1

Delgado McKinn was awakened by the shrill keening of the riverboat's steam whistle.

Sitting up too quickly, he winced at the stabbing pain in his head. It felt as though a stiletto of white-hot steel had been thrust through his temples. Too much cognac. He smiled ruefully. Ten dollars a bottle, imported from France. How much had he consumed? He could not remember—obviously more than he should have.

Guilt promptly insinuated itself, made him feel worse still. His father would have sternly disapproved of his actions last night. Angus McKinn was descended from Scottish Covenanters who made Quakers look like libertines. He viewed any form of recreation as a sign of moral weakness, indicative of a shameful proclivity towards self-indulgence. Ceaseless work was the only justification for man's presence on earth. Delgado admired his father, and the last thing he ever wanted to do was disappoint him. And Angus McKinn would most certainly have been disappointed had he known of his son's promiscuity. Getting drunk and gambling at cards! Devil's work!

Delgado swung long legs off the bed and groaned as the well-appointed stateroom began to spin. He closed his eyes and ran long fingers through tousled hair as black as a crow's wing, kneading his scalp. If a man took his pleasure, he had to endure the pain.

There was always a price to be paid. At least, mused Delgado, I did not lose.

Fortunately, from his standpoint, the game had been whist. He would not have fared so well, perhaps, at poker or keno. Three gentlemen had been looking for a fourth, and Delgado had just happened to be passing by their table in the grand saloon. They were Messrs. Horan, Wheeler, and Sterling. Horan, a planter's son. Pale, angular features. A full, selfish mouth. Pale blue eyes. Pale hair that curled down over his forehead in stubborn resistance to a generous application of pomatum. Wheeler, stocky, with a pleasant kind of bluff pugnacity, a jowly face framed by prodigious muttonchop whiskers, a loud, braying voice, a St. Louis merchant with an expert's grasp of the Mississippi River commerce down to its most intimate and obscure details, and a wealthy man as a consequence of this expertise. Sterling, thin as a rapier's blade, and with a wit as sharp as the tip of a duelist's sword, cool and collected at all times, impeccable in dress and manners, although early on Delgado had detected in him a streak of misanthropy. A newspaper editor. Delgado could not recall the name of the newspaper.

He had been fortunate to be paired with Sterling, a polished and utterly ruthless player. Wheeler proved too predictably straightforward in his play—whist was a game best played with guile. Horan was a daring player, and had fared well enough in the early going, but he hated to lose, which he had begun to do as the night wore on. The more he lost, the more reckless and erratic became his game.

One thing Delgado could remember with crystal clarity was the final game. A true masterpiece. Wheeler had dealt, turning up a heart as trump. Delgado had led with the king of hearts, a thoughtless opening on the face of it, and he had seen dismay flash fleetingly across Sterling's features. But the king of diamonds followed, taking the trick, and then the act of hearts, and the seven, and Sterling took the next trick with the queen, returning a diamond, as eleven hearts had by that time been expelled. Delgado passed the queen of diamonds. It was followed by the ace. Their opponents lost small spades to a seemingly endless onslaught of diamonds, and when the time was right Delgado played his ace of spades, followed by the four. Sterling knew now that his planter's had played a good hand with great skill. He finessed his knave, played the king of spades, upon which Delgado disposed of his singleton. The last two tricks were then Delgado's for the taking. Wheeler and Horan had held every trick in spades, and yet Delgado and his partner had made a slam.

Of course, gentlemen usually indulged in a friendly wager over cards. During his leisurely jaunt across the United States, Delgado had come to the conclusion that Americans had an insatiable appetite for gambling. Risk taking was deeply ingrained in the national character. Games of chance, horseraces, cockfights, wrestling matches—Delgado had even seen two men bet heavily on which of a pair of raindrops would reach the bottom of a windowpane first.

Wheeler and Horan lost a hundred dollars on the final round; Sterling had been the one to raise the ante all night, to and even beyond the point at which Delgado began to feel butterflies in his stomach. After all, this was his father's money, and Angus McKinn had not given it to his son to lose in a card game. Then, too, Delgado had the distinct impression that Sterling, for whatever reason, derived immense satisfaction from taking Brent Horan's money. It was more than a friendly wager for the newspaperman. He had used his wit, like sharp steel wrapped in silk, to prod Horan cunningly and mercilessly into ever higher bets. A dangerous game, since Horan was a Southern aristocrat, and Delgado knew such men were quick to take offense at even the most innocuous slight. Yet Sterling played his needling barbs with as much finesse as he did the pasteboards, enticing Horan into further costly flirtation with Lady Luck, pricking his pride and vanity, goading him to renewed recklessness. His senses dulled by strong spirits, Horan had been led like a lamb to slaughter, and by the end had lost several hundred dollars.

"I was at first concerned," Sterling admitted to Delgado as they split their winnings over one last drink, after Wheeler and Horan had departed the grand saloon. "I thought you might be a perfect tyro when it came to whist. But you have a masterful command of the game, sir. You play a good hand well and, even more importantly, a losing hand even better."

Delgado thanked him. "I had excellent teachers. I played whist every Saturday night for three years at Oxford, nearly without exception."

"Oxford? I didn't think you were an American, sir. English, then?"

Delgado smiled. "Not quite. My father is a Scotsman. My mother is the daughter of a Spanish grandee."

He left it at that, for by that time the cognac had the better of him, and he wanted nothing more than to retire to his stateroom and lie down and close his eyes. Sterling was intrigued; one look at Delgado McKinn and you could tell his was no ordinary pedigree. His black hair was wavy and unfashionably long, by American standards, to the shoulder. His clean-shaven features were aquiline, the eyes brooding and almost black. He was tall at two inches over six feet, and so slender in build that he seemed taller still. He spoke with a definite accent, but one Sterling could not quite put his finger on. One thing was clear—Delgado McKinn was endowed with a gentleman's grace, and had a gentleman's grasp of manners and vocabulary, and yet strong, almost reckless, passions surged just beneath that polished exterior. Finally, and with perfectly natural envy, Sterling conceded that Delgado McKinn was an extraordinarily handsome fellow. No young woman—and probably no woman of any age, no matter how well brought up—would be able to resist letting her gaze linger in speculative wonder upon this dark and rather mysterious stranger.

For his part, Delgado had learned to be vague about his citizenship. His home, Taos, was still part of the Republic of Mexico, and Mexico, as of May 13, 1846, only eight weeks ago, was at war with the United States. Technically, then, Delgado McKinn was traveling through enemy territory.

2

The sidewheeler's whistle shrilled again, and Delgado rose from his bed. Though it took considerable effort to do so, he was determined to demonstrate to the Fates that he still had a will of his own. He had slept in his clothes, so he changed into a clean white muslin shirt and donned a fresh waistcoat, fitted dark blue frock coat, and a fresh cravat, skillfully knotted to create an impression of deliberate negligence, which was the fashion of the day. He made certain to transfer his wallet from last night's rumpled coat to the one he now wore. One did not leave one's valuables lying about in a steamboat stateroom. Even a boat as reputable as the *Sultana.* On the river packets you met the wealth, the wit, and the rascality of the land. The passengers included ladies and gentlemen of unassailable propriety: businessmen, cotton planters, Creole lawyers, bankers, and commission merchants. But there were plenty of scoundrels riding the river as well. Gunmen and gamblers, courtesans and common thieves.

The Mississippi River was the carotid artery of Trans-Appalachian America. And dozens of lines branched off to service her many tributaries: on the Ohio System, the Cumberland up to Nashville, the

Kanawha up to Charleston, the Allegheny and the Muskingum. Steamboats struggled against the wild Missouri as far as Fort Benton these days, carrying supplies to military outposts strung all along the Big Muddy. On the "Lower River," the packets steamed up and down the Red, Arkansas, Ouachita, Black, and Yazoo rivers. Smaller boats made their way along the numerous bayous of Louisiana and to the very steps of the plantation houses to load thousands of bales of cotton every year and carry them to the docks of New Orleans for shipment overseas or to the New England mill towns. But cotton was not the only freight of the riverboat—corn, wheat, hemp, tobacco, and livestock came down the river from the young nation's heartland, while manufactured goods and luxuries were carried upriver from the great port of New Orleans.

Delgado remembered to pocket the pearl-handled derringer his father had presented him on the day he left home three years ago. Angus McKinn was of the firm opinion that a wise man trusted no one, and he would not permit his son to venture forth into the world unarmed. Delgado considered the short-barreled, large-bore, "over and under" hideout a useless encumbrance; he had never had cause to resort to it and never expected to. But he did not want the gun to fall into the hands of a sneak thief. The derringer was a gift from his father, and he cherished it for that reason if for no other.

With one last glance about the stateroom, Delgado stepped out into the long, gilded grand saloon, off which all the staterooms were aligned. Two rows of fluted columns, ten prism-fringed chandeliers, an oil painting—a misty and eye-pleasing pastoral scene—on every stateroom door, a three-hundred-foot blue and gold rug, custom-made in Belgium, extending from one end of the ornate room to the other. In stark contrast to the previous night, the saloon was nearly empty this morning. A platoon of cabin boys, looked natty in their plum-colored livery, were busy sweeping, wiping, and polishing up. The *Sultana* was no cheap, gaudy packet, but rather a genuine "floating palace," and it was Delgado's opinion that the saloon, as well as the adjoining staterooms with their brass and porcelain and velvet accouterments, were as splendid as the court of any Persian potentate.

He found the spacious "gallery," forward of the saloon on the boiler deck, already crowded, as ladies and gentlemen took advantage of the cool morning air. Finding a spot at the railing, Delgado glanced down the starboard length of the boat, admiring the graceful sheer of the three-hundred-foot vessel. Though she sat on an even keel, her decks—main, boiler, hurricane, and texas—all followed the same pronounced curve, for the boat rode high at bow and stern. The upper three decks were fenced and ornamented with white railings. The paddle boxes were adorned with the *Sultana*'s crescent moon emblem. A similar device dangled between the pair of soaring smokestacks capped with filigree crowns done in the likeness of oak leaves. At the base of the smokestacks on the texas deck stood the pilothouse, with glass and exquisitely wrought "gingerbread" all around.

Black smoke bellowed from the smokestacks, pluming behind the *Sultana* as she splashed resolutely against the strong current, making eight miles an hour. Delgado felt the rhythm of the wheels as they smote the shimmering surface of the mighty river, heard the muted roar of the inferno in the boilers through the open furnace doors. A half mile to the east, a line of trees, solemn old woods, marked the Illinois shore. Kaskaskia was behind them; today they would reach St. Louis.

St. Louis marked an ending of sorts for Delgado, and he contemplated his imminent arrival there in a melancholy light. Another eight hundred miles lay between him and his Taos home—long, arduous miles across the southern plains. Thus far he had enjoyed the trip immensely. Having dutifully applied himself to his studies at Oxford for the better part of three years, he had viewed his leisurely return via New York and New Orleans as a well-earned vacation. At the time of his departure from England, the United States and Mexico had still been at peace.

This had been his first exposure to the United States. The vibrant new nation had many wonders for a young man who had spent his twenty-three years in the insulated environment of Taos. He had been particularly impressed by New York City, where he had arrived three months ago aboard a steamship of the Royal Mail Steam Packet Company, founded six years ago by Sir Samuel Cunard. The voyage across the Atlantic had taken only a fortnight. The steam engine was revolutionizing sea travel and doomed the sailing ship to eventual extinction, and in a way Delgado regretted that. His voyage to England had been as a passenger aboard the *Flying Cloud*, one of the most famous of the clipper ships, and the experience had been an exciting one. Sadly, he predicted that in ten years the clipper ship would be but a memory.

No question but the times were a-changing, almost faster than the mind could assimilate. In Taos, life moved at a languorous and well-structured pace. In many ways life there was little changed from the way it had been a hundred years ago. The society was steeped in time-honored tradition. Life was to be savored. In the United States, life was to be spent—in a hurry, and in the pursuit of prosperity. Only recently were Americans learning to indulge in leisure.

New York City was a case in point. No one who saw the metropolis, in all its vitality and magnitude, could fail to be inspired by a sense of raw power and magnificent destiny. A forest of masts and spars rose from the hulls of hundreds of ships packed like sardines in the East River. The merchants and warehouses at the southern end of Manhattan Island handled half the imports and a third of the exports for the entire nation. Though London was still considered the financial capital of the world, Wall Street was coming on fast, and could already boast the greatest concentration of wealth in America. Forty-six years ago, at the turn of the century, New York's population had not exceeded 125,000; now almost 400,000 souls resided there, with hundreds more arriving every week, most of these refugees from the political unrest in Europe or, as in the case of the Irish, fleeing the grim prospect of famine.

Once Boston and Philadelphia had rivaled New York City as commercial centers, but no longer. The latter enjoyed too many natural advantages. Its harbor was broad and sheltered. It enjoyed ready access to a bustling, industrialized New England. To the north, the Hudson River linked the city with the Erie Canal, which in turn connected New York with the fast-growing regions beyond the formidable barrier of the Appalachians. The decade of uncertainty, deflation and, in some cases, ruination, which had marked the worldwide depression following the Panic of 1837 had been but a temporary setback.

New York City was symbolic of American power and progress. The city was brash, barbaric, hustling, arrogant, ostentatious, confident, unrefined. Delgado had visited the Astor Place Opera, and at the Chatham he had been entertained by a "grand national drama" entitled *The March to Freedom*, which featured General Taylor and the Goddess of Liberty vanquishing Mexican tyranny. He had dined at the Milles-Colonnes, sampled ice cream—the newest rage—at Contoit's, been accosted by a lady of dubious virtue as he strolled the enchanting woods of the Elysian Fields in Hoboken, seen the magnificent town homes of the gentry in Park Place and Washington Square.

He had seen the darker side of the city, too—the squalid ghettoes near Five Points, the ragpickers, hot corn girls, and apple peddlers who exemplified the thousands of unseen poor. Many better-off New Yorkers ignored these suffering masses, or contemptuously considered them the degraded overflow of European society. But many more, feeling it their duty to extend a helping hand to those less fortunate, contributed time and money to a host of benevolent charities like the Society for the Relief of Poor Widows and the New York Orphan Asylum. Delgado had concluded that while sometimes Americans could be small-minded, they were more often than not big-hearted.

After experiencing New York, he could not help but wonder what fate held in store for Taos. The Americans believed they were destined to own the continent, and Delgado did not believe the strife-torn Republic of Mexico could stand against the irresistible Yankee tide. Though Angus McKinn had never said so, Delgado suspected his father of sending him off to England to place him well out of harm's way, knowing that a clash was inevitable. This had suited Delgado; he was no warrior, and he could muster no allegiance, no patriotic enthusiasm, for any flag. Now a war was being fought, and territory would change hands. The Stars and Stripes would fly above the old Cabildo in the provincial capital of Santa Fe.

By virtue of conquest, whether he liked it or not, Delgado McKinn was destined to become an American. On that score he was ambivalent. Americans and their ways were fascinating, but remained strange to him. He wondered if he would fit in or forever feel like an outcast.

3

The *Sultana* was putting in to shore on the Missouri side, where a small village in a quick-cut clearing was coming to sudden life with the arrival of the "floating palace." In such a frontier settlement, drowsy in the summer sunshine, the day was a slow and dreary thing, yesterday's mirror image and a blueprint for tomorrow. But even as Delgado watched, the levee came alive with people as the cry *"Steamboat a'comin'!"* rang out. From every rough-hewn log and raw clapboard structure the denizens poured to gaze in awe at the wondrous sight of the sidewheeler, so long and trim and resplendent.

The whistle blasts that had awakened Delgado served to alert crew and passengers of imminent landfall. As the *Sultana* veered nearer the western shore, the big bell above the pilothouse rang out, two mellow notes. From the hurricane deck, almost directly above Delgado, the watchman called out, *"Labboard lead! Starboard lead!"*

The leadsmen rushed to their places near the bow, on the main deck. When the pilot rang the bell once, the starboard leadsman tossed out his knotted and weighted line to measure the river's depth, and called out, "Mark three!" At two bells the man on the other side performed the same ritual. "Quarter less three!" And soon, "Half twain! . . . Quarter twain! . . . Mark twain!" The pilot hailed the engine room, and the

Sultana slowed perceptibly. Steam whistled as it escaped through the gauge cocks.

Having visited the pilothouse earlier, Delgado could picture in his mind's eye what was occurring there at this moment. The pilot would be putting the wheel down hard to swing the boat into her marks. The cries of the leadsmen indicated that the water was becoming "shoal." "Eight and a half!" "Eight!" *"Seven and a half!"* Delgado felt a tingle at the base of his spine, and glanced about him surreptitiously to see if any of the other passengers presently occupying the deck realized that now the steamboat's hull was less than two feet from the bottom. *"Seven feet!"* Would they run aground? Surely not. A boat like the *Sultana* would merit the services of the best "lightning pilot" money could hire. At this speed, if they did run aground, the impact would be violent, and Delgado imagined himself hurled through a shattered railing into the murky brown water below. But he did not move or betray in any way his apprehension. Suddenly the engines stopped—he could no longer feel their pulse through the decking beneath his feet. The agile *Sultana* swung its stern sharply toward the shore as the pilot rolled the big wheel faster than the human eye could follow.

"Eight feet!" called the starboard leadsman, and Delgado breathed again.

Nice as you please, the sidewheeler came alongside a ramshackle wharf of gray, weathered timber. The mate, a big, burly, and profane man, took charge of the deck hands responsible for running out the gangplank. "Start the plank forward! Look lively, now! Damn your eyes, are you asleep, boy? Heave! Heave! You move slower than a damned hearse! Aft again! Aft, I say! Are you deaf as well as daft?"

Delgado watched four men with rifles tilted on their

shoulders come up the gangplank. They halted before stepping foot on the packet and looked up at the captain, who stood in his most imposing fashion by the big bell on the texas deck.

"Ahoy, Cap'n!" called the foremost of the quartet. "We be bound for St. Looy to join Doniphan's Volunteers. Will you take us free of charge? Our pockets are full of dust and not much else."

"Come aboard, boys," answered the *Sultana*'s captain with a sweeping and magnanimous gesture. "I would not accept so much as a redback dollar from brave men who are marching off to strike a blow for liberty."

The volunteers grinned and tipped their hats and came aboard, seeking some small space on the already overcrowded main deck, where those who could not afford the first-class comfort of the staterooms were packed in amongst the freight: sacks of rice, barrels of molasses, casks of rum, crates of imported goods, and a variety of livestock.

The four rifle-toting young men intrigued Delgado. Where were they bound? Who was Doniphan? No doubt it had something to do with the war.

A man appeared at the railing beside him. It was Sterling, a newspaper rolled up under one arm and a twinkle in his eye.

"Good morning, McKinn. No ill effects from last night's excesses, I trust?"

"I've never felt better," lied Delgado. The sharp, stabbing pain in his head had subsided into a dull, persistent ache behind the eyes. "Tell me, Sterling, about Doniphan's Volunteers."

"You mean the First Missouri Mounted Rifles. They are to join Colonel Stephen Kearny and his dragoons at Fort Leavenworth. Kearny is being dispatched to Santa Fe to protect U.S. citizens and property there.

In other words, to occupy New Mexico and—who knows?—California, too, in all likelihood. Alexander Doniphan is an acquaintance of mine, a young lawyer who was one of the first to answer Governor Edwards' call for volunteers. He enlisted as a private, but, as is the custom of our volunteer forces, the men elected him their commander. Whereupon the state of Missouri has honored him with the rank of colonel."

"I see. Santa Fe, you said?"

"Yes. They are calling Kearny's command the Army of the West. Have you not been keeping up with news of the war?"

Delgado flinched. "I have made it a point not to."

"May I speak bluntly?"

"By all means."

"You struck me at first as something of a ne'er-do-well. Someone who would not bother himself with the intricacies of current affairs, who would instead interest himself solely in the sporting life. Not unlike our young friend Horan. But, upon further reflection, I've changed my mind about you, McKinn. This war with Mexico *is* of grave concern to you, isn't it?"

"Yes," said Delgado, deciding on the spur of the moment that he could confide in Sterling. "Taos is my home. My father is a trader. His name is Angus McKinn. He is Scottish-born, a Highlander, but thirty years ago he established himself in Taos and became a Mexican citizen in '24. The new Republic of Mexico required all foreign-born residents to convert to Catholicism and swear allegiance to the republic and its constitution. My father was quite happy to do both."

"Even forsake his religion? I assume he was a Protestant."

"Even that. He had fallen in love with my mother, the daughter of a Spanish grandee. In order to marry her he had to convert. She could not have become his bride otherwise. At any rate, after the Texas expedition to seize Santa Fe, my father decided to send me off to England. He wanted the best possible education for me, and that meant Oxford."

"We have a few good institutions in this country," said Sterling. "Yale, for instance, and Brown, to name but two."

Delgado smiled. "My father had an ulterior motive. To place me as far away as possible from the war he knew was coming."

"I see. That explains England. But your return is a little premature, my friend. War broke out only two months ago. Mexican soldiers crossed the Rio Grande and killed some of our brave soldiers. American blood shed on American soil, as President Polk described it to Congress. Of course," added Sterling, with a wry smile, "Northern Whigs take issue with the 'American soil' part of that equation. As you must know, there is still some debate regarding which country holds legitimate title to the territory that lies between the Rio Grande and the Nueces River."

"War or no," said Delgado flatly, "I must get home."

Sterling leaned forward. "I may be presuming a friendship where none exists," he said, "but I ask you this solely out of concern for your welfare, which I value if only because your skill at whist provided me with the opportunity to best that pompous Brent Horan. Where does your allegiance lie, sir?"

"With my father," was Delgado's prompt answer. "No one and nothing else."

"And your father's allegiance?"

"He is a businessman."

"He swore an oath to the flag and constitution of the Republic of Mexico, did he not?"

"That he did," conceded Delgado. "But he will always put my mother and I, and his business affairs, before all else. I am not implying that he is without honor, of course."

"Of course not."

Delgado drew a deep breath. "He has a longstanding commercial relationship with a man named Jacob Bledsoe in St. Louis. Perhaps you have heard of him?"

"Indeed I have. I am well acquainted with Bledsoe. He is one of the leaders of the community, a highly respected gentleman."

"At my father's request I have come to St. Louis to visit Mr. Bledsoe. Perhaps he will have some ideas regarding how I am to get home, now that it appears that there is a war in my way."

A sudden commotion drew their attention. A stateroom door burst open and several men, locked in fierce combat, tumbled out across the threshold. A young lady shrieked. The knot of men careened off the railing, and Delgado was amazed that the railing did not give way and pitch all of the combatants into the river or onto the ramshackle wharf.

"Look!" exclaimed Sterling. "It's Horan."

So it was. Horan emerged from the melee, hat missing, cravat askew, an expression of savage elation on his features. He brandished a pamphlet over his head.

"We caught him!" he cried to one and all. "Caught the scoundrel red-handed. A damned abolitionist, come to stir up our Negroes into insurrection. I say we teach the blackguard a lesson he won't soon forget."

"Tar and feather him!" came one bellicose suggestion.

"No," said Horan, his eyes blazing with a lurid fever. "Get a rope. We will hang him, here and now, and be done with him."

4

Sterling stepped forward. "Let me see that pamphlet, Horan," he said sternly. It was more an order than a request.

Smirking, Horan surrendered the damning evidence. "Have in mind defending this rascal, *Mister* Sterling?"

Delgado had no doubts now—deep animosity ran like a river of black bile between these two men. What had transpired to set these two strong wills at odd?

Sterling studied the pamphlet. "The American Anti-slavery Society." He fastened a cold, piercing gaze upon the stout, disheveled man now held firmly in the grasp of two others. "Your name, sir?"

"Rankin. Jeremiah Rankin." He was afraid, but though his voice trembled he managed to conjure up a little defiance. Under the circumstances, mused Delgado, that was quite commendable.

"You are either a very courageous man or a very foolish one, sir," said Sterling. "Were your intentions to distribute this material among the slaves?"

"I have already done so, sir, in New Orleans, Natchez, and Vicksburg."

A man emerged from Rankin's stateroom with a parfleche valise. When opened, it could be seen that the valise was half full of pamphlets identical to the one in Sterling's possession.

"And these?" asked Sterling. "Bound for St. Louis, no doubt."

Rankin did not answer.

"What do we do with them?" asked the man holding the valise.

"Burn them," growled Horan. "Consign them to the flames of the furnace. Perhaps our abolitionist should meet the same fate. Give him a taste of the hell to which a just God will send him for daring to instigate our servants to revolt—to murder, rape, and pillage."

Delgado thought at first that Horan had to be joking. But there was nothing in his tone or expression to suggest that he was not in deadly earnest.

"Sterling," said Delgado. "May I see that pamphlet?"

"Certainly."

"Read it aloud, sir," insisted Horan, "so that these people may have no doubt as to the man's guilt."

Delgado glanced at the crowd of gentlemen and ladies who had congregated to the deck. He opened the slim pamphlet to a random passage and read aloud:

" 'We view as contrary to the Law of God, on which hang the Unalienable Rights of Mankind, as well as every Principle of revolution, to hold in deepest debasement, in a more abject slavery than is perhaps to be found in Any part of the World, so many souls that are capable of the image of God.' "

He paused to scan the circle of intent faces. No one seemed to be breathing. Clearly the pamphlet and what it contained fascinated even while it repulsed them. Delgado felt like a snake handler. Turning a page, he read on:

" 'What is meant by IMMEDIATE ABOLITION? It means every Negro husband shall have his own wife, united in wedlock, protected by law. It means Negro parents shall have control and government of their own children, and that these children shall not be taken away from their parents. It means providing schools and instruction for the Negro. It means right over wrong, love over hatred, and religion over heathenism.' "

"Immediatism," said Sterling with a hard look at Rankin. "Gradual emancipation is out of fashion these days, isn't it?"

"This all seems rather harmless," said Delgado.

Horan snatched the pamphlet from his grasp. Fuming, the Southerner turned to the last page of the document.

" 'Voluntary submission to slavery is sinful," he read triumphantly. "It is your solemn and imperative duty to use every means—moral, intellectual, and physical—that promises success in attaining your freedom. You must cease toiling for tyrants. If you then must commence the work of death, they and not you are responsible for the consequences. There is not much hope of redemption without the shedding of blood.' "

A murmur of shocked outrage rippled through those gathered near.

Horan raised a clenched fist. "Tyrants? Physical means? The work of death?" Infuriated, he slapped Rankin across the face with the pamphlet. "Defend that, Sterling. If you dare."

"But," said Delgado, "you've seen to it that your slaves are illiterate. Since they cannot read, those words are harmless."

"A few of the ungrateful wretches flaunt our codes and *have* learned to read," said Horan. "They will spread this vile poison to others, sowing the seeds of discontent. They think they want their freedom? They will suffer and starve as freedmen. Our Negroes are well cared for. They are clothed, fed, and housed. They are nursed to health when they fall prey to sickness. They want for nothing. Compare their condition to the plight of the poor in Northern cities, who labor sixteen hours a day in mill and factory, are paid starvation wages, and struggle to survive in plague-infested slums!"

Horan stabbed an accusing finger at Rankin. "This man is not concerned with the well-being of the Negro. The abolitionist is the tool of the Northern industrialist, who fears the political power of the South, and seeks to destroy our society by removing the cornerstone of its foundation. The South cannot survive without the institution of slave labor, sir. You should understand that, Sterling. You were, after all, born a Southerner."

"I am a Westerner," said Sterling.

"A Westerner opposed to expansion."

"I favor the expansion of republicanism, sir, but not the peculiar institution with it. And I will not allow you to hang these men. I may not agree with his ideas, or especially his tactics, but I will not stand by and let the fate which befell Elijah Lovejoy repeat itself here."

Delgado knew the story of Lovejoy. Ten years ago, Lovejoy, an abolitionist editor, had been hounded out of Missouri. Moving to Illinois, he continued his crusade against slavery. After his printing presses were destroyed on three separate occasions, his house invaded by an unruly mob, and his wife pushed to the verge of hysterical collapse, Lovejoy had armed himself, vowing to protect his family and property. When a mob came to wreck his fourth printing press, Lovejoy confronted them with pistol and hand, and was gunned down in the process. He had become a martyr to the abolitionist cause.

A boy broke through the press of passengers. By the condition of his dirty linsey shirt and ragged dungarees, Delgado took him for one of those less fortunate souls who were berthed on the main deck with the cargo. In his white-knuckled grasp was a length of braided hemp, and on his face was stamped the same mad lust for blood Delgado had seen on Brent Horan's narrow features.

"Here's your rope!" exclaimed the youth. "Stretch the damn Yankee's neck!"

Horan gave Sterling a look of defiance as he snatched the rope from the boy. Making a slip-knot loop at one end, he put it over Rankin's head and pulled the loop closed around the abolitionist's neck. Rankin renewed his struggle to free himself, but to no avail. The pressure of the rope seemed to make his eyes bulge in their sockets. Cold sweat beaded his forehead, and he began to mumble the Lord's Prayer. He could no longer deny his fate.

Seeing that Horan was prepared to go through with the lynching, some of the men in the crowd turned their backs, leading the woman away from the scene. But no one stepped forward to intervene—except Sterling, who clutched Horan's arm.

"Don't be a fool," rasped the newspaperman. "This man has broken the laws of several states by his own admission. Turn him over to the authorities, Horan, for the love of God."

Horan grinned like a wolf. "Let go of me, Sterling, or I'll hang you right alongside him."

Sterling removed his hand. The slump of his shoulders told Delgado that he would go no further to try to save Rankin.

As he stepped forward, Delgado reached into the pocket of his frock coat and extracted the derringer. He acted almost by reflex, without giving any thought to the consequences of his actions. Angus McKinn had always claimed his son was too impetuous for his own good.

"Pardon me," he said.

Horan looked at him, saw the pocket pistol, and froze.

"I was under the impression," said Delgado coldly, "that this nation was built upon certain unalienable rights. Are you acquainted, Horan, with the amendments to the Constitution?"

Horan just stared at him, rendered speechless by astonishment more so than fear.

"I refer specifically," continued Delgado, "to the right of free speech, not to mention the right to a public trial with an impartial jury and the assistance of counsel."

Horan was quickly recovering. "Stay out of this, sir," he warned, his words like cold steel. "This is none of your affair."

"I disagree. Is this a republic or a monarchy? The former is antithetical to the latter. Yet in recent weeks, during my sojourn in the South, I have begun to wonder if the United States of America is a republic at all. I have seen tyranny, aristocracy, hereditary privilege, restrictive land tenure, and servile obedience enforced by repression. And you, sir, you must be a prince of this aristocracy, since by your whim a man can lose his life."

Horan darkened. "I find your words insulting, McKinn."

"These are the facts which insult you," Delgado took a step closer and planted the derringer's double barrel in Horan's rib cage. "If this man hangs, Horan," he said, pitching his voice so low that only Horan could heard him, "you won't be alive to see it."

For a moment Horan made no move. He searched Delgado's face for any clue that this might be a bluff. There was no such clue. Delgado knew he might very well have to kill Horan. The man's towering pride might not permit him to back down, especially in the presence of so many witnesses. But Delgado realized that he could not back down either, if for no other reason than that Jeremiah Rankin's life depended on him. So he kept his nerve and did not flinch from the malevolence in Horan's gaze.

"Let the man go," Sterling told the two men who

were restraining the abolitionist. "Let him go, or Horan's blood will be on your hands."

It was a clever strategem. If Horan died, they would be responsible, because Sterling suspected, as did they, that Horan would not submit, preferring death to dishonor. This was a code they understood and strove to live by. The honorable course for them would be to release Rankin and save the life of their friend.

They let Rankin go. One of them removed the rope from around the abolitionist's neck. "I will turn him over to the authorities in St. Louis," he told Sterling curtly as he flung the rope over the railing.

The second man turned to Horan. "Come on, Brent," he said softly, with a wary glance at Delgado and at Delgado's pistol.

"This is not the end," Horan told Delgado, and turned briskly away.

Delgado pocketed the derringer and went to the railing, feeling suddenly nauseated, hoping only that he did not show it. Below him, in the brown water between the hull of the *Sultana* and the old wharf, the rope slowly squirmed in the river's current like a long snake. Delgado stared at the rope, unaware of all else about him. When Sterling put a hand on his shoulder, he flinched.

"That was a brave act, McKinn," said the newspaperman. "And it just may get you killed."

"Something had to be done. We have to live with ourselves. I think that would have been a difficult proposition had we stood by and watched a man hanged for no good reason."

"Slavery," Sterling shook his head. "It is an issue tearing at the very fabric of our nation. But Horan will not forget, or forgive, what you did. I thought for a moment he might issue a challenge."

"A duel?"

Sterling nodded. "It is still quite possible he will have his representative pay a call on you."

Delgado laughed sharply. "I am no duelist and refuse to become one."

"Well, perhaps nothing will come of it. Cooler heads may yet prevail. You are an unknown quantity, and that works in your favor. I hope we will meet again in St. Louis, before you leave for Taos. Perhaps you will be in the mood for another game of whist. Here is my card."

Sterling handed him the newspaper he had been carrying and walked away.

Delgado opened the newspaper. It was the *St. Louis Enquirer,* yesterday's edition. A few copies had come up the gangplank at this landing. The banner headline jumped out at him. Men from Commodore Sloat's naval squadron had seized the California ports of Monterey and San Francisco. Mexican troops were reported to be massing in the Los Angeles area, preparing to march against the American interlopers. A great and decisive battle was expected. . . .

Delgado grimly folded the newspaper, put it under his arm, and returned to his stateroom, wondering what the future held for Taos, his home, and his family.